CODENAME WILDCARD

BOOK I OF THE

"PATRIOTS FOR GOD & COUNTRY"

SERIES

A THRILLER BY

DIANA MACFARLAND

LIBERTY PRESS

LIBERTY PRESS
CreateSpace Books
7290 B Investment Drive
N. Charleston, SC 29418

ISBN-10: 1439271372
ISBN-13: 978-1439271377
LCCN: 2010905804
CreateSpace, North Charleston, SC

Printed in the United States of America
CreateSpace.com

Cover artwork by www.TomStackPhoto.com
Photography by Diana MacFarland
www.DianaMacFarland.com

DEDICATION

First and foremost, this novel is dedicated to all its readers, whatever their circumstances. While the story comes from the personal maverick lives of a real couple, it's not about them. It's about what they learned along the way that might inspire readers to call on the superhero that resides in each of us, in order to achieve more satisfying lives.

Equally important, this book is dedicated to the American forefathers who envisioned a new nation under God, blessed by divine providence, and so devoted the full measure of their lives, families, wealth, creativity and faith to give us the finest Constitution and nation of individual freedoms and prosperity the world has ever seen.

This story is also dedicated to all in military or government agencies who serve to protect our freedoms, including the clandestine operatives and patriots who serve without distinction or honor as earthly guardian angels helping protect us in our unseeing sleep.

In memory of Admiral Draper Kauffman, USN, and his wife, Peggy, whose lives set an inspiring example of living for God and country.

No, Posterity, you will never know how much it cost us to preserve your freedom. I hope you will make good use of it. If you do not, I shall repent it in heaven that I ever took half the pains to preserve it.

— John Adams, Founding Father and 2nd President of the United States

EYES WIDE OPEN

The husband-and-wife authors of this thriller have chosen to present their experiences from the sanctuary of The Great Cathedral of Fiction—with time shifts and embellishments for the sake of plot. All historical facts, however, are accurate—as are Jason's paranormal survival gifts, his incurable PTSD and how he learns to control it without debilitating prescription drugs.

The authors believe no one is automatically a good lover, and the Puritanical view of <u>Sex as Shameful Sin</u> derives from ignorance, hypocrisy and being ill-prepared for a life of sex, resulting in acts of self-centered gratification—as opposed to the <u>Act of Love</u> view, wherein both lovers learn how to give their all in mutually fulfilling, God-given multi-orgasmic bliss.

Even in today's Information Age, few Americans have been taught or have ever been given reason to imagine the lovemaking possibilities that have been enjoyed in highly civilized cultures for thousands of years. These abilities derive from training secrets handed down through the ages that have enabled enlightened people to transcend routine animal sex. (Recent master teachers' books are listed at the end of the novel.) This story reveals how Jason receives such multi-orgasm training in the Orient and shows his subsequent search for a heaven-sent mate he believes he must find. In the midst of his life-or-death adventures, he discovers the value of a caring couple's mutual giving and receiving—their uninhibited creativity producing endorphins for both that provide incomparable healing and energy. Such bliss nourishes unfading passion and laugher. It helps bond couples together in a life of seeking to be worthy of their gifts.

The unique lovemaking scenes integral to this story are offered not to arouse lust or to embarrass or to be skimmed, but <u>to show the power of the most magnificent force on earth</u>—available to all committed couples who want such acts of love for themselves and each other. Happy reading.

Diana MacFarland   The Florida Keys   July 4, 2012

PTSD

In the United States, 6,570 veterans commit suicide each year—an average of eighteen vets a day—far more than the soldiers killed in action.

The shocking figure became public on May 10, 2011, during a ruling by the 9th U.S. Circuit Court of Appeals.

Post-traumatic stress disorder and this tragic loss of life have been a hidden cost of war.

CONTENTS

PART ONE: NORTH KOREA

Chapter 1   South Korea. 1
Chapter 2   Deadly Crossing 5
Chapter 3   Torture. 10
Chapter 4   "Where Princess Ran Sang-hee?". 14
Chapter 5   Fantastic Connection. 18
Chapter 6   Weird Reality. 20
Chapter 7   Lifesaving Vision .24
Chapter 8   FBI Agent Thomas 29
Chapter 9   Suki 34
Chapter 10   Suki's Proposition 38
Chapter 11   Oriental Disciplines 42
Chapter 12   Sequim Anchorage 44
Chapter 13   Natasha 48
Chapter 14   Ivan 50
Chapter 15   Adrift 56
Chapter 16   Natasha's Nightmare 60

PART TWO: SCOTTISH HIGHLANDS

Chapter 17   Roots 67
Chapter 18   Gladiators 73
Chapter 19   Megan 79
Chapter 20   Aunt Rachael 85
Chapter 21   Highland Candor .90
Chapter 22   Caledonian Pine .95
Chapter 23   If At First. 100
Chapter 24   Scottish Fantasy 103
Chapter 25   Pinnacle Rocks. 109

Chapter 26   Telekinesis 115

Chapter 27   Highland Farewells 116

Chapter 28   Raison D'Être 121

PART THREE: U.S. NAVAL ACADEMY

Chapter 29   Shootout in Miami 127

Chapter 30   Business at the Fontainebleau 131

Chapter 31   Spetsnaz Realities 134

Chapter 32   Hooking Agent Thomas 138

Chapter 33   Submarine Down! 141

Chapter 34   Captain David King 145

Chapter 35   Serving America 147

Chapter 36   Dakota 151

Chapter 37   Warrior's High 155

Chapter 38   Reverse Weirdness 159

Chapter 39   Keeping Jason Alive 161

Chapter 40   Grandfather Steele 167

Chapter 41   U.S. Naval Academy 170

Chapter 42   Best Laid Plans 174

Chapter 43   Sybil 179

Chapter 44   Dangerous Beauty 182

Chapter 45   Do-Or-Die Seduction 186

Chapter 46   Friendly Persuasion 189

Chapter 47   Party To Blackmail 192

Chapter 48   Sybil's Gamble 197

Chapter 49   Soviet Progress 201

Chapter 50   Reprieve 206

Chapter 51   Hard Choices 208

Chapter 52   Wrenching Decision 213

PART FOUR: WAR NEUROSIS

Chapter 53   Starting Over 219
Chapter 54   Forks, Washington. 222
Chapter 55   Forestry 226
Chapter 56   Recruited 229
Chapter 57   Surveillant. 233
Chapter 58   Wolverine 238
Chapter 59   Heather's Information 242
Chapter 60   Inescapable Destiny. 247
Chapter 61   CIA Interest. 252
Chapter 62   Electrifying Interview 256
Chapter 63   Resourceful Profiler 260
Chapter 64   Suki's Secrets 264
Chapter 65   Quid Pro Quo 268
Chapter 66   Grand Design. 272
Chapter 67   White House Report. 280
Chapter 68   Onward 282
Chapter 69   Rejected By VAMC 284
Chapter 70   Revolutionary Movement 287

PART FIVE: VA HOSPITAL

Chapter 71   Flashback. 293
Chapter 72   American Lake Veterans Hospital 298
Chapter 73   Michael. 300
Chapter 74   Sadie. 302
Chapter 75   Containment Plan. 305
Chapter 76   Thuggery. 309
Chapter 77   Cost Of Winning 313
Chapter 78   Mission Accomplished. 317
Chapter 79   Suicidal Depression. 320
Chapter 80   Over-Volted 324
Chapter 81   Bridal Veil Falls 328
Chapter 82   Higgins' Resolve. 330

Chapter 83   Walter and Sebastian 333
Chapter 84   Strengths and Risks 337
Chapter 85   Visiting Jason 340
Chapter 86   Recruiting Jason 342
Chapter 87   To Die Or Not To Die 346
Chapter 88   Nurse Bonnie 349
Chapter 89   Hope 353
Chapter 90   Higgins' Motives? 355
Chapter 91   Bonnie's Gift 358
Chapter 92   Golden Fleece 364
Chapter 93   Focus On The Future 367

PART SIX: NEW BEGINNINGS

Chapter 94   Dougherty Enterprises 371
Chapter 95   Pioneering 374
Chapter 96   Higgins' Gamble 376
Chapter 97   Surprise Visitor 383
Chapter 98   Jason's Terms 386
Chapter 99   Persistence Pays 389

PART SEVEN: KEY LARGO

Chapter 100   Key Largo 393
Chapter 101   Rosa 398
Chapter 102   Lookout House 401
Chapter 103   Nice Duty 403
Chapter 104   Keys Cover 406
Chapter 105   Underwater 409
Chapter 106   Rosa's War Neurosis 413
Chapter 107   Estar Roto 418
Chapter 108   Catharsis 422
Chapter 109   Cuban Missile Crisis 426
Chapter 110   Picnic In Paradise 430
Chapter 111   Oh, Shit! 433

Chapter 112   Crunch Time 437
Chapter 113   Heaven's Mysteries 440
Chapter 114   Assignment 442
Chapter 115   All Bets Off 445
Chapter 116   Timeless Love 447
Chapter 117   To The Death 449
Chapter 118   Resourceful Women 452
Chapter 119   Redemption. 457

Acknowledgements. 460
Afterlife 461
Relevant Reading and Viewing 463
Glossary: Abbreviations, Definitions and Translations 466

CODENAME
WILDCARD

PART I

NORTH KOREA

CHAPTER 1
SOUTH KOREA

Jason Steele MacDougall felt a chilling heaviness. Felt his red-blond hair bristle at the nape of his neck. On his forearms. A premonition, sudden and undeniable.

Oh, shit! We're in trouble.

He went on full alert, like a lone Indian hearing a twig snap in the forest.

"Pull over, Tom." Jason kept his baritone voice calm. "Stop the truck."

Private Thomas Riley slowed to a halt on the single-lane dirt road six feet above the Korean rice paddies.

Why this overwhelming sense of doom? Sometimes his extrasensory gifts felt like a curse. Jason twisted his body in the open-top, three-quarter ton army truck and looked back toward Kimpo Air Force Base where the sun was about to set behind the mountains.

A propeller-driven cargo plane came in for a landing, the orange orb its dramatic backdrop. Then a liaison plane floated in, followed by three F-80 Shooting Star fighters. Finally an H-5 chopper came thumping in and put down. Everyone safely in for the night but him and Tom.

"What's wrong?" Tom's hoarse whisper betrayed his fear. The private wasn't ready to die. Not today.

"This road's not safe any more." Jason wanted to ignore the premonition, push on home to his base and to Suki. But he couldn't. He rubbed his knuckle across his brow. "Let's go back to Kimpo. We're going to be guests of the Air Force tonight. We'll call the 526th from there and let them know where we are."

And get word to Suki through houseboy Kim Kibonee so she won't become alarmed and try to leave Korea with Hyo and Yun Hee.

"Yessir." Tom reached for the gearshift. "Whoa. Taxi coming."

One of Korea's late-1930s black Ford sedans approached around a bend, its wizened driver coming towards them slowly. Tom pulled as far as he could to the side of the road without slipping over the edge of the dirt embankment.

"Something's not right here." Jason's throat tightened. "Be ready for anything!"

Tom rammed the gearshift lever into first.

The old Ford slowed even more as it edged past. A hard-faced young Korean woman popped up in the open rear window and aimed a U.S. military issue Colt .45 at Tom. "No move, GI."

Like hell. "Go, Tom!" In that instant the people and objects around Jason appeared to move in slow motion—while he continued functioning in normal time.

Both men ducked to the side as Tom floored the accelerator and popped the clutch. Jason saw the woman pull the trigger, but the taxi's mechanical brakes grabbed and jerked her arm so she missed. The heavy semi-automatic almost jumped out of her hand. Tom lurched the truck ahead, but the right rear wheel slid over the edge of the embankment, followed by the rest of the truck except its front wheels. It barely clung to the side of the slope. Before he and Tom could leap down into the rice paddy, three tough-looking men with weapons rose up in the taxi. One of them had a Thompson sub-machine gun ready to pepper the GIs if they tried to run.

It was over. Tom killed the engine and they raised their hands, trying to brace themselves with their feet to keep from falling out of the precariously positioned truck.

Jason's mouth was dry, his heart pounding in his ears. His face felt hot, then cold, then hot again as he waited for a supper of .45 caliber slugs.

The woman gestured for them to approach.

Last chance to run. To die fast. Jason whispered, "I'll get us out of this, Tom."

"I'm ready to do my part," Tom whispered back through his handlebar mustache.

They clambered up the steep slant of the truck and out onto the road. The Korean with the Thompson kept the heavy gun aimed at them while the other two men took their watches, tied their hands behind their backs with parachute cord and forced Jason and Tom to sit on the road. While the Koreans backed up the taxi to attach the cable from the truck's front bumper winch to the tow hook on the old sedan's frame, Jason tried to think of a way out. Tom was a logging truck driver from Oregon, and tried to appear calm, but Jason knew he was worried shitless. Only an idiot wouldn't be. So far, their kidnappers were too professional to leave any avenue of escape.

Using the winch and the truck's four-wheel drive, the Koreans pulled the American vehicle back up onto the road. The woman seemed to be the leader. After checking the gas in the hijacked truck, she told the old taxi driver to go on his way. The men shoved Jason and Tom into the back of the truck. The woman ordered one of the men into the driver's seat, and climbed in beside him. She gave more orders and off they drove. Jason studied their route, preparing for escape.

The three men were typically short, wiry, dressed in white cotton shirts and pants, white sweatbands across their foreheads—the usual attire of Korean farmers. But these men were armed for a different line of work. They seemed overly excited, as if high on something. Then Jason's head exploded, and his world went black.

* * *

When he awoke, he could swear he heard outboard motors running slowly with their burbly exhaust. He opened his eyes cautiously. He was lying lengthwise on the back floor of the small open truck, his body crammed between a bench-seat on one side and a row of feet on the other, where Tom and two of their kidnappers were seated. Jason worked himself up onto the opposite seat, despite the pain in the back of his head. The Korean with the .30 caliber carbine must have clubbed him with the rifle butt.

Damn. They were on some kind of makeshift ferry powered by outboards. And now he recognized the distinctive sound—British Seagulls, just like the motor on his family's dingy half a world away. Weird.

Tom signaled with his eyes, ready to follow Jason's lead. Jason wondered why their captors hadn't already cut their throats and thrown them into the river. He and Tom had nothing worth stealing except their watches and the truck, and the Koreans already had those. He could think of no reason for the kidnappers to keep them alive except … sport.

Shit! Shit! Shit! Don't fear dying; fear <u>how</u> you die.

CHAPTER 2
DEADLY CROSSING

South Korea
Friday, May 13, 1955

Jason's head was splitting. He fought the nausea. The guard with the carbine leered, his grin taunting. A big, lopsided moon illuminated the scene, and out here there were no artificial lights to handicap night vision.

The outboard operators idled their unstable craft under shadowy tree limbs, maneuvering their twin-hulled bows into a shallow dirt bank at the river's edge. The boatmen kept the engines running slow-ahead to hold the watercraft there. Jason paid attention to every detail, trying to formulate some plan of escape, pushing back the paralyzing fear of torture. He focused on the Koreans ashore. They dragged two heavy planks out of the trees and dropped the ends with connecting hardware over the forward ends of the planks on which the hijacked truck was parked. The driver started the engine and eased the truck over the plank track to the shore. The headlights illuminated wheel tracks meandering through the trees in front of them. Behind, men were already dismantling the planks that had supported the truck, removing two cross-members fitted to hold two open fishing boats together. Free of each other, the crews of the fishing boats headed downriver. Not one word was spoken throughout the entire operation.

Jason was puzzled. While he was unconscious had they crossed the Yeseong River near the Demilitarized Zone that separated South and North Korea? Kimpo was northwest of Seoul and that morning he had seen on his map that the DMZ ran close by—some of it north of the river. The DMZ was a booby-trapped no-man's land, stretching west to east a hundred-fifty miles across the peninsula, from the Yellow Sea to the Sea of Japan. It separated the enemy, communist North Korea, from the South Koreans, whom the North had tried to conquer. The Soviet Union had backed the North Korean invasion and MIG fighter pilots had been overheard speaking Chinese, confirming communist Mainland China's participation. Hostilities were supposed to be over now, but in reality, the DMZ remained the world's hot spot of the so-called "Cold War," so everyone was still extremely cautious. Added to continued military tensions, the black market had become a major enterprise. Theft was rampant.

He and Tom had been sent to South Korea as part of the United Nations forces, to keep democracy alive in this part of the world. A South Korean peninsula lost to Soviet communism would be like a dagger aimed at Japan, still recovering from World War II. Japan was rebuilding and reestablishing itself as the industrial center of the Orient. Without an armed allied presence in South Korea, a naval blockade by Russian ships could starve Japan into submission to the U.S.S.R., leaving communist Russia in control of Asia. Jason passionately believed in the goal of preserving democracy, despite the hellish reality he and Tom had just fallen into.

He appreciated the time he'd spent in this part of the world. If he hadn't been assigned to Korea, he wouldn't have experienced the challenges of rebuilding an allied nation— or met the awesome Suki and her ninja bodyguard, Hyo. But damn the joker who had rotated the road sign and gotten him and Tom lost earlier in the day. Their assignment had been simple—go to Kimpo to pick up a new throw-out bearing for the semi-tractor, and return that afternoon to their company compound at Ouijongbu. Traveling that lonely road as darkness fell was asking for trouble. *Damn.* And Suki. With her cruel aristocratic husband from Pyongyang looking for her everywhere, Suki would worry—perhaps flee—if Jason didn't come to her tonight as planned. He had to escape and get word to her.

After a short distance, the wheel tracks through the woods met a narrow dirt road. The Korean driver turned right and worked his way northeast up into the hills. The truck lurched through ruts and potholes. Groves of trees and grassy fields created a landscape different from anything Jason had seen in South Korea. He tried to size up the situation.

He believed they were still on the South Korean side of the DMZ, after clandestinely crossing the Yeseong River and traveling off-road to avoid U.N. guard posts. But where were they going?

Not across the DMZ, he hoped. When completed, the DMZ would be two and a half miles wide. But for now, in 1955, it was in the early stages of construction. Which meant when the construction teams ran into the countless unmarked minefields the North had planted, they would by-pass those hot spots. It could take years for unexploded ordinance specialists to find and defuse the explosives.

The woman ordered the driver, "Stop grinding the gears, and keep the rpm's down. We don't want to be heard by the American guard post ahead." She spoke in Korean, but Jason got the gist of what she said. And he realized "Ahead" was to the east.

The truck stopped by the edge of a field with a barbed wire cattle fence bordering the north side of the road. Attached to the fence were occasional identical triangular rusting metal signs with Korean characters Jason couldn't translate. Through the barbed wire he spotted a pile of animal bones, ghostly in the moonlight.

His captors prodded him out of the truck. They made him sit on the winch reel on the front bumper and lashed him to the grill. Jason felt as though his head would explode like a grenade, scattering in a dozen directions. Were they going to smash him into a tree for sport? Or just let his fearful imagination do him in for their amusement? He pulled himself together.

He had heard that Koreans were cruel to prisoners, and now he was beginning to believe it. A common practice with GI prisoners, according to old-timers back at the base, had been to place a garden hose up the rectum and turn on the water, blowing the GI's guts out through his mouth. He'd be left that way to die in the sun. Jason trembled and made his peace with God, then steeled himself.

One of the Koreans pulled cutters out of a GI duffle and cut a hole for the truck to pass through the barbed wire. Up ahead to the left, a faint glow indicated the lights of what he presumed was the city of Kaesŏng, north of the DMZ, suggesting he'd guessed correctly: they were still just south of the DMZ, a little east of where it angled south to terminate at the river. The truck lurched a few feet forward, then stopped right inside the fence while two of the Koreans repaired the barbed wire with splices, concealing their passage. No question now. They were going into North Korea.

Tom was ordered to walk twenty feet ahead of the truck, while their captors began driving hesitantly across the field. Bleached bones were strewn about the abandoned pasture. Dead cows or oxen. Jason saw that Tom was trembling. There was excited discussion of which way to go. The Koreans seemed to want Tom to go from one bone pile to the next.

Oh, shit! "Tom! It's a minefield! Be careful. Go to the skeletons. That's where the mines have already blown."

Tom turned back to the truck, eyes pleading in the vehicle's headlights. The Koreans held their guns as if they were going to fire at his abdomen, which would cause a slow death while the stomach acids ate at his organs. Jason prayed that Tom didn't know this. Yet he must have, because his legs seemed too weak to carry him. Still, he managed to turn and stagger across the field of bones in the direction the Koreans pointed. The truck followed at a snail's pace.

A nerve-shattering BAM!!! A blinding flash of light. Jason saw the exploding mine catapult Tom into the air, his left foot and pants leg missing, blood spurting from the remaining stump. Through the headlights Jason watched his fellow soldier land on his back screaming with his legs towards the truck.

Jason tried to force his body around as he shouted at the Koreans. "Cut me loose! He needs a tourniquet. Now, dammit!"

The woman signaled the driver to continue. Jason was horrified to see the left front wheel of the truck slowly advance up over Tom's legs and up his screaming body as his testicles were mashed. The driver stalled the truck.

The woman shouted orders at the driver, who re-started the engine.

"Damn you! Damn you! Damn you to hell!" Jason roared, as he watched the wheel lurch slowly up Tom's stomach, ribs breaking with a distinctive, crisp "snap" and squeezing thick, gelatinous ooze out his open, drowned mouth as his popping eyes pleaded and his hands, now free, reached up to Jason for help. Then the tire drove over his face. There was a hideous "crunch," and Tom disappeared.

In a rage born of absolute horror, Jason cursed his captors. They just laughed at his desperation.

Jason closed his eyes and tried to compose himself. *Thy will be done.*

The truck rumbled forward. He shuddered. Then he watched the ground between his legs with a mixture of fascination and terror. Heart thumping in his ears, he squirmed back on the winch, trying to protect himself. Could he survive long enough to reach the other side of this deadly tract?

CHAPTER 3
TORTURE

North Korea
Friday, May 13, 1955

When they finally reached the far side of the field the Koreans stopped, moved Jason into the back of the truck and drove on, along another narrow dirt road. They didn't check the line tying his wrists behind his back, and he discovered the knot had slipped when he'd struggled so violently to help Tom. They came to a set of tracks through the woods and drove in first gear, climbing steadily until they came out onto a regular dirt roadbed starting up a mountain.

Jason tried to memorize the road curves leading back to the turnoff, so he could find the trail in case—by some miracle—he got to come back down the mountain. They drove slowly for a couple of hours through heavily wooded, mountainous terrain.

He thought about his mother, an artist from a respected family in Washington, D.C. and his Scottish father, who had come to America to build a logging business in the Pacific Northwest. Both had been gymnasts in school. Jason had inherited their talents and their spirit of independence.

Even as a boy he had paranormal abilities, but his parents questioned them and insisted he keep this a secret so people wouldn't think he was crazy. His gift of premonition disturbed him. Inevitably it meant there was trouble ahead, never that something good was going to happen. On the other hand, he appreciated his gift of super-speed, which at times enabled him to see everything around him in slow-motion.

It made him virtually unbeatable in fights with loggers who felt compelled to challenge the boss's son. It proved invaluable in life-threatening situations. And then there were his occasional nightmares about being a Russian training to survive an enemy attack. Deeply disturbing, because he sensed these were not just dreams, but a parallel life he was somehow connected to. As though he had a twin counterpart.

The truck hit a pothole and jolted him back to the present. When the two men in back with him weren't paying attention, Jason tried to break the line tying his wrists together. While he couldn't break the nylon parachute cord, he did find his wrists had been tied with a granny knot. By exerting all his strength he loosened the slip-knot a little at a time until he had opened his lashings enough to free his hands when the moment was right. Hope began to replace fear.

They passed through a village where all lights were out and presumably everyone was sleeping. Eventually they came to a second village. They drove quietly most of the way through this dark village too, but turned left up an alley-like side street and stopped in front of a large building that extended out of the mountainside. The headlights illuminated a stone-and-timber construction like nothing Jason had ever seen in South Korea. He was certain that they had crossed the DMZ at the field of land mines, and had been driving in North Korea for as much as thirty miles.

Jason's captors pulled him out of the truck. They punched him, but just like when fighting, his body was able to tune out the pain. He was shoved through the door into a large room lit by a gas lantern hanging from the rafters. All sorts of U.S. military gear was heaped on the dirt floor.

Black marketeers.

A Russian soldier sitting at a rough wooden table greeted the Koreans and scowled at Jason. The Soviets had insisted they weren't involved in the Korean conflict. This raw-boned, blond giant wore the insignia of a sergeant on his sleeves. He seemed angry, and let the woman know about it in halting Korean. Jason got the gist—the Russian was upset they had let an American see him there.

Jason cooperated fully, praying they wouldn't check the cord at his wrists. They gagged him and stood him with his back against a rough-hewn post holding up beams bearing the earthen roof. The men tied a short length of parachute cord around his neck and the post. The man behind him tried to wrap the line twice, but it was too short, so he tied it with one wrap. Jason was surprised they didn't secure his feet and waist to the post, too. Then he realized, if for any reason he failed to stand, his breath would be cut off.

The four black marketeers took off their jackets and hung them over the backs of chairs around the table, less than eight feet from where he stood tied. The small, slender woman, wearing fatigues, revealed an impressive figure. Her face would be pretty if her expressions weren't so venomous. When she laughed coarsely and revealed her broken, yellow teeth, the spell was broken. Her evil was like a cloak. She was the one Jason feared most—her obvious hatred seemed to border on insanity.

The five began drinking something that looked like sake. Terrified about where he fit into their plans, his breathing became labored. Sweat ran into his eyes. And the gag hurt. Jason felt a wave of horror about what lay ahead. His eyes twitched with fear.

Fear canna serve any cause, laddie. Frightened, Jason looked around for his father. The words helped him regain control. His breathing calmed, his mind became alert, his body ready.

Jason could get his hands loose, but how could he free himself from the lashing around his throat before someone shot him? His captors were getting drunk and their weapons lay on the table.

The Russian soldier rose on unsteady feet and the woman laughed nervously as he dragged her out of sight among the stacks of stolen goods. Their activity was quick, noisy and obviously painful for her.

She returned half dressed and stood before Jason, her face reflecting her humiliation and hatred. Her shirt was buttonless now, and hung open, revealing large, purple-veined breasts. "Hey, GI, *you* want good time too?" she taunted.

"Do it!" the Russian growled in Korean, handing her his combat-issue bayonet.

She waved the knife back and forth under Jason's nose, enjoying the moment. Her rotten breath reeked of garlic.

Jesus! She's going to cut off my nose, gouge out my eyes. Or worse.

CHAPTER 4
"WHERE PRINCESS
RAN SANG-HEE?"

North Korea
Friday, May 13, 1955

Jason waited like a coiled spring, trembling, sweating, smelling his own electrified energy. His body concealed the fact he'd undone the line from his wrists.

Slowly, the woman's expression matched her eyes, turning grotesque, as she placed the bayonet blade against the gag under Jason's nose.

"GI, where Princess Ran Sang-hee?"

Suki! He held his breath and tried to remain expressionless. What did she know about Suki? About him? And how was he supposed to answer while gagged? The woman was crazy. Jason looked into a face twisted by evil.

Her eyes gave her away.

In them Jason saw the instant of her decision. Cords stood out on her neck as she raised the knife to slash his left eye and the side of his face. His gift of super-speed ignited.

The world around Jason slowed down and his captors seemed to move in slow-motion. He snapped his head to the right and lurched back against the post. He felt it give.

As if in a dream, the woman shrieked and slowly slashed at his eye.

Jason easily reached up with his left hand to grab the woman's wrist, and with his right hand to grasp the bayonet. With a powerful grip, he trapped her fingers between the palm of his hand and the bayonet handle.

A man at the table shouted and rose sluggishly, too late to help his leader. The drunk Russian standing behind her, slow to react, started to reach around her.

Jason used his left hand to draw the woman's arched waist to him as he forced her hand to slice the blade deep into the right side of her neck and her windpipe, cutting her carotid and jugular. Wide-eyed, with a strange rasping sound, she inhaled a huge gulp of air mixed with blood and tried to clutch her throat as Jason snatched the bayonet from her grasp, released her, raised one foot to her chest and kicked her backwards as hard as he could. The force of the blow snapped the defective post he was tied to. Overhead beams groaned as earth and rocks from the roof above sifted down. Clutching her throat, eyes agog, the woman slammed into the Russian and they fell against the table, turning it on its side, scattering weapons across the floor. Jason slashed the line holding his throat to the post, leapt to crouch beside the fallen Russian and slashed his throat before the soldier knew what was happening.

The soldier grabbed Jason's ankle in a vise-like grip. Jason crushed the back of his skull with the heavy bayonet handle, broke free and ran for the door.

One of the Koreans moved to block Jason's escape. Jason feinted for the man's face as Hyo had taught him, then jabbed his knife to the hilt into the man's unguarded chest, twisted hard, withdrew the blade in a fountain of blood and bolted for the door. The remaining two men scrambled for their weapons. Jason wrenched the door open and hurled himself through. He slithered past the truck, sprinted down the alley, rounded the corner and barreled up, not down, the village street, hoping to shake the men in pursuit.

He heard steps running after him—a very fast runner. Jason ducked into a side street, stopped, waited a second. Then he leapt out, bending low and thrusting the knife into the man's stomach. He ripped savagely up and out, spilling his enemy's guts. The man's Thompson hit the earth. Jason scooped it up and raced on up the main street.

After a short distance, he flattened himself in the dark doorway of a shallow porch and waited. Still gagged, he tried to quiet his noisy breathing so he could listen. Impatiently, he cut off the suffocating gag and took controlled gulps of precious air.

He heard more footsteps approaching.

The last man was running close to the house. He reached the porch. Leaping forward, Jason thrust the blade into the base of the man's throat. The force of the blow stopped the runner as if he'd hit a wall. The startled man's legs collapsed and he sat down abruptly. His eyes glinted in the moonlight as he stared wide-eyed at Jason. His eyes rolled back. Jason took the Colt .45 from the dying man's hand, un-cocked the weapon, and retrieved the bayonet, whispering, "Gamsahamnida," thank you. The last of his captors fell back motionless.

Jason's perceptions returned to normal time. He listened, fighting to normalize his breathing, straining to see or hear any indication of human activity. The mountain villagers had slept through the sounds of running feet—or, afraid of becoming involved, they were feigning sleep. *Thank God.*

He spotted the dead man's sandals, too big for the Korean's feet. Maybe they'd work for Jason. He removed them and walked between two houses, being careful to leave boot tracks in a garden. He headed up into the tree line behind the houses, as if escaping up into the mountain. Standing on a slab of rock, he took off his boots and slid his feet into the sandals. He'd leave no boot tracks in the dirt road heading back down the mountain. Staying in the tree line, he paralleled the road up the mountain for three houses, then returned to the road and cautiously headed down the mountain, through the sleeping village.

His stomach knotted when he looked at the two men he'd killed. As he passed each dark house, he tensed fearing a bullet would tear into his body. Hardly breathing, listening for any sound, he continued his fearful way.

CHAPTER 5
FANTASTIC CONNECTION

North Korea
Friday, May 13, 1955

At the first bend in the road beyond the village, Jason stopped. He wanted to roar at the night. He breathed in the invigorating mountain air. His heart pounded like a jungle drum thumping inside his chest. It wasn't the physical exertion of his escape, but something primitive awakened in him.

Raw emotion. He felt as pumped as a gladiator who looks about him and realizes that he has survived all the other gladiators in the Roman coliseum.

Jason smiled. It had been so easy to take the lives of his captors—almost too easy. In reflection he smelled the unwashed body odors and repulsive breath, the pheromones of fear mixed with gushing blood, the sickening stench of opened guts as he killed his captors. He felt like a Sioux warrior assuming the power of his dead enemies. Jason stretched, balanced on the balls of his feet, arms wide, invincible.

Then to his shame, he found himself lusting, possessed by an urge to take a woman—any woman—like an animal filled with life's energy and an inextinguishable will to live on. God, he had such a throbbing hard-on stretching his pants ... it ached so terribly he freed it, and groaning, dropped to his knees.

His mind swirled into another dimension and he saw a dark-haired young woman, muscular like an Amazon. She was on her back, arching up on her shoulders and separated feet, ravishing him wildly. Was he losing it? *Oh my god she's good.* His orgasm began to rack him, but she shoved him away and another woman, a blonde soldier with a striped tee-shirt, lay dying in his arms, her tear-filled eyes glassy, the lids like the petals of a rose withering and folding a final time. In that surreal moment, Jason saw the sad reality of nature—how fragile and precious life was, how fiercely it must be cherished even at the most elemental levels.

Having visited with the gods, he returned to earth.

Thank you, God, for allowing me to live.

Jason rubbed his forehead to recompose himself. The hallucination seemed so real. His human intellect brought him down. Harshly. This was North Korea and five people had just died so that he might live.

He didn't like what he'd had to do for the privilege of life. More, what he'd just *been* and felt at the expense of others.

But this was not about him. It was about *life*. Life would go on whether he lived or not.

With inexplicable insight, he reminded himself he was only a player in some plan too grand for him to see. Confused, he shook his head hard to bring himself back to the urgency of continuing his escape. His escape from North Korea.

And his escape from disturbing self-revelation.

He made himself focus on the village back around the bend. All remained still.

He put on his boots, figuring army vehicles coming up the mountain in the morning would obliterate his tracks in the dirt. He'd ditch the sandals far from here.

Jason began his hazardous journey towards the DMZ. Downhill was easy. He paced himself for distance running. It felt good. Damn good, just to be alive.

CHAPTER 6
WEIRD REALITY

North Korea

Saturday, May 14, 1955

As Jason pushed on through the night, his mind was sharp. What were his options? He had to assume that when the bodies were discovered with the hijacked truck, the North Koreans would figure out what happened, figure he was a GI and that he'd have to backtrack to escape. That should be some manhunt. Especially since a GI had seen the Russian.

He stopped where a driveway met the road. Barnyard odors—probably oxen. Hungry and knowing he needed nourishment to keep going, he looked for a chicken enclosure. He spotted one and was gathering eggs when the squawking and clucking brought a man's voice. "Eh? Eh?"

Jason raced up the drive before the farmer could see him, and continued down the mountain road. He stopped, ate two eggs raw, hiding the shells in his jacket pocket, then carefully placed the rest of the eggs in each pocket of his fatigue shirt and field jacket.

Carrying the Thompson impeded his running efficiency and threatened to break his eggs. Jason removed some of the .45 Parabellum bullets as spares for the pistol. He separated the magazine from the submachine gun and heaved them well apart into the wooded ravine below the edge of the road. One less weapon for the enemy. He continued running through the night feeling his steady heartbeat while his emotions returned to something more normal.

As he ran he said to himself over and over, *Think life, not death.*

Jason smelled wood smoke ahead just as pale fingers of light crept over the eastern horizon. He figured the aroma was coming from the first village they'd passed through while driving up the mountain road. Its residents must be waking up to the new day. He couldn't use the road any longer.

He looked for a place where water ran down the mountain and where there would be enough bare rocks so he'd leave no footprints. When the light was better, he found a rivulet and began climbing from rock to rock, being careful not to disturb the foliage or leave any trace of his passing. He climbed for almost two hours before he heard a motorcade advancing up the mountain road to the village where they'd find his truck and the bodies. *Good, that many vehicles will obliterate my tracks.*

He was up really high now. For the next twenty minutes he rested. He ate two more of the eggs raw. Hidden cocoon-like in a dense thicket, he had the trickle stream for drinking water. He dozed until he heard the Russian helicopters and a Russian liaison plane. He was worried about the intensity of the search. Perfectly concealed in the lush underbrush, he slept fitfully throughout the day. He decided it was safest to stay in hiding that night.

He worried about Suki and missed her. For months she had taught him three-thousand-year-old Taoist lovemaking disciplines, possibilities he'd never imagined. Remembering their happy nights together, he dozed off.

Jason, who rarely dreamed, found himself with the Amazon lover again, crowded in some tiny space. In the overhead light, Jason saw she had on a tight dress, but no underwear. Her dress was unbuttoned to expose perfectly-tanned breasts. The skirt was pulled up to her waist, revealing her open, seamlessly-tanned thighs and everything between. She was perched on a minuscule sink, zestfully taking him into her.

"Deeper. Come deeper. Find the source of life deep within me, then give me your little death." He straightened his knees, raising her off the sink, her dangling legs spread. She gasped, whispered hoarsely, "That's it, you've found the life—my altar for your *petits morts.* Now live the little death that gives life." Jason came so hard he woke to his cries of ecstasy.

First she'd come to him as a dim vision to keep him going while he was escaping, then as a vivid dream of life while he slept. Suddenly he knew what it was. His alter-ego, his other persona—whatever—had experienced his escape, knew his plight and was going to a lot of trouble to encourage him to live. But by sharing his woman ... ?

Strange thing though. The Amazon woman didn't have orgasms herself, just serviced her man expertly—albeit with love. What was it they didn't know, hadn't learned? It made no sense, because Jason knew his counterpart cared for her deeply. And when you cared about a woman, you didn't ... *my God, they don't know women can come too.*

Jason slept again. A bad dream took over. He saw the evil Korean woman's look of shock when he forced the knife across her trachea and jugular. Blood surging while she tried to stem the flow with her free hand. Gagging over the mixture of blood and air in her lungs, knowing she was dying and powerless to do anything about it, the air whooshing out of her as Jason kicked her away. Then he felt himself falling ... falling ... terrified. He awoke sitting bolt upright, sweating despite the cold, praying he hadn't screamed—praying if he had it wasn't heard.

Finally Jason had time to reflect on what he'd done. He'd never taken a human life before. After what they did to Tom Riley, the Koreans needed to die. He didn't mind about the men. He could move on from that.

The woman was different. He didn't think he'd ever be able to forget the malevolent hatred, the pure evil she directed at him. Did she hate him specifically, or just the fact he was American? He wished to God he'd never met her.

No question an evil man was after lovely Suki. Her cruel North Korean black market lord had organized people on both sides of the DMZ to offer tempting rewards for finding his runaway wife. Was the vast effort to get her back simply a cuckold's pride? Or was it more serious—like the fact Suki had taken off with his wedding gift to her of the family jewels, going back for centuries and worth millions? Sadly for Jason, Suki would be on her way to Vancouver by now, looking forward to her new life in the vastness of North America. That had always been her goal, and now that he had disappeared, she would have moved forward with her plan. God, he'd miss her.

Suki had taught him that women had to be responsible one way or another for their own orgasms, enabling them to enjoy and to be exciting in bed every time. She taught him how men could have multiple orgasms by learning the disciplines of the dry orgasm while building to a tsunami. She showed him that women are capable of such passion and endurance that they are more than equal to any man. Suki told him her endurance came from training the muscles in her crucible with a heavy jade egg. In the midst of this remarkable journey into the world of bliss, it had been important to him that the heat of their relationship was matched by their respect and consideration for each other. He was grateful for her companionship; her feminine civility was a welcome counterbalance to the rough, masculine world of the army. He fell asleep praying for her safety and wellbeing.

The next morning he heard voices all around. The Russian helicopters and small planes swarmed like dragonflies. It was now Sunday. He wondered if he'd left some sign showing where he'd abandoned the road and begun climbing the mountain, or was this all part of a massive general search? If so, then somebody high in command was reading much more into his escape than Jason knew about.

He decided to lie low, hidden in his thicket, for another two days and nights before trying to move down the mountain. That would give the Korean soldiers time to assume he'd made his escape. Hopefully, they'd call off the search. Exhausted and hungry, he lived on the raw eggs he'd stolen and water from the tiny stream.

Alone and waiting, he felt his optimism waning. It seemed like half the North Korean army was after him, along with those Russian liaison planes and choppers. The odds of his escaping appeared minuscule. Overwhelmed by thoughts of Tom's horrible death, Jason's chest and throat felt as if they would burst. He had no intention of being taken alive, and imagined what it would feel like when the enemy soldiers' bullets tore apart his muscles and organs, to lie there in shock and watch their faces grow dim.

CHAPTER 7
LIFESAVING VISION

North Korea
Monday, May 16, 1955

Jason's morbid thoughts were pushed aside by a beautiful vision, a lovely young woman with glorious hair. Her tear-filled eyes, like shimmering pools, seemed to say she couldn't bear to lose him.

The feeling that she was real was so intense he resolved to continue his ordeal, his effort to escape from enemy territory. In that moment, he *knew* she was his angel. He was being watched over and was on earth for a purpose, being prepared for something. But what? At peace finally, Jason slept.

When he awoke, he knew the answer. All his life, his parents insisted he ignore his premonitions and visions so people wouldn't think him odd, a misfit. Now it was clear he must accept his gifts and use them for good, no matter what other people might think. *Oh God.* The senseless cruelty of Tom's death flooded into his mind and Jason did something he hadn't given in to since his Airedale, Brutus, had been hit by a car and killed. He wept. Long, wrenching sobs.

* * *

The location of Kimpo U.S. Air Force Base was evident from the air traffic over it. Jason guessed it was about twenty-five miles away as the crow flies. He made himself wait. Finally the Russian helicopters and liaison planes stopped their incessant searching. He waited throughout another day of silence. Finally, on Tuesday, as soon as it was dark, he started back down the mountain to the village. He had to eat.

All was quiet in the village. A half moon rose in the sky, and Jason could see well enough to find a chicken shed. This time the chickens didn't squawk. He ate some eggs on the spot and placed the shells carefully in his pocket, leaving no trace of his presence. He put more eggs in other pockets. Eggs were the only safe food available. No time to get sick. He wished there was a way to get some bread. *God, that would taste good right now.*

Walking through the village, he spotted bicycles. Did he dare try the road? If he walked through the woods, he risked hurting himself in the dark and it would take days while growing weaker and weaker. He decided to risk the road with a bike. He selected a large, sturdy one, swung his leg over the seat and pedaled off, listening carefully for any sound of human activity. When the bike was discovered missing in the morning, the soldiers would know how to find him, but by then he'd be back across the DMZ. Or not.

After several hours of cautious, easy pedaling downhill, Jason spotted the pair of forked "schoolmarm" trees he'd noted at the entrance to the rough road they'd taken through the woods so many nights ago. The rutted, rocky trail was difficult to maneuver on the bicycle, but doable in the moonlight. He had to make time.

In places the trail disappeared altogether and he could barely track wheel marks passing several different ways around boulders and between the trees. When he sensed he was nearing the DMZ, he decided to lose the bike in a thicket. He jogged as quickly as he could with reasonable stealth, on downhill through the woods, listening and looking ahead, every sense fine-tuned.

Oh, shit. Where did that come from? Two Korean soldiers talking quietly at their guard post on a cleared road running east-west. His captors must have gone around them.

Jason had gotten off-track. Not good. How would he find the minefield crossing now? Was he trapped in North Korea? If he didn't make it across tonight, they'd get him.

Beyond the guard post was a barbed wire fence. Jason stalked the two soldiers by blending into the sparse woods beside the road. He'd expected more. This was a threadbare DMZ guard post. Was it a trap? He lay on the ground, watching and listening carefully, his heart thrumming in his chest. It really did seem to be just the two guards. He thought of Hannibal crossing the Alps in winter to conquer ancient Rome and remembered his historic words: *"Either find a way, or make it."*

Thankfully, the breeze was out of the south, so the Koreans wouldn't smell him approaching. Since these were the only guards, Jason guessed there must be land mines extending out from the roadblock into the woods on both sides of the road, so sneaking around them would be too risky.

Jason had nothing against these guys. They were only doing their job. But they stood between him and the American side, and would kill him if they had to. He said a little prayer, asking forgiveness for what he was about to do, and crawled forward, trying to still his fear.

Like most Korean soldiers, the men were small and wiry. Neither had on his helmet. They sat on their heels, surrounded by sandbags, chatting quietly. Their sides were to Jason as they faced one another, eating rice out of wooden bowls with their chopsticks. Their weapons were propped up against the sandbags beside them and a machine gun in its mount aimed south.

Pistol in one hand, knife in the other, Jason sprang over the sandbags. With a savage blow to the head of the older man on the right, Jason lunged with the knife for the throat of the second soldier. The youth's eyes bugged as he scrambled backwards and came up against the sandbags, where in stark fear the beardless teenager froze and waited for the death blow. Jason couldn't do it. With the pistol again, he knocked the soldier unconscious.

Jason looked up and down the road along the fence. Should he look for the crossover east or west? Something said west. He began running along the newly cleared road. Soon he was back in the terrain and foliage where his captors had crossed over, but at night he couldn't find the minefield again. Wait. Bleached cow bones ahead. He really didn't want to cross that field of mutilation and death. Once was enough. The word was the North Koreans lost many of their own people, and countless domestic and wild animals, in their unmarked minefields. But the South Korean edge of the DMZ had to be on the other side.

Jason pulled out his bayonet. He knew from basic training that the detonators were on the tops of the mines. He crawled on his hands and knees towards the first set of bones, probing the earth ahead with his bayonet at a shallow angle so it would hit the side of any mine buried in his path—warning him to go around.

Probing center, right and left, was taking too long. He switched to right and left, stabbing faster. He pushed onward, and heard a metallic thunk as his blade hit something hard. *Jesus!* He knelt there, sweat pouring off his face, and waited. *Oh, God. Help me.*

He worked his way around the mine and continued to the next set of bones, heart in throat. Then he saw the fence they'd cut, with the road beyond. The DMZ was only about a hundred yards wide here. This must be an old fence alongside an abandoned service road inside the DMZ.

Oh shit! Jason turned and began probing to his right, towards a dark object that smelled foul. Tom's eyes were gone, probably eaten by birds. Jason stood and looked to the fence, remembering the way they'd come to get here. Slipping the knife into his belt, Jason steeled himself and lifted Tom's mutilated body across his shoulders. He staggered to the fence and cut himself holding the barbed wire to climb through it with his grisly burden.

He was on the South Korean side now.

Time was crucial. When the guard changed at the North Korean post, there would be helicopters again, the works. He knew something big was going on. If he made it to safety, he might learn what it was. And he wondered, if he lived to get home, whether he'd find Suki waiting.

In the dim light of a dawning day, Jason headed east, where, on the night of his kidnapping, the woman had indicated there was an American guard post. He prayed he wouldn't step on a stray mine and trotted along the road as fast as he could with Tom.

There it was, with flag flying.

"We're going home, Tom."

Jason found new strength. Running towards the American post, he called out in his rich baritone voice that seemed to reverberate and echo in the foothills. "We're escaped Americans."

CHAPTER 8
FBI AGENT THOMAS

Kirkland, Washington
Wednesday, June 15, 1955

The soldier helping Jason lower Tom's body cried out in a horrified voice, "What's that all over you, man?" He leapt away, leaving Jason on his own to finish lowering Tom's weight. Then Jason saw the maggots infesting Tom—and crawling on himself. Hyperventilating, Jason tore off his uniform and began rubbing the writhing white flesh-eaters off his body and out of his hair. "For the love of God, have you got a water hose?"

Jason awoke from his recurring nightmare. He was home in his parents' Kirkland house, leaping around his bedroom in naked panic. This wasn't the first time. Once again, he stood under the soothing water of the shower and scrubbed himself with a washcloth—knowing the maggots were long gone, still dreading he'd find some.

Later that morning, he was working out when he heard a car drive up, followed by a sharp knock at the front door. His parents were in the Port Angeles main office, taking care of business, so he grabbed a towel and looked out the kitchen window. Parked next to the green family pickup was a plain white Ford sedan with blackwall tires and an unusual antenna mounted by the trunk. Wiping his sweaty face and torso as he walked through the living room, he opened the door. A tall, balding man in a business suit held out his hand, flashing a thin black wallet with an FBI badge and an identification card.

"FBI Agent Frank Thomas. May I come in and have a few words with you, Mr. MacDougall?"

Jason reached out for the hand with the card and held it so he could read the ID. "Franklin R. Thomas, Assistant Special Agent in Charge, Seattle." He invited the man in and watched him taking in the room, then the lakefront view out the picture windows. Ducks were feeding on the lawn between the house and wooden dock where his family's cruising ketch rocked restlessly in its berth. Lake Washington stretched on to the south. Open windows faced majestic Mount Rainier towering over the lake to the southeast. A cool breeze blew in from the snow-capped mountain. Jason offered Thomas a seat on the leather sofa.

The agent reached over to the coffee table and touched the open copy of *TIME Magazine* that Jason had been reading. Looking up at Jason, he said, "Fascinating article about the twins. Imagine them actually sharing what's happening even while separated, if one gets into trouble. That part about a twin trapped in her truck in an accident late at night on a lonely ranch road, somehow communicating to her brother to come sixty miles and rescue her. That's a hard one to buy."

Jason had been intrigued by the article. It confirmed the possibility of those otherwise inexplicable experiences in his life. "Only if you're not a twin," he said.

He decided to ignore the agent's look of inquiry. That dimension of his life was too strange to discuss with anyone, especially the FBI. He dried the sweat from his face and chest a final time, draped his towel over the back of a chair and put on his shirt.

"Coffee?" Jason offered, pouring himself a steaming mugful.

"I'd like to say yes, but my doctor says no."

High blood pressure? He appeared too fit for that. Looking down at the agent, Jason sipped his black coffee. "I thought my discharge after Uncle Sam flew me home meant I was free of government agencies for a while. What's an Assistant Special Agent in Charge anyway?"

The man smiled faintly. "Well, I could say it means I'm second in command of FBI operations in the State of Washington, working out of our Seattle headquarters on Third Avenue. But it's simply the government's way of saying I assist the Special Agent in Charge."

"Why'd he send someone as important as you for an unannounced meeting with a nobody, in an unsecured location?"

"It wasn't he who sent me, Mr. MacDougall. J. Edgar Hoover himself did. I've just returned from a meeting with him in Washington, D.C. So, you see, you're not such a nobody after all."

Shit. This man's trouble. "Is there a problem?"

"Not to my knowledge. Mr. Hoover had me read your military file, in his presence. He keeps it locked in a walk-in safe with files only he has access to. Your file is marked, '*TOP SECRET, EYES ONLY.*' It seems the State Department has asked Mr. Hoover to be responsible for seeing to it that no one ever learns of your misadventure in North Korea. He said the State Department remains nervous about North Korea finding proof that a lone American made the North appear toothless before their Russian allies and that this American could testify to the presence of Soviet operatives remaining in North Korea after the armistice. Mr. Hoover wants me to remain in contact with you regularly and be available if you ever have problems."

Jason didn't like the sound of this. "What sort of problems?"

Thomas spoke in an easy voice. "For example, if you start feeling people are watching you. We'll check them out and cover your back. Or, if, like a lot of vets, you were to start drinking and talking too much."

"Then what?" Jason challenged.

"Then we'd have to see," Thomas countered.

"So an honorable discharge isn't enough? I still have to answer to the government?"

"Fraid so, Mr. MacDougall. There's stuff going on you don't know about. Nobody does."

Jason paced, his face feeling warm. "And that's supposed to make me sleep better."

"It won't be a problem so long as the North Koreans and Russians don't learn it was you who made them look so bad."

"That doesn't explain why half the North Korean Army was searching for one man. I'd prefer it if you'd stop treating me like some barefoot yokel, Agent Thomas."

The agent passed a hand over his scalp. "The woman you killed was the drug-addicted daughter of one of North Korea's top generals. And there is no doubt that he'd start World War III to get you."

Jason thought about this for a minute, and decided to accept what he couldn't change. "So how do we handle this?"

Agent Thomas handed Jason his card. "Keep this on your person at all times."

Jason glanced at the card and handed it right back. "Okay, I've got it."

"Mr. MacDougall, this is serious. It's important for you to be able to reach me at a moment's notice."

"It's alright. It's in my head to stay. 1110 Third Avenue, Room 605; a generic switchboard phone number nobody could forget."

Thomas raised a brow, apparently impressed. "Even so, I want you to keep this card in your billfold at all times, so if anything happens, I'll be called." He handed it back to Jason. "I might try your coffee after all. Black, please. Are you planning to stay in Seattle?"

Jason brought him a mug of coffee and sat in a chair angled toward the agent. "I love Seattle. But I've come home to a changed America."

Thomas leaned forward. "How so?"

"Television. Everyone sits around their new plastic boxes watching the Jackie Gleason show and 'I Love Lucy,' instead turning it off and talking to each other or relaxing over a good game of bridge. And suddenly I can't handle people who complain about life in the States, because now I know people overseas who don't have our freedoms, and they would give an arm or leg to trade places with the least advantaged person in this country."

"So you're having a tough time making the adjustment back into civilian life?"

"You bet I am. What do any of you know about having to kill the enemy—real people, watching them die right in front of you—and then trying to fit back into society?"

"Combat veterans call it 'the long walk home'," Thomas said, closing his eyes for a moment. "I was in the slaughter they refer to as the Normandy Invasion. I still relive D-Day in my nightmares."

For the first time since his discharge, Jason felt comfortable with a civilian. He tried to talk about it. "It's like going through a revolving door into another world and coming back out a changed person. You've learned you have the ability to do terrible things. Now there's a raging monster hidden deep inside your former self."

Thomas nodded.

"What happened in Korea has made me feel like a loose cannon in society, but it has taught me that I should complete my education and serve my country by going to one of the military academies. At least there I'll live with people who don't take their freedoms for granted. My godfather teaches at the Naval War College and he's offered to help me qualify for the Naval Academy in Annapolis. I'm planning to take their entrance exams and then report with next year's class of plebes. Freshmen," he clarified.

"Don't the plebes start in the summer?"

"July. I'll be working with my father in his logging business for a year. Academy exams are next winter and I'll be studying like crazy."

Thomas made notes.

Jason looked at his watch and stood. "I've barely got time to shower and pick up our rebuilt starter for the boat. Can we continue this later?"

He'd escaped from North Korea and made it home alive, but now he still had to watch his back. If he tried to locate Suki in Vancouver, he could expose her to the same danger he was in.

CHAPTER 9
SUKI

"Fulfill Your Destiny"—the title of the Naval Academy material Jason had just received from his godfather. Destiny continued to be in his thoughts as he finished installing the new starter on the boat. He cleaned up and relaxed in an outdoor chair on his family's back lawn, taking in the magnificent view across Lake Washington to Mount Rainier. He pondered the possibility of destiny—a plan for his life that would give meaning to his special gifts, a reason for the extraordinary experiences with Suki and Hyo, an explanation for the angelic woman in his vision.

He thought back to his arrival at the 526th Engineer Company compound at Ouijongbu, Korea. Sent directly to the Orderly Room to report to the company commander, he was given a friendly greeting by Lieutenant Donaldson. The short, fit officer, in his early thirties, had Jason's file on his desk.

"MacDougall, I'll get right to the point. I see you were drafted right after your twentieth birthday. You got the highest scores ever recorded in the Seattle area for officer candidate school exams. In basic training the company commander at Fort Ord made you leader of the forty-man First Platoon. But after basic, instead of going to OCS, you were sent to Engineer Corps training at Fort Hood. What happened?"

"Before we graduated from basic, they tested our athletic ability. After the other men were deployed, they kept running me around a quarter-mile track, day after day, while they scratched their heads. Said they couldn't get my pulse or blood pressure to change. They flew in a team of doctors from Fort Benning to test me. The doctors never did figure out why my readings remained normal under stress, but they cleared me for OCS. That's when the sergeant in the Orderly Room told me they'd made me miss my cycle at OCS and I'd have to enlist for an extra year to attend the next cycle. I opted instead for engineering school, and wound up training at Fort Belvior to become a combat construction foreman."

"Where you graduated at the top of your class again." The Lieutenant looked squarely at Jason and said, "What really happened, MacDougall? Why aren't you standing before me as an officer?"

"Alright." Jason didn't see how he could avoid answering. "Near the end of basic, our company commander wanted to look good in the war bond drive, so he ordered me to make all my men sign up to buy a bond and the money would come out of every month's pay. That ten dollars was all the married men had each month for themselves, because it took the rest to support their families. I told the company officer why I couldn't, in good conscience, carry out the order. He was not pleased. I think he made me miss OCS deliberately. I didn't want to sign up for the extra year and risk spending it with another small-minded person like him."

Lieutenant Donaldson smiled. "We'll try not to disappoint you. We're stretched thin for the reconstruction. I'll assign you to the motor pool to lead convoys. I'll have the motor pool sergeant teach you to drive the semi with the bulldozer loaded. If you can get that rig through these tiny, curvy roads, the rest of the company vehicles can make it too. Also, since the ceasefire seems to be holding, we should start daily physical training. I'd like you to lead the full company in PT every morning before breakfast. And how'd you like to teach English to the KATUSAs a couple of evenings each week?"

"KATUSAs?"

"Korean Army personnel attached to the U.S. Army." He handed Jason a manual.

Jason flipped through the all-English text designed for teaching English with the help of a translator. "I'll do my best, sir."

Lieutenant Donaldson tapped Jason's file. "The fights in your file—how you took down the crazed soldier at Fort Hood who came at you with the machete, and the man you were boxing that tried to knife you. Your test scores and your fame as an unbeatable fighter from logging country precede you. Don't be surprised if the company's top dawg challenges you. Watch him. He fights dirty."

* * *

Sul Wan Kee, a civilian mechanic in the Motor Pool, already spoke some English. "Mr. Jason, my daughter needs an operation on her leg. You help me get money for doctor, I pay back." He said he adopted the little girl from next door after she was wounded by strafing from an American fighter jet that killed her parents and siblings. Jason didn't smoke, so he gave Sul his GI ration of American cigarettes. Sul turned the two cartons into enough *won* on the black market to pay the doctor.

Jason's fellow soldiers laughed. "You'll never see that money again."

"Surgery was success," Sul announced two weeks later. "You take money now."

"Keep it for your family, Sul, and I'll give you all my tobacco rations from now on."

A week later, Sul said, "Come my house, dinner, tomorrow." Jason was honored. Only Korean prostitutes invited GIs into the places they lived, and not for meals—and certainly not to meet their spouse and children.

Ouijonbu was a shanty town along a dirt road in a valley between high, de-forested hills. Typical of the dwellings, Sul Wan Kee's house was built from a mixture of hand-hewn and sawn lumber for framework and flooring, "reclaimed" plywood, mud and salvaged corrugated metal or flattened beer cans used like shingles for roofing. Jason left his boots on the ground in front of the porch and followed his host through the lightweight sliding door. Its wood frame was covered with paper that provided both visual privacy and natural light for the interior.

Sul, the bilingual one of the gathering, introduced each member of his family. Little Ho Sook, in her new plaster cast, gave him a shy smile. Then Sul turned to the best-looking young Korean woman Jason had seen. Her face was pretty by western standards and her breasts unusually curvaceous beneath her shirt. "This Suki," said Sul. "She not speak English."

Jason wondered why Suki was dressed in casual Sears Roebuck clothing, like all the local prostitutes, but bowed so regally, not taking her eyes off Jason's stare. He was curious that Suki knelt elegantly on the floor-mat throughout the cordial dinner, hardly eating, as hosts and guest sat cross-legged or kneeling, relishing the food. She never spoke while Jason and Sul Wan Kee's family learned about each other's lives through amusing stories.

When everyone had eaten their fill, Sul presented Jason a heavy bundle of black silk. Jason unwrapped it to reveal a hunting knife in a leather sheath. He unsheathed it and admired the thick-bladed tool, testing the blade's sharp edge and its balance. "It's magnificent, Sul." He handed it back.

Sul raised a hand, palm out. "You keep. I make for you be thank you. I forge from worn-out twenty-inch file in motor pool. I weld brazing rod both sides for thickness and make balance with bone handle."

Jason withdrew the blade from its sheath once more and admired the burnished steel sandwiched between the polished gold of the brazing rod. He was touched by such a special gift and locked eyes with Sul. "I don't know how to thank you."

Sul's wife and young children excused themselves and left the single-room home. Only Sul and Suki remained. They sat silently, facing him. Jason waited and wondered. The lovely woman must be here for him. But why? What did she need? Her hands and complexion seemed too perfectly cared for. Was she another kind of thank you?

CHAPTER 10
SUKI'S PROPOSITION

Kirkland, Washington
Wednesday, June 15, 1955

Jason recalled the way Suki seemed to float up on her feet. He rose with her. Before him stood a shapely young woman whose eyes suggested she was wise beyond her years. She spoke briefly in Korean to Sul Wan Kee. Her throaty voice carried an authoritative tone.

Sul led them out to the porch. "Suki ask you follow her. Is safe for you." Bowing, he stepped back through the doorway.

Curious but cautious, Jason laced his boots and hastened after her. Deep in the village of tiny homes, Suki turned up an alley and stepped up onto the porch of two joined houses set well back from the others.

Jason remembered how surprised he had been to see his young houseboy, Kim Kibonee, waiting on the porch. Kim Kibonee took care of the cleaning and laundry for him and the eight other GIs in his tent at the company compound. It was houseboy Kim who had introduced Jason to Sul Wan Kee when he needed help. Kim Kibonee opened the sliding door and Suki removed her shoes and entered the house. Kim gestured for Jason to follow.

Jason stepped onto the porch and removed his boots, surreptitiously looking back to get his first good view of the secretive person who had been following them. The shadow was a powerful, gladiator-like man in traditional white farmer's clothing. Kim slid the door open again and Jason walked through, tense and on guard.

Suki stood on a straw mat in the middle of an immaculate hardwood floor. Jason glanced around the room. Against the far wall, free-standing floor-to-ceiling bookshelves behind a partially closed silk curtain, a double-wide futon rolled up on the floor beside it, and in the corner, a magnificent wooden clothing chest, elegantly carved, with ivory inlay. Nothing more. No one else.

Kim Kibonee followed him into the room. "I interpret."

"Interpret what?"

Kim's eyes were bright as he shrugged. "Ask her."

"Tell her I'm not looking for a companion."

Jason watched Suki's eyes narrow as she replied.

Kim translated. "She say you not be here if she believe you are."

Jason felt his face smart. "Tell her I apologize for misunderstanding. Why the American clothing then?" He cleared his throat. "And why am I here?"

"Clothing is disguise for princess. She want make you pro-po-si-tion." Kim mispronounced proposition badly, as if he'd just learned the word from someone who couldn't say it correctly.

"Proposition with a princess. I understand." Jason smiled faintly, but knew his voice betrayed his skepticism.

Suki spoke again.

"She is hiding from cruel lord," Kim translated. "He never think to search for his wife as prostitute. She believes you are good man. Wants to make people believe she your prostitute. She want you teach her perfect English for new life in America. You promise you not speak about her, or she die." Kim's hand slipped into his knife pocket as he spoke.

Jason's stomach tightened. "And in such an event, am I to die too?"

Kim blushed and jerked his hand out of his pocket as if his knife had burned it.

Jason watched Suki listen closely and observe with seeming approval. Still skeptical, he said, "She's trouble. Why should I take such risks for her?"

After Kim's translation, she spoke through the houseboy.

"She say she place her life in your hands. Her real name is Princess Ran Sang-hee. From Pyongyang. Is capitol of North Korea. Reward for find her make anyone very rich. She say she give you choice: collect reward—or she can teach you three thousand-year-old arts of love for American goddess you marry."

Jason smiled. "I thought when I meet the right woman, all that happens naturally." Jason looked directly at Suki. "A goddess, huh. How would she know that, Kim?"

Kim interpreted and Suki spat out her response.

"She say after she teach you, any woman you marry feel like goddess. She talk to prostitutes here. They say Americans are culture that knows no more about sex than animals. Have orgasm and roll over and go to sleep. Easiest two dollars they ever make."

"How does she know about three thousand-year-old arts of love?" Suki spoke.

"She was student-teacher for four years"—Kim held up four fingers—"along with studies in special school to prepare princes and princesses for married life."

"You mean like a finishing school for Geishas?"

Suki spoke with a tinge of irritation.

"She say no. Geishas not royalty. Not taught royal secrets. Geishas only taught to entertain men, not secrets to help train princes."

Suki's eyes were flashing at him.

The challenge was irresistible, but this was a set-up loaded with trouble. "Why is her life threatened?" An image popped into Jason's mind. "Did she steal the family jewels?"

Suki gasped, her hand flying to her throat, and both she and Kim blanched.

"Her husband control many people who search for her. She choose die before go back."

"Why did she marry such a terrible man?"

"Marriage planned by her father and father of rich lord when Suki and her lord are children—so rich father take care of her poor father. Suki's ancestors, big name in royalty. Her name Sang-hee mean 'Benevolence and Pleasure.' Her father lose money in Japanese occupation. Her lord's family in disgrace, for helping Japanese during occupation. They not nice people. Suki's lord is chief of black market in North Korea."

"Why doesn't Suki escape to America now, and learn English there?"

"Papers take much time. Must make new identity. Find Korean baby born in America who die very young, with rich parents who die later. Take baby's identity. Forge perfect papers and history. Must make new identity for two others."

"And who is performing such difficult, specialized work?"

Kim drew his slender frame up proudly. "My uncle big man in local black market."

"And who pays him?"

Kim spoke questioningly to Suki, who gave him a nod.

"She has money. And two servants for life. One is Yun Hee, her handmaid. And man, Hyo, her protector."

"The one who followed us here?" Jason glared at Suki. "The warrior Hyo, waiting on the other side of that door if you give the word to make me disappear?"

Kim translated. It was Suki's turn to smile faintly. She spoke.

"She say you are rare man—one to be trusted—and save your questions until you teach her perfect English to answer them. She say it is time to begin, and I must go."

"Begin what, Kim?"

"Her part of agreement."

"Dammit, Kim, do I have *any* say in this arrangement?"

Kim muttered, "You got to be kidding."

Jason wondered whether Suki did understand English. Certainly she understood the tone of this exchange. Now when Kim translated she spoke angrily, turning her back on Jason.

Too late, Jason realized he'd hurt her pride.

"Princess say you dismissed." Kim bowed, placed a respectful hand behind Jason's elbow and guided him to the door. On the porch, he and Jason put on their footgear while Kim explained, "Not like princess to be so pissed. She say only way you see her again is get past Hyo. Nobody get past Hyo. Hyo is ninja."

Jason threw up his arms. "That's ridiculous. I won't do it. She's big trouble. And ninjas are comic book characters." He stood and headed back to the company compound.

CHAPTER 11
ORIENTAL DISCIPLINES

Kirkland, Washington
Wednesday, June 15, 1955

Jason remembered Kim Kibonee calling after him. "Now is chance to learn truth about ninja."

After a few steps, Jason stopped and thought about it. Some men seemed complete unto themselves—could take women or leave them. He was never such a man. Women fascinated him—commanded his respect, had extraordinary power over him. And Suki definitely interested him—fantastic offer, ninja challenge and all. His shoulders lifted in a great sigh.

Curiosity replaced his anger. He turned back to Suki's house. Kim was waiting on the porch, a wide smile on his face. Beside him stood a Korean couple. Jason presumed the lovely young woman was Suki's servant Yun Hee, and the gladiator was Hyo. The ninja stepped to the ground and planted himself in front of Jason—feet apart, muscular arms folded across his chest in unmistakable body language, a stern look on his Oriental face.

Provoked and determined, Jason walked towards his challenger.

As Jason approached, Yun Hee stepped forward, hands reaching out. "Your knife, my lord," she said softly in Korean.

Jason felt his face flush as he extracted Sul Wan Kee's gift from his waistband and handed the knife to her.

Yun Hee returned to the porch. Hyo stood on the ground, waiting. Jason rushed him, low, like a lineman. Hyo feinted to one side and somehow appeared on Jason's other side, leaping onto Jason's back.

In his slow-motion mode, Jason back-flipped, smashing Hyo down on the porch. Their impact broke the wooden floor beam supporting the outer edge. Jason spun away and found himself standing before Hyo, who still blocked his way to Suki. He moved in again, this time upright, planning to knock the wind out of Hyo—

A few minutes later, Kim opened the sliding door and Jason backed into the house, bowing with respect to Hyo. Jason slid the door closed as he rumbled, "We decided to call it a tie before the porch collapsed." Breathing hard, sweating profusely, bruised and bloody, he turned to look at Suki.

True to her agreement, she'd let her hair down and was slipping out of her clothing. Her face reflected fear of the unknown one moment, and pride the next. He held his breath. Through her exquisite veil of thigh-length hair she revealed her petite, ballerina-like perfection to him—

"D'ye ha' the starter installed and working, lad?" Jason snapped back to the present as his father called out from the house. He rose to go in and greet his father, reluctantly relinquishing his reverie. No wealth or accomplishment would ever be as fulfilling as the uninhibited passion Suki had shared with him. As her outstanding capacity for intelligence, grace, loyalty and love had unfolded, he'd learned to love her and was deeply distressed when she insisted that their stars intersected only briefly, then parted. She'd taught him skills and endurance to lavish on his one true partner, when he met her—the wife Suki insisted was fated to offer him far more than she ever could.

CHAPTER 12
SEQUIM ANCHORAGE

Sequim Anchorage, Washington
Friday, June 24, 1955

"Dad, everything in me is saying this is a terrible place to be anchored tonight. Please don't be stubborn about this."

"Holy Mither! Ye can whip any o' me loggers in a fair fight, and still ye be paranoid. I tell ye, lad, if ye donna let that anchor go, tis gonna be a terrible place ti be *richt now*."

Keeping the anchor line snubbed around the Sampson post, Jason tried his mother. "Mom, this is a really bad premonition. I know you wanted to spend the night here, but please tell Dad it's dangerous."

"Jason, dear, I'm the one who asked to come here for our first weekend together on the water since your discharge. You know it's a favorite spot of mine, ever since the woman on the fishing boat helped bring you into the world here, a perfect baby. And it's getting too late and cold to go to another anchorage across the straights. That crossing itself could be dangerous. This is a protected cove, no wind, and well away from boating traffic. What can possibly go wrong here? Now relax and let us enjoy some tranquility together like old times."

Not wanting to upset his parents, Jason gave in, lowering the anchor and paying out the line while his father put the boat in reverse to set the kedge.

A pea soup fog enveloped them as they ate supper in the toasty cabin of the cruising sailboat, warmed by its cast iron coal stove. Jason sat opposite his parents at the gimbaled table, wiping the last of his lamb stew juices with a piece of sourdough bread and admiring his mother's waist-length blonde hair, now down. "Thanks, Mom. That really hit the spot. You guys relax while I take care of the dishes."

His thoughts turned to FBI Agent Thomas. More than a week had passed since that unexpected visit. Since then he'd tried to put the horror of North Korea out of his mind, not dwell on the possible repercussions of the North Korean general. Instead he became preoccupied with the connections attributed to twins, in relation to his own experiences.

Clean-up completed, he rejoined his parents at the table, where they were ending a game of chess. Jason studied them for a moment. Finally he decided to broach the subject that had been tantalizing him. "Since Korea, I've been reading about twins, at the library, Mom. Is it possible I could have a twin brother?"

His parents looked at each other. Jason knew that expression: what would their off-the-wall, creative son come up with next? His mother answered. "I'd be the first to know, dear. I carried you for almost nine months."

"Right. 'Almost' nine months. Did you know it's normal for twins to be born three weeks early?" Jason took a sip of black coffee from his mug.

"Whoa, laddie. Donna be upsetting yer mither that way. Besides, she wis out like a light the entire time. But *I* wasna."

"But did you actually *see* the birth, Dad?"

His father blushed. Jason thought so. Both his parents had been outstanding gymnasts in school, and his dad could whip any one of the loggers he hired, but when it came to childbirth, fathers stayed out of the way.

"Please tell me exactly what happened that day, Dad."

When his father finished, Jason sat back, thinking, *So there could have been a second baby.* He saw the slow dawning of this possibility in his parents' eyes. He reached for their hands to reassure them—and became aware of a barely discernable thumping through the hull.

He jumped up. "My God, that's a tugboat propeller—a big one." He leapt aft, flipped on the switch for the cockpit spreader lights to illuminate their boat and threw open the companionway hatch to ring the fog bell.

"Check the anchor quickly, lad."

Jason raced forward to see if they'd dragged anchor and come adrift into the shipping lane of the straits, but the anchor was secure. He turned to his parents on the afterdeck. "All's well with the anchor." But all wasn't well. His gut was knotted in fear, his muscles tense and his chest ready to burst.

Through the thick fog emerged the bow of a commercial tug— moving slow-ahead toward the stern of the ketch. From the bow a sharp order: "Full astern! NOW!" The voice had a timbre oddly like his own.

He heard the loud clunk of a gearshift being rammed into reverse, followed by a locomotive engine's slow acceleration as it began thumping in full reverse. In seconds, the huge prop churned the water and slowed the tug's bow to a halt beside the sailboat's cockpit.

"Neutral," the voice commanded. The engine slowed to an idle, but remained in reverse. "Take it out of gear!" the voice shouted.

A man's soft Norwegian curses, a woman's voice shouting, "It's stuck. The lever won't budge."

Slowly the tug's bow began swinging towards the stern of the yacht, gathering momentum as the torque of the huge prop spun the tug. Jason's parents raced to place fenders where the boats would collide.

Jason shouted, "Mom, Dad. DON'T!" He ran towards them.

The tug smashed into the ketch, the deck lurched out from under his parents' feet and they tumbled into the water.

Jason stayed on his feet by holding a grab rail on the cabin top, then dashed to help his parents get back on board. But they were gone, swept away in the tug's prop wash.

The woman's voice shouted, "Fool, shut down the engine."

Jason leapt up to grab the tug's bow rail, and vaulted over it. He landed facing a bearded man whose jaw was clenched, whose eyes narrowed with horror. In that instant, Jason knew this was his twin. Without pausing in his desperate race to reach the control room, Jason dove right through the man, knocking him backwards. The man fell, hitting his head on a hatch.

As Jason reached the side door of the pilothouse, another man jumped out to stop him and Jason knocked him overboard in his rush to enter the pilothouse. A redheaded woman was struggling with the long clutch lever coming up through the floor. At the wheel, a grizzled man in a captain's hat was trying to kill the engine.

Jason reached around the woman with both his hands and grabbed the lever with her, braced his feet and pushed with all his strength. With a loud splintering of wood, the lever moved forward into neutral.

The woman spun in his arms, her body pressed between his and the lever he still held in both hands. She looked up into his face. He felt himself flushing hot and cold as he stared at the Amazon and mumbled in shock, "My God, you're real!"

Then her thumbs were pressing into his temples and he passed out.

CHAPTER 13
NATASHA

Sequim Anchorage, Washington
Friday, June 24, 1955

"Captain, we need privacy," Natasha ordered. "You and your crew go fix the clutch linkage in the engine room."

She looked around and spotted a coil of nylon parachute braid in the signal flag locker. With the concealed knife she carried, she cut off two pieces of the line, and tied Jason's hands and feet.

Ivan entered the pilothouse.

Natasha slid her hands under Jason's shoulders. "Help me lift him onto the aft settee."

Jason was solid muscle and surprisingly heavy. Ivan almost fainted from the effort, suddenly sitting at Jason's feet and feeling the back of his head. His hand came away bloody.

"What happened, Ivan?"

"He hit me like a speeding truck. I stumbled back into a deck cleat and fell so my head hit the corner of the forward deck hatch."

She inspected his scalp. "It's a nasty gash. Do you think you have a concussion?"

"Only a headache. If all the years of being knocked about haven't given me a concussion, this certainly won't have."

Natasha reached for the pillow on the berth behind the settee and pressed it down over their prisoner's face, smothering him.

"What are you doing? Stop that."

She continued her grisly task. "It's orders, Ivan. Anyone able to identify us must die at once. With his psychic connection to you, he sees through our disguises as if we weren't wearing them."

Ivan snapped, "Remove the pillow, Natasha. That's an order."

"I can't. He knows I've fucked him! He knows everything about us! He's got to die. It's orders."

"Up until now, everything's simply been an accident. But kill him, and you must kill the captain and crew. Do you want to do that, become a mass murderer and blow our cover?"

Natasha groaned in frustration and tossed the pillow back on the berth. MacDougall's eyes popped open and his chest heaved as he inhaled the air. She grabbed a rag and blindfolded him.

CHAPTER 14
IVAN

Sequim Anchorage, Washington
Friday, June 24, 1955

Jason gasped. "My parents ... ?"

"We all did our best, but ... they didn't surface." The voice of the man seated by his feet sounded like Jason's. And sad.

Jason turned his face away so they wouldn't see his tears if they leaked past the blindfold. He clenched his jaw and swallowed, took a long breath, and inhaled the scent of the woman. He sensed she was standing right next to him. Determined not to show weakness, Jason grinned up toward the Amazon who'd had incredible sex with him during his escape from North Korea and just now had tried to kill him.

"What's so funny, Jason?"

He faced his brother's voice. "She's an Amazon black widow. How do you survive her?"

"Very carefully, Jason. Very carefully."

Jason's temples throbbed. This felt surreal. "You seem to know me," he said. "Should I know you? . . ."

"In Russia, my name was Ivan. She was Natasha. You know exactly who I am. I'm your twin. Unfortunately for us, we're on opposite sides of this Cold War, raised with different ideologies, trained to fight for our own countries."

"How can this be, when my parents were convinced I was their only child?"

"You have a right to know before we kill you. My Russian mother was a doctor. I have a letter from her that explains. It's everything I know. I'll translate for you."

Jason heard the rustle of unfolding paper.

My beloved son,

I wrote this some day to be the prologue to your beautiful life, and to share all I know of your American parents and brother. I write about the most meaningful day of my life, one that has brought me both guilt and fulfillment every day since.

The afternoon you were born, we were anchored snuggly in a cove just east of Sequim, on the Olympic Peninsula of Washington State. The hail port on our commercial fishing trawler was Nootka Sound, Vancouver Island, British Columbia. The oceanographer-captain you know as your father, and I, were on one of our seasonal missions for Mother Russia, creating accurate charts of submarine depths in coastal waters and providing free medical care for the Nootka natives of Vancouver Island to assure their loyalty to us in our clandestine work.

We were in the pilothouse for tea when your father glanced out the window and said, "Now there's a pretty sight."

I looked where he pointed.

A splendid gaff-main cruising ketch under full sail was barreling east in Juan de Fuca Strait before wicked gusts of wind. I remember hugging myself, noting the ominous clouds racing by overhead. I told your father, "I'm glad that's not us out there." The morning's idyllic weather had turned foul around noon. Somehow, your father always knew when to seek shelter from upcoming bad weather.

Suddenly the sailboat jibed and headed straight for us in our sheltered anchorage. Heeled over on a broad reach, the boat tore through the water, creating majestic bow waves.

Your father put down his binoculars. "Trouble. There's only one man on deck with all that sail up." Switching to Nootka, he called his native crew up on deck to stand by.

The boat was coming like a projectile right at us. He shouted to his men. "Prepare for collision!"

When the sailboat was twenty meters away from our starboard side, its skipper spun the wheel, rounding up into the wind with a thunderous luffing of cotton sails. As the boat's momentum carried it forward, the young skipper lashed the wheel amidships, secured the mizzen sheet, hurried forward and dropped the port kedge anchor that hung ready at the bowsprit. He dropped the huge gaff main into its lazy-jacks, then the forestaysail and jib. With a speed born of skill, he lashed the jib and forestaysail, checked the anchor line for drag, threw out more hemp rode, secured it to the Sampson post and hurried aft to drop the mizzen. The sailboat drifted back until it snubbed up parallel with the beam of the trawler, a scant seven meters away.

My heart was in my mouth, and your father said, "That was the slickest piece of single-handed seamanship I've ever seen."

The skipper called out in a pronounced Scottish brogue, "Me wife is ha'ing oor baby three weeks early. Hae ye anyone who can deliver a baby?" (Your father and a linguist at the university helped me write the brogue, so you'll better know the man who sired you.)

Your father replied in English, "Yes. My men throw lines, pull you here." He gestured with his arms—that way he does when he speaks passionately. Then he instructed his Nootka crew, who grabbed the necessary lines and adjusted the tire-fenders alongside.

Turning to me, your father said, "Don't take your doctor's bag. Just what you may need. We don't want them to realize there's too much science on board this boat, that we're doing more than catching fish. Speak only Nootka. I'll translate."

Fast as possible I placed the supplies I wanted into a canvas ditty bag and we transferred to the sailboat as your father explained to the worried skipper, "My wife, sometimes, is midwife."

"Thank God. Thank ye for yer help. I niver should hae let her come while I wis taen the boat from Port Angeles to oor home in Seattle." He threw up his hands. "The morning's weather wis sae bloody perfect."

Below deck, a pretty young woman with long blonde hair lay on an aft double berth. She was panting hard and crying out with labor pains.

I checked her pupils and pulse, then the interval between her contractions, and spoke to my husband, who translated.

"Everything good. My wife give sedative now. Soon you have fine baby." The father-to-be looked so pale your father worried he might faint, so he helped the young skipper up the companionway ladder to wait in the fresh air of the cockpit, telling him, "I stay below, help my wife."

Unconscious under the anesthesia I'd administered, the mother felt no pain. I delivered a perfect baby. With my tiny hands, I always have. Except for my own babies, which, to our great sorrow, always miscarried.

I tied and cut the umbilical cord, cleaned up the babe and wrapped him in a beach towel. I turned to the mother to take care of the placenta.

I remember my shock when a second head appeared. "There's another one coming," I whispered in Russian. I knew instantly what I was going to do. "While I deliver it, you have our crew take the father in our launch to the nearest house ashore to arrange for someone to take him and his wife and baby to the hospital in Port Angeles."

"Baby? Only one baby?" Your father expressed his shock in a whisper. "You can't do that ... it's too risky ... our mission ... ."

Later your father told me the look I gave made clear where the greater risks lay if he didn't work with me on this. "We won't be caught," I insisted. "Her doctor didn't suspect she was carrying twins. Nor did she, because she didn't know it's natural for twins to come three weeks early. I sedated her fully, so she knows nothing of the birthing. She won't miss what never existed for her."

Your father went up on deck and arranged for the young father to be taken ashore by our crew. When the American was gone, he returned below. "You know what'll happen if we're caught kidnapping an American baby and taking him to Russia ... ?"

Your father told me later that I lifted up the second baby with a look of joy such as he'd never seen. I remember holding you to my bosom to quiet you, to cherish you as mine. "Now go on our trawler," I said, "and get a sheet to wrap our baby in. I want nothing to be amiss on their boat."

First he looked in the ship's log. "The father's name is Angus MacDougall, from Seattle. The mother is Ellen MacDougall," he flipped through some pages, "maiden name Steele. From her ink sketches, she's quite an artist. She's signed the drawings with her initials and—"

"Hurry," I interrupted. "We have to transfer the baby before the husband returns or the woman awakens."

Jason heard Ivan folding the letter. It sounded like he was tucking it into a pocket.

"How do I know you're not making all this up?"

"Because we share a telepathy peculiar to twins. I was there in Forks at sixteen when you were kicked in the face by the horse and through the painful operations in Seattle afterwards. I was there the scary night you were alone on the hundred-foot motor-sailor in the Port Angeles hurricane and let out all the anchor chain to stop its three-hundred-pound anchors from dragging ashore, and when the next morning you went in the chain locker and discovered your premonition had made you shut down the windlass with a scant four feet of chain remaining, dangling down through the port deck hawse. Because, when you had to fight for your life and escape from North Korea, I shared my woman with you to keep you going."

Jason stifled his shock. This weird reality was a two-sided phenomenon. And no one outside the three of them knew about the Korean connection. He heard cloth being torn, probably to bind Ivan's wounded head.

Ivan moved on the settee. "The psychic connection of twins. During times of extreme stress. However, the kind of events still relegated to UFO files and paranormal fiction."

Pissed, Jason said, "What's so special about you that I have to die so I can't identify you to ... whomever? Suddenly he had a flash that this couple was involved in some mission harmful to America.

"We aren't free to tell you. What's important is, I need you to know I'm sorrier than you about our parents' death. At least you knew them. I never even got to talk to my own parents."

"Why this way, on the water?"

"Curiosity. Cruising people have time to get acquainted. I wanted to get to know my birth parents without revealing who I was. We weren't told you'd be along."

"I realize the collision was an accident. More like fate." Jason gestured with his head to Natasha. "So, do you turn her loose on me now?"

He felt her pressing a pistol against his temple.

"Relax, Natasha. He can't talk. They'd put him in an insane asylum, and he knows it."

Then Ivan's voice was directed toward him. "We're both a bit groggy. I find I don't want to fight you to the death on this night. But soon we must have you killed. Fate has made us adversaries."

His thumbs at Jason's temples ended their traumatic encounter.

CHAPTER 15
ADRIFT

Seattle, Washington
Saturday, June 25, 1955

Jason couldn't place the ceiling, couldn't figure where he was. Or how he got here. Then it came back to him. His brother. The Amazon. His parents.

He jerked to a sitting position.

Big mistake. His hands flew to his throbbing temples.

A white-uniformed nurse came through the door. "Welcome back, Mr. MacDougall. You're at Virginia Mason Hospital. How do you feel?"

"My parents. What became of my parents?"

"Let me get the doctors."

* * *

"I'm truly sorry about your parents, Jason." FBI Assistant Special Agent in Charge Franklin Thomas sounded sincere, as if he'd dealt with losses himself.

Once again, Jason turned his face away, to hide the tears he still felt trying to emerge.

The doctor had told him his parents had drowned. Agent Thomas informed him the dismembered bodies had been found on the shore of the cove in the early morning. His father's business partner had identified them, and recommended cremation. The huge propeller hadn't been kind to them. In the first of several important decisions, Jason agreed, preferring to remember their beauty and vitality as they were on the boat.

Jason looked at the agent. "Please sit. Do you mind if I call you Frank? I seem to be fresh out of formality."

"Of course not, Jason." Thomas sat in a chair by the bed.

Jason looked around the private room. In an attempt to lighten the atmosphere, he said, "Thanks for the nice digs."

Thomas nodded, saying nothing.

"It was a simple accident in the fog, Frank. No Korean agents. Just a goddamn accident." Jason had decided to say as little as possible about the couple on the tug—because they'd lock the door and toss away the key if he mentioned anything about the psychic relationship.

Agent Thomas rubbed a big hand over his face and looked at Jason with sorrowful eyes. "I'm sorry. That won't wash with me today, Jason. The man you knocked overboard was on our unpublished ten-most-wanted list."

"How do you know I knocked a man overboard?" Jason didn't like the way this conversation was going.

"The tugboat captain and crew were chartered simply so a couple could meet your parents while they were cruising for the weekend. The man who went overboard was an ex-PI from Seattle, probably hired to locate and track your parents. We suspect he was a Russian agent on an important mission in this country. He ended up in the propeller."

"Am I in trouble? For killing him?" Jason rubbed his temples, which were still sore. *What the hell's going on?*

"No, the tugboat captain said the man was attempting to stop you from trying to save your parents." Thomas added, "The captain got real mixed up when I told him you were the son of the couple who went overboard. Said the woman told him her husband was their son. Said you recognized the woman, too." His brows arched in question.

Jason said nothing, his mind working furiously.

After a moment, Thomas said, "While I'm on the subject, the captain said he was really sorry about what happened." Thomas pulled out his notebook. "Said the engineer was adjusting the clutch linkage when the people showed up early for the charter, and the engineer forgot to install the cotter pin through the connecting clevis pin of the turnbuckle linkage, which came partly open and hung up on the edge of the wooden bulkhead hole the linkage passed through. Said you must have been on adrenalin, because you actually broke through almost two inches of wood to shift the gear. Whatever all that means. Said it was just fate and you being a man of the sea, you'd understand."

"God damn fate," Jason muttered softly.

"I've felt that way myself a time or two," the agent said.

After a long silence, Jason asked, "How'd I get here?"

"The couple had the tug return to Seattle, paid the captain extra, and told him to call for an ambulance. The hospital found my card in your billfold and called me."

Jason rubbed his temples again. "What did they do to me?"

"Captain said the woman pressed her thumbs into your temples hard and you passed out. Then she grabbed you and lowered you carefully to the floor. Her husband came in, still groggy from hitting his head. Asked if you were dead. She said, no, she hit you light."

Thomas shifted in his chair. "Seems the man left some hair and blood where he hit his head when you decked him. The CIA's been helping fund some exciting new research called DNA, that attempts to map each person's unique genetic code. Amazing stuff. I've sent samples of his hair and blood, along with yours for comparison. It takes a long time to analyze, but whatever you're clamming up about, I'm probably going to find out anyway."

Jason thought a moment, and returned to his original decision. "Frank, I'd help you if I could. But, parts of this story are beyond credibility. I *will* tell you the couple told me they're from the Soviet Union, are named Ivan and Natasha, and they intend to have me killed. I'm pretty sure they're living in Florida."

"How do you know that?"

"Because that Amazon-of-a-woman has a Florida-type tan with no swimsuit lines."

"She undressed for you?" Frank's voice was incredulous. All of them had been wearing turtlenecks and Mackinaws for the chilly weather.

"I told you there are things you'd find unbelievable."

"Okay. Why Florida? Why not California surfing?"

"Why not tanning lamps at an elite international hotel in Moscow, in preparation for life in Florida?"

"Why Florida, and not California?"

"If there's a reason, I don't know it." Jason smiled to himself. "Even though it's just a feeling," he looked Thomas in the eye, "You wouldn't want to bet they're not in Florida."

"You're starting to scare me, son." He rubbed his face that way he did, signing off on one subject and moving to another. "And they told you they're going to have you killed? Why didn't they just do that when they had you?"

"Killed, so I can't identify them. Not then, because I sense they're turned off by cold-blooded murder." Jason fingered his temples. "What they don't seem to know is Mother was a great artist, renowned for her portraits of people and animals, and she helped me learn to draw."

"We want any sketches you can provide."

"I'm sure they were wearing disguises—beard and wigs and such—and she blindfolded me, so I didn't get to see much."

"Even so." Thomas thought for a moment. "Jason, if you'd like, I can enable you to disappear forever in our witness protection program."

"Thanks, Frank. I appreciate that. But changing my identity, pretending I'm someone I'm not, doesn't appeal to me right now." He sat up a little taller. "After the doctors told me what happened, I had a long phone conservation with my godparents, David and Sarah King. Aunt Sarah is my mother's youngest sister. The Kings believe if I come live with them at Fort Adams and continue with my plans to go to the Naval Academy, the navy can protect me adequately."

"And living on the east coast where you believe the Russians who killed your parents live has a certain appeal, correct?" Thomas raised a brow.

"Do you know when I can go home?"

"No. But it won't be before I can arrange protection for you until your uncle can take over." He smiled into Jason's inquiring look. "I just want to hear the rest of the story you don't think I'm ready for."

"Frank, I intend to tell you what I can, just as soon as I can find a way to be sure you'll believe it."

CHAPTER 16
NATASHA'S NIGHTMARE

Flight to Chicago
Saturday, June 25, 1955

Natasha dozed in her window seat beside Ivan, just forward of the propellers on the commercial airliner. She was dreaming her familiar dream, reliving their last day in Moscow. Six weeks ago.

She lay on top of the bedding in the dimly-lighted Moscow Savoy hotel suite. The air conditioning felt refreshing against her bare skin, somewhat over-cooked by the hotel's sun lamp in preparation for their upcoming move. The high coffered ceiling and the red damask draperies at the long windows were an elegant contrast to the Spartan quarters where, since she was seven, she and her teammates had trained as Russia's best. She ran her fingers along the smooth skin of her legs, newly shaven for life in America. She was in her prime, twenty-one. She stretched her muscular body, ready to serve.

The wood floorboards creaked. Natasha turned her head on the pillow to admire the tall gladiator, her day-and-night partner of six years. Ivan joined her.

Two minutes later he was lost in the throes of release when Natasha stiffened. Across the room, she spotted the blue-and-white striped shirt of an élite operative. She barely had time to register what she'd seen before the silent intruder raced towards Ivan's back, bayonet extended.

"*Nyet!*" Natasha shouted with a rush of adrenalin. Her feet snapped down to the bed and with her strong arms she pushed Ivan aside.

Ivan whipped around in a blur of motion. Too close to the edge of the bed, he lurched to the floor. The wild-eyed attacker had already launched herself, flying over the foot of the bed, bayonet now aimed at Natasha's chest. Instinctively Natasha reached up with both hands to grab the fist holding the bayonet. She rotated the attacker's forearm and knife down and inwards as trained—twisting and thrusting with all her strength. Then Ivan grabbed the attacker's blonde hair, wrenching her body off Natasha's and onto the floor.

It was over. Ivan kneeled on the floor holding their dying attacker around her arms and chest. The long blade had entered at an angle under her rib cage. Blood pulsed out around the handle.

Lilia!

They had schooled with this respected élite forces agent since childhood. The wild look in Lilia's eyes vanished as they opened wide and filled with tears. She tried to speak. Natasha knelt over her comrade of so many years, her face close to Lilia's.

"Oh, Natasha. I'm so sorry." Lilia coughed blood. The knife must have pierced a lung on its way into her heart. "Ivan, when you injured Dimitri in training … you ruined us. They sent him into the army. A lifetime of work together … destroyed." She coughed again, then fought it. "My revenge … ." Lilia knew their habits, had targeted the strategic moment when Ivan would be off guard, the one instant she might overcome the élite of the élite. A new round of coughing racked her body. "I worshipped Dimitri … ."

Natasha held Lilia tenderly as she continued to cough. Ivan used the bedding to stop splattered blood from running into Natasha's eyes. Lilia rattled for air and attempted a smile while her focus drifted to the ceiling. She started to raise her arms then went limp.

Natasha held a finger to Lilia's carotid artery. *Nothing.* "She's gone." Gently, she closed Lilia's eyelids.

"Quick, Natasha. Into the shower. We've got to wash this blood off." Ivan stood. "I'll join you as soon as I notify Minister Zhukov."

She stared at him. Known as "Ivan the Terrible," his pride in being unbeatable had led him to use excess force with Dimitri, one of the best of the élite. Now he was seeing the consequences. He would take this imperfection hard.

Eight minutes later they were still scrubbing in the shower when the KGB entered their hotel quarters. They came out of the bathroom, soaking wet in the thick hotel robes, to explain what happened. Georgi Zhukov was only five minutes behind. When they repeated their story to him, he took charge, barking out orders to the KGB agents.

"There will be no investigation. Take her body to the morgue. Flip the mattress and get clean sheets and towels. Wipe up the blood on the floor and replace the bloody Persian rug with one from another room in the hotel. Be quick. These people have an important flight to catch in a few hours and they need sleep."

Housekeeping chores were not the purview of KGB agents, but Natasha noticed that when Defense Minister Georgi Zhukov ordered it, they were the best housekeepers in Moscow. Zhukov turned to her. "It's sad to lose a comrade, but you must put this behind you. Think about your future instead."

This was Ivan and Natasha's last day in Mother Russia. Soon they would be flying to Zurich, Switzerland, as American citizens Donald and Jeannie Dougherty. After bank appointments, they would be driven to Lucerne to stay at the Palace Hotel for three days of meetings. Then they would board a Pan American flight to Venezuela. Following two days of meetings, an Eastern Airlines flight would take them to Miami. They would work with Donald's wealthy "Uncle Richard," operating Dougherty Enterprises, Limited, from an ocean yacht berthed in Fort Lauderdale, Florida.

In the morning Natasha would style her jaw-length, straight black hair and apply makeup to set off her large, wide-spaced eyes and full lips so she would look like a fashion model from Paris, rather than the Olympic-caliber athlete and highly skilled élite forces espionage agent and linguist she was trained to be.

And the quick-sex specialist she'd learned to be with Ivan. Especially now that Ivan's mother had just informed him he had a twin brother in America, and Natasha had to help him keep his deep emotions under control, with what had been some of their wildest sex yet.

She was awakened from her reverie when Ivan gently squeezed her hand. The noise reminded her they were now aboard a plane from Oregon to Chicago.

Ivan's smile made his eyes crinkle at the corners. He leaned close and spoke directly into her ear to be heard over the engines. "You were enjoying yourself so much I thought you might like me to join you in the lavatory."

She shook her head, embarrassed. "I don't want your brother to have psychic sex with me, Ivan. It's too weird—and a psychological damper for me."

Ivan patted her arm. "I don't control it, Natasha. But I think I understand why it happened when it did, and never before or since. That's the first time we've had sex in the heat of a life-and-death situation, with all the emotions that generates. Besides, I thought it was one of the most exciting times we've had together, with you trying to double my pleasure."

"I hope you're right and it never happens again. It's unnatural to feel used in such a way." Natasha felt herself blushing. She turned her face to gaze out the window at the wilderness country far below. Jason MacDougall's shock to see she was real was an even greater shock to her. Had they opened some sort of door they couldn't close? Every time she serviced Ivan under such extreme conditions, would she continue servicing MacDougall, too? What had begun as Ivan's most impassioned time with her seemed to be developing into a paranormal bond between Ivan and his twin brother. That spooked her.

She turned to Ivan. "What are you going to tell General Kanokov when we meet?"

"The truth. We were meeting with our top west coast agent on a chartered tugboat when there was an accident in the fog that killed our agent and two people on a yacht."

"Why is the general flying from our embassy in Washington, D.C. to meet with us in Chicago?"

"Because he's the new KGB head of security there, and since he must report all our activities to Moscow, he doesn't want to meet where he might lead American agents to us." Ivan carefully moved strands of her long brunette wig away from her eye. "He wants us to meet at the apartment of the agent who will replace Bruno in Seattle, so we can brief her on our operation."

"Her?"

"Our old friend from training, Petra. Kanokov says she's become one of our best sex operatives in the U.S. She goes by 'Sadie Severance' here."

"Petra!" Natasha snorted. "All she ever wanted was to screw you."

"You know we were all ordered to circulate then, including you. In our line of work sex is one of the tools. And you've always known you come first with me." He squeezed her thigh reassuringly.

"I always liked Petra's what-you-see-is-what-you-get attitude. Actually she shared some things with me that were very helpful."

"I know. I asked her to."

Natasha snorted her displeasure. Ivan was about as romantic as a steam-driven sex machine with an oversized member that couldn't be taken lightly. And an unstoppable libido to match.

Her mind jumped back to Petra. It had been woman talk. Natasha had wondered. "How do non-athletic wives manage to service their athletic husband's extraordinary needs?"

"The husbands supplement with mistresses. Preferably ballerinas like me."

"Why ballerinas?"

Petra, who'd started in ballet and become a fellow gymnast with Natasha, assumed one erotic position after another. "Like gourmet food, gourmet sex is all about imaginative presentation. Who's more accustomed to ligament-straining, exciting flexibility than ballerinas? Variety is the spice of scintillating sex."

Natasha returned to the present and her concerns about Jason MacDougall. "What are you going to do about the fact MacDougall can identify us? He should be killed."

"Not at this time." Ivan rubbed his tired face. "Jason will tell what we told him. That we're Russian, our real first names—and that we cannot let him live to identify us. None of that information is useful to anyone. If he tells more, they'll decide he's crazy and put him away for us." Ivan spread airline blankets over both of them. "Sleep now, Natasha."

She snuggled closer to Ivan, pressing her leg against his and holding his hand under the blanket. She smiled as she thought how all of Russia's military might could not accomplish what Ivan and she would— the eventual defeat of capitalism in the United States.

PART II

SCOTTISH HIGHLANDS

CHAPTER 17
ROOTS

The Highlands, Scotland
Wednesday, July 6, 1955

Jason stood alone in the great front hall of MacDougall Castle and studied the stone walls in the gray dawn, trying to absorb the cold reality. His parents were gone. Forever. Now he was halfway round the world in the Scottish Highlands, to learn what he could from his father's older brother and the rest of the MacDougall clan. And what he was learning about the family heritage caused shivers to run down his spine as he imagined what might be expected of him with his secret abilities.

The day after Jason's parents died, his uncle, Lord Ewen Mac-Dougall, had flown through the night from Scotland to Seattle. His occasional brogue, so like that of Jason's father, made the whole tragedy even more eerie. After the funeral, he said, "Nephew, ye're alone now. There's no going back. But ye'll need time to deal with yer grief and set yer course. Ye're welcome to come live with us for a year, to discover yer ancestry."

His uncle's compassion touched Jason. Leaving the country for a while could be a safe way to separate himself from those two Russians who wanted him dead. Scotland wouldn't be as safe as the FBI witness protection program, but at least he could keep his own identity. In fact, Lord MacDougall's offer would be a way to learn more about himself.

Jason looked into his uncle's eyes and confided his guilt. "It's my fault that Father and Mother are dead. I knew something bad would happen at that anchorage, yet I allowed them to override my premonition."

Uncle Ewen's eyes lit up. He held Jason by the shoulders, excitement in his voice. "When ye get pumped—like in a fight—does everything around ye slow down but you?"

Jason's stomach muscles tightened. "Did Dad tell you about that?"

Uncle Ewen shook his head. "No, he didn't. Didn'a tell a soul." His uncle squinted at him. "But didn't he tell you they're gifts you've inherited from your grandfather Angus, and they're always meant to be used for a higher purpose?"

"I wish he had." Jason felt betrayed by his father for letting him believe he was some kind of freak. He swallowed bile rising in his throat. "Higher purpose?"

"Yes. Something we never seem able to know looking ahead, that only becomes apparent when looking back on life."

His uncle's voice turned sympathetic. "We can't know how it feels to a proud man like your father, growing up knowing his older brother inherits the title, lands and wealth in order to keep the clan MacDougall unified and powerful. Your father was a good man, but living as the second son may have made him bitter and selfish at times."

Despite Uncle Ewen's understanding, Jason felt compelled to defend his father. "We lived well. He was very inventive and had all kinds of ingenuity and energy."

His uncle reached an arm around Jason's shoulders. "Jason, what's done is done. If you want to learn where your gifts come from and why you have them, first you have to learn who you are. That can best be done in the land of your ancestors." He stepped back and with a twinkle in his eye, appraised his nephew. "Besides, my oldest son, Rufus, is off in Her Majesty's Service. We could use your brawn and brains to help us run the property and our Angus cattle operation."

Jason considered the Kings' invitation to Fort Adams, offered over the phone while he was in the hospital and again when they flew cross-country for the funeral. His mother's youngest sister and her navy husband could guide him on his way to the Naval Academy, but meeting Uncle Ewen convinced him that there was a step he needed to take first.

Like a drowning swimmer chancing upon a raft at sea, Jason grasped his uncle Ewen's invitation to live for a time with him and his cousins in Scotland; to learn more about the secret heritage of the Mac-Dougall clan.

"I want to say yes. But first, I should tell you I have a twin brother who wants me dead because I know he's in the United States working for the Soviets against America."

Uncle Ewen listened to Jason's story without a word. When Jason finished, his uncle said, "A MacDougall twin raised Russian to use his gifts to destroy America? That's no accident of nature. Your mission is clear to me, and it's all the more reason you *must* come to Scotland—to let us help you become who ye're meant to be."

Now, a week later, Jason was standing alone inside the front hall of the castle. Upon arrival yesterday he'd met his aunt Rachael and uncle Ewan's many children and all the household staff. He liked Aunt Rachael's down-to-earth warmth and his cousins, from teens to the five-year-old, were an exuberant bunch.

He turned in a slow circle. This foyer was larger than the living room of his parents' house. He traced his fingers across one of the stone blocks, tangible evidence of his new situation. Hearing footsteps behind him, he turned.

"Good morning, Jason." Uncle Ewen patted him on the shoulder. "You slept well?"

"Thank you." There was no point in seeming ungrateful and admitting he felt like a disoriented orphan.

"Now that you've met your cousins, would ye like to see where we've all come from?" Uncle Ewen's wink had a warmth and humor Jason had never experienced with his father. "A tour of your ancestry, lad?"

"All these paintings?" Jason gazed at the array of portraits covering the stone walls of the hall and the stairwells. Across from the tall, studded oak front doors, a pair of opposing, wide stone stairways with carved oak banisters curved up the turret-like walls to converge at either end of the high landing above.

"These are only your more notable ancestors. We go back to the fourth century." Uncle Ewen switched on the chandelier and pressed a bank of buttons that turned on small brass lamps extending over the

gilt frames. The lighted faces of his dour kinsmen in their Scottish fin-
ery emerged from dark backgrounds. Jason listened with fascination to
tales of the Chiefs with broadswords, stories about Lairds and Ladies
of the Clan MacDougall, who fought through the centuries for their
freedom. Uncle Ewen ushered him up the right-hand staircase. The hall
echoed with the legends of his forebears as the tour continued down
the other side and returned to the circular entrance hall. Standing with
their backs to the heavy front doors, Jason felt a chill run through his
gut. He was still wrestling with his new reality of having a determined
enemy, and now he was beginning to sense he had a role in this fabled
clan, as well. He didn't want to deal with it; right now it was tough
enough to handle his grief. Instead he pointed to the tapestries hanging
from the balustrade of the second floor landing. "The stories there?"

"Aye. These are two of our most famous battles." Uncle Ewen gestured to the left. "That's the sea battle of Largs in 1263, when the Clan
MacDougall's great fleet of galleys that commanded the seas attacked
and defeated the Norsemen. In the late 13th century the MacDougalls
were the rising force of Scotland's western seaboard."

"A seafaring heritage," Jason mused. "That might explain my love
of the sea." He cocked his head as he looked at his uncle. "My father was
a great sailor, but he never mentioned any of this."

Uncle Ewen nodded. "I expect your father downplayed your gifts
and his maritime ancestry because he wanted you to focus on taking
over his forestry business one day."

Managing his father's money and associates? A heavy responsibility. He turned back to the tapestries. "What about the other one, with
the red water?"

"The Battle of Red Ford. In 1296 the Campbells and MacDougalls
feuded over coastal lands between the two clans. Many lives were lost
at Lorn and the Ford River ran red with blood." His uncle made a fist
and punched his palm. "The MacDougalls fought first to secure their
lands, and then for their freedom in the Wars of Scottish Independence
from tyrannical English kings and nobles, who would use MacDougall
wives and daughters as spoils of privilege." His uncle's voice shook with
anger. "The family has paid a fierce price for freedom over the centu-

ries—fighting with men like Rob Roy, William Wallace and Robert the Bruce."

An avid reader, Jason knew of these famous men, but never realized his own family had participated in their adventures. Why had his uncle become so emotional when that was all so long ago? Or was it?

"Is there no portrait of my grandfather and grandmother?"

Lord Ewen smiled in answer. "Time for breakfast." He led the way into the dining room and stopped in front of the enormous fireplace. Above the mantelpiece hung the blue and gold MacDougall coat of arms. Two royal lions sat upright while two ships sailed beneath a knight's helmet and an armored shoulder and forearm clenching a sword topped by a red crusader's cross.

"The Clan MacDougall coat of arms, *Buaidh no bàs*," said Uncle Ewen, 'Victory or Death.' Now, look on the wall behind us." He turned. "Your grandparents."

Jason stared at what appeared to be a tall portrait of himself, only much older, and with a full red beard and mustache. His grandfather, Lord Angus MacDougall, was dressed as the clan chief in a MacDougall kilt and sporran, gold-colored Ghillie shirt, waistcoat and silver-buttoned Argyll jacket. His grandfather's head was turned to face the painting of his wife. Her face shone with character and a look of adoration that the talented artist had captured brilliantly. Jason was so absorbed in the paintings, he started when his uncle said, "Breakfast is getting cold."

Over their porridge, Jason said, "Dad told me his father was a World War II hero who was awarded the Victoria Cross. Said that was the equivalent of our Medal of Honor. What did Grandfather do to earn it?"

His uncle smiled ruefully and shrugged. "No one knows, lad. MI5 learned of his gifts and recruited him for some special mission—which we're told is still classified, to protect someone who hid him in enemy territory for months. I can tell you, he never revealed what he did, but he did say our Russian allies were up to no good, long term."

Part of the family secret? Awed by the centuries of freedom fighters' blood coursing through his veins, Jason was filled with a sense of their higher calling. *Victory or Death.*

Suddenly it dawned on him that his uncle expected him to measure up to the MacDougall destiny. Overwhelmed, he felt unprepared to live up to that calling. No way could he follow in footsteps like these.

Uncle Ewen broke through his bout of uncertainty. "My time in Seattle has left me with pressing matters to attend to. Your aunt Rachel and I have asked her young assistant to accompany you and show you around. Her name is Megan. She grew up in MacDougall Castle."

Walking out of the dining room together, Uncle Ewen placed his heavy arm across Jason's broad shoulders. "Largs, Lorn and English lords are history now. Today it's the Soviets. Churchill warned us about the Russians at the end of World War II—possibly in part with information supplied by Father. It may be a *cold* war, but it's not difficult to see their goal. They want to take away our freedoms and make us all their serfs, to serve their lust for power and resources." Lord MacDougall's blood seemed to boil again. "Folk are sae bloody blind no ti see it."

Was Uncle Ewen telling him more than he was saying? *Forget it.* Someone else could save the world.

CHAPTER 18
GLADIATORS

Despite her linguistic skills, Natasha had to concentrate to understand Seán Kelly's Irish brogue. "Uncle Richard Dougherty" had brought Ivan and Natasha, alias "Don and Jeannie Dougherty," to Dublin to meet the IRA leader. Ultimately they would replace Uncle Richard in leading Ivan's grand plan and it was important to meet all of Uncle's contacts who might provide useful services to help in their takeover of America. It suited Russia that the outlawed Irish Republican Army was a nuisance to Great Britain, creating havoc in Belfast and elsewhere in Northern Ireland, and that the IRA was ripe for being influenced by communist ideology. The Dougherty Foundation was a substantial under-the-table contributor to the IRA terrorist organization. Natasha listened attentively as Seán Kelly charmed them with a tour of Dublin sights, pubs and eateries.

"Irish-American contributions to our cause enable us to buy vital information from London." Seán raised his tankard of ale. "To the Doughertys and a free Ireland!"

"To a future with us in control!" Richard Dougherty toasted in return.

After supper, as Ivan and Natasha prepared for bed at their inn, Ivan asked, "What do you think of Seán Kelly?"

"On the surface, the man's charming. But behind the smiles and charisma, I feel there's a double-dealing, ruthless politician at work.

Like we're in the company of a cobra. I hope we never have to rely on his kind."

"You're good. Exactly what I sensed."

Reading the glint in his eye, she smiled. "Do you think your unique ability to sense what others can't and to perform faster than others can might be rubbing off on me?" She backed across the room. "For example, I sense I have about three seconds to get ready for a personal coup of spontaneous proportions." Laughing, she dove under the bedcovers with Ivan in determined pursuit.

Moments later, her duty done and their mirth subsided, Natasha asked, "What's on the schedule for tomorrow?"

"Richard will conclude some business here with Seán, who has kindly set up a meeting for us with a contact in Scotland. The rendezvous is in Inverness at an annual gathering of clans for Highland games. We'll have an early breakfast, fly to Glasgow in a private plane, be met by a maroon Bentley and driven to Castle Grounds where the games are held. We'll be back here by nightfall."

Alarmed, Natasha said, "The Highlands? That's where your brother is. You didn't tell me because you're going after him and you didn't want me pointing out how risky that is in a foreign country."

Ivan smiled as he lay back. "You know me too well, Natasha. We'll see if he recognizes us despite the blindfold at Sequim and our present disguises. If he does, we'll have to arrange for his demise."

* * *

Tuesday, July 19, 1955

Natasha stepped out of the Bentley to the wail of bagpipes from across the fields. She found their Scottish host, Lord Burns, easier to understand than their Irish contact had been. Of course, seeing men in skirts took a bit of getting used to. But what powerful legs they had from walking the Highland hills. Ivan looked handsome in his kilts, with his bushy brown hair and beard concealing his features. Natasha wore a long blonde wig with unsecured straight hair that usually covered one eye or the other, making her full face look narrow.

Lord Burns was a clandestine affiliate of the IRA—even if Scotland remained under British rule, there was still a chance for Northern Ireland to break free. Secretly near bankruptcy, the lord maintained his Highland castle and London townhouse through financial support from the IRA. His important connections in London made him privy to useful information for the organization, and given his indebtedness, his loyalty to the IRA was considered absolute. He made every effort to be a gracious host as the threesome strolled past solo bagpiping and Highland dancing competitions.

Ivan squeezed Natasha's arm and stopped. "Whoa. What's that?"

She looked where he was focused and saw a powerful man running with a long, hefty pole held upright in his cupped hands. With a mighty heave he threw his end up so the top, thicker end landed on the ground with the inverted pole upright. It teetered for a moment. The crowd encouraged the pole, "Turn, turn." But it fell back towards the man, who moved out of the way and let out a growl of disappointment, audible over the onlookers' groans.

Natasha was intrigued. She and her partner were extraordinary athletes. With a shine in his eye, Ivan turned to their Scottish host. "Perhaps you'd explain this competition."

The lord was delighted. "Aye. It's called 'tossing the caber,' and symbolizes our Highland games. The caber is the trunk of a fir tree, with the limbs and bark removed. It's usually about seventeen feet long, weighing some ninety pounds. The pole is held by the small end and thrown so it turns end over end and comes to rest with the small end pointing directly opposite the tosser. Competitors are judged on how closely their throws approximate the ideal twelve o'clock toss."

Natasha saw Ivan wet his lips and realized there'd been too little athletic challenge in his life of late.

Then their Scottish host said, "Aha, we're in for a treat. Here comes Lord Ewen MacDougall. He's been the caber toss champion for nigh twenty years—ever since his younger brother left home. As you can see, he's a regular bull of a man."

Natasha heard a hiss of breath. Ivan was looking at his brother in the crowd and whispered, "He's staring right at us."

Ivan turned to Lord Burns. "What do you know about the powerful-looking young man over there, standing beside Lord MacDougall?"

"Aye," their host exclaimed. "I'd wager that's Ewen's dead brother's son. Sad. The lad's parents drowned. Word is Ewen's taken him into the clan." Looking again towards Lord MacDougall, he said with excitement, "Here comes Ewen's toss."

Natasha noted how Lord Burns made a point of dropping first names to show how "in" he was with the rich and famous.

Lord MacDougall's explosive toss was not perfect, but easily the best of the day, judging by the cheers. Natasha saw Jason looking at his uncle with frank admiration as everyone gathered around to congratulate Lord MacDougall.

"I'd like to try that," said Ivan.

Natasha was shocked. She looked at him sharply, cautioning him with a hand on his arm that they mustn't bring attention to themselves. Baffled by his uncharacteristic behavior, she watched him looking at Jason as if the twin were a young stallion that Ivan, as the dominant stallion, had to challenge. The only other time she'd seen Ivan in such a primordial state was when he almost killed the three élite forces trainees who forced themselves on her during maneuvers in Siberia.

"Have you ever tried tossing the caber?" asked Lord Burns.

Ivan shrugged. "No, but it doesn't look that difficult."

The Scotsman raised a brow. Ivan clenched his jaw. "This is something I must do." He turned to Natasha and said in an undertone, "Move aside with Lord Burns so he's not seen with me. I'll join you at the car, after."

After what? Natasha knew there was no stopping her partner. Ivan, the visitor, the stranger in this crowd, had the bit in his teeth.

Ivan's lips were pressed thin as he strode towards Jason, eyes challenging him. The American stood ready for anything, his muscles defined and nostrils flaring.

Ivan said nothing. He stepped forward and hefted Lord Ewen's caber, getting the feel of it. His run to the line was longer and faster than the other competitors she'd watched. The airborne pole sailed in a snappy arc and made a perfect turn, landing exactly in the twelve o'clock position. Though not officially in the games, Ivan had made the perfect toss of the day. He stood proudly at the throw line, feet apart and hands on hips, breathing heavily, clearly challenging Jason—who nodded his head to Ivan in salute.

Suddenly Jason walked to the far, small end of the caber where Ivan had tossed it. Saying not a word, he unfastened his dress sporran and chain and placed them like a marker line at the end of the pole where it lay. He stood straddling the end of the log, held up his hands like horse blinders and sighted between them at Ivan where he stood. Then Jason raised the heavy end of the pole and walked it up until it was standing vertical on the ground. Squatting down with the pole propped against his shoulder, he worked his hands under the small end and stood. As he walked directly away from Ivan, he balanced the vertical log on the heel of his right hand and raised it one-handed, high over his head. Stopping, he turned to face Ivan, transferred the pole to his other hand and lowered it with the one hand. The onlookers were frozen in silence by this display of control and strength.

Holding the caber in his cupped hands, Jason took his long run and, at the sporran chain, pitched his pole with such force it seemed to snap through its arc, aimed directly at Ivan still standing on his own throw line. The spectators gasped as Ivan stood his ground despite the caber turning straight towards him—the tip missing his sporran by fractions of an inch to land squarely between his feet. Ivan gave a faint smile and nodded in salute to the defiant MacDougall standing with hands on hips, and the crowd burst into a roar of cheers.

Ivan walked up to Jason and Natasha read her partner's lips. "There is no place on this planet you can go to escape us, Brother."

* * *

Undressing for the night in their room back in Dublin, Natasha asked, "What happened at the games? What was it about Jason MacDougall that got to you? You *never* give in to your emotions like that."

"I wanted him to know running away to Scotland does him no good. I realized blindfolding him at Sequim was pointless, he *feels* my presence. He must die."

Natasha gave Ivan's hands a reassuring squeeze. "I take it you saw that without the weight of his sporran, his kilt flew up on his toss, and that he's just like you in other ways?"

"I saw. But you already knew that. From the times I've shared you with him."

Devastated by Ivan's cold remark, Natasha resorted to her training in deception to hide her feelings. She pressed Ivan's face into her breasts. "The way you tossed the caber, and then gauged the closeness of MacDougall's throw, I knew your powers were at work. You were brilliant today, and I intend to be your most special prize." In keeping with her unwritten directive from Mother Russia, she pushed Ivan backwards on the bed, climbed up over him and with all the skill she possessed, gave him memorable release to keep him mentally fit for the arduous challenges ahead.

CHAPTER 19

MEGAN

Jason awakened to a raspy tongue grooming his hair on the pillow. One of the long-haired cats that kept him company through the night. He reached for the lamp on the nightstand and turned it on to look around the great bedroom that had been his father's while growing up. The fireplace at one end was ready to ward off winter cold, the three-inch thick door was a barrier to sounds in the hallway, and the antique oak bedstead was larger than his twin bed at home. Now the room was littered with enormous Maine coon cats and beautifully marked Norwegian forest cats. More than a half dozen furry felines. The Baby Ben read 4:00 AM.

He needed time alone to think and to try to deal with his emotional wounds. He was in trouble, and knew it. He felt yesterday's encounter with his brother confirmed his passage into a kill-or-be-killed life from which he couldn't return.

Until he found a way to shake the impact of the loss that enveloped him, he certainly couldn't come to grips with having a twin who wanted him dead, much less live up to the family expectations. He arose to the damp chill of the castle and walked across the room to the old oak desk. Perhaps writing about the events of the past few weeks could help him out of his funk.

When the grandfather clock bonged six, he stared at the pages of scratched-out words, put down his fountain pen, and dressed for the hills. Like faithful dogs, the cats followed him out of the bedroom and down the stairs to the pine-paneled dining room. Three small logs crackled in the fireplace, dispelling the early morning chill. The embers glowed as red as the hue in his MacDougall tartan.

Megan entered from the toasty kitchen with its coal stoves and chatty staff who were preparing breakfast for the Laird and Lady and Jason's numerous cousins.

"Morning, Jason."

The warmth of her voice surprised him. Heretofore, this dark beauty had treated him with reserved civility while showing him the world-famous MacDougall Angus breeding operations. Megan was "family." Her mother ran the house staff and her father was the farm manager, so Megan had grown up in the manager's wing of the castle on the other side of the huge kitchen, playing in the main house and going to school with his cousins. Her admiration and affection for his aunt Rachael MacDougall seemed to know no bounds. After a year of assisting Jason's veterinarian aunt on a breeding project, she would head off to Edinburgh Veterinary School. Megan's responsibilities didn't include household tasks.

Jason smiled. "Hi, Megan."

Her cheeks were flushed with heat as she placed a generous breakfast of eggs, venison and muffins at Jason's setting on the eighteen-foot long dining table. By now the cook knew he had little fondness for haggis.

Intensely aware of her physical presence, Jason tried to avoid watching her bountiful breasts threatening to spill out of her square-necked cotton blouse as Megan slowly filled his large cup with steaming tea. He said, "Isn't this above and beyond the call of duty for you?"

"I've got the day off, and Annie asked me to set the table for her. Bit of morning sickness. By the way, congratulations on your caber toss, saving the family honor." Megan waited by the end of the table. "Will there be more? Anything."

Jason looked up, startled by the innuendo in her voice. Explicit eyes were challenging his, her sultry smile dazzling as she gushed vitality. *What's changed?*

Jason considered Megan strictly hands-off. She'd just completed advanced-level secondary school at the top of her class. But since first meeting her, he found it difficult not to be caught staring. She was slender, curvaceous, with a tiny waist—a Celtic beauty with a superabundance of long, coal black hair which she wore down and free, making him think of a brunette Lady Godiva.

Jason struggled to maintain his composure and smiled up at her. "Yes, Megan. I want to spend the day in the hills. It's why I'm wearing my kilt." *Dumb. Dumb.* He handed her a small leather shoulder bag. "Please have someone pack a lunch."

"That sounds lovely." She swept her hair behind her shoulder. "Since I've got the day off, would you like me to change and accompany you?"

* * *

They crossed the back lawn in the retreating early morning fog and were quietly joined by three of his uncle's dogs—two great Danes and one of the mastiffs. A red stag and three of its hinds appeared out of the mist. The deer, Jason and the dogs froze in the excitement of being together in such unusual circumstances—until a wave of grief hit Jason as he realized the stag was doing a lot better job of protecting its family than he had. Finally the deer walked on to forage elsewhere and the dogs trotted over to smell where they'd been. Jason said, "I don't see how Aunt Rachael managed to train the dogs to leave the deer alone."

"Actually, the word is she trained the dogs to terrorize any strangers attempting to poach on MacDougall lands." Megan tossed her hair. "Your aunt and uncle are fierce conservationists and love all life."

Continuing their walk with the dogs, they skirted the farm pond and admired the elegant mute swans leaving a barely discernable ripple as they swam. Mallards paddled about among the reeds, ducking their heads underwater for breakfast. The track to the hills led them through a glen thick with birch, aspen, red-berried rowan, wych elm, holly, oak and even beech trees with lichens.

The woods were alive with birds calling out their early morning exuberance. A blue tit and a goldfinch tried to outdo each other. Jason spotted a Scottish crossbill watching him quietly from a birch limb over the trail. A pair of red squirrels chattered down at them harshly for interrupting their chase.

Filled with a sense of the wonder at all of God's creation, Jason recalled the opening lines of William Cullen Bryant's "Thanatopsis:" *To him who in the love of Nature holds communion with her visible forms she speaks a various language; for his gayer hours she has a voice of gladness, and a smile and eloquence of beauty, and she glides into his darker musings, with a mild and gentle sympathy, that steals away their sharpness, ere he is aware.*

Nature was offering him her healing bonds, calling him to over-come the despair that engulfed him. He felt emotionally dead, and it scared the hell out of him. Megan seemed to sense his mood, and he appreciated her silence as they walked through the woods. He soon dis-covered, though, that if his emotions were deadened, his basic instincts certainly were not. Following her, he couldn't help admiring her mus-cular calves tapering to trim ankles and feet that moved so silently the wildlife wasn't disturbed.

As they emerged from the woods he and Megan began the steep climb through a scattering of ancient Scots pine and juniper. Green vis-tas of pastureland opened up before them. Fragrant sage and purple heather blanketed the moors and clung to the rocky slopes.

Rock was everywhere. He'd never seen so much rock. Rock hills, rock mountains, rock promontories, rock embankments and rock-strewn fields. Rock walls, houses, churches, castles, roads, bridges, wharfs and seawalls. It seemed all Scotland was one huge, sparsely pop-ulated, cold rock.

They reached the pasture for the prize bull and Megan stopped short. "Something's wrong. The upper gate's wide open—and he's gone."

The magnificent Angus was nowhere to be seen.

"This is serious, Jason. That stud is the culmination of many years of unique breeding."

They ran uphill to the gate. Jason noticed the dogs sniffing where two sets of feet had disturbed the dew on the grass leading from the gate up into the trees to the southwest. He called the dogs back to them and joined Megan examining the latch.

She gave him a puzzled look. "It's not broken. Perhaps the brute just leaned into the gate and bent it enough for the wooden slide to disengage."

Jason said in a low voice, "Two people opened the gate and went up into the woods over there."

She studied the tracks in the wet grass. "You're right." She frowned. "But nobody on these lands would be so irresponsible."

They picked up the bull's trail to the west in the wet grass and gave chase with the dogs.

Over the first hilltop they spotted the massive animal grazing in a grassy hollow. Megan called the dogs and said, "We'll go back for help." But the frisky dogs had other ideas and ran barking around the bull. The bull snorted and pawed the ground. Then it decided to give chase.

Now the disobedient dogs obeyed the command to come, as they fled towards the safety of Megan's side, with the bull in close pursuit.

"Oh, shit!" he muttered as Megan exclaimed "Bugger!" They raced to a large Scots pine a few yards away. At the tree he grabbed her waist between his hands and lifted her to sit on his head so she could get her feet on his shoulders. "Stand and pull yourself into the limbs," he said, looking up and giving her an immodest boost with a hand against her kilted bottom.

Jason sprinted to the bull's enclosure as hard as he could run, with the bull closing the gap. The bull's snorting breath sounded closer and closer. Was his bright MacDougall tartan the red flag? He glanced over his shoulder. Inches from being gored, he reached the rock wall and vaulted over the top to safety.

The dogs swerved and went through the open gate, taking the bull with them. Jason vaulted back over the wall and shut the gate, hastily latching it while the dogs skedaddled through the rails to escape the agitated animal. Not a scratch on himself from the bull or the stone wall, but a performance he'd never care to repeat.

Sweating profusely, Jason returned to the tree and caught Megan as she dropped from the lowest limb. As he stood her on her feet, she said, "I thought he had you. I've never seen anyone run so fast."

"I've never been so motivated."

She clung to him, pressing her body into his with extraordinary familiarity. "This morning I awoke knowing we must pursue our fate together, or perish. The bull was a sign." She stepped back, looking at him with a bemused twinkle. "I confess, it didn't occur to me that fate might include the bull."

They drank from his water bag and rested, seated under the shade of the tree. *Pursue our fate together? Or perish?* This morning the dangerous bull, yesterday his brother's threats at the caber toss—were these foreshadowings of his time in the Highlands?

Megan's soft giggle developed into contagious belly laughter, a release of tension that left them rolling on the grass in uncontrollable hilarity. When they'd caught their breath, they resumed their walk up into the hills, but now hand in hand.

CHAPTER 20
AUNT RACHAEL

Scottish Highlands
Wednesday, July 20, 1955

For the next half hour Jason climbed with Megan. He appreciated the freedom of movement and airiness of the kilt. They continued hiking hand in hand.

Finally, he broke the silence. "I apologize for putting my hand ... ."

"Thanks for helping me up into the safety of the tree." Smiling, she said, "Don't be bothered by whatever you saw. Not after yesterday at Inverness. Without your sporran, your kilt flew up on your toss, revealing more manhood than we're accustomed to seeing."

He felt his neck and face burn with embarrassment. "Do you always speak so bluntly?"

"'Tis the custom here. We're breeders, and have little use for people who beat about the bush."

They ascended with the dogs to one of the higher ridges at the northwest corner of his uncle's land, defined by three lone pinnacle rocks standing tall on the ridge top. Breathing hard and sweating from the exertion of their climb, he looked back to the southeast and marveled at the panorama that unfolded before them. Black Angus cattle dotted grassy hills and valleys with wooded streams. His uncle's castle and orderly estate and farm buildings seemed less imposing from this distance and altitude. Two miles beyond and below the castle was the large village where his cousins attended school. Established as it was on the banks of a loch, the village was postcard picturesque. Beyond the loch stood the Grampian Mountains.

Building clouds brought a chill breeze, despite the warm day. "Look at that," said Megan. "The dark shadow from the scudding clouds, racing across these treeless moors like some avenging angel condemning what man did to the hills that once were endless forests of Scots pine."

"I thought this land was always grassy meadows. And rock."

"You're a logger. The Scottish Highlands are a classic example of what your aunt Rachael calls ecosystem impoverishment resulting from elimination of the top predator. First it was logging, then bringing in sheep, and finally killing the last wolf in the middle of the eighteenth century, which changed the land permanently."

"Killing the wolves did all this?" Jason swept his arm across the heathered hills and lush meadows.

"Unfortunately. Without the wolves, the population of Scottish red deer expanded and fed on the young seedlings so no new trees grew. Except where the deer were fenced out, only the huge pines dating back to the time of Bonnie Prince Charlie remain."

Jason studied the landscape. "The unforeseen consequences of what we do."

They sat on a low, flat rock where they could use one of the pinnacles for a backrest. Jason was glad he had the seven woolen layers of his pleated kilt insulating him against the cold stone. Megan snuggled against him for warmth as the chill wind cut through their Ghillie shirts, wet with sweat. The dogs already knew the drill and plopped down to snooze beside them. Jason absently rubbed the mastiff's head and thought about the staggering changes in his life. Despite the beauty all around him, he was tense with inner conflict.

The pace and values of life in the Scottish Highlands were not so different from the logging communities like Forks, Washington, in the Olympic Peninsula. For the most part, Highland people were quietly reflective, if you didn't stir up their fierce pride and independence. He liked that. It gave him time to consider what he needed to learn and decide—if he could somehow shake his agony at the thought that he was at fault for his family's death.

"I'm glad for the company of the dogs," he said, "even though they remind me of the loss of my Airedale, Brutus. He was always my best friend, accompanying me through the Olympic forests while I practiced the hunting, shooting and knife-throwing skills my father taught me. I never understood why it was so important to Father that his son be the best at everything, but I did like winning."

Megan looked at Jason strangely. "Trying to be the best doesn't seem like a bad way to grow up."

"Not without knowing the reason for it." Jason rubbed his back against the rock like an old bear. "Over the years Brutus and I lay beside streams while I pondered the natural order of everything I saw around me and wondered where I fit into that picture. I always believed I had a mission. After Uncle Ewen explained the source of my gifts, I hoped that with the help of the family here in Scotland, I could figure out what I'm meant to do."

"You can start by thanking God for the time with your Airedale instead of mourning his loss." She shivered. "Then you can keep me warm in this chill wind." She moved to sit between his legs in the circle of his arms, with her back against the warmth of his chest.

Jason smelled the fresh herbal scent of her glossy black hair and turned his thoughts to yesterday's Highland games. When Uncle Ewen was practicing for the annual games, he told his nephew, "Before yer father left for the States to make his fortune, he was the one man who could best me at the caber toss." Jason realized his father had rarely mentioned his older brother. Curious, Jason tried some tosses alone and discovered his father had taught him with a pole that weighed at least ten pounds more than the ones here. That had given Jason quite an edge tossing a regulation Highland caber, an important advantage when he was challenged by Lord Burns' guest. His brother. Jason shuddered at the memory of that athlete.

The concern he felt was counterbalanced by confidence in his ability in self-defense. His father had taught him unorthodox Highland fighting tactics so he could stand up to Pacific Northwest loggers and their sons, who couldn't resist testing the son of the strange-talking man who financed their gyppo logging operations. Uncle Ewen, on the

other hand, insisted, "Use yer brain for leadership lad; dinna be brawl-
ing when ye can take charge instead." Nevertheless, he'd already begun
teaching Jason, the hard way, a few tricks his father hadn't—for those
times when fighting was unavoidable. His uncle's agility and strength
took Jason by surprise.

His thoughts were interrupted by the dogs jumping up as they
were joined by two golden retrievers wagging their tails. Jason became
aware of a new scent, followed by the sound of a pebble rolling downhill. He started to look around his pinnacle backrest when two wool-
stockinged, muscular calves descending from a green and blue kilt
moved into his line of sight. The bulging calves tapered to petite ankles
and leather walking shoes.

Surprised, he looked up into his aunt's sweaty, freckled face,
crowned by her thatch of red hair hanging loosely over her shoulders.
Her cheeks were flushed and her ample figure looked as if it would burst
the top buttons of her sweat-soaked shirt. She looked and breathed as if
she'd chugged up the steep trails.

"What a grand breeze you've found here today," she said cheerily.

"Aunt Rachael." With proper respect, he started to stand.

Removing her small leather backpack, she plopped herself down
opposite Jason and Megan before he could get to his feet. "Thought this
is where ye'd be. Your uncle got called into town so he asked me to join
you. He thought you might want to talk a bit."

"I'm fine, really," Jason fibbed. "The gate to the bull pasture was
open." He tried to sound matter-of-fact. "After the dogs herded him
back in, we closed it."

Rachael gave them a quizzical look. "Those aren't herding dogs,
lad."

"Well, we sort of outran the bull." He chuckled. "By the skin of
our teeth."

Rachael joined his laughter. "That's not the way I'd have chosen to
distract you from your sorrows. I'm glad you're both in one piece." She
shook her head. "Thanks for corralling our prize stud. We'll check the
gate on the way back. Somebody was very careless."

Jason caught Megan's eye. She nodded. "There were two sets of human tracks in the dew, leading from the gate to the woods." He cleared his throat. "The bull was released deliberately."

Rachael looked at Jason intently. "Ewen told me about Lord Burns' guest who challenged you at the games. That he was looking for your parents when they died, and he turns out to be your brother! On top of that shock, he wants you dead." She turned her head sideways to squint at him with one eye. "Now someone releases the bull. Do you think your brother's responsible for that? What do your MacDougall gifts tell you?"

"That I was tuned in to Megan," he quipped. Jason shuddered. "I wonder if my brother's as spooked as I am."

"Spooked?" She peered at him. "You do look haunted."

"Aunt Rachael, I'm certain that man never tossed a caber before in his life. He's scary."

She leaned toward Jason. "Why did you wait until late last night to tell Ewen who the challenger was?"

He shrugged. "The man disguises himself, hides his face behind a full beard. It all seemed too melodramatic—like the imaginings of the frightened guy I am after running into him halfway across the world yesterday."

Rachael leaned forward and patted his knee. "Jason, your uncle and I will never doubt any sixth sense you have. I'll talk with him tonight, and we'll try to sort this out."

CHAPTER 21
HIGHLAND CANDOR

Scottish Highlands
Wednesday, July 20, 1955

A cold wave washed over Jason as he acknowledged the danger that stalked him and now threatened the relatives who'd taken him into their life. Then he recalled Uncle Ewen's family history lesson, and took heart. It felt right to be up here in the Highlands with Rachel and Megan.

His aunt opened her pack and handed them each a sandwich wrapped in waxed paper. "Let's eat."

With the hunger of hikers, they munched their venison sandwiches and quenched their thirst with bottles of ale. They were silent as they looked out over the MacDougall properties. Suddenly Rachael flung open her arms and burst out with enthusiasm, "*God* I love this land!"

Jason laughed. "Is that why you married Uncle Ewen and bore him so many fine children?"

Rachael smiled reflectively. "He wanted to hire a veterinarian. I was just out of the Royal College of Veterinary Studies at Edinburgh and the only woman to respond to his query, but in the interview we discovered we shared a dream—to improve the Angus breed of cattle and to improve conservation practices for the sake of future generations. We became infatuated during that interview. Being a Campbell, I was leery of working for a MacDougall, but he insisted—said I could be his gamekeeper and train his fine dogs, too. All things he knew I loved."

She stopped and smiled again, her cheeks rosy. "We planned and worked side by side. God I was attracted to him." She laughed. "I was Lady MacDougall before I knew it. Lord help me, a Campbell conquered by a MacDougall! What irony. I was sure me parents would never approve o' me marriage."

Jason found himself caught up in her story.

"We've bred a lot o' cattle together." Rachael gazed at the heifers in the grassy glen below. "Ewen's a fine bull of a man. His kilt just brushes mine and I'm ready. It seems the most natural thing in the world."

Jason felt his face flush. He'd give anything to have a wife like Rachael. She was the most wholesome, natural woman he'd ever met. "Uncle Ewen's a fortunate man."

"He is that, Jason. But so'm I. And so will be any woman who shares herself with you."

Jason noticed Megan didn't seem at all embarrassed, but he didn't know what to say.

Rachel opened another bottle of ale. "You're grieving the loss of your parents, Jason. You've discovered your father let you believe you're a freak. You've met a twin brother you didn't know existed, who seems to have your gifts. And now you've met a girl you think is taboo and you wish she weren't. Mind you, that's a lot for one young man to handle alone." She paused. "How tall are you?"

"Six foot one."

"And muscled like a gladiator." Suddenly her eyes were penetrating. "Jason, I came up here to tell you something. You have choices. You can use this time just to grieve your losses. Or you can take the bit in your teeth and prepare for whatever challenges life has for you."

He let that sink in.

Finally, he spoke. "What should I do?"

"Let us in, Jason. You have emotional walls protecting you nobody can penetrate. I see how the lassies look at you—especially your cousin Shamus' siren daughter, Lil. Why do you hold back?"

Jason was in shock from such candor, especially in front of Megan. His face became as hot as any oven.

"You're twenty-two, Jason."

"But Lil's my cousin."

Megan moved to sit cross-legged opposite them. He noticed her control a smile that tugged the corners of her mouth as she watched the interchange.

"Lil is nigh twenty, Jason, and old enough to make a man of you, believe me." Aunt Rachael laughed. "She's a handful, that one. Because she's the granddaughter of your grandfather's brother, she's your second cousin. And take this from a veterinarian-breeder, being second cousins is no deterrent. It's when you're first cousins there can be health issues with children." Rachael took another draught of ale. "But I'm not suggesting you *marry* Lil."

Jason squirmed.

Rachael didn't ease up on him. "You're shy with strangers, Jason. But surely you have some experience with women."

"Actually—" Jason was going to mention Suki, but thought better of it when he glimpsed Megan blushing. He saw Aunt Rachael notice the blush too.

"After your performance at the games, half the single women around here will be vying for you. Your uncle and I think there are things you should know. Pertaining to your gifts."

Jason exhaled, deeply curious.

"You're a real catch, with your fine looks and family background. A lot of women will think they want you, until they discover they can't handle you—not because of your physical attributes—but because you need someone who can remain by your side while you slay dragons. A woman who can stand up to the enormous love you'll have for her and she for you."

Jason felt himself blush. "How do you know more about me than even *I* know?"

Her green eyes bored into him. "It takes one to know one. Such women are few and far between. But we do exist. So hold out for the one who's right for you. It's the most important thing you must succeed at in life."

Jason smoothed his kilt along his outstretched legs and listened.

"Every gifted MacDougall has had to have an extraordinary woman at his side to complete him and to offset his unbearable aloneness. Ye should hae seen yer grandfather Angus with his Angie." Aunt Rachel's touch of brogue seemed to summon his grandparents out of a bygone era.

She glanced at Megan. "You can learn about them through Megan, who grew up sitting at yer grandfather's knee."

Jason gazed at the distant mountains. "How will I know when I've met the woman for me? That she's the one?"

"Because when you meet her, she'll be the best of all the women you've known and you'll want no one else—only her—and you'll never give up on her. Until then, there will be other lassies you make verra happy," Rachael said with a smile.

Jason's embarrassment gave way to wondering how such things could be. No one he knew besides Suki had ever talked to him with such candor. His heart still questioned how anyone could replace her. But he was grateful for his aunt's advice, for the opportunity to move forward.

Rachael stood and Jason grabbed his day-pack and helped Megan to her feet. While the dogs explored ahead, the three of them walked side by side down the steep slope.

"This is breeding country, Jason, and Highland women are verra liberated. We know you'll want to be responsible. You've no doubt seen the wee packets in your nightstand drawer."

There was that face-in-the-oven feeling again. He said nothing.

After walking a long time in thoughtful silence, Jason stopped. "I'll be darned. You've set us up, haven't you?"

His aunt turned to face him. "We haven't done a thing, Jason. Your uncle and I are just giving you our blessing. Think of it as customary European preparation for the challenges ahead."

"But Megan's not ... ."

Rachael put her hand on his forearm. Her green eyes flashed. "You're right. She's not. But there's greatness in you, Jason. *You* will be the remarkable member of our existing family. Both Ewen and I know it, as does Megan here. But only if you don't let your loneliness get you hooked by a needy woman along the way—something Megan would never allow. And that's the practical reality of your life right now." She turned and resumed hiking down the trail with the dogs.

"Anything more?" he asked, a tinge of finality in his voice.

"Always," Rachael added cheerfully over her shoulder. "Your father left here before it became customary to wear bloomers under our kilts. I'll confess, your uncle and I still don't—unless we're going into town. I really don't know how many of our children to attribute to that little indiscretion."

Jason erupted in a chortle. "Why *Lady MacDougall!*"

Her laughter rolled across the moors and echoed back from the hills.

He felt Megan's hand slip into his.

As Rachael forged ahead, Jason whispered out the side of his mouth, "You reveled in my discomfort while she set me up at the pinnacle, didn't you?"

"Best performance I've ever seen."

Jason was pleased he'd refrained from mentioning his experience with Suki. "I'll get you for that."

"I'm counting on it."

CHAPTER 22
CALEDONIAN PINE

That evening, Jason felt the loneliness of an outsider looking in as he watched his cousins gather in the great living room before supper. He stood taller when they were joined by Megan and her parents.

His younger cousins rushed Megan. "Dance, dance," they clamored.

"It's suppertime." Megan smiled down at the children and stood erect and proud before them, her hair cascading over her shoulders and down her back.

"Please, please," the children insisted. Two of the older boys took a pair of swords from the wall and placed them in a precise cross on the floor in front of the fireplace.

Megan looked at Jason's Uncle Ewen.

"It would be a treat for all of us, Megan. It's not every day we get to see the regional champion perform."

Megan removed her shoes while Cousin Terry placed a record on the turntable. Like a ballerina, Megan stood by the swords as the huge Klipschorn corner-speakers filled the room with rousing bagpipe music accompanied by a heart-quickening drumbeat. She raised her arms so her fingers touched and stood that way a moment, joining with the battle-dance music. Then she placed her hands on her hips and raised a knee under her kilt, toes pointed down gracefully, and began dancing the dangerous Highland sword dance with such dazzling speed and accuracy that Jason forgot to breathe. Her pointed toes high-stepped between the blades with uncanny precision. Her dance was punctuated with pauses that gave the illusion of flashing feet suspended from a body floating free of gravity. As she twirled, her hair wrapped around her face. Minutes later, the dance was over and she stood as she began, except her chest was heaving and her hair wild.

The family cheered and clapped, Jason most of all.

He held Megan's chair as she took her seat beside his at the long dinner table. Food usually attracted his full attention, but he found Megan an irresistible distraction. When the meal was over, everyone returned to the living room for family time with Ewen and Rachael.

* * *

As the family drifted off to their bedrooms, Jason walked out on the back terrace to greet the night.

Megan caught up with him. The energy between them was tangible. She slipped her small hand into his and he noticed the top of her head came to his shoulder. That was taller than Suki, who was only four feet eleven inches and not quite ninety pounds.

A full moon illuminated the ancient Caledonian pine that stood proud and inscrutable on the far side of the lawn. Megan led him across the grass to stand beneath the tree and touched its scaly bark with seeming affection, then looked up at Jason.

"Do you know this Scot's pine has stood here for over five centuries?"

His logger's eye told him the healthy trunk was more than seven feet in diameter. Massive roots spread out into the ground and the first great limbs began a dozen feet above their heads.

"Can you imagine the things this tree has seen?"

Megan guided him around to the far side. She stood with her feet apart, elevated on two raised roots, her eyes now almost level with his, and leaned back comfortably against the tree trunk like it was an old friend.

"I *know* what it's seen—and has yet to see, Jason. Can't ye feel it, understand, at least a wee bit, why I'm meant ti be here wi ye?

Jason inhaled the pine-scented air and the aura seeped into his being.

She touched his arm. "I wish ye'd known yer grandfather Angus."

He thought about the character and love he saw in the dining room portraits. "Me too."

Megan twined her fingers through his. "Niver mind. Ye'll know him through this tree when the time comes and yer gifts tell ye what he knows."

He heard the mystique working its spell. "You speak differently here—dialect."

"Under this auld tree, I'm in another time—like when yer gifted ancestors were referred to as dragon-slayers by their clansmen." Megan squeezed his hands. "Some already call ye that."

He squared his shoulders. At the pinnacle rocks, his aunt had spoken of slaying dragons. "I trust you and Aunt Rachael are speaking figuratively."

"Yer grandfather used to hold me on his knee, while sitting on this root here under ma foot."

He followed her glance down to the giant root.

"He was a bull of a leader—a gladiator who fought to keep Scotland free. I love ma parents, but I worshipped him. Once I asked him, 'Where do yer gifts come from?' He patted the trunk and said, 'From the wisdom o' this ancient tree.'

"When I was a wee lassie, he told me stories of the clan once-upon-a-time. Then one day when I was older, he said the best story was yet to be—a story about me, and a dragon-slayer from the future. I would be 'the fair maiden to show the valiant one his power,' by bringing him back to a time when men and women lived more simply and their purpose in life was clear.

"When yer uncle Ewen brought you to MacDougall Castle, I wanted no part o' men." She smiled. "But while I was showing you the property, yer magnetism completely undid me. Last night I dreamt of yer grandfather and he reminded me of all I must do. This morning I woke so desirous of you I fair died."

Jason studied her face, shining in the bright moonlight. His rational mind questioned the spell. "We're not talking magic here are we?"

"No magic, Jason. All I can say is, things happen here we dinna try to explain." She smiled and kissed his eyes tenderly.

He trembled. Her lips were as soft and velvety as rose petals.

"Jason, are ye familiar wi' *Brigadoon?*"

Her hushed tones excited him. "Who isn't?"

"Think of this place as yer Brigadoon, not for one enchanted day, but for all yer time here. Let us shield ye from the harsh realities of the world while each of us passes on to ye all the knowledge and love we possess."

Overwhelmed by such a generous focus of attention, he questioned her with his eyes.

"Because ye're the one's got the gifts, Jason. That makes ye our dragon-slayer—our hope in the face of a foreboding future."

The details were vague, but his own sense of having a special life's purpose had now been voiced by a woman who made him want to measure up to her faith in him. Megan squeezed his hands again. Mesmerized by her nearness, Jason found himself glancing at her cleavage, then felt awkward as she caught him looking.

With a smile she took his hands and held them. "I've noticed ye're attracted to ma long hair." She placed his hands on her thick tresses where they lay over her collar bones. Her grin turned impish, "and to ma more feminine attributes." Gently, she drew his hands down her hair until his palms covered her abundant breasts.

Jason inhaled sharply.

Megan pressed his hands firmly against her, moving them in slow circles over her softness. "Hold me so I feel it, Jason. Harder. I'm not fragile." She shuddered sensuously. "I'm no flame-spewing dragon, but when ye want, I expect I'll make things plenty hot for ye."

Suddenly her brow creased. "Too much, too soon?"

Electrified, Jason shook his head.

Her eyes reflected the moonlight. "Yer grandfather tells me to be here wi' ye now."

"My grandfather? What about you? Do *you* want to be here with me now?"

She must have felt him tense, his guard go up, because she said, "I do, with every instinct in me," and added hastily, "I'm not crazy, Jason, and if ye'll open up, ye'll ken it, too."

He took a deep breath. "You sound crazy, yet I know you're not."

"It's the tree, Jason. Ye'll see."

He wondered if *he* was crazy.

Megan spoke faster, a tinge of excitement edging her voice. "Remember the first day I showed you around the property, when the bull broke down the fence and took the cow, how he bulled into her so she let out a bellow but didn't try to get away? Women are no different, Jason, when that's what they want."

She wrapped her arms around him. "I dreamed I need ye to be the bull tonight, Jason." She kissed him passionately, pressing her body against his hardness. Her low moans promised everything Jason craved. All his senses coming to life, he released the last clasp of sadness.

Too good to be real? He opened his eyes to the ancient branches overhead. He sensed that somewhere deep inside she carried a hurt and needed him as much as he wanted her. He broke off the kiss, holding his lips an inch from hers. She was panting and they were engulfed in a glow of mystical energy. *Dear God, I am crazy.*

Suddenly he realized, Suki had taught him lovemaking, but nothing about subtly inviting a woman into bed with him for the first time.

Unsure of the next move, he said, "Would you like to come up to my room?"

Her kiss reached into his mouth, her answer clear. Jason decided to follow Megan's lead tonight. After all, nothing but good had come of that with Suki.

They stepped out from behind the tree and he noticed the lights were out in the castle.

"Go to yer room, Jason. I'll join ye there."

CHAPTER 23
IF AT FIRST

Scottish Highlands
Wednesday, July 20, 1955

Jason was sitting naked on the edge of the bed looking out the window at the Caledonian pine when he felt Megan enter his room silently and heard the door close with a quiet click. He turned his head. The light of the full moon shone through the window and like a cloud, her filmy white nightgown seemed to float across the space between them. He stood to honor her and was rewarded with a substantial hug, nothing cloud-like about it.

"You're a fine man, Jason. I want to be yer best friend and yer lover."

He kissed her gently.

She stepped back and slid her gown to the floor. Bathed in moonlight, she let him admire her femininity.

Fascinated by her flat abdomen, he placed a hand on it. She pulled her stomach in further, making it concave. He was hooked. Irrevocable, throbbing-with-passion, hooked—and realized from that touch she knew it. Her skin felt warm and soft against his as she stood on her tiptoes and kissed him fervently. Her breasts pressed into his chest, her electrifying body inciting his manhood.

Taking the measure of him in both her hands, she encircled him one slender finger at a time. "A strapping man you are, and I see by your frown that suddenly you're wondering how a wee hundred-pound woman like me can bed with a fine bull of a man like you." Her eyes locked with his. "Watch me."

Jason thought Megan was laying it on a bit thick—but found he appreciated her kind encouragement. He remembered feeling humbled by doll-like Suki, amused at his conceit that he might overwhelm her where babies were able to pass. He smiled and remained silent, admiring the matter-of-fact way Megan gave of herself. It seemed so natural that this lovely Celtic lass should be his mystical new friend.

Megan lay back on the bed. Her dark hair spread in disarray across his pillow, a stark contrast to the pale linen. Her breasts glowed white in the moonlight, with dark peaks on top.

Awed by her beauty, Jason lay beside her, where she encouraged his touch. Their ardor blossomed.

Her low, husky voice trembled in his ear. "It's not my physical size that matters, Jason, but the size o' ma readiness." She placed his hand where he could stroke and caress her while she opened her thighs.

As Suki had taught him, he gently stretched and explored her till she began pressing, moist and welcoming, up into his hand. Reaching for the nightstand drawer, Jason pulled out one of Aunt Rachel's "wee packets" and opened it.

"Here," said Megan, deftly slipping the latex over his anticipation, while hungrily kissing his mouth.

Every detail imprinted in his innermost being, Jason knew he would always remember this exquisite act as the sexiest, most promise-filled monument to the launch of their courtship.

Megan drew her calves to her thighs and pressed the soles of her feet together.

Jason poised himself over her on hands and knees, holding up his chest and head to keep his weight off her. He watched her face. Megan guided him as, with reverence, he eased into her enveloping warmth. Her hands pressed his buttocks to her, demanding all. He gasped in wonder at the magical working of her hips under him and began moving with her. Soon the rhythm took on a life of its own. Jason held back, waiting for her to peak. But after a long while it still wasn't happening. He stopped.

She frowned. "Don't you want to come?"

"After you." He tried to sound gallant.

Tears shimmered at her eyes. She covered her face with her hands. "What are you afraid of?"

"It's a long story, Jason. Not one I care to share right now."

"Then let me tell you a short story our family doctor told us." With one hand Jason removed her hands and wiped her eyes dry with a corner of the sheet. Throbbing with desire, he pulsed within her.

She gave him a sad little smile.

Jason felt her inside muscles contracting around him, still encouraging him, even as her private trouble suppressed her own release.

"Our doctor said a mother brought him her three year old daughter, because the little girl was eating the heads off the kitchen matches. He ordered tests, and learned the girl's system was deficient in sulfur."

Megan's eyes shone.

"The body knows what it needs, Megan. Your body is telling you what it needs. You asked me earlier to open up. Now you tell me what you meant by your dream about the bull."

Jason watched her face brighten with sudden understanding. "Take me under the auld tree, Jason, and I'll show you Highland legend come to life." The life in her pelvis echoed her words.

Jason held back with the discipline he'd learned from Suki and gave Megan a kiss. "It would be a privilege."

"Let's go then." She squiggled out from under him. Her voice filled with resolve. "Put on your robe." She crossed the bedroom, donned her thick terrycloth wrapper she'd left by the door, and stepped out into the hall.

CHAPTER 24
SCOTTISH FANTASY

Jason followed Megan down the stairs in barefoot silence. They passed through the high-beamed living room and the library, onto the back terrace. An errant cloud blotted out the moonlight. On the way across the dark lawn, Jason prayed for the ability to give her whatever she truly needed. Suki's lessons took on a whole new importance.

"Here, under the Caledonian pine." Megan breathed deeply. "We'll become part of its history."

Its history? He shivered at the thought of all the tree had witnessed. And what it was about to see right now. He took Megan's hand and led her around to the far side. Then a strange sensation traveled through him, nothing to do with the heat of his arousal. He was aware she'd been here with another before him—*a man who'd hurt her.* Where did that knowledge come from? The secrets hidden in the ancient tree?

The cloud moved on and the moon shone bright. As she had earlier in the evening, Megan stood with her feet apart on the two giant roots, her back against the trunk, her hips level with his. She gathered her hair away from the rough bark and draped it in front, where it cascaded over her breast. Her robe fell open on either side of her, a protective blanket against the bark.

Jason dropped his robe. The moon through the branches spotlighted his straining manhood.

Megan gasped, a hand clutching her throat. Slowly, she reached out and took him between her palms. "The lighting effect on the

rubber spooked me. Yer a bit much and this is going to be primordial."
She pulled him against her and half-whispered in his ear, "It's alright if
the rubber breaks; I'm protected too."

He kissed her reassuringly. "Just envision the things you were
dreaming about this morning, and the reality will be better than the
dream."

"The dream began like this." She took him in and pressed against
him with urgency. Her hand atop his shoulder, she flexed her legs, sliding herself up and down. He held her breasts. She began making startled
gasps, then tensed, her fingers digging into his shoulder. He clasped
harder. "Good. Good," she panted, while her pelvis jerked as Jason felt
her contractions begin. He worried she was too sensitive to endure
more, but she said, "Don't stop." He held her against the tree until her
first orgasm was well under way. *Now* she was ready to keep coming
with him.

Her Celtic eyes were pools of mystery. "It's time, Jason. Listen to
the tree. For the love of God, do it now."

"Do what?" he groaned in frustration.

"Do what the bull did. Don't ye feel the wisdom o' the tree? Don't
ye feel ma need? It's all so clear."

Bursting with passion, frozen in confusion, he blurted, "I don't
want to do anything to hurt you."

Her eyes begged him. Jason willed himself to sense whatever he
didn't understand. Then, inexplicably, he possessed the wisdom of the
tree, understood her emotional paralysis from deep hurt, recognized
her need to lower her guard against betrayal and to feel again. He leaned
his palm against the rough bark above her head. Just as he saw her pain,
and how he could relieve it, he suddenly felt his guilt and anger at letting his parents die by not acting on his premonition. Could the act she
craved heal him, too? As though a starting gun had gone off, he thrust
up into her so she was lifted off her feet.

Her loud inhalation froze him as she bit down hard on his shoulder
muscles, muffling a shriek.

He was horrified at what he'd done. Yet something ... *yes, primordial* ... made him hold her dangling there against the tree, his own

emotional pain beginning to quell from the pain of her teeth clamped on his shoulder.

Slowly, she relaxed her bite and raised her strained face to his, the cords on her neck standing out. She set her jaw and her expression changed to steely resolve. Pinioned on him, she let go of his shoulders and held her arms and legs out to the sides, showing she was alright. "Again," she whispered hoarsely. "Expiation first." She hugged him, her feet once more on the roots.

He kept thrusting hard, her muscles gradually welcoming him as she embraced the forces lifting her. Her orgasm reignited. A throbbing vein stood out on her forehead. Jason admired her wide-eyed determination. She pressed her open lips over his and her mouth-to-mouth cries reverberated in his skull.

He continued, praying this was what she needed. Perhaps it was the wisdom of the tree, perhaps an awareness of his own journey that told him the tears flowing down her cheeks bespoke the joy of emotional release. His own self-doubt seemed to vanish. He hadn't wept since his family had drowned and now he felt tears spilling, a healing and bonding taking place while they exorcized each other's pain. Strange. Her face had become serene in the midst of this fierce act.

Megan broke into a radiant smile. "Now show me yer need o' me." He lowered her feet to the roots again to give her the control. She began a slow, sensuous rhythm. He let her set the pace. He could feel her passion mounting. She strained her loins to receive all of him, until she took him with her. Once more, he held back his fluid as they exploded together. She crushed her mouth to his, muffling her cries of intense pleasure.

Jason flamed her orgasms of growing magnitude and wondered how long she could keep this up. Megan amazed him by stepping off the tree roots, arms around his neck, her heels seeking purchase at the tops of his bulging calves. She raised and lowered herself over him with flexes and twists that drove them heavenward. Her multiple orgasms grew to a muscle-jerking, tendon-wracking climax. It was time. Jason released at last.

Thrilled that they were in unison, he became one with Megan and the universe. It was a dazzling ride to the stars, a little death that flirted with eternity. Haunting strains of *Scottish Fantasy* enveloped his soul. The mysterious beauty and power of Bruch's music echoed his experience—the violin, the harp and the orchestra were himself and Megan, and this wise old pine.

The cool night air, scented with pine needles, gradually brought his reeling senses back to their earthly surroundings. Megan clung to him, softy kissing his neck, quiet laughter mixed with heavy breathing. Finally she spoke, a touch of wonder in her husky voice. "That was more than a woman hopes for." She looked up, eyes sparkling with excitement. "I felt like I could go on forever with ye." She nuzzled the hollow beneath his throat, her heartbeat thumping against his. "I felt *every*thing, just as ye did." He heard the passion in her voice. "Tonight ye restored me to womanhood—and more."

He felt indomitable. Like the bull in the pasture, but with a caring and a desire to give that the animal didn't have.

"You're right about the tree," he murmured. The pulse in her neck was still throbbing as he kissed it tenderly. "Let's come here often."

She pressed up to receive more of him. "I've never imagined anything could be so wonderful."

Seeming unable to stop completely, she continued to pull him deep within her. "Aren't you supposed to be soft now?" she said.

"Not while you keep that up."

Without warning, Megan delivered a playful blow to his jaw. "Well, you got even, like you warned this afternoon." She frowned. "How is it possible for you to keep us coming? I've never heard of such things. I feel as if we'd made love a mile high in a balloon, revealing unimagined vistas. You've exploded my horizons of what can be. Where did such sex come from?"

He brushed her lips with his fingers. "In Korea, I helped a woman. In return, she taught me an ancient Taoist discipline allowing me to achieve the control needed to reach unusual heights. She taught me to hold back my fluid while having repeated orgasms that build to a tsunami. I learned multi-orgasmic sex transcends what most people know or imagine about lovemaking."

Megan gripped his shoulder, her eyes round with wonder.

"At first my teacher thought it amusing when night after night she was able to make me wake the neighbors with uncontrollable cries of delight." He laughed in recollection. "Later, to her embarrassment, I learned to give her such pleasure it was her cries awakening everyone." Jason grinned. "Would you like me to get even with you some more tonight?"

Megan's eyes glistened. "Good lord, could ye?"

"After a bit. We're young."

She slid her hands along his shoulders. "Jason, for a year I've wanted nothing to do wi' men. Do ye realize what an appetite ye've given me tonight? I promise ye'll get no rest wi' me till ye've shown me everything ye know. I never imagined anything so amazing." Her eyes widened. "No wonder sex runs the world."

She smiled, her teeth like pearls in the moonlight. "Before you have to return to the States, we can grow together. We'll share unstoppable passion until we're both satisfied. People close to us will know, but that's alright." Smiling, she said, "Did ye hear the laughter coming from the voices in the tree?"

"I thought that was us."

Megan hugged him so fiercely she took his breath away.

When she relaxed, she looked up at the branches and back into his eyes. "We have months to build ourselves up for the challenging times in our futures."

Jason's curiosity overtook his inculcated social reserve. "Megan, do you wear anything under your kilt?"

Her throaty chuckle reassured him. "Not anymore. Not after this night."

* * *

Alone in his room, Jason thought about the way he'd seen his life that morning, and how he saw it now. His grief and uncertainty had retreated into the night—replaced by an eagerness to move forward, daring to forge a future for himself that not only accepted the risks, but faced them boldly. He would embrace his destiny. Fate had brought them together, Megan and him, not forever, but for now, to heal life-threatening emotional wounds with life-giving passion. This physical and emotional connection was their gift to each other. Suki had not only taught him the secrets to amazing pleasure. She had given him the key to the engine that would sustain his life, a key he could share. He could scarcely wait for morning.

CHAPTER 25
PINNACLE ROCKS

Infatuated, filled with excess energy, Jason and Megan raced to the pinnacle rocks marking the northwest corner of the MacDougall lands. "My legs are like rubber," Megan gasped, leaning against a rock.

Jason removed his kilt and shirt and made a bed for them. After a month of daily lovemaking, their ability to satisfy one another knew no bounds. Megan added her clothing to the bed and flopped down to remove her sturdy brogues and knee-stockings. Jason grabbed his pack and joined her, pulling out a fresh waterbag to offer her. The three big dogs that accompanied them settled down nearby.

"Do you think we've become too addicted to sex?" he teased.

"Only if we write our memoirs." She grinned. "Publishers might be a wee bit more conservative."

Megan removed his shoes and kneesocks and lay back beside him, stretching luxuriantly. "Your grandfather told me all dragon-slayers are born with an emptiness only a special woman can fill. Rachael told you the same thing, when she joined us up here."

"What makes a dragon-slayer's woman different?" Jason rested his hand in the hollow of her stomach.

She caressed the hand, taking a long while to answer. "She's born with an emptiness only a dragon-slayer can fill." Megan propped herself up on her elbow and looked him in the eye. "A man she can give herself to in absolute respect and trust—for life—knowing this is the man she will joyfully die beside when his time is up. Whether fighting shoulder-to-shoulder with him, or growing old together."

So there it was. For him and that woman, life would be a continual search until they found the one meant for them—the one they must die with—so they could be complete and free to throw themselves into the rest of their mission. "Aunt Rachael said to hold out for her, yet in the meantime ... ."

"You and I pursue our fate together."

"Hungry, yet?" Jason asked, pretending to reach for his knapsack.

"Ravenous." She laughed. "Have been since I awoke."

Jason swiveled his head to look down her body. She was self-loving, preparing.

"You want company?"

"Thought you'd never ask."

He pressed his hand into her, stretching her while she laughed with excitement as if he were tickling her.

She rolled over to kneel above him and unfurl a Trojan down his expanding lengthiness. "I dreamt that today I would make love worthy of a dragon-slayer."

"How was it?"

"Hard on the body. Soul-satisfying." She moved so her breasts swung over his mouth.

Fascinated, he cradled them in his hands. "Mmmm." His impassioned lips caressed them.

She shuddered as she smothered him in succulent flesh. "Oh-h-h-h-h." Slick with readiness, she buried him deeply within her, laughing her pleasure. "Oh, Jason. This has to be the best feeling in the whole world."

Her rhythmic contractions intensified, taking him with her, while Jason held back with all the discipline he'd learned. He wanted his dry orgasms to keep her coming.

Their first climax left her breathless, but even more charged, more unstoppable. She began rising up off him, then coming slowly down as she devoured him over and over with cries of ecstasy. Her magical energy emanated in waves. "Do something fiercely difficult,

Jason. Be my dragon-slayer, and I'll be everything ye need right now. I promise."

Jason felt his grandfather's presence, his strength. "Just don't let anything I do stop what you're doing."

Locking eyes with her, he arched his body and raised himself up on his hands and feet under her. Megan continued her controlled strokes as she stood to stay with him, then added astonishing hip rotations, stretching her crucible to its limits.

His whole being vibrated. "That's incredible."

"Good. I want to be ready for anything."

Jason reached out one arm. Megan grasped his wrist while he pushed up off the blanket of kilts. Her muscles bulged as she gripped in counterbalance while he pulled himself up on his feet, where he could thrust deepest into her insatiable orgasms. She shrieked in pleasure. When he stood erect he pressed his hand against the base of her spine and her feet left the ground.

"Hold me tight," she gasped, and arched back, flinging out her hands and feet in trusting abandon and a burst of laughter. Her hundred-pound body hung in orgasmic contractions on his dragon-slayer's sword. "More," she cried, "I want more."

Jason cupped his hands around her hour-glass waist, and thrust his deepest. As her body jerked in response, she cried out encouragement. Megan hooked her insteps against his shins and arched further, her hair brushing the kilts at his feet. Their shouts of tsunami climax ricocheted off the rocks as they exploded in muscle-wracking bliss.

Slowly Jason knelt, sitting on his calves and resting her shoulders on the kilts while her legs kept him locked within her.

Megan gasped. "Sweet Mother of God, every time is like a circus performance with you."

"Would you rather lie quietly on your back while I service you?"

"Not a prayer, now that I know how it can be between us. A month ago I never dreamed how exciting it could be between a man and a woman." She squeezed her thighs around him, laughing wickedly. "You've tapped into a heritage of wild Celtic sex I look forward to unleashing on you in the months to come."

His laughter joined with hers. "Wild Celtic sex it is then."

The dogs growled, a low rumble at first, then louder, ominous, as the mastiff and two great Danes rose up on their haunches. Jason went on full alert, *his hand streaking into his open knapsack.*

An unfamiliar voice called out, "If ye don't want them dogs shot, hold 'em."

Two scruffy men dressed like gamekeepers stood behind a fallen pillar rock, with rifles pointed toward the three huge dogs. In a flash, Jason sensed they were assassins from his brother. Only a dozen feet from the bed of kilts.

Jason rolled violently to one side to draw any shots away from Megan. One of the men fired his Manlicher bolt-action carbine. Earth sprayed across Jason's hand. The shot had missed him. Jason rose up on his knees and threw his heavy Korea knife into the throat of the slower rifleman on the right, then sprang to his feet and leapt up on the rock. Behind it the first rifleman was slamming a fresh round into the chamber of his carbine. Jason flew at him, delivering a sledgehammer fist to the man's left temple. The rifleman tumbled backwards and Jason fell on the dying accomplice. He yanked his heavy knife out of the man's throat. His mind flashed back to North Korea.

A cultured Scottish voice behind the tall rocks to his left brought Jason back to the Highlands. "Come out unarmed, MacDougall, or the lassie dies."

Jason whipped his head around to spot Megan, on her feet, facing the voice, the man he couldn't see behind the rocks. She stood stripped of everything but her wits and courage and the three huge dogs gathered round her—all four poised like sculptures. A scene he would remember forever.

"Mach ihm!" she shouted to the dogs and screaming like a banshee with centuries of rage at abusive men, charged with the dogs. Jason catapulted into the fray. The hundred ninety-pound mastiff leapt at the man and a shot cracked out just as Jason grabbed Megan, trying to insert his body between hers and the challenger.

"I'm alright, I'm alright. Let me go!" she insisted.

The dogs were mauling the man and she desperately tried to call them off, kicking at their rumps with her bare feet while Jason held her around her chest so she didn't get caught up in the melee of flashing teeth. Finally, the dogs obeyed her fierce spirit and Jason lowered her to the ground.

Back in normal time, Jason became alarmed when Megan cried out in horror as she turned and buried her face in his chest. He looked in shock at the mauled man's missing face in the jaws of the wounded mastiff.

Jason stroked her hair. "Storm saved you," he said.

* * *

The castle slept. But not Jason. After the ambulances and constables had left, an inspector from MI5 had started a line of questioning that made Jason feel like the assassin—until Uncle Ewen told the interrogator Jason was the gifted grandson of Lord Angus MacDougall. With an immediate change of attitude, the inspector said, "We've been watching for IRA sympathizers. Those assassins were in bed with the IRA. The one who lost his face is Viscount McTeague, from south of Glasgow."

* * *

Jason was pacing, still wired, unable to come down from his warrior's high, when Megan slipped into the bedroom with him. They held each other tight.

She beamed up at him. "Good news. I've been helping Rachael with Storm. She's staying the night with him. She believes he'll live— even be fine again."

"Thank God. What a wonderful animal. Can I take a shift with him?"

"I offered, too. But she wants to be the one with him if anything goes wrong."

"Megan, why on earth did you charge into that loaded rifle? It was a suicidal move."

"I'd just promised I'd be everything you need, remember?" She smiled. "If you'd come out disarmed, he'd have dropped you with a shot through the head, and I'd ha' fared verra badly at the hands o' those men. Better to go out fighting than whimpering."

"If you're not destined to be a dragon-slayer's wife, God help me when I meet the real thing." Jason looked sideways at Megan and mimicked her. "'Tis said Rachael trained the dogs to go after poachers." He looked into Megan's eyes. "What duplicity. The nine large ones are a trained force protecting the property, aren't they? And you grew up helping my aunt train them, correct?"

Megan pressed her lips together in a little grin as she nodded affirmatively. "At least ye can be easy the rest o' yer time here. Now that they know, nobody will come for ye. With me and the dogs by yer side, ye'll be better protected than by yer American Secret Service.

She stared into his eyes, her face radiant. "I need ye verra badly, Jason. I don't understand what I'm feeling, but if ye don't take me now, take me hard, I'll by god take ye with the verra knife ye used today ... ."

CHAPTER 26
TELEKINESIS

Natasha used the marine toilet on their boat in Fort Lauderdale and returned to bed with Ivan in the dark. As she knelt to join him, he rose and grabbed her from behind. Her first emotion was fight or flight—until his hands began pulling on her breasts and she realized he wanted sex a new way. They had always faced each other. Her shock turned to relief and nervous laughter as she helped him find her entrance even as her body mobilized for his surprise onslaught.

In minutes Ivan's probing shaft drove her to spasms she didn't understand. It felt good. Then Ivan climaxed and her body responded in a way she'd never experienced. Her head swam and she buried her face in the sheets to stifle her startled shouts.

Before she regained control, Ivan turned her on her back with her legs hanging over the edge of the bed and kept her in spasm as he came into her again. She wondered what was happening. He'd always climaxed once and then rolled over to sleep or gone back to work on his projects. And she'd just felt an exhilaration she thought only men enjoyed. On into the night he screwed her to paradise and back, doing things she and Ivan didn't know how to do.

Finally, Ivan slept. She lay beside him, reliving her amazing new experience. Until she sat bolt upright, mid-breath: her partner had been sharing a warrior's high following a deadly challenge to his twin. And Natasha had to deal with the scary fact Jason had won again.

CHAPTER 27
HIGHLAND FAREWELLS

Scottish Highlands
Wednesday, April 11, 1956

Jason had wanted to sleep longer. But the cats were creatures of habit who knew perfectly well what time he usually began petting them. So he took out his grandfather's letter and reread it, while absently stroking their magnificent coats.

Dear Jason,

In his mind he heard his grandfather's brogue:

MacDougalls hae always fought for freedom—
Independence and a government that serves the people.
Each man serves God, according to his individual talents.
The great threat to freedom be Soviet communism:
Individuals be insignificant, subservient to The State—
Collectively men serve The State,
Atheism be their religion.
I hae seen yer special gifts
Be to counter Russian subterfuge and takeover.
May the best ye hae ivver seen of freedom fighters,
Be the warst ye'll ivver encounter.
God be wi ye.
Affectionately,
Grandfather

Grandfather Angus had penned the message a few years before he died and Uncle Ewen gave it to Jason to open shortly after he arrived at MacDougall castle. Jason put the letter away for the umpteenth time and closed his eyes. His ten-month sojourn in Scotland enabled him to understand that he was seeking redemption for his parents' death. He would find it by using his gifts to serve God and freedom.

Now he would return to America and stay with the Kings between his six-week tour of duty in the submarine reserves and the start of plebe summer at the Naval Academy in July.

The day had arrived to say goodbye to his MacDougall family and Highland acquaintances. Megan and his aunt and uncle had shared everything they knew about his grandfather and the extraordinary, supportive relationship with his wife Angie. Thanks to Megan, what could have been a devastating time in Jason's life had become a rewarding one. Despite his enthusiasm for his coming year in America, he didn't want to leave her.

Aunt Rachael and Uncle Ewen were already at the table when Jason came down for breakfast.

"You came to Scotland to make some difficult decisions. Are you comfortable with what you've decided?" Aunt Rachael scanned his face.

"I think so." He smiled, hiding his ambivalence about Megan. "At the U.S. Naval Academy, I can kill three birds with one stone. One of the best educations in the world, test my attraction to the sea and discover if I can be an asset to the military."

Because the Academy turned down the highest percentage of college applicants in America, he'd studied hard for the entrance exams, which his uncle David had arranged for him to take at the American Consulate in Glasgow. Uncle Ewen gave him ongoing training in the time-tested techniques of Highland fighting. The months spent with Megan—running in the hills and learning to share their passion as an energizing daily way of life—had taught him to believe in himself and want to build on his foundation of differences. No longer centered on himself and his grief, very little slipped under his radar as he tuned in to other people's masked feelings.

Comforting letters from his mother's sister Sarah and his responses to that aunt had led to correspondence between her husband, U.S. Navy Captain David King, and Uncle Ewen. Both men were agreed about the dangers of the Soviet communist government and viewed what the Russians had been doing in Korea as a first step toward trying to control Asia. Uncle Ewen knew Russia was a major threat to the free world and believed Jason's MacDougall gifts and unusual intelligence would make him an invaluable asset on the side of democracy.

Before going upstairs to pack, Jason walked out to the back terrace and whistled for the dogs. Storm trotted over, too, fully recovered, and nuzzled Jason's hand for his usual vigorous ear-rubbing.

Aunt Rachel joined the farewell. "I come to comfort the dear departing."

Jason chuckled at her gallows humor and they sat down on a green wooden bench.

"You made the right decision, Jason. I told you we see greatness in you. So will Sarah and David King when they get to know you as we do."

Jason turned to her. "What of Megan? Will she be alright with my going?"

Aunt Rachael patted Jason's hand. "Her heart is just as torn as yours. But she knows you have different futures. She'll always be happy for the foundation you forged together, to build your lives on."

"She's taught me to believe I can face anything with the right woman by my side. I hate leaving her." He swallowed back his emotion. "Life will seem empty without her."

Jason looked his aunt squarely in the face. "I think someone before me trashed her heart. So much so she was afraid she couldn't feel again."

Aunt Rachael looked at him in surprise. "You *are* perceptive." She gave a deep sigh. "Unfortunately, one of the more painful lessons of life— trying to get through idealistic adolescent love to the realistic give and take of adult love."

She stood, looking down into Jason's face. "When you arrived, both your spirits were as low as pregnant cats' bellies. Together, ye've given each other a can-do spirit. Unquenchable determination.

Achievement. Fulfillment that will sustain ye both throughout yer separate destinies. Tell me, Jason, what finer gift could ye ha' been for one another?"

With that, his aunt walked back into the house. Jason patted the dogs and went in to pack.

* * *

Suitcases nearly ready to close, Jason felt the pangs of his imminent departure. Dropping a pair of slacks on the bed, he stopped his final folding to go take a walk with his uncle.

"I'm glad for a moment alone with you, Jason." Uncle Ewen's sober tone alerted Jason for serious news. "MI5 has just contacted me to say that anyone Lord Burns was with should be considered very dangerous."

Jason felt his mouth compress.

They passed under the ancient pine and Uncle Ewen stopped to look Jason in the face. "Over time, your premonitions may occasionally become visions—sometimes seeing what's hidden on the other side of a wall, at other times glimpses of the future. Like your grandfather knowing your destiny from a painting your mother sent him of you as a wee laddie with your Airedale. He just studied the portrait and smiled. I realize now he saw that you had the gifts and eventually would come here to learn about them. He was so certain, he didn't have to tell anyone. He just let events unfold as he knew they would—so you could believe in what you've been given." Uncle Ewen patted the tree trunk. "At first, you'll think you're imagining things. Don't. Trust your visions as you've learned to trust your premonitions."

They walked on towards the pond. "You'll find you have unbelievable survival skills for fulfilling your purpose in life."

"I'm not entirely comfortable with the idea that my life is not my own."

"Aye, you're an individualist—" his uncle winked—"so think of it, then, as our prayers holding you up through all the mischief you'll encounter."

They arrived at the pond. "My time with Megan and you and Aunt Rachael has been the happiest of my life. I have you and Aunt Rachael to thank for making everything possible."

Jason gazed at the azure surface of the water, a pretty reflection of the sky, hiding the reeds and muddy bottom—and the fish eating fish, in turn being eaten by other fish. Life could be like that, reality camouflaged by a socially acceptable surface.

* * *

That night, his cousins and Megan gave Jason a farewell party, with much ribbing and laughter, followed by emotional goodbyes and best wishes for life at the Naval Academy. Cousin Terry offered the final toast. "Remember another Scot who began his career as a midshipman—Lord Thomas Cochrane, Earl of Dundonald—whom Napoleon Bonaparte called 'my nemesis.' Here's to Jason, the next 'Sea Wolf'."

CHAPTER 28
RAISON D'ÊTRE

Trans-Atlantic Flight to New York
Thursday, April 12, 1956

On the flight across the Atlantic, flashes of lightning outside the windows drew Jason's thoughts back to his fireside farewell with Megan. After everyone had retired, he waited for her on the library sofa and dozed off in the mesmerizing light of the burning logs.

When he awoke she'd raised his kilt and mounted him. She wore the terrycloth robe, open, and her face shone in the firelight.

"You'll forever be a part of me," she said, and became the accomplished seductress who aroused him to unspeakable desire.

Their free-spirited giving carried them slowly forward in a wave of passion, rising high on its crest, quickly curling and crashing off that wave, confidently picking up another until it curled and crashed on the beach, and raced forward on the sand, then retreated to the sea, leaving them both exquisitely fulfilled.

When their hearts stopped pounding so hard, he said, "It seems an eternity ago I was afraid of hurting you."

She kissed him with tender intensity. Her eyes said, "I love you," but her lips never did.

"Remember our first night, under the auld tree?" she whispered.

"Every second of it." Jason clasped her hands. "*God* I'm going to miss you in America."

She smiled. "You've always known I'm inseparable from this place." Megan stroked his chest. "Tonight I want to tell you something our time together has done for me."

He kissed her fingertips. "I never wanted to pry."

"Thank you for respecting my privacy." She cleared her throat. "Last Christmas I received a letter from your cousin Rufus. You've known he's serving as a Royal Engineer with the U.N. forces in Korea." She paused. "We began corresponding."

Megan hesitated and took a deep breath. "This morning I received a letter with his proposal of marriage, which I've thought about alone ever since. I want you to be the first to hear that when Rufus is discharged from Her Majesty's Service and returns home, we'll announce our engagement." She squeezed Jason's hand.

The initial shock took Jason's breath away.

A feeling of loss percolated through him, followed by an unexpected relief that he wouldn't be leaving Megan all alone. "Rufus is the eldest son—you'll become the future Lady of the clan." That was a good surprise. The pieces were falling into place. "Rufus is the one who hurt you?"

Megan nodded. "The only man who ever could. We grew up best friends, became enthusiastic but terrible lovers when I was sixteen—uneducated beyond animal husbandry fundamentals, unskilled, no finesse."

She coughed. "He was home on university holiday when I . . ." She hesitated. "Well, let's just say ... he'd violated my trust." Her eyes squeezed shut for a moment, as if holding in the pain. "We had to go to the doctor. It was gonorrhea. Thank goodness for penicillin." She looked directly at Jason then, her eyes hiding nothing. "We'd expected to marry when we both finished university. I was devastated, and he was so upset by what he'd done, he left home and joined the military."

Jason stared at her. "And what makes you think the leopard's spots will change?"

"Because he's really a good man who made a terrible mistake one night along with his university friends, and the surprise result was more than either of us could deal with then." She held Jason's face between her hands. "He'd been gone for a year and I still had no interest in any man when you arrived at the castle." She smiled at Jason and looked into his eyes. "Eventually, I sensed *your* pain, your need, and realized I might ... that as your grandfather had told me, I was the fair maiden to help the valiant one."

Megan stretched her legs on the sofa, drawing them together between Jason's, holding him tightly. "Before Christmas I felt I couldn't bear to let you return to the States without me—that I was willing to give up the future I'd always dreamed of here in Scotland. Of course it made no sense. You'd have to live in the Academy barracks for four years and might get to be with me on a Saturday night. Then, through you I discovered I still love Rufus—love him enough to forgive him. When I heard from him, I was too conflicted to know what to do. I couldn't understand how I could go on craving the hours with you and loving him at the same time—until I realized life isn't perfect. In fact it's downright messy."

Jason kissed her moist neck, arched his head back and looked into her face. "You're changed, Megan. He'll know."

She reached up and kissed Jason's forehead. "He'll handle it. Especially when he learns you're our dragon-slayer and it was my destiny to help you, and in return learn your ancient arts of love to carry us through our own life and to pass on to our children."

She nuzzled his neck. "Before you and I made love that first night, I thought I could never love again. You not only turned my life around, you showed me the brass ring."

He kissed her eyes. Her heartbeat resonated in his chest, filling him with confidence and contentment. He thought about last weekend, leaning against the pinnacle rock. And how on the way back to the castle they'd laughed and chased each other, pausing with nostalgia at each familiar stone formation and fallen tree they'd used for months like pieces of furniture to nail that brass ring every way imaginable. Before they emerged from the woods by the west lawn, Megan had launched them yet again, astride a springy fallen sapling.

"There'll be none to match you," he said, while she straddled his lap on the sofa, with her knees bent up against his chest. Megan bit down on her thumb-joint as he kept her exploding like a string of

firecrackers—until her excitement sped him to his uttermost fulfillment again, leaving them both with a euphoria that neither could handle
too often. But when they did, their exhaustion was matched by a surprising energy.

The crackling logs in the fireplace had consumed themselves to
embers. "Take my word for it," said Megan, "there'll be more lassies for
you. Each with something you need."

"Promise?" Jason smiled. "Or are you just trying to ease me off
your hook gently?"

She squeezed his hand. "Let's walk out to the tree."

Together they crossed the grass for the last time, enveloped in the
nighttime mystique of the ancient Caledonian pine.

Max Bruch's *Scottish Fantasy* would always remind him of
Megan, whose greatest gift of all was to remove her hook and
return him wiser and unharmed to the ocean where he belonged.
And hadn't he just relinquished Megan to her own destiny rather
than impose his uncertain future on her? After all, Aunt Rachael
told him he'd never be able to give up on the one woman meant
for him.

So he'd said his heart-wrenching goodbye to a tearful Megan
under the mysterious old tree. In the many nights beneath its branches,
she'd been a magical conduit for him to become charged with the heart
and spirit of the MacDougall dragon-slayers—an advantage his brother
Ivan didn't have.

* * *

The plane hit turbulence, jolting Jason back to the present. His
thoughts turned to the warning from both his Scottish and his American
uncles. Totalitarian communism was already crushing Eastern Europe,
China and North Korea. A miserable future was in store for the free
democratic countries if they didn't work together to stop the spreading
Russian aggression. Jason still was uncomfortable with the idea of being

"destined" for something, but he knew he must fulfill a higher calling to protect the free world.

Aunt Rachael was right. Thanks to Megan, he felt like a roaring lion, ready to take on anything. Even the Russians. He smiled, ready at last to take on Ivan.

PART III

U.S. NAVAL ACADEMY

CHAPTER 29
SHOOTOUT IN MIAMI

Miami Beach, Florida
Thursday, April 26, 1956

Natasha had an uneasy feeling about the meeting just completed at the Fontainebleau Hotel in Miami Beach. Their bodyguard, Sampson, chauffeured the Rolls Royce limo, while she and Ivan sat on either side of "Uncle Richard Dougherty," listening to his take on the conference to explore recruiting the Mafia. Dusk was settling over Collins Avenue as they crossed Haulover Inlet Bridge and the famous art deco buildings of the Beach gave way to a wooded park.

"Two cars, come fast!" Sampson interrupted in his limited English. He pointed to his rearview mirror. As in countless training exercises, Natasha and Ivan instantly pressed a spot on the right and left rear door panels that opened hidden armrest compartments holding large semiautomatic pistols with silencers affixed. Grabbing her pistol, Natasha saw a black Pontiac speed around them on Ivan's side and slide sideways in front of them to block their path.

She and Ivan opened their rear side windows and were assaulted by the outside noise. The heavy Rolls Royce screeched to a stop and backed up with a roar of power, to smash into a second car stopping behind them to box them in. Sampson's maneuver scattered the men trying to get out, while she and Ivan fired into their frantic bodies. Then Sampson rammed the gearshift into first and floored the accelerator again. The Rolls jerked forward, smashed into the men with machine guns emerging from the Pontiac, then hit the back quarter panel of the vehicle and spun it around.

"Back, Sampson," Ivan said as calmly as if he were ordering a drink. The Rolls raced backwards while Natasha and Ivan finished off the men in the road with shots to their heads. Machine gun fire from the car behind them shattered their rear window and tore up the headliner. Natasha couldn't see the gunman, but Ivan stopped him with a burst of shots. Through their open windows, she and Ivan dispatched the remaining men.

"Are you alright, Natasha? Sampson?" Ivan's voice was tense.

She checked herself. "Yes," she answered in unison with Sampson.

"Well, I fear Comrade Richard took a fatal blow. Sampson, find a quiet spot with a public bathroom."

Natasha switched to a jump seat facing Uncle Richard so she could see what was wrong. He was slumped, a hole through the side of his neck. Blood pulsed out despite Ivan's hand compressing the wound. Uncle Richard sounded chagrined as he was dying. "Who would have believed it? Taken out by a crime boss consigliere from New Jersey that I was trying to recruit in Miami."

Ivan added, "He's very perceptive to have figured out what we're up to. His conversation in Italian with his cohorts didn't conceal his contempt for 'Ruskies' and 'commies'." Ivan cleared his throat several times and Natasha realized he was squelching his emotion over the loss of this comrade who had, in fact, been like an uncle to them as well as an indispensable component of Ivan's covert setup in America. Natasha reached into the breast pocket of Uncle Richard's jacket and thrust his white linen handkerchief into Ivan's hand. Ivan pressed it against the wound. "I can't stop this bleeding, Richard. It's the carotid artery."

Perhaps shock from loss of blood masked the pain, but Uncle Richard managed a laugh as he said, "Imagine. Patriotic mobsters."

Sampson parked in the shadows of a great ficus tree and shut off the steaming, clattering engine.

"Sampson, call in the standby crew with the Lincoln limo and additional car. Use the coded transceiver."

The head of the Dougherty Foundation looked with affection at the young couple. "You'll have to go back to the hotel and kill all of them before they know there's anything wrong, or you'll have their formidable crime syndicate after you."

Ivan placed a hand on Uncle Richard's shoulder. "Consider it done."

"Ivan, I didn't always believe it, but I'm convinced now that your Grand Acquisition plan is brilliant, mostly because it's so unstoppable. People's self-interest and greed make it so." He coughed blood onto Natasha. "Sorry, dear." He wheezed. "I also believe you're ready to take over the Dougherty Foundation and I so notified Spartak Kanokov in my report last month." Comrade Richard coughed again, gasped in and exhaled with a rattle. He took their hands and held on hard. "I'm going to sleep now." His eyes closed. His face looked peaceful. He took a deep breath as he relaxed his grip and died with a faint smile on his face.

Natasha was overwhelmed with sadness. Then she started shaking as the intensity of the past few minutes hit home.

Ivan held her chin up, riveting her with his intense stare. "We have work to do. Will you be alright?"

She forced herself to be calm. "Yes, Ivan. You can depend on me."

"Good, then go to the restroom over there. If the door's locked, shoot out the lock. Take the bag of evening clothes that's in the trunk, clean up and put on the black evening dress, blonde wig and high heels. Glamorous jewelry."

Ivan stepped out of the Rolls and hurried around to open the bullet-riddled trunk. "Ah, good. Looks like the luggage escaped their bullets." He reached for a suitcase and handed it to her. "Go now." Before she turned towards the bathroom, Natasha saw him open the weapons attaché case and begin screwing the long silencers on the automatic SIG Model P210-1 9mm Luger pistols.

While she changed, Ivan joined her, washed off the blood, and donned a dinner suit.

As they exited the restroom together, their team drove up quietly with the Lincoln limo and the car. "Take the Rolls with the body and run it to the remote deep-water canal we scouted in the Everglades last fall," Ivan instructed them. "Remove all identifying numbers, papers and possessions and dump the car and body. Then return to the boat."

He turned to Sampson. "Your uniform escaped harm. Be sure to wear your hat low to make you harder to identify. You'll drive us back to the Fontainebleau and accompany us through the hotel in your uniform, carrying the spare weapons attaché. We'll return to the suite and do unto them before they do unto us."

"Do what?" asked Sampson with a puzzled expression, unfamiliar with the American saying. He held the door of the limo for Natasha to get in.

Seating herself, Natasha answered for Ivan. "Kill them, Sampson. Kill them before they kill us."

"Oh. Yes. Of course." He adjusted his chauffeur's cap. "Comrade Dougherty was good man."

CHAPTER 30
BUSINESS AT THE
FOUNTAINEBLEAU

Miami Beach, Florida

Thursday, April 26, 1956

Each one of them knew exactly what they had to do. At the hotel, they parked under the building and took an elevator directly to the top floor. Natasha had her large pistol tucked under her left arm, concealed by the elegant Thai silk stole that covered her bare back and shoulders. Checking that the corridor was empty, she signaled the men and stepped out. Ivan and Sampson flanked her as they walked on the plush carpeting towards the suite.

They stopped at a small table near the door. Samson placed the attaché on the tabletop and silently opened the case. He and Ivan checked the silencers, placed extra mags in their pockets and took the precision semi-automatic pistols in each hand. They released the safeties and cocked the weapons. Natasha draped her stole over the case, pushed her abundant cleavage up to expose as much flesh as she dared above the revealing cut of the dress, and pressed the doorbell.

A voice inside asked, "Who's there?"

She made certain her décolletage was in view of the peephole and replied, "Me." To her amazement, the door opened immediately. A man stood there, pistol in hand, but she shot him between the eyes before he could shoot her. He hadn't even collapsed to the floor in the time the three were around him and racing across the suite foyer to the luxurious living room. An armed man appeared. Ivan's bullets dropped him.

They hurled themselves into the room firing at anything that moved. In four seconds it was over. Three Mafia soldiers. The consigliere. And a voluptuous hooker who'd joined them after the meeting. Natasha felt sorry for her.

Suddenly Sampson dove at Natasha, knocking the wind out of her as she was driven to the floor, while muffled shots vibrated in her ears again. She saw Ivan firing his pistol into a soldier who'd emerged from the bathroom. Sampson had protected her. At first she seemed okay. But now she had to fight for her breath. It was a terrible sensation—not being able to breathe. She heard Sampson's relief as he told Ivan, "She not hit, just her air go." Sampson sat her up and banged her on the back, but it didn't seem to help. Through her distress she watched Ivan dump his empty mag, slip in a fresh one and chamber the first round so skillfully it was actually beautiful to see. Then he was off to check the rest of the rooms.

After a long, painful moment, Natasha began to inhale again. Sampson supported her where she sat on the floor as she took in deep breaths of welcome air.

"I sorry. You okay?"

"Thank you." She saw blood running down his wrist. "Oh, Sampson, you took a bullet for me. Let me check that." Natasha rose to her knees and helped him remove his jacket. She drew a knife from a garter sheath under her dress and cut the bloody shirtsleeve off his arm. Under his arm, in the side of his chest, a flesh wound was bleeding heavily. The bullet had grazed him from behind. She looked around. *What can I use?* Jumping up, she rushed over to the dead hooker and removed her elasticized tube top. She grabbed a bottle of whiskey, returned to Sampson and soaked the shirtsleeve with the alcohol, then poured some directly on the wound while Sampson grimaced and stiffened. With Sampson's cooperation, she slid the tube top down over his chest and stuffed the whiskey-soaked sleeve between the wound and makeshift elastic bandage. She was helping Sampson back into his chauffeur's jacket and cap when Ivan returned and put a bullet in each gangster's head. "To make it look like a Bugsey Siegel style, gang-related execution."

Ivan stood before Natasha with a strange look on his face as he helped her to her feet, where she saw in a wall mirror what she looked like—wig askew and full cleavage hanging out of her dress. She spun away from Sampson and put herself back together.

Looking down at her feet, she whistled. "I can't believe these high-heeled thong sandals stayed on through all that. Have to give credit to the American engineers."

"I thought those were Italian shoes."

"I guess you're right. Have you got all the brass? Any fingerprints?" She used a curtain to wipe her prints off the whiskey bottle and dropped it on the thick carpet. "Don't forget the empty mags."

Natasha walked out to the corridor and picked up her stole, held the attaché for the men's pistols and mags, then handed the considerable weight to Sampson to carry. A rush of ebullience swept through her. She placed a hand on each man's arm. "Shall we go, gentlemen?"

In the Continental limo, heading up route A1A to Fort Lauderdale, her euphoria grew and she experienced something new—a primordial drive. Despite Natasha's reservations about the possibility of sharing herself with Jason again, she stroked Ivan's thigh, looked into his intense eyes. *Yes.* Ivan reached for the switch that closed the privacy screen. They were unstoppable, like two trains colliding head on.

CHAPTER 31
SPETSNAZ REALITIES

Route A1A, Florida
Thursday, April 26, 1956

Still exuberant, Natasha knew that once they were aboard their yacht she would offer herself again, to help them settle down. While Sampson drove them home to the Bahia Mar marina, Natasha held Ivan's hand as her mind traveled back over their exceptional life together.

Her thoughts turned to the other time she'd had to kill. She clenched a fist, recalling that terrible moment when Lilia went berserk and tried to knife Ivan in the back and Natasha had been forced to kill her long-time friend and associate. Natasha probably was the only person alive who knew how Ivan had been humbled, his life altered by Lilia's death. Ivan was Natasha's whole life, *even ahead of Mother Russia* she admitted with a twinge of guilt.

It seemed so many years ago she and her partner had been Natasha Piroumov and Ivan Goldelenov, Russia's élite trainees. Ivan had an I.Q. said to be above genius. Their special treatment began after his first-year university research paper, *How the Soviet Union Can Win the Cold War Without Breaking Gosbank* (The State Bank). The paper was passed immediately to GRU, the Chief Intelligence Directorate of the General Staff. Defense Minister Georgi Zhukov ordered a feasibility study. Joseph Stalin personally met with them. The project was given the highest security clearance, held by less than a dozen leaders. Without knowing any details except they were financing an espionage coup from within the United States, Gosplan, the State Planning Commission, had accepted it. Utmost secret, a carte blanche, multifaceted long-term operation to turn American capitalism from the indulgences of one nation to the socialist benefit of the world masses.

Ever since Georgi Zhukov became Ivan and Natasha's immediate superior, they'd been honored with privileges. For their final trip to Moscow to report to Comrade Zhukov, they'd been billeted in the world-famous Moscow Savoy, the hotel for wealthy visitors. She remembered marveling at the grandeur of their suite and its furniture. It even had a private bathroom—something every American took for granted—not one down the hall that had to be shared by everyone on their corridor.

Natasha regarded Ivan as a national treasure. She was his chief protector and operative partner, always at his side, intensely proud to have been raised to complement such a great man with her own outstanding mind, body and talents. She and Ivan knew each other better than anyone else alive.

When they were seven years old, they had been chosen to become part of a large cadre from all over the United Soviet Socialist Republic, selected to be specially trained for insertion into American society as future espionage agents. They lived and trained in a special compound where they spoke only accent-free English. Eventually some were trained to become equally fluent in Spanish. When they were fifteen—more than seven years ago now—the most promising of them had been partnered and housed like husbands and wives. Each member of the couple was taught to depend on the other for their very lives. They were tutored intensively, and academically were far ahead of students headed for university studies.

They became the product of a lifetime of specialized schooling and strenuous training regimens, during which time they learned motorcycle and horseback riding, escape maneuvers with cars, foreign dress and customs, disguises, acting, swimming, skiing, scuba diving, boat handling, flying and reconnaissance, and land and water combat skills to aid them in their mission in America. They even spent a couple of summers in the United States assisting other agents while perfecting their language and "fitting in" skills, learning about American sports and establishing their American identities. She remembered her shock at seeing the profligate consumption by Americans. The two observed the capitalistic society wasting more water, food, electricity, fuel and hard goods than most people in the world had to live on. Clearly communism would bring purpose and balance to the utilization of America's vast natural resources.

As a *Spetsotedelyi*, or small team, she and Ivan became the best in the élite special forces now called the Soviet Voyska Spetsial' Nogo Nazrachenniya, or *Spetsnaz*: Forces of Special Designation. Of those who began as élite special force selectees, only one in ten—the toughest, most intelligent, determined individuals—made the cut.

It seemed all *Spetsotedelyi* trainees had an inner rage—from being deprived of their families and youth, if nothing else. Controlled rage and emotional detachment were job requirements for Special Forces. As a woman, Natasha realized she had to be smarter and tougher than her comrades. Theirs was not to reason why, but always to do exactly what was ordered—even to death. The prize was to wear the blue-and-white striped T-shirts that designated them "the best of the best."

Natasha sighed. She couldn't even imagine life without being constantly at Ivan's side. He was like a drug that kept her high. She made certain it was the same for him. They complemented each other in all the important ways. Together they would orchestrate the Soviet communist takeover of America from within.

Their first mission in America involved frequent travel to counteract the damage done by McCarthyism. Money was made available to hire top lawyers to defend the good names of individuals whom Joseph McCarthy exposed as communist infiltrators in the State Department. Dougherty Enterprises surreptitiously enabled the Communist Party USA, hurt by the Wisconsin senator's investigations, to move underground and start up long-term operations. The Doughertys financed lobbyists who helped get McCarthy censured in the Senate. Now, no American communist ever had to stand alone, especially newscasters, teachers and legislators. With growing ease, the movement planted their activists in universities to advance their political agenda. Their goal, from the University of California to Harvard, was that universities abandon their mandates for teaching students *how* to think by allowing the radical professors to teach *what* to think. The subtle social pressure to agree with the teacher and the students' desire to get good grades in the course were easy ways to influence the young people's views. Eventually, capitalism and American democracy would be decried as unjust imperialism.

Ivan broke into her thoughts. "It's good that our late comrade sent that endorsement to Kanokov. The full scope of our plan will take years to accomplish. We need to keep working daily, with patience. Over time our efforts will tip the scale. Then we'll win."

Natasha smiled with satisfaction. Until Ivan added, "Just before we set out for our Mafia meeting, Uncle Richard received information from Lord Burns through Seán Kelly. Jason MacDougall has returned to this country to live with an uncle who teaches at the Naval War College in Newport, Rhode Island. My brother's been accepted at the Naval Academy."

Her stomach tightened. "He knows us, Ivan. Can identify us. Even worse, he can share our most intense experiences." *Like tonight?* Natasha hugged herself, shivering. She squeezed his hand. "You know what must be done. We should do it now."

A great sigh. A strong squeeze from his hand. "You're correct, of course. I will contact Kanokov by courier, to have MacDougall killed so it looks like an accidental death. I will instruct him to use his best mercenaries."

"Why mercenaries?"

"Because we can't afford to risk *Spetsnaz,* who are too highly trained, too few and too important to our mission to be replaceable. I have a feeling that trying to assassinate my brother may be as difficult as trying to assassinate me."

CHAPTER 32
HOOKING AGENT THOMAS

Fort Adams, Rhode Island
Thursday, April 26, 1956

Jason chose the submarine reserves to fulfill his final requirement for entering the Naval Academy, and gladly accepted his godparents' invitation to stay with them at Fort Adams prior to reporting for duty. The Kings' spacious wooden house on Officers' Row was one among many well-maintained properties for officers and their families stationed in Newport, Rhode Island.

Captain David King instructed admirals and generals at the Naval War College and was in an excellent position to tell Jason more about the Soviet threat. Almost Jason's height, but very slender, Uncle David didn't look like one of the most decorated heroes of World War II—until one perceived his leadership skills and empathy, and realized that whatever this quiet, deliberate man had was what others strove for. Jason was eager to learn how his career Navy godfather viewed the world and to know why the captain and his wife believed so passionately in his military work. Jason hoped his godfather would have time for that discussion soon.

Meanwhile, at the War College, Uncle David had met a Navy instructor who studied some of Jason's writing and figured out that Jason had been born left-handed but was schooled to be right-handed. That switch was now known to handicap a person's reading skills. Jason still remembered as a first-grader reciting the alphabet backwards faster than the other children could say it from A to Z. Dyslexia wasn't understood in those days and his grade school teacher thought he was being a smarty-pants. Now this Navy instructor offered to tutor him and Jason seized the opportunity to overcome his handicap.

For the moment, however, he was dealing with a different problem. Last night had produced killer dreams, and several euphoric dreams with the Amazon woman. Jason laundered his sheets and remade his bed while his aunt was doing her family errands in town and his three young cousins were in school.

After much thought, at ten o'clock in the morning, he made a long distance call to Seattle.

"Agent Thomas here."

"Frank, it's Jason. In Rhode Island."

"Jason? What a coincidence. I was going to call you today."

"I'm all ears."

"First, welcome back to the United States."

"Scotland was amazing." The memories flooded Jason's mind. "But it's great to be back, too."

"I want to reestablish your monthly check-in calls; we'll set up a schedule that works for you. Now tell me, what's the purpose of your call this morning, at 7:00 AM Pacific Time?"

"I need you to find out something for me."

"If I can, Jason."

"You can. Last night, I'm guessing in Florida, eight men were shot on a road by the sea, and then five men and a woman in a luxury hotel suite not far away. So far it's not on the news. Can you find out where that was and call me back at NEwport 3-2104?"

"How do you know such things happened, Jason? Something like that would make headlines."

"Don't worry, it happened."

The Kings' phone rang five minutes later.

"It was on U.S. A1A. Miami. Eight soldiers from the New Jersey syndicate. Maids found the other bodies in the Fontainebleau Hotel less than fifteen minutes ago. Five men and a woman. They're all New Jersey syndicate. Bugsey Seigel-style executions. We're having the police keep the story under wraps till we know more. Talk to me, Jason."

"They were killed by the couple who killed my parents. With the help of someone in a chauffeur's uniform. I can't describe the chauffeur, except he's big. Don't ask how I know, or I'll not help you again."

"So much for your 'They're not cold-blooded murderers' theory."

"They're not. They were capable soldiers defending themselves. The head-shots were to make you think it was mob business as usual."

"Who's your informant, Jason?"

"If you'll check my uncle's phone records, you'll see the only long-distance calls in or out this morning have been to or from your number."

"Then who's your informant, God?"

Jason smiled. "Not God, per se. But I imagine he has something to do with it."

There was a long pause. "Jason, the DNA information came in. You and the Russian appear to be very closely related. Like the DNA of siblings."

"Really? Well, you said it's a brand new science. I'll be interested to know what the technology can discover in the years to come." Jason felt an urge to refocus the FBI's attention. "Let me tell you, Frank. That man's a chameleon when it comes to disguises—even his eye color and his ways of moving are always changing."

CHAPTER 33
SUBMARINE DOWN!

New London, Connecticut
Friday, May 18, 1956

Jason heard someone shout, "Red light! Red light! Forward torpedo room hatch!" Stationed at the trim planes in the control room of the World War II fleet-type submarine, Jason's ears were assaulted by the nerve-wracking "Ahooga-Ahooga" of the warning claxon. The sub had just dived with a green board, indicating all hatches were sealed.

"Blow all ballast!" the skipper commanded. "Hard rise on planes! All ahead full. Start the forward pumps!"

Like a hovering hawk the chief petty officer watched his new reservist as Jason turned the wheel to adjust the trim planes and confirmed, "Hard rise on planes, aye, sir."

The noise from blowing the ballast sounded as if his head were inside a toilet that wouldn't stop flushing. He tried not to be spooked. Behind him a voice on the starboard side called out, "Forward torpedo room pumps operating at full capacity."

A naval career. That's what his uncle David had encouraged if Jason really did want to do his part. And it would be a way of honoring his parents, his country for all it had given him. Now, with lights flashing and people shouting, he questioned the wisdom of his decision.

Over the intercom, a scared voice shouted, "Flooding in the forward torpedo room! We're trying to secure the inner hatch! There's a lot of water coming in here, Skipper!"

Tense moments passed. Then the first voice, with palpable relief, said, "Green light! Green light! We have a green board, sir." The boat was sealed again.

However, the weight of the water in the forward torpedo room was too great. The boat kept going down. The chief petty officer began calling out readings from the depth gauge as the hull started to make loud cracking sounds. "Chrissakes, this boat ain't certified for these depths any more." He said it softly so only Jason could hear. But the chief's profuse sweating spoke louder than words. Jason's non-com was scared.

The skipper's voice commanded, "All stop." Perhaps shutting down the engines would reduce vibration on the overstressed hull.

The cracking noises grew worse. All they could do was pray.

While he waited, Jason reflected on the circumstances that brought him to this moment. His parents' death and his unexpected departure for Scotland before seeking a congressional appointment to the Naval Academy meant qualifying for admission through the competitive exams and the organized submarine reserves. Training took place at the submarine base in New London, Connecticut, on diesel fleet-type submarines with seasoned crews from World War II. Today the navy was conducting exercises with a group of destroyers and sub chasers above, in preparation for the increasing conflict between Russia and the U.S.

As the submarine continued to sink, Jason wondered if he were a jinx. Was his presence somehow responsible for their predicament? Had he chosen the wrong calling?

The sub settled to the soft bottom and the apprehensive crew waited for the pumps to overcome the negative buoyancy.

Suddenly Jason's ears were assaulted by a shattering BAM! The explosion popped flakes of cork off the hull and into everyone's face.

BAM! BAM! BAM! Cork and paint chips everywhere. There was nothing Jason could do but watch, register the details.

The skipper shouted into the radio mike, "CEASE FIRING! CEASE FIRING! YOU'RE TOO CLOSE! I REPEAT, YOU'RE TOO CLOSE!"

BAM! BAM! BAM! Overhead lights shattered. Red emergency lights came on.

The men held their breath in silence. Jason's heart was racing.

The chief petty officer's face looked strangely pale in the dim light. Was it embarrassment Jason saw? Then he noticed a foul odor coming from the vicinity of the chief's wet pants. Jason realized the experienced men were all scared shitless. Obviously he should be, too.

In the midst of his own fear he had a vision. The angel who'd given him hope to keep going despite his despair in North Korea. Now her presence reminded him that he still had a destiny to fulfill, he had the MacDougall gifts. Jason experienced a strange calm. He sensed he wasn't a jinx: this was just more training to prepare him for whatever he was destined to accomplish. Then the vision was gone.

Jason reached out a hand to the chief's forearm and spoke in a deep, controlled voice. "I know you have the experience to recognize when to be afraid, and I haven't been where you have, but let me assure you this isn't our time—no matter how bad it seems to you."

"Easy for you to say. What do you know?"

"I just know it isn't our time yet."

BAM! Then silence.

Jason thought he detected a faint sigh as the chief petty officer left the control room. When the chief returned from the head, he announced, "This was meant to be a practice depth charge run, but at a safe distance. Some inexperienced lieutenant on the sub chaser really screwed up. Chrissakes, they even had our air bubbles to go by." He shuddered. "Heads will roll."

Jason understood the veteran submariners' fear. These men had survived the war, but many of their fellow sailors had been killed by enemy depth charges. They knew all too well that this exercise error could be fatal. The uninitiated new reservists hadn't known this and assumed the racket and shaking was just nerve-wracking realism.

Jason took a deep breath, glanced at the green board and studied his controls again. The crew had experienced two unexpected, life-threatening challenges in a single day's training, and the danger wasn't over yet.

The pumps kept operating in the forward torpedo room. Finally the sub went from negative to positive buoyancy and rose slowly to the surface, making loud cracking sounds again as it passed through the pressure differentials. Once safely on the surface, the boat headed in to port.

The chief stood beside Jason and looked sidelong at him. "What you said to me—what was that about? How did you know?"

Jason thought a minute. "That was about me finally learning to accept my fate. Kind of a premonition, I suppose."

The World War II veteran raised his eyebrows and said nothing.

CHAPTER 34
CAPTAIN DAVID KING

New London, Connecticut
Saturday, May 19, 1956

"Uncle David!" Jason was astounded when David King showed up at the submarine base the next morning. The captain had driven down from the War College to see how Jason was handling his close escape.

They moved to a room where the captain wouldn't have to return salutes every few seconds. After they were seated, his godfather said, "What do you think of submarine duty?"

"Actually, I've already developed great respect for it. Subs are amazing technology. Submariners are outstanding. Sub duty is the ultimate hunt—in stealth, stalking and shooting straight. And if an American sub kills, it isn't for sport. It's for something you can believe in, defending freedom."

His uncle looked relieved.

"Thank you for coming," Jason added. "I really wasn't worried."

Captain King snorted. "So I heard from the chief who was with you. What are you, suicidal? Psychic?"

Jason was silent for a moment. "In retrospect, it *was* scary." Jason shook his head. "I don't know if I'm meant to play confident superhero." He shrugged. "At the time, reassurance and calm seemed appropriate."

The captain smiled knowingly. "Only the ignorant or stupid, or the psychotic or suicidal aren't afraid in battle. It's what you're able to go ahead and accomplish *while* you're afraid that counts."

Jason smiled. "Let's just say it didn't feel like my destiny was to die that way."

The captain shook his head. "I wish I could have felt like that each time I deactivated a booby-trapped time-delay 500-pound bomb in England or was swimming off a Pacific beachhead with Japanese soldiers all around me in small boats shooting at me every time I came up for air."

Jason felt immeasurable admiration for his godfather. "I've never understood how you came through so much stress unchanged."

"You have no idea how much I'm changed inside, Jason. Or how much Sarah and the kids have had to adapt to my changes. It's why I took off right away to check on you."

Jason choked up with appreciation and just looked in silence at this great war hero.

His uncle leaned close to Jason and spoke in a low voice. "Before seeing you, I met with the base commander. He told me the 'accidents' were no accident. The o-rings sealing the forward torpedo room deck hatches were replaced the night before with defective ones. In addition, the sub-chaser's sonar pinger-timing had been recalibrated to indicate a submarine was further away than it actually would be. The people who did this knew exactly what they were doing and wanted the sub to go down with all hands. Why, nobody knows. You don't have any ideas, do you?"

Queasy, Jason felt the blood drain from his face. Who would do such a thing in peacetime? Risk an international incident? Supposedly the North Korean general would, but this operation sounded like too much of an inside job for that mad enemy to accomplish. Who else? Possibly Jason's brother? He shook his head slowly. "When I decided to explore my MacDougall roots in Scotland, I told you someone I met in Seattle wanted me dead. But he'd never do it with such needless carnage."

"Well then, it's not your problem. But security on this base is going to be a top priority from now on." The captain rose. "You look like you could use a good meal. Let's go to a restaurant in town before I head home."

CHAPTER 35
SERVING AMERICA

New London, Connecticut
Saturday, May 19, 1956

Jason automatically selected the shooter's seat, where he could spot everyone entering the restaurant.

His uncle smiled, sadly, it seemed. "How long have you been doing that, Jason?"

"I'm sorry, did you want to sit here?"

"No, thank you. How long, Jason? Since Korea?"

He nodded. "I need to see what's going on around me."

"Yes. I see it in your restless eyes, all the time."

The waiter came and they ordered.

"Uncle David, tell me why you stick with the navy when year after year United States Lines keeps trying to hire you as the CEO of their fleet of ships at ten to twenty times navy pay."

The captain thought a while before answering. "Before World War II my work took me to Europe." He dipped a shrimp in the spicy sauce.

"Working for United States Lines?"

"Yes. I was graduated from the Academy without a commission because of poor eyesight." He tapped the edge of his eyeglasses. "The depression had hit and the government was looking for any excuse to cut back. When I became engaged to the daughter of U.S. Lines' owner and they learned I was a Naval Academy graduate they offered me a wonderful job that included travel abroad."

"Neat." Jason was enjoying his shrimp cocktail.

"Not so neat. What I saw in Germany so alarmed me that I gave lectures back in New York trying to alert people to the growing dangers there—including my concerns for what lay ahead."

"People don't like getting involved, do they? Especially if it involves them taking risks."

"Unfortunately," he sighed. "My views proved sadly accurate, but at the time few wanted to hear the bad news. Mothers didn't want their sons going to war and most Americans were focused on their own lives and preferred to live in denial of the possible threat posed by problems across the oceans. Only after the Japanese attack on Pearl Harbor was our country open to the words of President Roosevelt, 'There is no such thing as security for any nation—or any individual—in a world ruled by the principles of gangsterism.' Today that describes the Russians, Jason. Gangsters who want to control America's resources and future."

Jason frowned and rubbed his chin. "Why would the Russians, our wartime allies who suffered so harshly at the hand of the Nazis, want to control *America*, half a world away on another continent."

Captain King leaned forward in his chair, his voice filled with a new urgency. "Because even more than leveling the global playing field with their totalitarian ideology, they want to expand their communist empire to access the whole earth's resources." He sipped his scotch, then with his finger stirred the ice in his drink.

"Since the end of World War II, America has been leading the creation of a new world order of democracy and freedom. What other nation in history has gone to war to save so many nations, and then put them back on their feet—even their enemies—and helped them to prosper with the best system of government and economics ever devised?"

Anxious to benefit from this hero's perspective, Jason asked, "Our Marshall Plan?"

"Unique, unprecedented action by a victorious nation to rebuild lands decimated by war. We've aided the recovery of sixteen countries throughout Europe." Uncle David was on a roll. "We have international laws and treaties with countries that believe in freedom and democracy and a market-based economic system. There's the General Agreement on Tariffs and Trade, the World Bank and the International Monetary Fund. Huge advances for democracy and freedom."

Jason shifted in his chair, proud of his country's leadership, but feeling overwhelmed personally. He tried to visualize ways his future navy career would contribute to the success of such positive outreach in the world.

Uncle David paused and sipped his drink. "Unfortunately, the world is still in danger. The Soviets tried helping North Korea drive the American and U.N. presence out of South Korea in order to swallow up that territory, blockade Japan and take control of the Far East. But below the media radar, the Russians aided the Viet Minh to drive the French colonials out of a far-away country, on the South China Sea. A place called Viet Nam." Captain King contemplated his scotch and took another swallow. "We can't be naïve, Jason. Powerful nations want our wealth, and will do anything to get it. We need to maintain a strong military. The good news is we have mutual security agreements with thirteen other countries through NATO and with Japan, so our troops aren't alone against the Soviets or other aggressors. And we're part of the United Nations forum for our collective security and international cooperation."

His godfather finished his drink, loosening the tension that seemed to weigh on his shoulders, even as his voice remained confident and persuasive. "Our military and economic alliances come out of shared ideals and have been entered into voluntarily, so yes, I see real possibilities for peace and prosperity—as long as our executive branch and legislators continue to adhere to the principles of our forefathers that made democracy work. We need presidents who understand the workings of men and of history, presidents who can explain their own policies to the nation so there will be a consensus on foreign affairs."

The captain nodded thanks to the waiter who brought over the lunch special, homemade meatloaf. He continued, enthusiastic, intense.

"Divided, our young nation found it could never endure. Our forefathers set up our unique republic in the belief that if we remain unified under God's laws, we at least would have a chance of accomplishing the miracles they envisioned. Our Constitution is the foundation of our prosperity, for power and for performing good. If our schools and churches ever lose sight of that, we as a nation will lose our freedom and wealth so fast there will be no stopping the forces that move in to enslave us."

Jason tried to imagine where he fit into all this. His uncle's eyes zeroed in on him. "Jason, our peace and prosperity are going to require help from young people like you, with all your faith and talents. We can't walk away from our responsibilities. You're a MacDougall. You've never walked away from a fight in your life. And there will be fights, mark my words."

Standing, he said, "Which is precisely why I remain in the Navy— to help keep us ready to preserve the United States as a free nation for my children and your children to grow up in."

CHAPTER 36
DAKOTA

Fort Adams, Rhode Island
Friday, June 22, 1956

Jason completed his submarine training without further incident and returned to Fort Adams. In ten days he would enter the Naval Academy for plebe summer. It was time for a break. His aunt grinned. "Check out the action next door. New neighbors. And let me tell you, Lieutenant Commander Dupré's daughter is *all* about character."

The girl next door helping unload the moving van wore shorts and a tight-fitting polo shirt. She had a woman's curves, but a concave stomach and trim hips. She was so spare, her limbs showed classic muscular definition when she moved. She had a remarkable way of walking—like the wind passing over the ground without disturbing a leaf.

Jason stepped outside. "Let me help you with that box ... ."

* * *

Jason was taken with Dakota's bright-eyed openness and enthusiasm for life. She made no secret of the fact his invitation to dine out thrilled her.

She wore no makeup or jewelry, but dressed with a gypsy flair in a strikingly colorful ensemble of scarf, loose-fitting blouse and swirly skirt hanging from her raw-boned frame. Her shoulder-length dark hair matched her piercing brown eyes. With her chiseled face and dark complexion, Dakota was a willowy, rawhide-and-sinew beauty.

He drove her to a modest restaurant on a seventeenth-century street in historic Newport. Over dinner Jason learned her grandmother was a full-blooded Cherokee and Dakota loved painting and acting. Jason liked her reserved wisdom in conversation and the banked fires he felt were just beneath her surface.

"Forgive me if I seem personal, Dakota, but I find you unusually natural and comfortable with yourself—as if you were a younger version of Aunt Sarah." He raised his wineglass. "My highest compliment, by the way."

She smiled. "Don't be fooled. It's a girl trick. I told you, I love acting. In the here-today-gone-tomorrow life of a Navy junior, you have to learn to make friends and grow up fast—or go through life awkward and lonely. What a waste. I want to taste everything there is. I think it's the artist in me."

He was taken aback. "So what are you saying?"

Her eyes hinted mystery as they read his face. "That I find you interesting, too, and we don't have a lot of time to fool around."

Jason didn't dishonor her by making her explain. "Just like that huh?"

"So it seems," she sighed. "In your case, at least." Her wry, Mona-Lisa smile seemed to speak of centuries of women who'd embraced the inevitability of submitting to Nature's Plan.

When he ushered her out of the restaurant, he said, "Would you like to drive back to the fort and walk barefoot on the beach?"

Her quiet smile and sparkling eyes were his answer.

They walked through the parking lot and around to the back of the restaurant where he'd parked his uncle's Chevy sedan. Jason was reaching to open the passenger door for her when two men approached them from behind a dumpster. The men were separated to trap Jason and Dakota against the car. He saw the glint of blades in their hands.

As if launched from a catapult, Jason charged the big man on his left.

The man slashed expertly, but using a maneuver Hyo had taught him, Jason used both hands to grab the wrist of the attacker's knife hand, spun his own body clockwise and raised his left knee sharply to break the man's forearm faster than one could see. He heard snap-ping sounds and the man's howl as his bones broke, then a clatter as the heavy knife hit the paving stones.

The second man, knife extended, rushed toward Jason. With a bloodcurdling yell, Dakota leapt on the wiry attacker's back, wrapping her heels around his shins, clawing furiously at his eyes from behind while wildly trying to kick his legs out from under him.

Jason finished the first man with a devastating blow to the right side of his head and lunged, grabbing the wiry man's knife wrist with his left hand before the attacker could turn his blade on Dakota. The first man's collapsing body was in Jason's way and threw him off-balance.

The wiry man managed to cut Jason's wrist, but Jason didn't let go. He didn't want to risk clobbering Dakota, so with his free hand he grabbed the attacker between the legs. Adrenaline reinforced Jason's iron grip. With a falsetto shriek the attacker dropped his knife.

"Dakota, let go!" She dropped to her feet, and Jason felled the man with a sledgehammer fist to his jaw.

Jason and Dakota stood facing each other, the unconscious men between them. She stepped around the inert attackers, removed her scarf, and wrapped Jason's wrist tightly to stop the flow of blood. Then reaction set in, and Dakota began shaking. Jason hugged her willowy frame. She held him tightly, breathing heavily in his ear, her body trembling. They said not a word. When the chips were down, neither had been wanting. That was enough.

Ten minutes later the police insisted they ride in an ambulance to the hospital, where an emergency room physician stitched and bandaged Jason's wrist. "The knife missed all your tendons and nerves," the doctor said. "You're a very lucky man."

Jason asked about the attackers. Another ER physician told him both had concussions and remained unconscious. The big man's forearm was being set. The shorter man was in emergency surgery for repairs to the serious damage to his eyes. Then he would need to have his broken jaw wired.

Jason and Dakota's medical care completed, the police took them to the precinct for questioning.

First, Jason asked to use a private phone, so he could leave a message for Agent Thomas.

Jason told the officers, "You might want to guard the assassins. I expect the FBI will be here to question them and take charge of them. I'm sorry, I can't tell you more. Talk to the agents."

The precinct detectives phoned the Kings' but the sitter didn't pick up, and no one was home at Dakota's house.

"My parents are at a party with the Kings," she said, "—where, we don't know."

The detectives finished asking their questions. "The officers will drive you home now."

"We have to drive my uncle's car home," Jason said, "so he has it for work in the morning."

The officers looked at each other. "Okay. We'll take you to his car at the restaurant."

Sitting silently in the back of the police cruiser, Jason experienced a warrior's euphoria he had difficulty suppressing. He sensed the same smoldering in Dakota. Like him, she wasn't showing it to the police, but despite her stoic expression, he felt manic energy between them.

It was after eleven. Everything was closed and dark for the night. The squad car turned into the empty parking lot and pulled up beside the Chevy behind the restaurant. Jason held the door for Dakota and walked around the car to get behind the wheel. He started the engine.

The policeman waved, rolled up his window, and the squad car drove off.

CHAPTER 37
WARRIOR'S HIGH

Newport, Rhode Island
Friday, June 22, 1956

Jason felt Dakota's hand on his, gently turning off the ignition key. Her lips were almost touching his ear, her breathing in quick gasps, as if—

Damn, she's ready, fighting to hold back.

"Jason . . . ." The way she said it expressed everything—her womanhood, her imperative.

Jason whipped a packet out of his billfold and slid across the sedan seat to Dakota.

"Hurry," she urged, kicking off her shoes and skirt, squatting on the seat as he slid under her. She tore her blouse off over her head. Underwear wasn't a problem; she'd worn none. Taking the condom from him, she tossed it. "I'm wearing a diaphragm." Jason squeezed her firm breasts hard enough to subdue her orgasm briefly. But she remained unstoppable, opening his slacks and unceremoniously yanking everything down where he could kick off his loafers and pants. She jerked his polo shirt over his head and pressed his hands onto her breasts again. "Hard is good right now."

He felt her grasp his urgency to place at her slippery entrance. "Holy—" Suddenly her hand was taking the measure of him as she looked into his face with wide-eyes and a furrowed brow. Her need drove her to begin taking him into her incautiously. She kissed his mouth—gently, at first, but more and more greedily as she discovered she could have all of him. That's when she lost control and became the savage from hammer county.

He tasted blood from their fierce, open-mouthed kiss, and without the condom was so sensitive he had to fight extra hard for control. He let her bring him with her as he arched up into their explosive orgasms together, but reserved the tsunami for later, the way Suki had taught him.

Spent, Dakota hugged him tight. "Oh, Jason, that was perfect."

"Shall we keep going?"

"I'm too sensitive. Besides, I heard you come. It was wonderful."

"Would you like to see what we can have?"

She looked at him strangely. "But ... we're both spent."

Jason arched up hard into her sensitivity, making her gasp. "Do I feel spent?" he said, and shifted them to the middle of the bench seat that way.

She tensed. "That hurt. But this is good." She rose up and down on him, testing. "You're telling me there's more?"

"I'll show you." He raised his right knee onto the seat. "Stay with me." He rolled his body up onto the seat with her, maneuvering her spine into the seatback. With his left leg he raised her right leg with his over the seatback. "This is going to take strength, Dakota." He felt her nails against the impenetrable muscle of his buttocks. She made guttural sounds as he thrust deeply into her, each penetration forcing her body up with his until she was lying precariously on her spine along the top of the seatback, with him squeezed in over her. Balanced with one foot on the front seat and the other on the back seat, she reached out for the steering wheel to steady herself. Her hand hit the horn ring.

The loud honk shattered the silence of the night. They froze, on edge again. Dakota laughed nervously. After a long moment, Jason felt the tendons of her thighs straining as she stuffed her blouse under her, clearly signaling she wanted to see where this spontaneity would take them.

Jason had just been trying to get them into the back of the car without disconnecting, but if she was good with doing it on razorback ridge ... . With his fingers he woke up her nipples while he kissed her softly, opening their mouths wider, and wider still, to engulf one another. He gentled his penetrations to awaken every sensitive nerve in her, making her want more, and more, as she flexed her animated pelvis up to receive him. Her nostrils flared and she made tiny noises that made him think if an eagle could purr that's how it would sound.

When he felt her falling into the river of no return, he kept her going as they cried out into each other's engorging kiss.

"Men can't do this," she protested, even as her jerking pelvis brought him with her twice more in as many minutes.

Breathless, she exulted. "A pinnacle experience. If we lose our balance, we fall off our precipice."

Jason worried about the seatback breaking down. Placing a hand under her, he moved them onto the back seat while she alternately laughed and cried out sounds of bliss.

"Is there more?" She teased, "I want more."

Jason couldn't feel her right leg and realized she had it folded back under her, leaving her other calf over the front seatback, ready for anything. She reached up and held his face, kissing him into oblivion while he made love to her so tenderly she shuddered and moaned with every measured stroke.

Their petite orgasms brought tears to her eyes.

Then he felt her contract around him with new force, uncontrollable, and she arched up on her elbows and legs as her body strained high off the seat to him, offering everything she had.

Jason increased the tempo, pushing harder.

Her tears gushed and wet her breasts. "Anything, Jason. Everything." Her husky voice defined Mother Nature at the peak of arousal.

He had a flash vision of Dakota with a young Indian chief—a naval officer, studying at a university—and Jason knew how it would be for her in life.

He slowed. "Tonight's not about you and me, Dakota. It's about you and your chief. Time for us to soar with the eagle high over the mesas." He wasn't sure why he said that, but he knew it would mean something to her.

Dakota's dark eyes grew huge. Then they signaled recognition, as if she realized what some spirit wanted her to know.

Hands on the seat under her, she raised up to glide in and out over Jason's enthusiasm, moving her pelvis so seductively he no longer wanted to be in control. As he hammered into her need, he gave himself to her, body and soul. He heard Indian drums, danced with her. When their orgasm took off he felt himself soaring like an eagle with her, to the melody of an ethereal flute,—higher, higher, higher ... over all life on earth—until their eagles' heart-piercing muscle contractions made them screech in ecstatic agony as they fell back to earth.

Dakota's face glowed. "The Great Spirit was with us. I helped you survive tonight. In return, you've loved me like I've never been loved. You've encouraged my faith that I'm meant for a certain man—that I can be worthy of him." She contracted around Jason. "Teach me how to enable him to be capable of many orgasms, like you."

It was four o'clock in the morning when Jason drove her home. Dakota stopped on the path to her front door and hugged him fiercely. "Thank you. Thank you." Finally she pulled away, let go of his hand, and entered her house. Jason gave a great sigh and walked next door. In a couple of hours he'd be telling Uncle David about the attack.

CHAPTER 38
REVERSE WEIRDNESS

Fort Lauderdale, Florida
Saturday, June 23, 1956

Natasha hurt. But it was a good hurt. She lay atop Ivan, aboard their yacht at its berth in Bahia Mar Marina. He was falling asleep bathed in their sweat after hours of the most intense sex they'd ever experienced together. Finally his eternal hardness was shrinking within her. She smiled contentedly, feeling split to the ears. Sex certainly evoked strange emotions.

They'd gone to bed early, had sex, and fallen right to sleep entwined on top of the bedding. A little before nine, Ivan began having a nightmare. It was clear to her his brother was in trouble, so she let the dream play out, and brought towels from the bathroom to dry Ivan when he awoke in a cold sweat from the stressful dream.

Ivan inspected his left wrist carefully. "It felt so real. The assassin cut my brother's wrist with his knife. I wonder how much damage it caused?" He rubbed his wrist. "What a magnificent woman he had with him—instead of wringing her hands, she jumped into the fray to even the odds."

Natasha wiped Ivan's face and chest with a moistened wash cloth, then rubbed him down with a large bath towel.

"It's as I feared. He and the savage woman just destroyed two assassins who were attacking them with knives. Why do I feel so strongly he's the greatest threat to our work in America?"

"It just means we'll have to kill him ourselves."

Eventually, they slept again.

Without warning, Ivan needed her. He'd practically assaulted her.

She knew exactly what was happening. Jason and the girl were experiencing the warrior's euphoria while Ivan was still caught up in their activity. Natasha assaulted Ivan right back despite her discomfort at being unprepared. She was astounded by his endurance and additional orgasms till two in the morning. *What is his brother, some kind of sex monster?*

When they awakened at daybreak, Ivan would be sorry for the assault, but she wouldn't. She'd been able to respond in kind, and that pleased her immensely.

CHAPTER 39
KEEPING JASON ALIVE

Fort Adams, Rhode Island
Saturday, June 23, 1956

Jason awoke to a loud knock on his bedroom door. Alarmed, he realized he'd overslept. "Just a minute." He yanked the summer-weight blanket off his bed, wrapped it around himself and opened the door. His uncle looked stern, or was it puzzled.

"Would you be good enough to jump into something more appropriate and join us in the living room?"

"Us?"

"Your aunt and myself." He turned to go, then hesitated. "Also, MPs from the base. And the Newport police." He turned back. "Oh yes. The FBI. And then there's Dakota Dupré's mother, who seems to have lost her daughter." The captain did an about face and marched down the hall.

"I can explain about Dakota," Jason said weakly, closing the door and dropping the blanket. *Boy, is he pissed.*

In less than two minutes Jason joined an army of uniformed people in the living room. "I'm sorry I overslept. I wanted to tell you everything when you and Aunt Sarah came down to the kitchen this morning."

"Don't berate yourself," Sarah said. "I forgot to replace the guestroom clock when the alarm switch became unreliable." Then she introduced Jason to everyone in the room.

Captain King addressed the gathering. "As Sarah will tell you, I have no fondness for the inner workings of automobiles." He turned to his godson. "When I tried to start Suzabelle to go to work, nothing happened. Naturally, I opened the hood to see if I should call the police if there was no engine, or a mechanic if the car still had one."

It wasn't a reprimand, but his voice conveyed trouble. His face muscles were tight, his expression impassive. "Have a seat, Jason."

"I'm so sorry." Jason sat on the edge of a chair, across from his uncle. "The car started hard and ran a little rough for a moment on the way home last night, then worked fine again. Everyone was sound asleep when I got here. I take it you found the note I left for you. I wish you'd awakened me."

Sarah said, "We assumed you were out on your usual early morning run on the beach."

"I may not be an expert on cars, but one thing I do know well is bombs." The captain reached into a brown grocery bag beside his chair and pulled out a plastic bag with what looked like three sticks of dynamite taped together with a primer and two capped red wires and a black one dangling from the device. "I found this under the hood. Apparently, you showed up before the men finished installing it, so they attacked you directly instead. You beat them, so they failed to kill you and remove this other evidence."

Jason stared at America's foremost unexploded-ordinance expert and his face flushed hot and cold—as if it were being held alternately in a freezer then an oven. His eyes twitched and his mouth was dry. There was a pause, as if his uncle wanted to give him time to gather his thoughts.

"The FBI told me that during interrogation, the man Dakota temporarily blinded admitted he and his cohort are ex-Navy—now mercenaries from Boston. He was heavily medicated and confessed that a stranger paid them a great deal of money to kill you so nobody would suspect it was a hit. They wanted to impress their new employer, so they rigged the submarine to make your death look like an accident." Uncle David peered at him. "Why is someone so anxious to kill you that they'd kill sixty-some innocent men to make your death look like an accident?"

Jason's stomach knotted. "If they wanted to make last night look accidental, why did they resort to a bomb?" He clenched his fists. "Uncle David, I've told you I know a man who wants me dead. He's prepared to kill. But not indiscriminately, like on the sub. He'd never approve that. I'd stake my life on it."

For the next twenty minutes, the various agents asked questions of Jason, then departed, until only Mrs. Dupré was left. Like her daughter, she was a dark-haired beauty. A worried beauty at the moment.

"Jason, yesterday Dakota was a girl. This morning a woman went off to the airport to marry her man. For the love of God, what happened last night between when the police dropped you off and four this morning?" She wrung her hands. "I really need to know."

Sarah and his uncle stood up. "We'll give you some privacy," said his aunt.

"No, no." Jason gestured for them to say. "Dakota told me you're her godparents. You should hear this too."

The Kings sat again, this time together on the sofa, holding hands.

Jason turned to Mrs. Dupré. "Do you approve of the man?"

"He's Lloyd Welch—Eagle Eyes, son of the Chief of the Cherokee Nation. Top of his class at the University of New Mexico law school, specializing in Native American law. As the quarterback on his college football team he was called 'Ashwin,' for 'Strong Horse.' A giant among his people, determined to move the Cherokee forward in the twentieth century, but without losing their identity. One day he'll be their Chief. He's loved Dakota since childhood—calls her 'Krita,' which means 'A Work of Art.' He's ROTC, going to be in the Navy for a few years. What's not to approve?"

Jason thought about his answer. "I believe some things are fated, that it was no accident Dakota was there to help me survive the assassins. That it was no accident I was destined to be alone with her through most of that emotional night—to help her resolve troubling self-doubts about being worthy of her exceptional chief. Because that's all that's held her back." Jason looked at his godparents and Mrs. Dupré. "When I asked her if she and Lloyd were best friends, like her parents and godparents, that's all it took." Jason stood and took Mrs. Dupré's hands.

"Dakota's spirits worked through me, Mrs. Dupré. I know you understand. Your daughter is an amazing woman. You must be very proud."

Tears filled her eyes even as she smiled. "Thank you." Her quick hug was heartfelt, and then she was gone.

Jason turned to his godparents. "I have something rather difficult to share with you—something possibly even pertaining to national security." He hesitated. "Something so weird that even my father and mother couldn't believe me."

The Kings were the best listeners Jason knew, and it took surprisingly little time to tell them about his secret gifts and twin brother. "So if whatever my brother is doing here in America is important enough, I suppose the fact I can identify him and his partner could be reason to remove me as a risk." With that he slid back in his chair to wait.

His uncle stood up and mixed three milk-and-scotch toddies, one for each of them.

Jason added, "If you want documentation, I decided to create some with an FBI agent in Seattle—just in case I might need proof someday." The scotch smelled good and he took a big swallow, which made him cough.

"Agent Thomas called me last May to verify that you'd not flown in from Miami on a certain morning." The captain sampled his drink. "He seemed at a loss for words when I assured him you'd been here all evening with the children while Sarah and I were out, and joined me as I had my nightcap before retiring." He squinted. "Wasn't that about the time of that Mafia mass murder in Miami?"

So Jason told them about sharing his brother's traumatic experience in Miami in the form of a nightmare. He left out the part about the psychic ménage à trois.

"Agent Thomas called me this morning. Passed on the information they got from the short man, so you'd know someone's after you. Now I realize that 'someone' is your Russian twin. What more can you tell me about your brother?"

"I can't. Except we've grown up on opposite sides."

The captain set down his toddy. "Soviet communist dictatorship versus the free world."

"He thinks I'm some kind of nemesis."

"You haven't told Agent Thomas everything you've shared with us?" Sarah sounded puzzled.

"Thomas can only benefit from information he can pass on to his superiors, because they would certainly question his judgment and my sanity if he told them about the relationship I experience with my twin."

David King nodded. "I'll tell Thomas just what you've said, and no more. Alright?"

"Coming from you, it might sound more credible." Jason studied the relatives who'd given him a home. "But I can't stay here and endanger you and your children and people like Dakota."

"Considerate of you, as always." The captain's face relaxed, a reassuring smile at the corners of his mouth. "In a week you enter the Academy, to live under the protection of the United States Navy—which I'll ensure you have. In the meantime, I've arranged special security for you. Sarah called her father—your grandfather Steele—and he's invited you and my two best men to stay with him at his house in Bethesda."

"Your two best men?"

"My old Underwater Demolition Team. We've selected a few promising new members to train like Russian *Spetsnaz* élite forces."

"What's *Spetsnaz*?"

"Soviet naval élite forces trained from childhood to be the best infiltration-assassin forces in the world. It's Soviet *Spetsnaz* who win most of the Olympic medals for Russia. They're outstanding athletes, linguists and special force team members in the air, land and sea."

There was a knock at the front door. Jason arched his brows.

"My men," said his godfather. "You drive through the night."

Sarah opened the door. "Thanks for coming on such short notice, Dirk, Tim." She gave each of them a hug as they came into the house.

The captain made the introductions. "Jason, these are Chief Petty Officers Dirk Sullivan and Tim Johanson. They'll be your day and night guardians until they deliver you safely to the Academy."

Both men wore slacks and sports shirts and had the physique of circus trapeze performers. But Dirk stood out to Jason. Like Jason, his eyes reflected an inner flame and his hard, defined muscles and features exuded some sort of invisible energy. Their handshake was a constrained test of strength, and they liked each other at once. Tim's handshake was firm but respectful as he said, "Sir."

"Call me Jason."

"In a week, we'll have to call you 'Sir'," Tim said. "Thought we'd get off to the right start."

Jason smiled. "Jason, for now. We'll worry about the rest when the time comes."

CHAPTER 40
GRANDFATHER STEELE

Bethesda, Maryland
Sunday, June 24, 1956

Jason suppressed a grin at Tim's incredulity. "God almighty, Jason! How are we going to keep an eye on you in all this space?" Grandfather Steele's house and grounds occupied more than half a block on the outskirts of Bethesda, adjacent to Washington, D.C. "How many rooms inside your grandfather's house?"

"Nobody seems to know for sure. Sarah once told me 'Everyone's agreed, it's over fifty'." A door swung open. "And here comes our host." Jason climbed out of the car to greet his tall, ultra-thin grandfather.

During the next week, Jason spent hours with the gentleman from another era and regretted not growing up close to him. As a young man, Grandfather Steele had been a great hunter and Jason relished his stories and the photographs and trophies hanging on his office walls. More evidence of his family's love of boating and the sea. He admired the sixty-foot motoryacht his grandfather had owned before donating it for shore patrols during the First World War, and he imagined how thrilling it must have been to sail on his great-uncle's one-hundred-twenty-foot America's Cup gaff sloop with its thirty-two man crew.

There was much to take care of on the expansive property and Jason loved helping his grandfather. In appreciation, Grandfather Steele gave him his personal, custom Mannlicher-Schoenauer Model 1903 .30/06 rifle with double-set trigger, from his expeditions in Alaska. His grandfather had been part of the 1909 Boundary Survey expedition with Tom Riggs, who later became Alaska's territorial governor. Jason admired the rifle and felt deeply honored that it was passed on to him.

When Jason's grandmother was alive and her daughters were in their teens, Grandfather Steele closed in the courtyard to create a ball-room for banquets and dances and wedding receptions. He still enter-tained interesting guests, and east coast family members often gathered at his house. One of his frequent guests, Countess Czècheni, came for tea on Saturday and brought her granddaughter, Gwendolyn.

"Will you be staying with your grandfather over Christmas?" the countess asked.

"I hope so," said Grandfather Steele.

"Wonderful. We'll put Jason on the list for all the debutante par-ties." She turned to Jason. "You do enjoy dances?"

Jason glanced around the elegant living room and felt unprepared for the east coast social life his mother had left behind. "I grew up in logging country. Tell me about the dances here."

"Come," said Gwendoyn, "I'll show you." She looked at her elders, who smiled their approval.

"Everyone but Grandmother calls me Gwen," she said over her shoulder as she led him into the ballroom. She turned on the record player and placed a seventy-eight on the turntable. "I'll show you the dances we like," she said smiling at him. "Let's start with a foxtrot."

Jason watched her glide around the wooden parquet floor.

"Here's how you hold your partner," she said, putting his right hand at the back of her waist and taking his left hand in her right.

Off they went. The basic step was easy. "This is fun."

"You're a natural." They danced over to the Victrola and she put on another record. "Now let's try a waltz."

The waltz became his favorite and he loved twirling Gwen around the ballroom. This part of Washington life didn't seem at all old-fash-ioned and stuffy. By the time she and the countess said goodbye, Jason was eagerly looking forward to the Christmas parties.

The afternoon before he was to leave for the Academy, he took a final walk in the large stand of great oak trees his grandfather had planted years earlier behind the house. Jason always felt at home in the woods. Dirk accompanied him. The two men were silent, deep in thought.

Jason spoke. "What makes you think I'm a fighter, Dirk?"

"How do you know what I'm thinking?" Dirk's voice was matter-of-fact.

"Since we first shook hands at Fort Adams, I've known. Why do you want to fight me?"

"Because you're the first man ever made me wonder if I was the best."

Jason sighed. "I guess no one can see us here among the trees." He unbuttoned his shirt. "This is going to hurt, you know."

"Always does." Dirk's shirt came off, revealing rippling muscles. "Tell me, Dirk, what'll we prove?"

Dirk replied without hesitation, "That we remain fit to keep freedom alive for America."

"Good answer, my friend." Jason took off his shirt.

* * *

Annapolis, Maryland
Monday, July 2, 1956

When Tim and Dirk dropped him off at the Naval Academy, Jason was a battered, bruised man reporting for duty, and Dirk sat in the back seat, his arm in a sling, the other hand holding an ice bag to an eye still swollen shut.

As Jason thanked the men and said goodbye, he told Tim, "I'll always be Jason to you."

He turned to Dirk, who said, "I've never been up against such a fast or deceitful fighter as you. Fighting you is like taking on a cyclone." Dirk still looked puzzled.

Jason grinned. "It's the ninja in me, Dirk. Would you like to call it a tie, then?"

I'd consider it an honor, sir."

"*Jason*, Dirk, Jason."

CHAPTER 41
U.S. NAVAL ACADEMY

Annapolis, Maryland
Monday, July 30, 1956

Getting into the Academy had been no cakewalk. Tens of thousands applied. In the three days of scholastic entrance exams, Jason had placed one hundred forty-seventh. Only one thousand sixty-four were admitted—and less than eight hundred would graduate as commissioned officers from this prestigious and demanding military academy.

Assigned to the Sixth Company, Jason loved plebe summer, where admitted candidates received indoctrination while all the upper classmen were away for summer training at sea. The plebes learned to march, shoot, handle boats, and even cast machinery parts in the foundry and perform rudimentary lathe work in the machine shop. Jason became a sensation on the rifle range for his shooting ability. Under Lieutenant Siatkowski, he was the first plebe in the history of the Naval Academy to receive a command of the big Alden sailing yachts moored off the seawall. He excelled at marching and manual of arms, and found inspiration in the naval history classes about dedicated leaders like John Paul Jones. For Jason, the hard work, the new skills and his successes were truly satisfying.

September brought the first hint of fall and the return of the upper classmen for the next academic year. And hazing began. Hazing was intended to help weed out those individuals unfit for naval life—physically or mentally. Fourth classmen were called plebes because the first *rule* of military co-existence was conformity, and nothing sorted out those who didn't fit in like having to survive as plebeians at the bottom of Naval Officers' social structure.

Plebes had been taught that the first *law* of every midshipman was to speak only truth. If a midshipman said or wrote anything in a misleading way he could be packed, discharged and out the gates within three hours. The Naval Academy operated above all by its honor code system.

An Academy *rule* was never answer a question with, "I don't know." Jason and his fellow plebes learned the proper response was, "I'll find out, sir." They were required to find out by dinnertime. During hazing that could mean having to memorize servile ditties and long ridiculous poems at the same time as trying to learn academic material in class or complete course homework, then shout out those passages flawlessly, while standing on a chair in front of the whole brigade of four thousand men at supper.

Midshipman First Class Karl Kloski had entered the Academy at age twenty-six after serving on submarines, and was now the peacock-proud midshipman company commander of the Sixth Company. He relished hazing the fourth classmen, compulsively using the power of his rank to bully people under him.

Kloski focused much of his perversity on Jason, possibly—Jason guessed—because the first classman sensed that Jason knew him for what he really was underneath the leadership image he projected so well. Jason's gut told him Kloski was a fake and that the first classman feared him for knowing that. His hazing of Jason quickly became flagrant abuse of power, obvious to anyone who wasn't one of his vassals. At mealtime, Jason could see disapproval on the upper classmen's faces as Kloski made his unrelenting demands. But hazing and conformity seemed to hold sway, for none of them spoke up. And Kloski's inflated self-importance rendered him oblivious. His obsession became so extreme that Jason couldn't get to his homework and his two roommates found Kloski's regular evening visits to their room during study hours equally disagreeable. As plebes, the three were careful not to show their disrespect for this bully who wasted their time and prevented them from doing their best academically.

One morning while Kloski was the Battalion Officer of the Watch, he targeted the entire Sixth Company of fourth classmen and inspected every plebe's room in Bancroft Hall. It wasn't hard to find some infraction, as it was very difficult to leave a room perfect every time the men went to class, and neat and clean was not considered perfect.

"You're all on report," Kloski barked. "Report to Midshipman Robertson on Saturday to march off your extra duty." Jason seethed. A whole company of plebes was denied their Saturday time off because someone had a wrinkle in his bed sheet.

Saturday dawned sunny and by midmorning was unseasonably hot. At eleven Kloski took over from Second Classman Robertson and forced the group to march on the brick pavement without stopping, until three men collapsed in the heat. The third one broke his jaw when he fell in a faint and would be unable to complete the academic year. At best, he would be able to return the next autumn and endure another full year as a plebe. While Jason helped the fallen midshipman, he had a disturbing vision of Kloski endangering twelve men under his command at sea—sending them ashore in a personnel boat while waterspouts threatened. Jason didn't see the outcome in the vision, but he had a premonition the worst would happen.

Back at his room in Bancroft Hall, Jason worried about the best way to handle this revelation. For days he agonized over what to do. Under the honor code, he was bound to tell what he knew, but undoubtedly he'd be thought mentally unbalanced if he did. He realized he faced a life filled with choices and responsibilities beyond those of most. Fitting into the brigade with his gifts, even trying to explain them, seemed an insurmountable challenge. No military organization was set up to handle his unique abilities.

Kloski continued coming to his room every evening to harass him and "frap" him so that Jason was required to march off the demerits each weekend. By the following Saturday, Jason knew he needed a break. He rose before dawn to complete his marching by lunchtime, and with Siatkowski's permission, took one of the big yawls out for an afternoon on the bay. It was a blustery day with whitecaps on the water and the other Academy boats remained at their moorings. But Jason was desperate to get away from his quandary, away from Kloski, and into the refreshment of a strong sea breeze and the soothing motion of a hull gliding through the water. He had already selected his crew of class-mates and set sail feeling like an innocent man released from prison.

The exhilaration of tacking across Chesapeake Bay drove all thoughts of Kloski from Jason's mind. But as he headed back to the mouth of the Severn River he felt a new uneasiness. It had nothing to do with Kloski or with the challenge of picking up the mooring buoy off the Academy seawall. This was the same tension he'd felt just before the tug appeared through the fog and killed his parents.

CHAPTER 42
BEST LAID PLANS

Stealing the small Chris Craft cabin cruiser should be a breeze. Natasha had found it the day before, docked at the end of Spa Creek by an uninhabited house that was being remodeled.

She and Ivan and Sampson parked their rental car up the street before dawn. Quietly, they grabbed their bags with food, water, binoculars and the break-down rifle they needed for the day's work. Walking onto the deserted property, they checked for any lights turned on early in the houses sprinkled along the shore of the cove. The homes were still dark. Perfect.

They donned clear surgeons' gloves and boarded the boat with their gear. While Ivan picked the cabin lock, Sampson opened the panel below the helm and placed his alligator clips to jump the ignitions. Both engines started easily and ran smoothly. They breathed a sigh of relief.

The gas tanks were full, so they cast off and idled out Spa Creek past Petrini and Trumpy shipyards to starboard, then the U.S. Naval Academy to port. Several large Academy racing yawls danced on their moorings off the Academy seawall. Beyond the seawall, Natasha could make out a track-sized obstacle course and tennis courts, then the impressive buildings of cut granite blocks, and a pale green dome. This secure navy yard was MacDougall's safety zone. And only she knew their target was Ivan's brother. Ivan's strategy was to keep his family relationship a secret from everyone else. Ivan headed across the Severn River and putzed up and down the northeast shoreline like other local boaters relaxing on the water for the day.

Despite the whitecaps whipped up by the fifteen-knot easterly breeze, Natasha's long, chestnut wig became uncomfortably warm in the hot sun, and she removed her yellow foul weather jacket. The three of them wore shirts and pants that looked like the other weekend boaters' apparel from Fawcett Boat Supply. They needed to blend in, not draw any attention to themselves, and had to be difficult to describe in any way that distinguished them from the others. Ivan's dark brown beard was short and well groomed, like a naval officer, just enough cover to disguise his features. His shirt and shorts were sufficiently baggy to hide his gladiator shape and rippling muscles. Sampson had grown heavy since his gold medal days at the Olympics, his thighs bigger around than Natasha's waist, with shoulders and arms to match. Long pants covered his muscular legs. Nondescript visor-caps and dark sunglasses completed their costumes.

After eating some hard-boiled eggs and bread Natasha had packed, they relaxed over cups of black coffee. Sampson asked, "Why you know he come sail today?"

Natasha caught Ivan's eye for permission. "His midshipman company commander works for General Kanokov, and assures him that MacDougall is signed up with a crew to take out one of the big sailing yachts we passed on the way here."

"Company commander works for General Kanokov?" Sampson sounded puzzled.

"No, no," Ivan explained. "The general has very talented girls working for him. He sent one to seduce the midshipman—his name is Kloski. She plays the part of a wealthy, spoilt brat who tells Kloski that MacDougall seduced and jilted her and she wants to pay Kloski in sex and expensive party-weekends to make certain MacDougall flunks out of the Academy. So Kloski knows nothing, except he's got a sweet deal. Turns out Kloski's a cruel, drunken date, the girl says, and she can't wait to have us put an end to her assignment."

After lunch, the wind began blowing stronger. Sampson frowned. "Much wind for sailing."

"Don't worry," Natasha reassured him. "We were told the officer in charge of the boats, an old-time mustang named Lieutenant Siatkowski, lets MacDougall go out when no one else can. No other fourth classman has ever qualified to command these big boats. It's one of the reasons Kloski hates MacDougall."

Sampson kept on idling along the northeastern shore of the Severn River, waiting for MacDougall to go sailing in the afternoon. Finally a yawl sailed out into Chesapeake Bay.

"That's Jason MacDougall at the helm." Natasha handed Sampson her binoculars.

She didn't like Ivan's silence and tight-lipped expression. When he went in the cabin to assemble the sniper rifle with its scope and silencer, she followed.

"You're tense, Ivan. Do you want Sampson to make the kill? After all, he won the Olympic gold for this kind of shooting."

"No. I have to do this myself."

"You're too uptight to make such a difficult shot from a rocking boat. You've got to relax."

He looked up. "What did you have in mind?"

"Something fast." She closed the hatch and unbuckled her belt.

When the Academy yawl returned from the bay, Sampson steered the Chris Craft back across the Severn and idled off Trumpy's shipyard. The yard was closed for the weekend, no one in sight. The yawl was on a course to pick up its mooring buoy upwind of the seawall.

Ivan studied the sailboat. "With this wind he's really barreling in. Those boats don't have engines. If he misses, he's on the seawall. Might be interesting to watch."

Sampson checked through the binoculars. "Comrade Ivan, you study skipper?"

Ivan reached for the proffered field glasses, studied the midshipman and caught Natasha's eye. She shivered at the recollection of her partner's brother. Ivan put a cautioning hand on her shoulder. "Let's stay inside, where we can't be seen." Looking at Sampson, he said, "Wait till he's passed our bow, then move slowly down Spa Creek so I can shoot through the open starboard window."

With the field glasses, Natasha reconfirmed it was MacDougall at the helm. She heard his deep voice call out, "Ready about. Hard alee. Slack all sheets. Stand by to pick up the mooring line." A midshipman at the bow stood by with a boathook, with another sailor behind him ready to help.

The ten-ton boat's momentum enabled it to round up into the wind and slow gradually as it bore down on its mooring buoy. In this strong breeze the snap of the luffing sails sounded like the cracking of whips. Ivan explained through the open hatch to Sampson, "If the skipper misjudges his turn and momentum, he can either overshoot or fall short of the buoy. Whichever way, he ends up on the rocks by the seawall. But he won't misjudge. The boat will stop dead in the water exactly at the buoy."

The boat did just as Ivan predicted. Its crew secured the mooring line and quickly lowered the luffing sails. Sampson said, "How you know skipper be successful?"

Ivan smiled. "Because I would have been successful."

Sampson looked again through the binoculars. "He balances like cat on rolling boat—like you. He looks for something. He looks at us."

Ivan was sighting through the telescopic sight of the rifle, ready to fire. He whispered to Natasha, "He senses danger. He knows I'm here."

She tensed as Ivan's finger began squeezing the trigger.

She imagined the cross-hairs of Ivan's sight on Jason's forehead and admired Ivan's calm demeanor. Sensitive to the fact her partner was deeply troubled over killing his brother, she placed a steadying hand on Ivan's shoulder.

Suddenly MacDougall pointed behind their Chris Craft. She looked.

Fuck! Natasha sank her fingernails into Ivan's shoulder. "Don't fire," she said in a low voice.

They'd been so focused on MacDougall's hazardous maneuver, they hadn't noticed the Coast Guard boat that was motoring down Spa Creek behind them. Had someone reported the Chris Craft missing? She held her breath. No, the Coast Guard was headed toward the yawl. Perhaps standing by to pick up the sailboat if it missed its buoy.

Hastily, Ivan broke down the rifle, packed it in its short travel case and tossed it into a duffle.

Natasha watched MacDougall wave goodbye to the departing Coast Guard patrol boat and their "borrowed" Chris Craft and return to the business of securing the Academy yawl, while a navy personnel boat stood by to carry him and his crew ashore.

This was the *fourth* time Jason MacDougall had avoided death at their hands. Natasha watched dark clouds blot out the low sun, and felt despondent—finally realizing why Ivan felt Jason was protected by some "destiny" they couldn't understand.

CHAPTER 43
SYBIL

Bethesda, Maryland
Wednesday, December 26, 1956

The Christmas holiday offered a welcome break from Kloski's hazing and Jason was eager to spend more time with his Grandfather Steele in Bethesda. He had already accepted invitations to several of the dinner dances in Washington, D.C., and Gwen asked him to be one of her escorts for the party given by her grandmother. It was a friendly introduction to the world of tuxedos and strapless evening gowns. Fortunately, military dress uniform was a socially acceptable alternative to a black tie dinner suit. In fact, the young ladies found it exciting.

Despite his grandfather's Harvard degree from the distant past, Jason felt like an outsider with the Ivy League men at these balls. They were urbane and clever conversationalists. He was a straight talking logger with military experience. Then, at a party the night after Christmas, he met Sybil Sibelius and forgot about everyone else in the ballroom.

Sibelius. His mind jumped to *Finlandia*, some of his favorite music. "Your father is a diplomat with the Finnish Embassy?" Her answer was a smile that made categorical questions unimportant.

Sybil danced with verve and warmed up to him as if he were what she'd been looking for all her life. Her gown was deep blue moiré satin, which complemented her blue eyes and shoulder-length blonde hair. Jason was captivated by her luscious figure and vivacious manner, and had difficulty not staring at her extraordinary cleavage. She seemed ecstatic, laughing frequently. Yet occasionally, when she thought he wasn't looking, her eyes appeared troubled.

After the last dance, Sybil said, "Could you give me a ride to my apartment? I'll make you a cup of Finnish coffee." It didn't take Jason a blink to accept her invitation.

She twirled and flashed a brilliant smile. At the cloak room, she handed him her wrap and said, "Would you hold this while I duck into the ladies'?"

As Jason waited in the marble hall, he wondered why a sense of impending danger clouded his happiness. Why did he feel she was more mature than the other eighteen and nineteen-year old girls at the dance? Something wasn't right.

He liked her directness. Her English was nearly flawless, with barely discernable traces of a foreign accent. From some of his Finnish schoolmates in the Northwest, he knew the Finns were among the happiest, most honest and liberated of nations. His hand felt something metallic in her coat pocket.

He stepped into a corner and felt in the pocket. Keys. Curious, he pulled them out. A Jaguar logo key-ring. Two car keys, and another he assumed was to the apartment. A pocket within the pocket contained a few Kleenex tissues. *What's this?* Wrapped in one of the tissues was a tiny test-tube vial with a colorless liquid and eighth-inch stopper. *Shit!*

Poison? For him? In a flash he knew that the enemy had tracked him down. He held his breath as a shiver of fear ran down his spine and then enveloped him like the tentacles of a giant octopus he'd seen while snorkeling off the Olympic Peninsula.

Trying not to panic, he glanced around the lobby for help. Everyone else had gone. Uncle David had told him bodyguards like Dirk and Tim should be unnecessary in the rarified confines of these well-chaperoned parties. The polished granite columns created solid support for the coffered ceiling, but offered no security for his precarious situation. Every atom of his being shouted, *Flee!* Jason turned to run out of the building—but something held him fast. *Think.*

He stood motionless. *Flee where?* Neither the FBI nor the navy was at hand, and he wondered whether even they could help him against this enemy. It was only his paranormal gifts that identified the seriousness of his situation. He had no proof other than the vial, which he only sensed contained poison intended for him. Jason needed proof and incontrovertible documentation, or he was a dead man.

Sybil's coffee seduction must be a set-up, but if she was planning to poison him, it seemed unlikely there would be other assassins waiting at her apartment. He wanted more information.

Frustrated and angry, he decided to handle this himself. He took the vial and slipped it into an inside pocket of his dress uniform. What about her wrap? He ran his hands over the fur, feeling for weapons. Nothing.

He managed a smile as she came out saying, "Are we the last to leave? Let's go." With a big smile she said, "I can't wait."

On the way to his car, Jason placed her fur around her bare shoulders. He guessed she'd stalled in the ladies' room because she wanted to avoid being seen leaving with the man she was about to kill.

While he drove them to her place, he discovered the extent of her craziness and intentions as she did everything with her tongue and hands to distract him from his driving. Sybil was the flagrant antithesis of any girl he'd met in Washington. When they stopped alone at a red light, she kissed him so passionately he took advantage of the opportunity to explore her eager body under her dress. At least she didn't have a dagger or derringer strapped to either thigh or hidden between her bountiful breasts. In fact, her high-heeled dancing slippers and long evening gown were *all* she was wearing. "What happened to your stockings?"

"That's part of what took me so long."

"Oh, my," Jason heard the deep rumble in his voice. Dear God, he wasn't acting. Despite his fear, he craved Sybil's offering. Only his realization that she intended to assassinate him prevented him from turning down the nearest side street to consummate her offering.

CHAPTER 44
DANGEROUS BEAUTY

Washington, D.C.
Thursday, December 27, 1956

Jason studied the deserted marble lobby as he walked Sybil to the elevator. It was well past midnight. After their amorous ride to the third floor, Sybil took his hand and waltzed him down the carpeted hall to her front door. Jason played along, but in the shadowy hallway, he felt like a lone bull culled from the herd and surrounded by predators. Without taking her eyes off him, she reached into her coat pocket for her keys, then turned to unlock the door.

Once inside, Sybil flipped a light switch and, as he'd hoped, the apartment appeared empty. Alert for any sound behind him, he removed his midshipman's overcoat and draped it across a chair. She laid her fur coat over it, placed her purse on top and kicked off her shoes.

"I should have used the bathroom too, before we left."

"Through the bedroom," she said pleasantly.

On his way, Jason glanced at the kitchen and dining area. No one in sight.

He came out of the bathroom, satisfied no one lurked in waiting.

Sybil stood where he'd left her, leaning provocatively against the front door. She reached both arms back to unzip her dress.

"Let me give you a hand."

She turned sideways for him.

He watched the dress fall to the floor, verifying she had no weapons other than her shocking naked beauty.

Aware that she was laughing prettily and undoing the brass buttons of his dress uniform with expert haste, Jason just stared down at her in hypnotic admiration. The women he'd known had athletic builds. Sybil's feminine figure, on the other hand, shocked him. Her lovely face was matched by an eye-boggling slender body supporting enormous breasts. Jason couldn't take his eyes off her. What an alluring killing machine.

As she deftly removed his shoes and socks, he said, "What do you weigh, Sybil?"

"Fif—a hundred twenty-eight." She straightened up, rolling her shoulder and enticing him with a sly wink. "Think you can handle that?" She dropped his pants, revealing his uncontrollable arousal.

"I'll do my best. But I want to be responsible." He forced a grin. "I'll just—"

"I'm already protected," she said with a candid smile. "Just in case we stopped on the way here." She held his erection tightly. "Oh, I want you inside me, Jason."

And I want information, Mata Hari. He ran his hands through her thick hair as if admiring it, but in reality checking for any potential weapon hidden there.

She slid her hand up his chest. "Bend your knees, Superman." Her voice was rich with humor.

He kept his eyes on her as he lowered himself to her eye level. She was incredibly ready and got right to it, dropping herself over him with hardly a groan of discomfort.

"A little short on foreplay, aren't we?" he said.

She shrugged. "Foreplay is highly overrated. Now stand with me."

Jason held her abdomen against his and slowly straightened his legs. She held on but let her legs dangle, while her intense eyes squinted into his and a slight smile played at her full lips. She began undulating her stomach muscles to work him. Jason smiled at her agility. "You certainly know how to excite a man, Sybil. Does this excite you as much as me?"

Her glance faltered for an instant, and it dawned on him that her obvious experience had always been one-sided—she seduced while men took. But right now his life depended on information about the vial and learning how he might save himself. He forced himself to concentrate on staying alive, rather than the feelings that were driving him wild.

Yet even if she told him everything she knew, then what? No agency could protect him every night and day of the year, unless he changed his identity and dropped out of life as he knew it. That was still unacceptable to him. Jason's mind raced through the scenarios. *Of course. Blackmail.* The masterminds who sent her, the enemy themselves, who already feared his ability to identify them.

Blackmail might save him—if he could get enough on the enemy so they feared him dead more than alive. A rush of hope recharged him—if only he could turn Sybil into his *ally* instead of his assassin. Wouldn't that be the seduction of a lifetime!

He studied her face. "Sybil, you've learned to cut to the chase, but can you handle feelings?"

She misunderstood. "Watch me, Jason." She placed an arm around his neck and wrapped a shapely thigh and foot around each of his legs as she worked the hardness engorging her.

Jason placed unyielding hands at the small of her back and pressed fully up into her fine frame.

Her head snapped back, face grimacing, eyes wide with concern.

Jason glared at her. "Now *I'll* cut to the chase." His voice was guttural. "Who sent you to poison me?"

Her eyes flashed instant understanding. Her body arched, then fell limp in surrender. She whispered hoarsely, "People who'll punish my entire family if I don't do exactly as they say." She looked away, hesitated. When her eyes met his again she said, "Something about you ... you saw right through my seduction ... I feel all I can do is to be honest with you and accept the consequences of my failure."

"Then tell me, why were you given this job?"

"I've become such a success at seducing and drugging my assignments into sleep so I can memorize their papers, that my boss made me your assassin. For my family's sake I couldn't refuse."

Jason thought how wise she was to recognize that only complete honesty would help her now. "I'm truly sorry about your family problem, but I have to know who your boss is and why he wants me dead."

"I cannot name my superior." She clenched her teeth. "And I know nothing of why." Her eyes filled with terror, her muscles taut in preparation for his attack.

Beneath the assassin he saw a conflicted young woman. "Has anyone ever tried to be nice to you—to give you as much as they take?"

"Why should they?" she said bitterly. "They have all the power." Her tone was defiant.

"Have you ever cared for a man—loved anyone besides your family?"

"Of course not. We're taught a woman loses power over a person she cares for."

Jason softened his grip. "Make you a deal. I'll show you what real power is. In return you reveal who's after me. I need information to make them leave me alone."

She tried to push him away. "I can't tell you, Jason. I'm sorry I was going to kill you. Kill me if you must. My life ... being used day and night by men I work for ... isn't so wonderful anymore."

He looked into her empty eyes. She meant what she said. "Your life *could* be wonderful, Sybil, if you worked like a sixteenth century Venetian courtesan instead of a twentieth century sex-slave."

Her eyes flickered with curiosity.

CHAPTER 45
DO-OR-DIE SEDUCTION

Washington, D.C.
Thursday, December 27, 1956

Still not releasing her, Jason carried Sybil into the bedroom as she beat his chest and kicked his legs. He felt her apprehension, her fear as he closed the door and pressed her back into it, pinioning her there. She fought to get free, but Jason kept her firmly impaled. "Listen to me." He spoke with passion. "The fact is, love is where women's power over men really begins."

Her mouth dropped open. "You catch me trying to kill you, and you lecture me about love?"

How could he convince her? *Not with words.* Jason bent his knees, lowering her feet to the carpet. With a fervent prayer, he thrust up into her the way he had under the tree with Megan, jerking Sybil's feet off the floor. She let out a sharp cry of surprise, then looked at him defiantly, her jaw set with determination, as if accepting her penance.

"Again?" he said.

"*Nyet,*" she whispered hoarsely, but nodded her head in surrender.

Nyet? So she was Russian. No question Ivan was behind this. What organization was his brother working through this time? A flash of anger possessed him, but he forced himself to focus on his mission.

With Jason's next thrust Sybil screamed, a heart-rending cry, expelling years of pent-up anguish and pain. At least, he hoped that's what it meant, but he let her recover before he said, "Again?"

She just waited, tensed for the next assault, tears leaking out between closed lids.

"Look at me," Jason commanded, and ran a finger over her tear-stained cheeks. "Don't you understand," he said more tenderly, "without love you're only going through the motions?"

"My job is sex, not love for my targets or their love for me—just their lust."

She tried to turn away, but he held her jaw and turned her face to look at him, to really *see* him as a person—as a man. Very gently, he kissed her eyelids, her tears, her quivering lips as she clung to him.

"You're worth more than that," he whispered. "You deserve to love and to be loved."

Jason began again, battering down her mental doors of resistance until he saw surrender in her eyes, in the relaxation of her face. He moved more tenderly and felt her discovering the joy of sex as inner muscles awakened to embrace it. To slow her, he carried her to the bed and lay her on a corner, standing between her twitching thighs.

"Don't stop," she whispered, and uttered something in Russian as she grabbed him with a fierce need and arched her body for deeper fulfillment. He reached for her erect nipples to explore their sensitivity. Sybil came with such child-like wonder that the experience seemed almost spiritual. He came with her in a controlled rush, holding back hard, and continued thrusting to bring her again as she moaned her astonishment.

The turbulent crescendo of *Finlandia* thundered through him as he soared over the magnificent storm-tossed landscape of her breasts, surging under the wooing embrace of his hands—until her unleashed contractions brought him again in the most penetrating, muscle-wracking explosion he could endure.

Sybil lay sobbing, her powerful legs holding him within her. Jason clutched her body to his, crawled across the bed with her and rested her head on a pillow.

"Please don't leave me," she begged. He lay on her lightly, keeping most of his weight on his forearms. With an odd feeling of guilt, he slipped a hand under the pillows, surreptitiously checking for weapons, telling himself he didn't dare forget that this place had been set up for his assassination. Sybil stopped clinging and wept quietly as she relaxed under him. He stroked her face and her blonde hair, wet and matted on the pillow. Finally she stopped crying, and he blotted her tears with the sheet.

As she gazed up at him in silence, Jason said, "Which will men risk death to return to—the woman who fakes rapture or the one you just were with me?"

Her emerging smile and bright eyes assured him she understood.

Sybil sniffled. "That's the first time I've cried since I allowed myself to be taken when I was fourteen." She ran her fingers across his chin. "Someone must have loved you very much, for you to have learned to make love like that. Why isn't she still with you?"

Jason swallowed hard. "We were two ships sailing together for protection, until we had to resume our separate courses and destinations." He looked into Sybil's eyes. "But you're right. We loved each other deeply. Always will."

She hugged him tighter. "Different destinations." She smiled sadly. "And that's how it's to be with us, yes?"

"Depends."

CHAPTER 46
FRIENDLY PERSUASION

Washington, D.C.
Thursday, December 27, 1956

N ot forgetting he was in the apartment selected for his assassination, Jason looked down into Sybil's face. "I never could have shared all that with you if I hadn't believed you're a good-hearted person."

Her brow creased in a frown as she seemed to be making a decision. She stroked his jaw, almost lovingly. "For whatever it's worth, I never was comfortable with the killing part. I've watched how the distinctions between good and evil become blurred by the complexities of minds trying to survive in a world run by power-hungry, evil men. They say it's for the good of the people they're meant to take care of, but now I can see it's all about serving their personal greed and lust for control." Sybil gave an introspective smile. "Since I was fourteen, my looks have been a curse that makes such men use me as their honeypot."

"Honeypot?"

"A bedroom spy. Eventually I understood that their interest in my training was for their own gratification. I got screwed—as Americans would say—screwed out of my adolescent years, forced to go from puberty directly into adulthood. All my mother ever told me is women submit to sex for three reasons. To service their men, to get pregnant, or to get information. It took my enemy to show me a fourth reason."

Another silent tear brimmed over, and he gently wiped it away.

She shrugged. "Fortunately, I liked the attention. In the final analysis, it was my decision to go along with it. Maybe it was my curiosity about sex, or entrée to fun parties, wonderful food and clothes—

now even a Jaguar and private apartment—all just for being cheery and spreading my legs for a few seconds whenever required. But it was so much better than growing up in a home with little food and not enough heat."

He looked sideways at her. "How old are you, Sybil?"

"I'm supposed to say eighteen," she said, "but really I'm twenty-two. I work in my embassy as a receptionist. I'm also a dove," she volunteered.

"Dove?"

"A plant, usually an office worker, who keeps an eye on her superiors for their leaders back home. Nobody fully trusts anyone in the embassy." Sybil cleared her throat and wiped her nose. "A dove may have sex with her bosses to gain information in an unguarded moment—anything to ascertain deviation from the approved party line."

Had Sybil really turned, or was she just stringing him along until she could carry out her assignment? He sensed she really wanted to repay his gift of kindness and, perhaps, wanted the courage to improve her own life. However, if she was going to do that, she needed to learn a few other things first. "When you're telling your weight, don't start to give it in kilos." He winked. "As for *Nyet*," he raised a brow, "obviously you're working for the Russian embassy."

She bit her lip and said nothing.

It was time for Jason to control the next step in this dangerous predicament. "I think you should try to convince your superiors you'll spy for them, but not kill for them. Tell them you can serve them well as a bedroom spy, but that you're not cut out to be an assassin. They should accept your terms because they have too much to lose without you. They'll treat you with more respect, too."

"I like respect." She paused, appearing introspective. "Jason, what's it like when two people have sex tenderly?"

"None of it works well as mere sex—there's got to be caring and romance to express the empathy, respect and appreciation I was able to feel for you tonight. It's the relationship that matters." He watched her eyes soften. "Foreplay is an expression of that—or should be."

Her eyes opened wide—deep blue, unguarded. "Show me."

Jason started slowly, watching her professional mask melt, morph into true pleasure and then ecstasy. He kept her at the peak of her passion so long he was able, to drive her laughing across the bed, onto the floor and across it until she was draped over a chaise lounge by the window. His heart almost stopped as she cried out in appreciation. For a few brief moments they remained like that, when suddenly she pulled back, looked at her watch and jumped up. "Dress quickly, Jason, we have to go right away."

Had she fooled him? Was this still a trap? He needed to stay on guard. "What's the hurry?"

"This apartment belongs to strangers who are away in Europe, but a crew is due here any minute to clean up the place so the owners never know we were here—no trace of us." She hesitated. "That means they are coming to dispose of your body. Your car, too."

Jason raised his brow. "And how was that to be accomplished?"

She smiled brightly. "It seems we own a crematorium in the area. And a junk yard with a car crusher."

He tried not to show his horror over their plan to exterminate him. He never took his eye off her as they dressed, making sure she didn't go for his jacket or a weapon concealed in the apartment. He breathed a silent sigh of relief when they were safely outside the building and driving away in his car. As they drove, he formulated a plan. Before he dropped her off for the night, he needed her to agree to help him—or surely he would perish.

CHAPTER 47
PARTY TO BLACKMAIL

"What was the poison?" Jason glanced at Sybil while driving her to the Russian embassy.

"*Was?*" She stared at him in surprise, and searched the pockets of her wrap. "I brought it with me in case you said no to coffee at the apartment, but yes to just taking me out for drinks."

He patted her knee. "You didn't think I was going to let you keep it, did you?"

Sybil cleared her throat.

"Well?" he pressed.

She licked her lips. "They told me a designer drug—tasteless, a nerve toxin—shuts a person down in seconds." She paused. "Are you going to report me?" She sounded worried.

"To whom? Besides, you're not the enemy, but your replacement might be someone who doesn't mind killing. The people calling the shots are the enemy. They're the ones I must address." He glanced at her. "Of course, everything *could* fall apart for your superiors if someone did succeed in killing me after tonight."

"What do you mean?"

"The poison, and my accompanying letter describing everything that's happened to me with a perfect description and drawings of the persons responsible, would be made available to the FBI, CIA and MI5. The letter will detail everything I know—including the crematorium and vehicle compactor. The investigations would shut down question-able Russian activities connected with their Washington embassy."

Jason stopped for a traffic light. "Naturally, I don't want anyone to hunt me down before I set everything up. So after I drop you off to make your report, I'll go directly to another state, and not return until my legal business is concluded."

"Blackmail?"

He nodded.

She smiled. "I take psychology courses at George Washington University and, with my photographic memory, the studies are easy." Sybil stroked his thigh and looked at him out of the corner of her eye. "You're a man who stands on his own two feet without help. Few accomplish that—at any age."

A surge of satisfaction rushed through him, but Jason refused to be distracted. Victory wasn't his yet. The light turned green, he drove through the intersection, shifted into second gear and then third. "Sybil, you've got to be the most amoral, unnaturally happy, self-accepting person I've ever met."

Her delighted laughter filled the car and he trusted the sparkle in her eyes, vivid blue in the bright dash light.

Jason reached over and squeezed her hand. "Would you deliver a message to your superiors for me?"

"For you, anything. Anything except betray Russia. As imperfect as it is, it is my country, my identity. I said I wouldn't give you my superior's name, but you need something powerful against your adversaries, so I will tell you he's the KGB general in charge of security at the embassy—and he is the one who ordered me to kill you. I must tell you also, he's a good man and an honored soldier."

A KGB general. Giving Jason that lead could cause her untold grief if discovered and he knew without question she, too, needed his blackmail to work.

Sybil twisted on the seat to face him. "Since you have the vial of poison with my finger prints on it, I'm going to tell him you threatened me with blackmail if I didn't fuck you and after that you opened a whole new world of possibilities for me that for Russia's sake I couldn't resist."

She bit her lip and stared at the roof of the car. "I hope you're right about my value, that they don't kill me for failing this assignment." She straightened her shoulders and looked into Jason's eyes. "What's your message? I'll type it verbatim as soon as I get to the embassy."

"Tell your superiors, if I die I'll have left behind enough evidence with the FBI, CIA and MI5 to put all of them in the biggest spotlight America has. So I advise them to see that nothing happens to me. The general can tell a man named Ivan to come out of hiding and do his own dirty work. And he can tell Ivan I know he's operating in the Miami area. Also, I sensed his presence on the small cabin cruiser that windy day I was picking up my mooring buoy at the Academy while the Coast Guard boat stood by. Tell him it's not my destiny to be easy for him to get."

"What audacity." Her voice was filled with awe. "Who *are* you, Jason?"

"Just a student trying to make it through college. But it's obvious your people think I'm something more."

"Well, aren't you, if you know how to get help from people trying to kill you?"

Shortly before reaching the embassy, Jason turned onto a side street and stopped at the curb. "Are you going to be alright?"

Sybil gave him a dazzling smile and laced her fingers through his. "I'm going to be fine."

"Good luck." He put the car in first gear and prepared to pull away, then changed his mind. How could he make sure his blackmail plan succeeded? *Of course.*

He shifted into neutral and set the hand brake. "Tell your people, if they must kill me, I want you to do it." He grinned. "In fact, let's put them to the test. How would you like to spend the final weekend of my Christmas break in a clothing optional suite at the Mayflower Hotel? Followed by weekend encounters in Annapolis? There's lots more to teach you."

"You're crazy, Jason. That's putting your head in the mouth of a Russian bear. I'd love weekends like that with you. But they'd never let me. And what if they kill you despite your blackmail? What if they kill me?"

He drummed his fingers on the steering wheel as he thought. "Okay, what's the most important information your boss needs that no one's been able to get for him? Seduce whomever you have to, get that information and surprise your boss with it by the end of next week. Then see if he won't let you meet with me." Jason laughed. "Tell him I put you up to it and he owes me."

"I love it." She put a gentle hand on Jason's sleeve. "But what if they want to kill you anyway? It's too dangerous to meet again."

"Why is it more dangerous for me to meet with you than not? If my blackmail plan doesn't work, I'm a dead man anyway—no matter where I go."

Jason placed a hand over hers. "Sybil, these people don't care about collateral damage. They tried to sink a submarine with its entire crew just to kill me. What if my grandfather or friends are with me when I start my car and it blows up? I refuse to live in fear—that doesn't work for me. So let's find out if the blackmail will work." He grinned. "At the Mayflower January 5th?"

A mixture of elation and sadness played across Sybil's face. "What's the American saying, 'Give me liberty or give me death'?" She caressed his cheek, brushing his lips with her fingers. "Saturday the 5th by 3:00 PM I'll leave a yes-or-no message for you at the pharmacy counter of People's Drug Store in Bethesda. If our rendezvous is a go, pick me up at the embassy at five."

"The embassy? For all to see? That's pretty bold of you. You sure?" She nodded.

"Okay. The 5th at five." He put the car in gear.

As Jason dropped her off at the embassy entrance, Sybil gave him a kiss and whispered in his ear, "You get lots of sleep, my friend, for the upcoming Russian assault—to the death of our personal cold war. I'll be party to your blackmail, but be forewarned that I'm a spy who intends to learn all I can from you in the little time available to us." Her laughter filled the car.

He gave her a victory sign, flashing a smile. "I'll expect nothing less than a grand sex opera to keep us soaring."

Jason headed for the Pennsylvania state line. He couldn't tell the FBI or even Uncle David. They'd be obligated to question him about what he'd learned from Sybil and he'd lose his clout, his hold over the Russians. Jason would create his safety net with a Philadelphia attorney he'd read about in Time magazine. Risking his own career in an old, respected law firm, this lawyer went out on a limb for his clients in a way Jason found unforgettable. Jason sensed the man would be intrigued by this international blackmail scheme and just hoped he wasn't out of town for the holiday. When breakfast time arrived in Bethesda, Jason would phone Grandfather Steele to let him know he'd be back at the house for New Year's.

He ran the blackmail plan through his mind—all the angles and loopholes he could imagine. Had he overlooked anything? He felt a tingle behind his ears. Would he still be alive at the end of vacation?

CHAPTER 48
SYBIL'S GAMBLE

With Sybil still aboard, Natasha maneuvered her launch alongside the Burger yacht and stopped by the stern platform, with its steps up to the aft deck. The "Doughertys'" floating home base was anchored off the main channel of Nassau Harbor, where Ivan and she had been conducting business for the past month. This was the only commercial port she'd ever seen where the water was aquamarine and so clear you could see the fish swimming over a clean sandy bottom.

Their yacht was manned by a crack Spetsnaz team of male-female partners. One of the tanned, muscular crewmen took Natasha's lines, secured the launch and gave the women a hand onto the platform.

"Thanks, George."

George didn't move. "Ivan said he wants to see you in the salon as soon as you return."

Natasha raised her brows, noting that General Kanokov's seaplane remained anchored behind them.

"Okay." She pointed to the launch. "Bring up the ice chest. I grabbed twelve lobsters and speared a black grouper for supper for everyone tonight. Take care of my snorkeling equipment too, please. And we won't be using the spare anchor after all." She noticed George was trying not to stare at her and Sybil in the new two-piece swimsuits from Venezuela. "Relax, George. When in Rome——" She beamed. "Get one for Elsa and tell her how incredible she looks in it. She'll like that."

Through the entrance of the salon, Natasha saw Ivan seated on a sofa across from the general.

At the arrival of the women, both men stood courteously. Kanokov stared at their revealing swimming attire, but looked relieved to see Sybil.

"General," his honeypot said softly, "good to see you again."

Natasha had taken Sybil offshore to have a talk about this honeypot's double allegiance in the Jason affair. Natasha's job was to determine whether to keep Sybil in the operation or to dump her at sea, wrapped in the chain and spare anchor that she'd had George place in the bow of the open boat.

Sybil still looked shaken. She'd known the score, and had convinced Natasha that Jason had taught her skills that made her a greater asset for the Soviets than a liability.

Ivan lifted a brow. "The crew haven't seen you like that, have they?" Natasha and Sybil had been wearing cover-ups when they'd headed out in the launch.

"Get used to it, Ivan. It's the new style for liberated women. No flap across the front, lots of bare midriff and back. It's still much more conservative than a French bikini." Men could be such a pain.

Ivan looked at his watch. "Why don't you tell Madeline to serve lunch as soon as you can get dressed?" It wasn't really a question.

Natasha ushered Sybil to the guest stateroom where she'd changed earlier, then went straight into the shower of the elegant master stateroom. What a morning this had been.

It had started when George reported a seaplane "with a General Kanokov and the most impressive woman I've ever seen. They want to come aboard the yacht."

When Kanokov stepped onto the teak deck, Natasha thought his yachting shoes, slacks and blazer seemed out of place on the KGB general. His hard line philosophy and his loyalty to the party cause exuded from him like piety from a pope, so however he dressed, he wore it like a military uniform, the only attire that fit his character.

The general introduced Sybil as his honeypot protégée. "I sent out a well-trained young party girl to seduce and poison MacDougall. She returned hours later a completely transformed woman and telling me what she would and wouldn't do." Kanokov's face reddened. "She boldly admitted her disobedience in helping Jason blackmail us. I brought her here immediately to determine with you how best to handle this unsettling matter."

Sybil stepped forward with an envelope. "This is Jason MacDougall's message, which I wrote down verbatim."

Natasha and Ivan read the neatly typed paper, and looked at each other in disbelief. This was a message from a first-year college student to two of the most capable killers on the planet? Ivan decided Natasha should take Sybil boating and determine if she should live or die for helping Jason blackmail them into keeping him alive.

Natasha had been impressed with Sybil's exceptional intelligence and straightforward integrity. But the clincher had been when Sybil described what Jason had shown her and the pleasure she experienced.

Of course, Natasha and Ivan were the leaders, and she couldn't disclose her naiveté, but she felt a deep surge of resentment towards Soviet rulers who kept men and woman in ignorance about sex, simply to serve their selfish purposes. Her Soviet government controlled access to all information and only disseminated ideas that they believed promoted the communist cause. The subject of sex was taboo and the fact women could have orgasms was basically unknown.

She resolved to find out what secrets had changed Sybil's life overnight. Something about learning sex that enabled her to be Russia's best courtesan ever. Sybil had proved it two nights later when she went out on her own and extracted information from an American Joint Chief's aide, whom Kanokov's best honeypots had reported was unassailable.

"How much should we trust General Spartak Kanokov?" Natasha had asked.

"One can never know another's innermost thoughts, but I think he will prove trustworthy insofar as he believes you are serving Russia's best interests. As the head of security at our embassy in Washington, he's been a straight shooter from the old school. I've only seen him try to be a loyal Russian." Sybil smiled. "And don't be fooled by his gruff exterior. Underneath, he's a teddy bear."

"He's been intimate with you?"

"Of course. I'm his dove."

"Sybil, life has taught me to trust only Ivan. But today something tells me I can rely on you, even though it is against my nature. How'd you like to work for us—first a while longer with Jason MacDougall, and then seducing bright college students all over the country into taking courses taught by our underground cadre of socialist professors?"

"You mean as an alternative to feeding fishes?"

"I mean as an alternative to eventually getting caught stealing top secrets from America's best scientists and military men and spending years in prison."

"The general allowed Jason and me to survive our Mayflower Hotel assignation, as more research for courtesan work and intelligence-gathering." Sybil shrugged. "And you could have left me out here for the sharks."

Natasha watched her shudder, but she recognized this young woman's audacity and daring.

"Jason wondered if I could meet him occasionally in an Annapolis hotel. He doesn't know it, but one of the girls already goes to Annapolis almost every weekend to see a midshipman she's been assigned to." Sybil looked at the speargun. "I'm in awe of the way you operate boats and hunt for supper, but I'm confident in my area of expertise."

Natasha had brought the seductress back to the yacht as an addition to Ivan's plan for bloodless subversion. Hastily putting the finishing touches on her hair, Natasha poured herself into a dress that showed off her legs and figure to best advantage. As she strode up to the salon, she realized how fortunate she was that it never had occurred to her to warn Sybil she'd finish what she'd set out to do this day if Sybil ever tried to be Ivan's dove.

CHAPTER 49
SOVIET PROGRESS

Natasha's simple dark blue halter-dress and pearls complemented Ivan's nautical blazer. Madeline, partner of their Spetsnaz boat captain, served them a healthy meal of mangrove snapper and fresh steamed vegetables. All spoke perfect English. Natasha listened as Ivan tried to explain to General Kanokov why their plan could work.

"Here's the problem. The United States is a nation of virtually untapped natural resources and wealth. Today's citizens forget that people from all over the world came and took this great plum from the native Indians, and then from the British—" Ivan speared a red-skinned new-potato with his fork—"not forgetting the French and the Spanish." He chewed fast and swallowed. "America has had great leaders, mostly, who worked to build up their country—nationally and industrially." Ivan clutched his fork like a weapon.

"But communism cannot coexist with capitalism, and now we need America's wealth in order to improve conditions all over the world. The United States is allied with so many other capitalistic industrial nations that in a direct confrontation they might overwhelm us. We can't let that happen. So our plan for subversive takeover must succeed."

Natasha felt the excitement as she interjected, "Our plan is simplicity itself. By encouraging human nature to pursue its least noble self, we'll let America conquer herself from within through greed, selfishness and apathy."

The general tapped his glass for Madeline to pour more wine. "Allegiance to Mother Russia and a superior military are paramount to our world leadership."

Ivan nodded acknowledgement. "Russia's achievements to date bode well for our future. Our U.S.-born comrade George Abramovich Koval's intelligence about Oak Ridge and the chemical components of U.S. atomic weaponry was an invaluable contribution to our military capability. Thanks to Alexander Feklisov's recruiting genius, Klaus Fuchs gave our scientists vital information while working on the atomic bomb at Los Alamos and the Rosenbergs stole atomic secrets for us. All that made it possible for us to test our own bomb years ahead of schedule."

The general squared his shoulders in pride.

"*Pazdravlayu!*" Ivan hoisted his glass to Mother Russia's nuclear accomplishments.

They joined his toast. "*Na zdarov'e!*"

Natasha signaled Madeline to bring in the dessert and hid her impatience as she waited to hear Ivan explain the importance of his own plan to Kanokov.

"General, we're meeting our objectives with the Communist Party in this country. Mother Russia funds the CPUSA substantially and controls its policies and we often recruit American party members as spies. Of course, right now CPUSA has to operate underground, for the most part. Senator McCarthy exposed fifty-seven of our people in the U.S. State Department and fueled American fear of our ideology. But we influenced the press to censure him and managed to ruin his reputation and influence. Nevertheless, the House Un-American Activities Committee and the Senate Internal Security Subcommittee are thorns in our side, and all the private loyalty-review boards and anti-communist investigators are interfering with our plan to destroy this country from the inside. Even the communists in the arts and entertainment industry had to go undercover. The past president of the Screen Actors Guild, an actor named Ronald Reagan, testified before HUAC and stands against any political party that's proven to be an agent of a foreign power."

Kanokov frowned. "This actor, Reagan, is he going to be a problem for you?"

Natasha wanted to answer, but the general was old-school and only trusted men for policy decisions. Back in Chicago she'd caught on that he was uncomfortable with the gender equality advocated by communism.

"Reagan is just pursuing his movie career. He's not even one of the top stars." Ivan nodded his thanks to Madeline as she set his dessert in front of him, but clearly his focus was on the importance of the Grand Acquisition plan, as he continued.

"Our goal is to insert and maintain our people in local, state and federal government, in universities, and in Hollywood—where we can subtly convert the American consciousness through entertainment with a socialist viewpoint. That's our strategy for a bloodless takeover of this nation. So it's urgent that we undermine the agencies, the committees and the individuals who are obstructing our sabotage."

Natasha noticed Sybil's eyes open wider, almost imperceptibly, as a subtle smile crossed her face. Apparently this student of psychology thought Ivan's plan a clever strategy.

Madeline poured coffee and the general sipped from his cup. "Tell me, comrade, what's the bottom line of your plan?"

Ivan leaned forward earnestly. "To break America financially by radicalizing it, over decades, until the United States is too weak to resist our peaceful takeover."

"What's your secret?" The general snorted. "This is the wealthiest, most powerful nation on earth."

"You know our escalating proxy wars around the globe should make them spend themselves into massive debt as they send their military to help other nations fight communism."

Military might was the general's overriding interest. Ivan set down his cup in its saucer. "Now, on their own soil we infiltrate their schools and news media to promote disloyalty and practices that, over many years, will bury the American economy. Bury it under the weight of greed and dishonesty. The greed of the next generation of capitalist business leaders. The dishonesty of the politicians who, ahead of all other considerations, seek to keep the power of their office."

They moved from the dining table and settled onto the settee and easy chairs.

"What I see," said Kanokov, "is a powerful, well-run country, so charged with pride and entrepreneurship it even has the ability to rebuild its defeated enemies. What could possibly enable you to believe such a nation can be taken without a war to end all wars?"

Natasha poured the general another cup of coffee. "History, General. History."

Ivan sat back, deferring to her.

She perched on the edge of a chair opposite the general.

His frown challenged her, but she was determined not to be intimidated.

"Take the Chinese. The oldest civilization in the world." She felt confident, on a roll. "Brought down by foreign trade for enough opium to bring corruption and destroy the working class people throughout that great nation. Until the violent anti-foreign, anti-Christian Boxer rebellion put a stop to drug use. The decadent Qing Dynasty ended with the establishment of the Chinese Republic."

"That's why you work so hard to increase the flow of illegal drugs into the United States?"

Natasha nodded vigorously. "Absolutely," she and Ivan said in unison.

"What makes you believe it will work here, that lawmakers won't stamp out drug use?" Kanokov sipped his coffee.

Ivan answered. "For the same reason we had the Bolshevik Revolution. Party differences. Lenin's Bolsheviks had to defeat Martov's Mensheviks to eliminate democracy and establish his supreme power. The Bolsheviks used guns. Americans can do it with voting power. Voting power that serves the duplicitous legislators, rather than the people."

Kanokov looked puzzled. "This country is run by good people. They wouldn't tolerate the things you're predicting."

Natasha jumped in. "Think about it. The people running America today have fought for their freedom. Worked hard to build their great corporations—the Rockefellers, Fords, Kaisers, Mellons, DuPonts, Vanderbilts and Hiltons ... the great entrepreneurs. The presidents and legislators were raised to appreciate the freedoms so many of their ancestors sacrificed for. But what are these people doing to prepare their children to take over the responsibilities?"

The general shrugged.

Sybil seemed to be studying all three comrades.

Natasha tossed out her hands. "They spoil them, want their children to have everything they lacked. Bail them out of whatever trouble they get into. Buy them whatever they want. Keep too busy at work and socializing to spend time teaching their children the values and common sense their parents taught them."

"So?"

"What Ivan said: We support professors who'll allow students to cheat, to knock the only system of government they know, to rebel, to take whatever they can get away with—from corporate wealth to social services. When those former students and their children take over, many will rob their nation blind—and a nation dumbed down by excessive good living and drugs will tolerate such behavior."

The general stood. "How can you be so confident things will work out as you say?"

Ivan answered. "Greed for power. For the rich life. Once begun, it never sleeps."

"So a great nation destroys itself from within?"

"More effectively than we can from without."

"Hmm. Interesting." The general rose from his chair. "Good plan, if it works the way you say."

CHAPTER 50
REPRIEVE

Nassau, Bahamas
Tuesday, January 8, 1957

Their visitors were well on their way back to Washington as Natasha watched Ivan pace the salon. "Of course, I can't tell General Kanokov my concerns," he said, "without revealing that MacDougall is my twin and our paranormal abilities." He stopped in front of her. "You tell me the honeypot Sybil says MacDougall got hold of our new nerve toxin and has it as evidence of the attempt on his life, in addition to a description of you and me. And the fact her boss ordered the hit. Plus knowledge of our crematorium and car crusher. She says MacDougall has those proofs in secure hands as blackmail to ensure nothing happens to him. None of those things is insurmountable in itself, but a misstep could set off an international incident and the last thing we need is to draw attention to ourselves and our long-range plan. So Kanokov and I have agreed to leave him alone." Ivan paused. "For the present, at least."

"Sybil's convinced Jason is not an agent working against us, just a patriotic American war vet trying to find his way in life." Natasha looked into Ivan's eyes. "But you and I know he's a man of consequence, a problem for our project."

"Well, at least we know where he is. Meanwhile," he grinned, "how do I know you've decided to have sex with me in the next few minutes?"

Natasha rose from the sofa and took Ivan's hand. "Have I ever told you, you have a real knack for taking all the fun out of it?" Exasperated, she led him to their stateroom. If MacDougall was going to be a thorn in their side, at least she could keep Ivan at the peak of his abilities. They would succeed with their Grand Acquisition.

This evening, when Natasha serviced Ivan, her experience was no different from their usual. Back in 1953, when Natasha had tried to order the Kinsey Report on Sexual Behavior in Women, she'd been told it only reported the number of times people did it, so she'd written that off as being useless information, since people normally don't have the excess energy of Olympic athletes. When MacDougall fought off the assassins in Scotland and Ivan's shared euphoria brought her spasms of exhilaration, she realized sex could be more than they'd learned in Russia. Now Sybil had shared her discovery that women as well as men can enjoy a climax. Natasha did a rough calculation in her head: servicing Ivan an average of twice a day, over the past five years equals—Unbelievable. That's over three thousand orgasms Ivan and Mother Russia owed her. Damn men. There had to be a way.

Of course. She'd order Sybil to write a detailed analysis of everything Jason had taught her and how it affected her physically and mentally. A secret document for Natasha's eyes only. Natasha smiled at the simple solution.

She lay beside Ivan as he slept. General Kanokov appeared sold on their strategy. Good. But what about MacDougall? She'd take him out herself if he hadn't guaranteed he was a bigger pain dead than alive. There had to be a way around the blackmail. Neutralize him without killing him. Make him a quadriplegic? Why not, so long as he didn't die?

What a terrible thing to do to a fellow athlete. Ashamed she'd had such a thought, she worried. *We're becoming as bad as the low-lifes we're turning against their own country.* After all, what had the magnificent young man done but fight to defend his life and prove himself a brilliant adversary. Dammit, why didn't MacDougall just go away.

CHAPTER 51
HARD CHOICES

He was a mere plebe, a midshipman fourth class, but Jason knew he would make history today—one way or another. He took his bayonet out of his locker and checked its ungainly balance for throwing. Outside the window of his large Spartan room in Bancroft Hall, the rainy grey sky matched his dark mood. Yesterday's bright yellow daffodils and forsythia were obliterated by the foggy drizzle.

He'd been awakened at dawn by another vision about Kloski. In it he saw a waterspout whirl down from the black clouds and capsize a P-boat, drowning a dozen sailors in the roiling funnel of water. Jason knew this callous bully would endanger his men, even cause their death. It seemed Kloski's primary interest in the navy was to glorify himself. Once again Jason pondered his responsibility to act on his premonition.

A month ago, at one of Jason and Sybil's clandestine trysts in the Carvel Hall hotel, she confided that Kanokov was adding fuel to Kloski's hazing efforts. Last fall, the KGB general had sent a honeypot to seduce the first classman at a party. The woman pretended to have been jilted by MacDougall and was willing to do anything for Kloski if he would make Jason's life absolute hell. Furthermore, any plebe who received too many demerits would be forced out of the Academy. But the action Jason contemplated now was not about revenge. His vision this morning confirmed the danger to future sailors under Kloski's command.

Jason peered out at the unending drizzle, then at his bayonet. The drizzle turned to driving rain. He listened to the large drops pelting the window and decided it was time to use his gifts in a new way. He would try to save those sailors from certain death by getting Kloski out of the military once and for all. Even if he risked his own career in the process.

He fingered the cold steel in his hand. The balance was way off center, low down on the handle. That meant as the bayonet spun through the air, the tip of the long blade would be turning much faster than that of a balanced throwing knife. A very precise, practiced throw would be required to hit a target with the blade forward where it would stick. The three-inch wide doorjamb was the only visible wood in the room. The bayonet handle was so heavy that only an extremely hard throw could make the tip penetrate the door frame sufficiently to arrest the rotational momentum and support the weight on the long fulcrum. Such a forceful throw would increase the risk of it going wild. What could he use for practice?

The desk chairs were steel, but the seats were padded vinyl over thick plywood. Jason placed his chair by the doorjamb so the plywood bottom faced the room. From behind his steel desk, facing the fireproof door, he threw the bayonet across the room, again and again, with a loud thunk into the bottom of the seat. He practiced for an hour, summoning up all of the eye, mind and muscular coordination achieved in the past throwing hunting knives. Finally, he was satisfied.

Desperate measures for desperate men—

Having steeled himself for what was to come, he put the room back in order, sat at his desk, placed his bayonet in the drawer, and began studying his Spanish irregular verbs.

There were lots of reasons not to create a showdown with first classman Kloski. At the minimum, Jason probably would be expelled from the Naval Academy—a terrible disappointment to himself and to his Uncle David. Worst case? Missing his mark and going to prison for murder. A long bayonet had to be the most unbalanced knife ever devised. Jason could be off as little as two inches and seriously handicap or even kill the man. But he intended to take the risk, to play the hand he was dealt.

He put aside all thoughts of the possible consequences of today's plan, balled his boxer's fists and waited for the test ahead.

After supper, Kloski arrived at his usual hour and stood at attention just inside the doorway. Jason's roommates snapped to attention, exclaiming, "Sir!" and stating their names. But this time Jason remained seated and silent. He leaned back and put his feet on his desk facing the vain upper classman. Jason tried to appear calm.

Red in the face, Kloski snarled, "Mr. MacDougall, I'll see you marching every waking hour for this insubordination."

Jason let out a short, contemptuous laugh. "Sorry, Kloski, you already have me doing that." Well, no more. Jason narrowed his eyes and dropped his baritone voice to an eerie rumble.

"Kloski, I'm only going to say it once. Leave this room. And never come back." Kloski froze as Jason removed the bayonet from his drawer and stood.

He saw his roommates stare in astonishment and raise their hands in slow motion while he continued to operate in regular time.

Almost leisurely, Jason raised the bayonet by its blade and threw it with force. He watched it rotate slowly, perfectly, through its half turn as it floated across the room to bury its blade with a resounding thunk into the doorjamb exactly where Jason aimed. It quivered just two inches from Kloski's right ear.

Kloski remained frozen, eyes bugged. Without turning his head, he strained his eyes hard right to see the bayonet handle by his eye. He blanched. His mouth opened and closed, opened and closed, but no sound escaped. He swallowed hard, did an about-face and left the room.

The world around Jason returned to normal time. His heart was racing, but he felt no righteous satisfaction. He was just doing something he believed he had to do. Still, he knew he'd almost lost his emotional control, burying the bayonet so deeply in the jam that he had to yank it out. Clearly he'd be on the carpet for what he'd just done.

The next morning the order came scheduling Jason to see the Academy psychiatrist at 0800. The doctor leaned forward as he listened to the entire story.

Following a series of tests, the psychiatrist said, "Mr. MacDougall, I see you arrived in Korea right after the armistice, but did anything traumatic happen there?"

The details and ramification of his misadventure in North Korea were classified information. "After my discharge, I lost my parents in a horrific sailboat accident."

"I'm sorry to hear it." The doctor laced his fingers together. "I'm checking for possible causes of 'war neurosis,' what they used to call 'battle fatigue' in the Second World War. Sometimes it takes years before it surfaces as an unacceptable behavior." He handed Jason a mimeographed sheet describing a stress disorder cropping up in veterans of the Korean Conflict.

Silent, Jason revisited the horrors of his kidnapping and escape. That was the past. He figured he could handle it. "I expect I'm just a bit stressed out from Kloski's harassment." He thought hard, knowing his future weighed on his responses. "If you're thinking I was angry, of course I was. But don't overlook the fact, it was *controlled* anger. Survivors learn to operate that way."

The psychiatrist raised his brow. "All the same, I'm scheduling you for further testing next fall. Meanwhile, you're free to report to your company officer."

Now, two hours later, Jason hoped his quiet exterior concealed his inner turmoil as he entered the officer's chambers. Here's where his future would be decided. Would he be kicked out of the military? Court-martialed?

The lieutenant ordered Jason to stand at ease. "Mr. MacDougall, you've performed a serious and flagrant breech of conduct. After reading the psychiatrist's report, I spoke to the other midshipmen in the company and learned that Mr. Kloski has been severely out of line with his hazing. I've ordered Mr. Kloski never to bother you again."

"Thank you, sir." Jason breathed a sigh of relief, then felt surprising weakness. His eyes twitched as he fought for composure.

The fit-looking lieutenant leaned back in his chair and peered kindly over his desk at Jason. "Mr. MacDougall, my report in his file will ensure Mr. Kloski will be watched for any further behavior of this sort. If it continues, he'll be eased out of the navy."

"Sir, Kloski's cruelty and lack of common sense are going to get men killed. Why can't you act now?"

The company officer looked down at the papers on his desk. The ticking of a ship's bell clock on a nearby bookshelf filled the silence.

"Because," the officer said, "we have too much invested in Kloski not to give him another chance—just as we are giving you."

Jason swallowed his disappointment over Kloski's continued leadership, but didn't feel he could push the issue further.

The lieutenant leaned forward. "Mr. MacDougall may I make a personal observation?"

"Of course, sir." He felt the beating of his carotid pulse against his uniform collar.

"In the time I've served here, I've never seen a midshipman stand with his feet planted midstream and attempt so hard to walk against the current. And might I add, it can't be done successfully."

Jason thought he'd been doing his best to go along with the system, despite his unique capabilities and his rugged individualism. He loved feeling at one with the brigade during the Academy parades. He felt a powerful connection to the people throughout history who had marched proudly for their country. The band music and precision moves inspired a fierce identification with the traditions of American freedom, with patriotism. On the Navy crew team he loved the sense of unity with the seven other rowers in the shell. And he exulted in racing aboard the Academy yawl, Royono, piping up a wind with his harmonica for superstitious Lieutenant Siatkowski.

The company officer appeared businesslike again. "Return to your studies and resume normal activities here. You won't be reprimanded for insubordination or throwing the bayonet and terrifying a superior officer—not this time."

But Jason heard the warning in his tone.

CHAPTER 52
WRENCHING DECISION

Annapolis
Tuesday, April 2, 1957

"Stand against the current." The lieutenant's words echoed in Jason's mind. After all his hard work to get into this esteemed Academy, Jason now questioned his role here.

Maybe he was the wrong horse for the job. Horses—he loved them, loved riding. He felt like a thoroughbred hunter whose heart is for galloping sure-footed through challenging woodlands, across rough fields and jumping fences. He didn't fit in with race horses trained for flat, groomed tracks. Sometimes, in the east coast society his mother had left behind, he felt like a socially inept, independent woodsman rather than a polished insider. Perhaps he was too independent for the military hierarchy and the Academy. It was a wrenching possibility. One he couldn't get out of his head.

Kloski. The CO back at basic training. Ambition with a mean streak, putting themselves ahead of their men. Sabotaging the advancement of any man who they feared might expose their self-serving orders or incompetence.

Several days later, he requested another appointment with his company officer.

"Sir, I believe my place is elsewhere, that I have a different destiny."

"I'm surprised to hear that. I know how hard you've worked to be here." The lieutenant placed his hands on the desk in front of him. "We believe you'll make a good officer, and will make valuable contributions to the navy. I hope you'll reconsider."

On Saturday, Jason's uncle David flew to Annapolis to take him out for lunch and have a serious talk. During their past conversations, Jason heard stories of patriotism, honor, duty to country and love of freedom. He'd been inspired by tales of sacrifice and leadership and courage.

Jason looked at his godfather across the table in the Carvel Hall restaurant. What fatherly advice was he about to hear? The captain took a swallow of his scotch.

"Jason, I had a call from your superiors. They want you to continue at the Academy. You got away with breaking Kloski because your extraordinary skills make you a prime candidate for the new elite navy Sea, Air and Land team being planned as an outgrowth of UDT."

Jason sat taller. David King had organized, trained and led the Underwater Demolition Teams, during World War II.

"You're as natural a leader as I've ever met. But it's essential for you to fit into the military hierarchy. If you could do that, I'm convinced you could become one of the most skilled and respected officers in the navy."

Jason flushed, flattered by his uncle's observation. The legendary hero believed in him. That made it even harder to explain how he felt.

"I've discovered I'm too creative a thinker to fit into the military system." He sighed. "No matter how hard I try, I'm a loner and I don't know how to stop trying to be the best in everything I do, even at the expense of not fitting in. I've learned my gifts are incompatible with this system. I see why military organizations can't be expected to alter course because of one man's premonitions. And I realize there will always be someone like Kloski over me to try to bring down an individual like myself."

That night while the brigade slept, Jason walked along the seawall beside the Severn River and listened to the wavelets lapping against the rip-rap. His premonitions and visions were incompatible with military thinking; clandestine response to the guidance of his gifts was impossible in a military structure. When he returned to the silent corridors of Bancroft Hall, he knew he was going to have to disappoint the family he loved and who believed in him.

He lay in bed thinking his gifts were a mixed blessing. They seemed perfect for military ops, but in a world that didn't believe in the paranormal, his premonitions just caused doubt and confusion in an otherwise orderly organization.

His life was filled with struggle, but growing up close to nature, in the solitude of the Olympic forests, he'd seen extraordinary order, came to feel he was part of that order and that his life had a purpose. He was being readied for something special—some unusual mission that required a unique combination of talents. It was a truth that he and his brother alone could know. An unrealistic code that they alone had to live by.

Several weeks later, Jason met with Sybil in her usual weekend room in Carvel Hall. At supper in the dining room, her eyes sparkled.

"When my work for the Russian Embassy is over, I want to create a legitimate institute where PhDs in Sexology will teach the secrets of rewarding sex."

He recalled the fun they'd had while she learned what he'd been taught. "I applaud your vision."

"I've observed that in America, innovation and hard work can reap success."

Her left hand rested on the tablecloth and he covered it with his. "I believe in you."

This was their last rendezvous before his final exams, and her laughter-filled new bedtime skills made it memorable. About midnight, they fell into an exhausted sleep.

Jason awoke quietly from his usual escape nightmare—this time taking the bicycle in the Korean village and peddling, heart in throat, down the mountain by the light of the half moon. He reached for Sybil. Nothing.

He saw a crack of light under the bathroom door. He didn't move.

After a half hour, the light went out. In the dim illumination from a street lamp below the curtained window, Jason watched Sybil open the door. She placed a book under the clothing in her overnight bag, and rejoined him in bed, careful not to disturb him. Jason tried to make his breathing sound as if he were still in a deep sleep. Soon her breathing complemented his.

When he was convinced her sleep was genuine, he rose as if to go to the bathroom, and slipped a hand in her bag to take the book on the way. He closed the door, turned on the light, and sat while he checked out what she'd been reading. *Reveille for Radicals,* by Saul Alinsky, copyright 1946. He hardly paused as he slipped the book back under her clothing in the bag and slid into bed, cuddling her.

"Mercy," she said in an exhausted voice, and slept on.

* * *

After passing his final exams in May, Jason resigned from the Naval Academy, receiving an honorable discharge. It was a wrenching decision. The Academy officers tried to dissuade him, and he knew part of him would always regret leaving. Still, he was a survivor. He would continue to serve God and country, but in his way, no one else's.

PART IV

WAR NEUROSIS

CHAPTER 53
STARTING OVER

Kirkland, Washington
Friday, June 7, 1957

"I'll take the year-old black Buick Rivera with the red leather seats and stainless trim interior." Jason pulled out his checkbook. "How much?"

"The price is $500, but you're planning to pay everything now?"

"Yes, if a local check's alright."

"Wait a moment, please?" The salesman stepped into the office. He returned smiling. "The owner says since you're paying up front, it's $400."

Jason had just moved back into his parents' house in Lakeview at the south end of Kirkland. Funny, he still thought of it as their house. The dock looked barren without the wooden sailing yacht tied there, but he'd sold it before going east. Low-maintenance fiberglass boats were all the rage now.

The professional cleaning and grounds service he hired to spruce up the house and property had done such a fine job, all he needed to do was to stock it with groceries and supplies.

Ever since he'd decided to leave Annapolis, Suki had been on his mind. He assumed she'd reached Vancouver safely and was moving forward with her plans to settle in the United States. He had fully accepted her insistence that their relationship was only for a season, that they had different destinies, but he still wanted reassurance that she was okay.

Megan had written to him at the Naval Academy to say everything was working out with Rufus, and they were blissfully happy. He'd written back, pleased for both of them and for the rewarding closure for himself.

He bought some heavy wooden lawn furniture and spent hours by the dock, looking out over the lake to Mount Rainier, reading and thinking—trying to reassess his life and create a plan.

He'd only been home a few days when he found an envelope had been slid under the kitchen door while he was down at the dock. His name was penned in calligraphy on the elegant parchment. There was a line drawing too, a sailing junk towing two small boats and starting to change course to leave the company of a modern sailing yacht.

Jason raced out the door and up the driveway to the road, but saw nothing out of the ordinary. Wait. A taxi pulled out from behind a parked car and began turning around. He sprinted towards it, waving the letter. When the taxi was sideways to him, he spotted the passenger in the back, by the window. Hyo. Jason stopped running and bowed deeply, his hands holding his forearms. Hyo raised a hesitant hand as the taxi sped off. Jason smiled. Hyo had kept what Suki had referred to as his warlock's braid, which extended well below his waist. Jason hurried back to the house, eager to read the missal from Suki.

Beloved,

This is to let you know the three of us are well, and that all has gone as planned. We are Americans in the United States of America, free to live as we will.

Freedom to live without boundaries still takes our breath away. It is a concept so unbelievable it remains difficult for us to grasp the wonder of it.

Fate has sent the man into my life whom I will respect and serve all my days and nights. Like you, his passionate mind and body set me on fire, and keep me there.

We live on a grand estate where he manages his affairs and we love, read, exchange ideas, work, ride horseback, swim, hike and share the fullness of life.

It is with sympathy I watch your lonely struggles. I can tell you, your stars are in alignment so good things will happen for you in the foreseeable future. But then, I fear you will be tested greatly!

Keep your faith, Jason. You have much to accomplish.

Your Princess,

S.

Throughout the afternoon Jason sat by the dock with Suki's letter in hand, reading it over and over, thinking about his exquisite past with her. And the formidable future he seemed fated for. In Korea, Suki had assured him there was a remarkable woman being prepared to be at his side—just not Suki herself. Oh God, how he'd love to meet that woman.

Meanwhile he'd try to live a normal life for a time, even if it was an illusion. He wanted to be able to earn a living, so he signed up at the Forestry School at the University of Washington. On a clear day he could see the university stadium from his house, to the southwest across Lake Washington. When his credits arrived from the Naval Academy, the Forestry School would determine his course requirements.

In the interim, he found a summer job with the State Forestry Headquarters in Forks, on the Olympic Peninsula. He rummaged through the back of his closet for the logger's boots and tin pants he'd not worn since he'd left home for the army. The tough canvas britches protected him from the rough underbrush and the steel calks in the boot soles enabled him to trek across tree trunks that lay like trestles high above impenetrable windfalls on the ground.

Jason was ready to reconnect with the forests and to hang out with some of the people he grew up with in Forks and Port Angeles. He longed to return to the Upper Hoh River Valley and looked forward to revisiting old Virgil, who'd carved out a small farm deep in the rain forest and fermented blackberry wine in the attic of his cabin. It was Virgil who'd shared his experience as a woodsman and hunter with the admiring son of a Scottish logger.

Forks was known as the logging capital of the world. Jason hoped that when he emerged from the woods on the weekends, one or two interesting single women would be free to spend time with him.

CHAPTER 54
FORKS, WASHINGTON

On Friday afternoon Jason reported to the State Forestry Headquarters, where he met Isabella, the cheerful dark-haired secretary. "Izzy" greeted him warmly and introduced him to the forest engineer in charge. Jason met the rest of the experienced crew he would be working with and reflected on Izzy's bare wedding ring finger, her bright look and spare energetic figure. He decided it could be a good summer.

After settling into the ranger station bunkhouse, Jason drove his Buick out the Sitcum-Solduc road to Virgil and Reeva's homestead up in the western foothills of the Olympic National Forest. The last part of the way wound through imposing trees on two tracks better suited for Virgil's old military jeep. When the trail broke out into a hay-filled meadow, he followed the track to the small one-story log cabin, and was glad to see that Virgil's open-topped blue jeep was there.

Reeva was sitting on her porch rocker, snapping beans in a large bowl on her lap. Her collie, Buck, stood protectively by her side. When she saw who was getting out of the shiny black car, she broke into a welcoming smile.

Jason leapt up the three steps onto the porch and gave Reeva a bear hug while Buck's enthusiastic tail-wagging made the dog prance for balance. As Jason greeted Buck, he saw Virgil striding up from the tool shed.

The grizzled woodsman stood his ever-present hunting rifle by the front door and extended a hand. "Thought you were away in the Navy."

"No more, Virgil. I've decided to transfer to Forestry School back here. Trying to follow in my father's footsteps."

Reeva bade them "set" while she fixed some "refreshment."

Virgil sat silently, looking out over his homestead. He didn't speak often, but when he did, his observations were sometimes profound.

"Sorry to hear about your parents' accident. I remember when your father came here to check out business prospects in the logging business. Then with all the demand for lumber during World War II, everyone prospered. I liked working for him once I could figure out what he was saying in that strange Scottish way of his. Only man who ever paid me to teach what I love most—forest life."

Jason sat quietly, enjoying the view with Virgil, listening to the subtle cacophony of forest sounds being carried to them on gentle breezes. After a while, Jason spoke. "I had to escape in the mountains of Korea with half an army hunting me. The only reason I made it was the training John Huelsdonk passed on to you that you shared with me while my parents lived in Forks."

"Glad it worked out for you. Sometimes I felt you listened to the forest even better than I did."

They sat in comfortable silence, each reflecting on the past.

The Upper Hoh River Valley was a lush world of its own—noted for twelve feet of rainfall a year, more than anywhere in the continental United States. In this temperate rainforest, timber grew so fast that areas which had been harvested three times since the 1800s already stood tall again as healthy mature forests.

Virgil had spent much of his life working and hunting with John Huelsdonk, the Olympic Peninsula's most famous pioneer. In 1892 John and his wife Dora were the first settlers to homestead on the Hoh River. The Huelsdonk cabin was seventeen miles from Forks, and for thirty years there were no roads—not even trails fit for pack animals. Everything had to be back-packed in on foot.

Hired by hunters, surveyors, timber cruisers and geologists, John earned the pay of two men for carrying heavy backpacks and equipment weighing up to two hundred pounds. He was called the "Iron Man of the Hoh." In time he became so successful at trapping fur-bearing animals and hunting predators for state bounties imposed to protect the Olympic elk and deer that he became a legend.

Jason recognized that most people today weren't aware of John's respect for the interconnectedness of all life. He had passed that on to Virgil and to a very young Jason, open to the ways of the wild. John told him, "To live here we've had to compete with the trees and wild animals to have space to build our homes and establish our crops and access roads. When we live in the forest, it speaks to us a thousand little ways. I don't think Virgil or I ever took the life of a tree or animal we didn't respect and send on to its maker with appreciation."

With gratitude Jason realized how much he'd relied on that training throughout his escape from North Korea—listening to the forest telling him in many voices the way ahead was safe. It was the silence of those forest voices that signaled danger.

* * *

Jason had hired on to spend the summer as part of a five-man survey team establishing benchmarks and mapping the first of a series of logging roads into the virgin timber of the Olympic National Forest. That meant cutting a trail while back-packing everything they'd need to establish a base camp from which to operate for five days at a time.

Their first day out, he noticed that the camp cook, a retired logger and the oldest man on the team, was clearly overburdened. During a rest stop, Jason quietly shifted the man's heavy bedroll to his own pack.

When they arrived at the pre-selected base camp site, five miles deep in the forest, he saw why the bedroll was so heavy. It contained three number ten cans of peaches for the smiling crew.

Throughout the week the team cut trails and pulled chain, crossing ravines and windfalls, calling out transit numbers and marking their maps. Evenings around the dinner-pot over the fire pit prompted tall tales of days gone by and exaggerations of current exploits. Overhead, their meat and dry provisions were well wrapped against mice and hung from tree limbs too small for bears.

Friday afternoon the men packed back out to the truck they'd left at the end of a logging trail, and drove down to the station for the weekend. The cook invited Jason for supper with his wife and stepdaughter.

Jason arrived at the trailer in a pleasant neighborhood, and discovered that Izzy was the stepdaughter. She had divorced several months before and moved back in with her mother and "Cookie". After supper, Jason and Izzy talked enthusiastically. Izzy was trying to learn the truth behind the local Quileute tribal legend that their people were created from wolves by a supernatural transformer.

"I have an appointment tomorrow morning with the head teacher at Quileute Tribal School on their reservation in La Push. It's only twelve miles away. Would you like to join me?"

With that question, a beautiful summer began as Jason encouraged Izzy in her quest to understand the inexplicable—and he sought further to understand the outside forces of his paranormal abilities and destiny.

CHAPTER 55
FORESTRY

His summer in the wilderness reaffirmed Jason's love of the woods and his awe of the ancient trees. The largest Sitka spruce in the world, the hemlocks, Douglas firs and red cedars were home to elk and deer, cougars and bobcats, and the bald eagles that symbolized America. This was home.

He returned to the comfort of his house, happy about the future he anticipated. Back from his first day of classes at the University of Washington, he settled down to study, mug of coffee beside him. He was engrossed in his ecology textbook when he became aware of a vehicle coming down the driveway. Since Korea he'd found himself hypervigilant and jumped up to look out the window. A black-tired white Ford, typical government car, now parking. FBI agent Thomas climbed out of the vehicle.

Jason crossed the room and opened the front door.

"All's well, Jason. Just wanted to stop by in person to see how things are working out." His eyebrows arched. "Whether perhaps you've given thought to a career in the FBI?"

Jason ushered him into the living room. "Coffee?"

"Black. Thanks."

Jason sat in a chair facing the agent. "We both know Ivan and his cohorts have been leaving me alone. I'm still resolved to help stop the Russians in this Cold War, but I'm too independent for a career in any highly structured setting. I believe I've made a wise decision. I can develop my own logging business, providing needed jobs and products we don't have to import, all with a strong preservation focus."

Thomas took a swallow of coffee. "Sounds like you've made a good choice."

"I'm concerned that Americans are taking their resources for granted." Jason thought about Rachael's conservation concerns, back in Scotland. "Did you know the Scottish Highland moors once were forests?"

Thomas looked surprised.

"Or that South Korea has been stripped of all trees, with just a small woodland park remaining? It's patrolled by soldiers with orders to shoot anyone taking so much as twigs from the ground. Americans could take a lesson from that bit of history."

Thomas pressed his lips together and nodded in agreement.

"I love the sea, and was always torn between the navy and the woodsman's life I already knew." Jason rolled his shoulders back in a stretch. "I want to make a good living, and I'm probably best equipped to learn tree harvesting methods that will conserve the forests and wildlife. Eventually I'll get married and buy another boat for cruising Puget Sound and Alaska."

He looked directly into Thomas's eyes. "Since I have enough income from my father's estate to continue my studies on the GI Bill, the first step is forestry school and a bachelor's degree." But he did wonder what trials would test him along the way.

"Good plan. I'll expect you to continue your monthly calls. The Korean DMZ remains a hot spot and State hasn't forgotten your incident in North Korea. Soviet communism is more a threat than ever." The agent rose. "Meanwhile, study hard, and don't forget time out to have a little fun."

* * *

For the next two years, on campus and in town, Jason kept an eye out for the person who might become the wife Aunt Rachael said he needed, the one Suki said would be his. He enjoyed the company of a young divorcé who loved dancing and became best friends with him. He spent time with a charismatic graduate who had her own children's television show. And he went horseback riding with a sweet gal whose dad owned a cattle ranch in Goldendale. He cherished these relationships, but eventually each woman recognized his destiny was a world apart from one that would fulfill her dreams.

CHAPTER 56
RECRUITED

Kirkland, Washington
Saturday, September 5, 1959

Jason inhaled the sweet scent of fresh cut grass. He enjoyed mowing his lawn. It gave him time to think. With only three college quarters left to earn his degree, he could scarcely wait to build his forestry business. It seemed the blackmail was working and Ivan was no longer a personal threat, although Jason remained concerned about his brother's role in the Cold War.

When he stopped mowing to wipe the sweat from his brow, he heard the phone ringing. He ran up the slope and into the kitchen.

"Agent Thomas, here."

What could the FBI want now? Jason had made his monthly check-in call less than a week ago.

"Jason, I need to meet with you in person. Today. Can you do that?"

Jason wondered at the urgency in Frank's normally deliberate manner. "Where?"

"Meet me at the University Arboretum. I'll be in corduroys and a sweater, trying to look like a professor. How soon can you be there?"

"It's Saturday, no problem parking. I need a quick shower. Forty-five minutes."

* * *

Driving into the city, Jason imagined a dozen different scenarios, none of which he wanted anything to do with. He spotted the "professor" strolling back and forth at the top of a grassy hill near the parking area. Reserved as always, Agent Thomas simply said, "We'll walk down the hill towards the lake while we talk. It's a good open space. We can see if anyone is close enough to overhear us."

Thomas appeared to be admiring the trees beyond Jason as he spoke in a quiet voice. "How would you like free room and board a few blocks from school? Save you that hour you spend every morning getting to the Forestry School and looking for a space during the parking rush. A studio-room on the second floor of a boarding house, with parking for your car? It's on Northeast Forty-fifth Street near Roosevelt Way, a pleasant walk to the University."

Why the odd offer? What was the agent not telling him? Jason squinted as he looked into the man's face and answered cautiously. "Why would the government want to provide my housing? After two years back here you need to keep closer track of me?"

Thomas surprised him by showing a trace of amusement at the edges of his eyes. "Don't flatter yourself. We've leased the apartment to keep an eye on a man who owns the house next door." He gazed around at the trees. "A university student working assorted hours at a desk facing windows overlooking the man's property would work very well for us right now." He handed Jason a black-and-white photograph. "Here's a surveillance picture of the man and his family."

Jason studied the photo of a broad-shouldered man, who towered over two women with noticeably attractive figures and hair. He handed the picture back. "Sorry. You've seen where I live. Why would I give all that up? What's wrong with using one of your own people?"

Thomas looked uncomfortable. "Jason, I'm in trouble. I've known you long enough to believe you're trustworthy. May I tell you something in confidence?"

Jason had experienced enough trouble in his life. He wasn't about to get dragged into some FBI operation. "I'd prefer you didn't. Especially if it means moving into a boarding house with rules. You know I'm a loner. My own house is just right for me and my social life. Surely there are other people you can call on." Jason turned on his heel to head back up the hill.

"Jason . . ."

The tension in Thomas's voice made Jason stop. He turned to face the agent.

"Since I was promoted to Special Agent-in-Charge of the State Division four months ago, I've uncovered a serious problem at my headquarters office."

Jason's stomach knotted. Maybe doing this job for the FBI was a ploy; maybe *he* was a target. He zeroed in on Thomas's eyes. "Does that mean my cover's blown? I'm in danger?"

"No. No, nothing like that. Nobody knows about you but me, and I keep your file in a safe that can only be opened by me and, in an emergency, J. Edgar Hoover's appointee."

Relieved, Jason looked at a patch of bright blue in the cloudy sky, but he didn't drop his guard. "Then what's your problem?"

"It's quite awkward, really." Thomas shifted his feet on the grass. "A cherubic looking woman has started appearing at parties my men attend. Apparently, she's the most blatant seductress the men have ever encountered—and she's managed to get information out of the best of them. Says she's fascinated by FBI men and her passion in life is to bed every agent in the country who'll have her. Even worse, the stores across the street from headquarters have apartments on the upper floors and she's rented one overlooking our entrance on Third Avenue. She could even photograph everyone going in and out of our building. Which is why I need help from someone who can't possibly be connected to the Bureau."

I've got to nip this in the bud. "I really don't want to get involved. And if I did," Jason laughed, "I'd prefer it be to take the seductress off your hands."

Agent Thomas's lips compressed into a thin line, so Jason dropped his attempt at humor.

"The fact is, every time I tried to do something for my country through the military, I wound up with my neck in a noose. Why should federal agencies be any different?" He paused. "Already I'm getting a bad feeling about this. No. Get someone else. There are a lot of G.I. vets at the university who'd jump at the opportunity to help in exchange for free room and board. Why not one of them?"

"This is too important, Jason. I need someone I know I can trust. Right now, that only leaves you. Everything tells me you're the man for this job."

Jason struggled to remain patient. "You can't help out any starving G.I. student—trust any of them? Then, what about an agent from Ohio or Michigan who can pose as a student?" He turned again to leave. "Let's go. Mr. Hoover can send you someone."

"No. If anyone checks, you're already an established student. You're perfect for this surveillance task. And so is the timing—the start of the fall semester, when a student would move into an apartment for the school year. " He tapped Jason on the shoulder. Jason wheeled around and their eyes met. "Don't make me beg."

Jason reached for the photograph and studied it again.

"We're only interested in the man," Thomas said. "He recently married the taller woman, a widow from an old Seattle family that owns a popular waterfront restaurant. She's already borne him an infant son. The teenager is his stepdaughter. He's away for long periods."

Jason looked up from the picture. "What's your interest?"

"If you knew any more, you might give yourself away."

Jason didn't want to get trapped into working for a bureaucratic government organization. "Exactly what do you want me to do, besides noticing what goes on outside my windows? Is this guy dangerous?"

"Just keep your eyes open. Assume he's dangerous. Report when he's around. Report anything suspicious. We just want you to live as usual, do what you normally would. There's a secure phone in the nightstand drawer that connects directly to our switchboard and can't be tapped without alerting us. And I'd expect you to continue reporting to me how you're doing."

Jason thought awhile. It wasn't the way he wanted to serve his country, but the assignment shouldn't rob him of his independence, and his gifts might enable him to aid the FBI in a unique way. He extended his hand. "Okay. I'll give it a try."

As they shook hands, the premonition came—and Jason felt with terrible certainty that he'd just entered a portal which somehow could redefine his life forever.

CHAPTER 57

SURVEILLANT

Seattle, Washington
Monday, September 7, 1959

Jason moved into the room in the boarding house on Labor Day and kept an eye out for his next-door neighbors. The tall woman looked like a model and occasionally worked in her garden in the morning. The sixteen-year-old daughter was a shorter carbon-copy of her mother. When he saw them working outside in the mild autumn weather, Jason couldn't help appreciating their natural beauty. It was two months before he saw the husband—all six feet six inches of him. Slender, exceptionally wide-shouldered, muscular, with craggy features under a shock of brown hair.

The man just hung out with the wife and stepdaughter, and didn't seem to have a job. One day Jason was working on his car when the husband strolled over and introduced himself.

"I'm Leif Olsen." He extended a hand.

Jason noted the Scandinavian name and the trace of an accent. He shook hands firmly. "I'm studying forestry at the university."

The man wanted to talk and even offered useful advice as Jason continued timing the engine of his Riviera.

"Thanks for your suggestions," Jason said, and looked out from under the hood. "You know a lot about engines."

The man smiled. "Have to if you operate a workboat. Summers, I'm a deep sea diver in Alaska."

"Now *that* interests me." Jason shut off the engine and unclipped the timing light, to begin pumping the man with questions.

"I have a business raising liberty ships torpedoed off the Aleutians during the Second World War."

"The Bering Sea? That water's freezing, even in summer."

"We sell them for scrap. It's good money."

"Where do you refuel?"

"Port of Wales, on the Seward Peninsula."

Jason knew that was just sixty miles across the Bering Strait from the Russian mainland. He was fascinated by Leif's work and the possibility he might learn something useful for the FBI, until he remembered he had to go study for tomorrow's exam.

Leif asked, "How'd you like to come for a nice home-cooked supper and meet my family sometime next week? Would Monday work for you?"

Jason jumped at the opportunity. Maybe he'd get something for Agent Thomas.

* * *

The beautiful wife was named Ann, the look-alike daughter was Heather, and the proud father introduced his son as Little Leif. Ann took Monday nights off from running her restaurant, and this evening she served a chateaubriand with an excellent Beringer Brothers red wine.

Heather devoted most of her attention to helping her mother and caring for her baby half-brother, and Leif regaled Jason with his past summer's tale of woe. Leif and his crew ran into so many problems raising the sunken liberty ship, that they'd been late in the season for towing it to their client in Japan. Leif's ocean salvage tug and its tow were clobbered by a storm with huge seas. The hawse jerked taut against the massive towing bitt with such force it opened the tug's afterdeck. Leif had to tack-weld plating over it, while tied with safety lines to keep from being swept overboard. He told his story with humor and Jason laughed frequently. He noticed the women wore fixed smiles, but assumed they'd heard all this a few times before. Leif's towing predicament turned even more dangerous when the hawse got wrapped in the tug's enormous propeller. Then the liberty ship started to sink rapidly and Leif had to jump into the frigid sea and cut the hawse with a hacksaw to keep it from dragging the salvage tug down with the ship. By the end of the evening's sea stories, Leif had a true admirer in Jason—who now was as curious as the FBI to know more about this man.

Jason never knew why Leif wanted his friendship, but was lonely and flattered by the attention. Leif seemed fascinated with Jason's Scottish and American ancestry. Sometimes it was hard for Jason to think of himself as a surveillant who had to remain objective about a man he admired and whose company he enjoyed. Leif's friendship seemed genuine and Jason got only positive vibes from him.

Frequently when Jason was outdoors, washing his car or simply returning to his apartment, Leif dropped by to see him. If Heather was home from school, she accompanied her stepfather. She always carried Little Leif and focused on him, never speaking unless addressed. Ann might join them in the morning, but in the afternoons and evenings she managed her restaurant. Jason admired their family closeness and had nothing significant to report to Agent Thomas.

* * *

In December, when his first quarter exams were over, Jason decided to teach himself to type and bought a used Smith-Corona portable. He thought he was doing pretty well, until the January afternoon he walked past Leif's house and through an open window heard someone rat-a-tat-tatting at tremendous speed on the keys of a typewriter. He knocked on the door. It was Heather at a new Royal portable her stepdad had bought her for Christmas.

"I want to type like that. How did you learn to be so fast?"

Leif answered for her. "Let Heather teach you, Jason." He seemed eager to be helpful and turned to his stepdaughter. "You can do that, can't you, honey?"

She looked up from her work. "I've still got my exercises from typing class at school. I could set Jason up with those and give him some pointers a couple of afternoons a week."

"Well, how about that, Jason?" Leif was enthusiastic. "Can't get a better offer than that."

"Are you sure it wouldn't be too much trouble?"

"Of course not." Leif smiled broadly. "That would be okay with you, wouldn't it, honey?"

"Of course, Leif. Should I get them now?" Heather's brown eyes seemed strikingly large in her petite face.

"Why not?"

She carried her typing books to Jason's, started him on the exercises, and left.

Heather came to coach him for an hour every Tuesday and Friday afternoon. Jason worked steadily and became quite proficient.

He reported to Agent Thomas, "Nothing for you, but a perk for me. My typing's great, thanks to Leif and Heather."

"Don't let your guard down," Thomas warned.

Early in March, after two months of lessons, Jason wanted to repay Heather, but Leif said no, so Jason took the family out for supper on a Monday, when Ann could join them. Heather seemed withdrawn, and Jason tried to include her in the conversation.

"Heather, I never notice you with other young people. Why is that?"

She looked tense. "I have to baby-sit my brother."

"Sure, but what do you do for recreation?"

"I read books. And I belong to a ballroom dance group after school. I love dancing."

Jason grinned. "That's what *I* do to relax. I go to a dancehall with several other students who love dancing, too, and we dance till we drop. Fast Viennese waltzes, polkas, tango, foxtrot, jitterbug, Charleston, you name it." He hesitated, then asked, "Would you like to join us some Friday night? I could take you, bring you home."

Heather looked at Jason with startled eyes and then cautiously at Leif.

Leif said nothing.

"She'd love that!" It was Ann's enthusiastic voice. "How about next Friday? Wouldn't that be lovely, dear?"

"Yes. That would be good," said Heather, looking down at her plate.

That'd be good for me, too, Jason thought, wondering if he could learn anything about Leif from his stepdaughter, information that might be valuable to Agent Thomas. It was doubtful, but worth a shot.

CHAPTER 58
WOLVERINE

Seattle, Washington
Friday, March 11, 1960

Jason knew that Heather would be one of the prettiest young women at the ballroom, but was surprised to find her rigid in his arms and a disaster as a dancing partner. She tried to get through a slow foxtrot with him, finally gave up and left to make a call at the payphone. He watched her cross the room in her blue satin, off-the-shoulder dress with a flared skirt, and gold high heels, and wondered if he made her nervous. When she returned, her mouth twitched and she stared down at her shoes. "We have to go. Leif wants me home right away."

Something was terribly wrong. Jason held out his arm to escort her from the dancehall.

Once in the car, Heather begged, "Please drive as fast as you can!" She sounded panicky and broke down crying.

The stores in the block ahead were closed for the night. Jason pulled his Buick into the row of empty parking spaces, turned off the engine, twisted to face her on the bench seat and said firmly, "All right, Heather. It's time to get a grip and tell me what's going on. We're not going anywhere until you do." He reached out and tried to blot her tears with his handkerchief.

She batted his hand away. "My baby brother's in danger. Leif's threatening to kill him if I don't get home right away and I think he's crazy enough to do it this time. Jason, you've got to get me home as fast as you can!"

Jason didn't move. Nothing he was hearing made any sense. "Why would he want to hurt his own son?"

Hysterical now, she knelt on her side of the seat facing Jason so her youthful cleavage showed in the scoop-neck dress as she screamed, "Don't you *see*? Doesn't *anybody* see? *That's his hold on me!*"

"Hold? For what?" *Oh, my God!* Leif was forcing himself on his stepdaughter and using her little half-brother as a hostage. Jason's face flushed hot while hers turned red in the streetlight as she hid it in her hands.

Naïveté about this kind of family situation had blinded Jason's usual instincts. Now they were fully functional. All his admiration for Leif morphed into blind fury. For the first time in his life his hands shook uncontrollably. He sprang into action, grabbed the keys from the ignition and rushed to a store-front payphone. Hands still shaking, he fumbled a nickel into the slot and dialed the FBI Seattle headquarters.

"FBI."

"This is Jason MacDougall." He shook so hard he could hear the vibration in his voice. "Tell Agent Thomas Leif Olsen's gone crazy and I'm racing to his house with Heather as fast as I can to stop him from harming his baby son."

Jason slammed the receiver down on the hook and ran to the trunk of the car. He grabbed the tire iron, slid back into the driver's seat as he handed his weapon to Heather, started the engine and raced out into traffic, passing vehicles recklessly, honking, bumping cars, screeching around corners, going up on the sidewalk, causing cars to collide— anything to get the attention of the police and get back in time to save the child. *Damn, where are the police when you need them?*

"There's more," Heather shouted over the roar of the engine.

"You don't have to tell me. I believe you."

"No. I mean *more!* I think he's a Russian spy." She paused. "He's dangerous. He works out every day like some kind of trained killer. He has guns and a dagger."

It all made sense. Leif's work in the Bering Straits, Heather's obsession over her half-brother, her lack of a teenage social life because of her controlling, incestuous stepfather. A manipulative spy. Like

Milton's Satan, Leif possessed every admirable quality, yet, by some cruel fluke, was driven to serve evil. Jason was about to confront that evil. Wired for the danger, he deliberately focused on cool control.

"Okay, Heather. Dry your face and calm down. We're a block from the house. I'm slowing to a normal speed. We'll drive up like ordinary people. Then I'll help you from the car and walk you to the front door. You'll be on my right side. Just act normal. But carry the tire iron in your left hand, concealed in the folds of your skirt, and be ready to put it in my right hand when I reach out to you. The door latch is on the left and opens in. If he has a weapon, throw yourself to the right on the porch."

"Don't let him get you, Jason." She sounded terrified. "He'll kill us. He's a wolverine."

"I know that now. Trust me."

As they approached the front door, pretending to chat and laugh, he saw Leif peering through the window blinds. Jason made sure Leif could see there was nothing in his hands. When Leif left the window to unlatch the door, Jason reached out for the tire iron and Heather smoothly transferred it to him. Suddenly the door was flung open and Leif's right hand shot out to thrust a dagger into Jason's heart.

Jason rotated his chest to his left and backwards, out of the way, knocking Heather sprawling on the porch, while he brought the tire iron up in a blinding-fast blow to Leif's elbow. Leif screamed and dropped the dagger. With all his strength Jason swung the iron up again, between the man's legs. Leif turned white. Then Jason deliberately broke the villain's jaw with the tire iron.

Before Jason could turn to help her, Heather was scrambling over Leif's unconscious body in the doorway and dashing to the baby's room. Jason pulled their adversary aside, closed the door and locked it.

When he joined Heather with the baby, she was holding her little brother and comforting him. She looked at Jason with such defenseless humility and thankfulness, he felt ashamed to have seen so deeply into her soul.

But his job wasn't finished. "Heather, I need line to tie him up."

"In the storeroom, off the kitchen."

Returning with the line and a sharp kitchen knife, Jason bound Leif's hands and feet securely. He then opened the man's mouth to clear out several broken teeth so he wouldn't choke on them. The man's jawbone and elbow were shattered. Leif's pulse was erratic and when Jason checked his eyes, they were rolled back. *Not good. I really lost it for a second.*

CHAPTER 59
HEATHER'S INFORMATION

Seattle

Friday, March 11, 1960

Jason's breathing was still heavy. "Did you see what's in the fireplace?" He stared at Heather's partially burned typewriter in its white case and the baby's burned clothes and toys. "You really did save Little Leif."

Jason turned to look in the nursery, where Heather was cleaning up the baby in his crib. "Brave girl. Are you okay?"

She pressed her lips together and nodded.

"I assume your mother knows nothing."

Heather let out a sob. "She worked so hard for years after my father left and seemed so pleased to be remarried, I didn't want to ruin her happiness." She blew her nose. "Besides, I was too embarrassed to talk about it ... ashamed. And scared." She tried to reuse her Kleenex and Jason handed her his handkerchief. "Then Leif began threatening that if I told Mom he'd use me and her baby to control her like he used the baby to control me. He's crazy."

Jason boiled with anger, but he needed to learn all he could about this man she claimed was a Russian spy. "Can you tell me more about Leif?" He tried to put a reassuring hand on Heather's arm, but she drew away, hugging herself.

"Sometimes he got drunk and mean, then hurt me ... inside, where it didn't leave marks. He threatened to kill me if I cried out, to take me where no one could hear me. He threatened to hurt the baby, too." Heather shuddered, hugged herself and stared at her brother in his crib.

By now Jason realized it wasn't so much Leif's lustful craving for sex as the man's obsession with domination and control. But Heather still hadn't revealed why she thought he was a Russian spy.

After a long moment, she fixed her eyes on Jason's. "Last week when I got home from school, he was drunk, speaking a foreign language. It sounded like the Russian you hear on TV news." She glanced at the fireplace and squeezed her eyes shut, as if to deny the reality.

"The day after you took us out to supper, he got really drunk once Mom left for work. When I got home from school, he bragged that soon all American women would be free for any Russian soldier to use like he used me. Spoils of war, he called it. He mumbled a lot."

Heather fell silent and Jason waited, not wanting to push her too hard and risk having her shut down. Finally he asked gently, "What did he say?"

"Things that sounded like 'keys' ... 'drugs' ...'border' ... 'middle class' ... 'central command' ... crush government ... and something about 'submarine detection devices' ... 'Aleutians.' After that he passed out." She hugged herself again and shivered at the memory.

"The next day I was so scared of what he'd do if he remembered what he'd told me, I kept throwing up. He told Mom it must be stomach flu and I should stay home from school."

Jason didn't need to be told what happened next. It was evident from the look of anger and grief on Heather's face that Leif had abused the poor girl.

"He threatened if I told anyone about our relationship, he'd kill them and take me and my family out on his tug and when he was through with us he'd tie us to weights and dump us in the ocean."

Heather hugged herself and swayed back and forth as she relived the abuse. She sobbed. "Thursday after school was worse. And today was so horrible I almost couldn't get ready to go with you, but I was desperate to get out of here, away from him."

Jason felt his heart thumping. Leif must have been afraid after Ann encouraged Heather to accompany Jason to the dancehall. Must have feared losing his absolute control over his stepdaughter. Thank God the man turned to drink instead of murder on Tuesday.

"He was crazy, getting worse by the day." Heather put her hand to her throat. "You're ex-military and the only person in my life I thought . . ." Her voice trailed off as she sat huddled on the sofa, tears flowing down her cheeks.

Suddenly Jason realized he'd been so enraged with Leif he might be in legal trouble for the damage he'd inflicted. He needed an influential ally. "I've got to make a call immediately." He stepped to the phone on the kitchen counter, picked up and dialed zero. "Operator, I need 202-OLiver-1362. Collect, please. Urgent, from Jason."

When he finished telling Uncle David everything, his godfather said he'd call colleagues in central intelligence. Then Jason phoned the FBI again and was given the duty officer. "Agent Thomas is on the way with backup. Is everything alright, sir?"

"It's over. We need an ambulance. Please hurry." When Jason hung up, he turned and saw Heather, still slumped on the sofa, looking pathetic.

He wanted to reassure her. "I won't even try to imagine what it's like to be in your shoes right now, but I do know you won't have to bear your burden alone any longer. Just know that I respect you for doing everything possible for your little brother. And you pulled it off, did everything right. He's going to be able to have a good life now, thanks to your love and sacrifice."

Eyes glazed, she stared at Jason without saying a word.

"People will be arriving soon. You might want to change into slacks and a shirt. And perhaps pack an overnight bag for you and Little Leif."

Heather nodded and left the room.

Jason stood looking down at Leif. A wave of nausea fogged his vision as he thought about the evil perpetrated on this innocent family by the stranger on the floor. He grew angry with himself for being naive and missing the signs. *How could I have been so dense?*

Then it hit him. His reason for being. His mission. Like a lightning bolt of empowerment that left him dazzled by the clarity of it. When he stopped Leif he performed the first act in the mission he'd been prepared for in life—to stop the Russians—to enter into a battle from which there was no escape this side of death. He'd picked up the gauntlet and fought to protect his countrymen and women. He sensed there would be many unexpected challenges before his job was done. His face flushed hot and cold, alternating exhilaration and fear.

The first car swooshed in silently, with a Cadillac ambulance close behind. No sirens. Followed by another sedan. Jason picked up the tire iron and, holding it behind him, opened the door a crack. He left the safety chain in place and ordered, "Show your ID through the gap."

CIA cards and FBI badges. At least they looked official. "It's Agent Thomas, Jason. Open the door."

He opened the door wide to face their guns and deliberately placed the iron back on the floor, careful to keep his hands visible. The agents were clean-cut types who appeared both competent and respectful. He nodded grimly to FBI Agent Thomas, who apologized. "I was out with my family. It took a few minutes for the duty officer to locate me."

While the two medics checked Leif's vitals, Thomas bent down to feel for a pulse at his neck, then looked at Jason in shocked surprise. "Between this and the other matter I'm seeing you about, I get the impression you don't much like Russians."

So you knew he was Russian.

To the medics Thomas said, "Get this injured one to emergency as fast as you can."

One of the CIA officers told Jason in a quiet aside, "We need to find out what he knows."

Jason called out, "Heather, can you come in here with Little Leif? We have company."

The medics were giving Leif oxygen and strapping him onto a transfer board while Thomas called for another ambulance. The CIA officer carefully bagged the dagger and the .38 semi-automatic Smith and Wesson pistol they found in the back of Leif's belt.

Heather looked pale as she walked in with the baby. One of the medics quietly seated her on the sofa and asked her if she and the baby were alright. Her responses and a quick check of their pulses and eyes appeared satisfactory. He turned to the head CIA officer. "They seem OK."

The officer said to one of his men, "Joe, you go with Mr. Olsen. Don't let him out of your sight. I'll have another officer sent to the hospital to join you. I want to know if doctors think we'll be able to interrogate him eventually." The medics left swiftly with their patient and the CIA officer.

CHAPTER 60
INESCAPABLE DESTINY

Seattle
Friday, March 11, 1960

A female FBI agent appeared at the front door with Ann, who looked ashen but in control as she walked over to Heather and the baby. She sat on the sofa holding her children and stared into the fireplace.

An FBI and CIA pair worked to record Jason's story in the living room while another team, including the female agent, took Heather's report in her bedroom. Agent Thomas questioned Jason. "Was it necessary to attack him so viciously? How could you know the girl was telling the truth about him?"

"You mean besides the fact he tried to run a dagger through my heart?" Jason didn't want to mention his premonitions. "I just knew."

"What proof did you have to justify destroying the man like that?"

"Just look in the fireplace. There's your proof."

Thomas looked around. "You couldn't see into the fireplace from the front door. Not while he stood in the entrance, blocking your view."

"Well, I just knew it was him or me if any of us were to live to tell what Heather had learned about his espionage. And I acted accordingly, with the force I felt was necessary."

"You didn't leave much for us to work with. His pulse was erratic. He could be in a coma, the way his eyes are turned back."

"You already have a lot more information than you would if I'd allowed him to kill me." Jason stood. "Why is it you're more concerned about the Russian than the innocent women and child whose lives and happiness he trashed? Where are medics to look after *them*?"

Thomas didn't back down. "I want to know what made you take the law into your own hands and practically kill another citizen. How did you *know*?"

"I just knew." Jason clenched his teeth and turned away.

The agent grabbed his shoulder, spinning him around. Barely in control, Jason looked at the hand on his shoulder then at Thomas, who quickly dropped his hand. "We need to know. It's either here or downtown. Your choice."

Jason paused, thinking. "Alright," he said with a nod. "For a moment, on the way back here, Heather lost it and let me *feel* all her pain and fear, so I simply knew her story was real, without needing more proof." He hesitated. "Sometimes I just know things."

"I haven't forgotten your call from Rhode Island. Jason, you're telling me you're psychic?"

"What, and have you think I'm psychotic? I'm not going down that road with you. Report it as an intuitive judgment call." Jason folded his arms with finality, and noticed the CIA officer writing rapidly.

Then the second ambulance arrived and took Heather and Little Leif to the hospital for a complete checkup. Ann went with them, appearing to need medical help more than her children.

FBI Agent Thomas stayed the night with Jason, on the sofa in his studio-room. The CIA officers wanted to make sure that no one connected with Leif got to Jason.

Thomas said, "I'm sorry I got you into this mess."

Jason answered ruefully, "Take my word for it, it was meant to be. It confirms what my life is about. So in a way, I should thank you."

The agent raised an eyebrow. "More intuition?"

"Something like that."

Jason was curious. Had the FBI known all along that Leif was a Russian?

"I can't tell you what led to our surveillance," Thomas said. "But only when we arrived here at the same time as the CIA did we learn from them he was Russian." He raised a brow and peered at Jason. "The CIA. You have some extraordinary connections."

The next day Agent Thomas informed Jason that Leif had gone into shock and died in the ambulance. Thomas was instructed to deliver the message that there would be no murder charge against Jason and he could begin renting the studio-room for forty dollars a month as long as he wished.

No murder charge? Some thanks.

Thomas reported that as a precaution, Ann, Heather and the baby were moved out of their house and placed in a witness protection program so the Russians couldn't learn what happened to Leif.

Jason felt a guilty relief that the Russians would have no way to trace his involvement. He'd helped uncover a really big covert operation, another Russian Cold War plot. But was he home free? "Do you think there's any way the Russians could learn that I know about their plan, too?"

"I asked Heather that. She didn't know if her stepfather remembered babbling while he was so drunk and she had no way of knowing who he might have contacted while she was in school." Thomas chewed on his lip. "Safest thing is to assume they could suspect you. You could go into witness protection, if you want."

Dark thoughts clouded his thinking. What had he gotten himself into? No, by God! He wasn't going to live like that. His mind cleared.

"I'm going to gamble that even if he remembered blabbing, Leif wouldn't want to admit he got drunk and compromised the subversion project," Jason narrowed his eyes as he looked at Thomas, "so he would have figured he'd take care of his problems on his own."

"That was my thinking." Thomas raised his brow. "But I'd still watch my back. If you feel uncomfortable about any strangers, call me. We'll investigate and provide protection if warranted."

There'd been no threats to his life since Jason had blackmailed the embassy and his brother. But after last night he could be a target, there was no turning back from that. His heart tugged at him to enter the fray, however he realized for the present he had to accept his place on the outside looking in, while others more qualified took over.

Thomas's eyes studied Jason. "If you want to reconsider the FBI Academy once you've completed your bachelor's degree, I'll give you my highest recommendation."

Jason smiled his appreciation. In his heart, he believed his future would always lie outside the conformity of government organizations.

As Thomas left, he handed Jason a book. "This was published two years ago by Mr. Hoover. It's received such bad press, it doesn't sell well in bookstores, so you probably haven't heard about it."

Jason glanced at the cover. *Masters of Deceit: The Story Of Communism In America And How To Fight It*, by J. Edgar Hoover. He thumbed rapidly through the substantive pages with surprise. "Thank you. I didn't know such a book existed. I'll read it today."

The next morning, Jason phoned Thomas on the secure line. "My god, Frank, why isn't Hoover's information about the Communist Party USA in the news every day?"

"I'm afraid some politicians passed the book off as scare tactics by Hoover to coax more money out of Congress for the FBI budget, and a war-jaded population bought the excuse to ignore Hoover's warning."

* * *

Jason kept up his school work, but his thoughts often shifted to his run-ins with Russians. He had to live watching his back at all times—Thomas's advice came from FBI experience. Like most forestry students, Jason wore soft leather lace-up boots under his Levis. But now he carried a heavy, thick-bladed sheath knife in the top of one boot—quickly accessible by hiking his trouser leg a few inches.

Jason wondered if the Russians thought Americans would just roll over for them. As a Russian spy Leif had done unspeakable things to his American family. Korea had been an ocean away, but Leif was right next door in Jason's hometown. In annihilating that enemy Jason knew he'd crossed a threshold beyond which there was no return. With the blackmail he'd been protecting his own life, but now, in his mind, he'd given the Russians notice: No way he'd let them abuse his country and its women. From his perspective, Soviet communism was the antithesis of the brotherhood and equality-for-all it claimed to be. He would do his part to thwart it.

Seated at his desk in the boarding house, Jason's mind focused on the Soviet Union while his eyes read the text of his forestry book. The Cold War was an inescapable reality and the primary concern of everyone involved in foreign policy. He knew that everyday Americans worried about Russia dropping an atomic bomb on the United States and some even built their own bomb shelters. Nevertheless, he felt lonely. It seemed most Americans couldn't—or wouldn't—acknowledge the genuine threat of the more subtle communist goal.

His thoughts turned to Suki. She believed his was an inescapable fate, a dangerous destiny, with the help of a unique woman being prepared for him. It was time for him to find that woman.

CHAPTER 61
CIA INTEREST

Washington, D.C.
Wednesday, March 16. 1960

Walter Higgins' head snapped up as the conference room doors burst open in the E Street headquarters of the CIA.

"Ah, there you are, Walt. I've been looking for you. Am I interrupting anything important?" The Director of Central Intelligence came on in anyway. Even in age the director was slender, wide shouldered, fit and retained his military bearing. The retired admiral was a distinguished man with straight white hair and wore a dark blue jacket, gray flannel trousers and dress Gordon tartan tie.

Higgins stood up from the array of blueprints spread out over the large conference table. As Deputy Director of Operations, he'd been working overtime to keep pace with the constant flow of problems to build a larger, state-of-the-art headquarters facility across the river at Langley. "No, Admiral. Nothing I wouldn't welcome a break from."

He offered a comfortable chair and settled himself into another. Walter Higgins accepted the fact that he looked like the antithesis of his boss, who was his friend and his neighbor in Bethesda. Higgins knew he looked soft, out of shape, with his watery pale blue eyes and wispy, prematurely graying hair. As always, he wore the rumpled tweed suit that made him look like an absent-minded intellectual.

Admiral Zantzinger handed his DDO a folder marked *TOP SECRET, EYES ONLY.* "In here is a file I've just received from J. Edgar Hoover himself. Haven't had time to read all of it, but it's the military records and FBI follow-up of a fellow named MacDougall. He's the nephew and godson of a good friend, Captain David King."

Higgins sat up with interest. "America's first frogman, the demolitions-expert war hero?"

"That's the man." The DCI smiled faintly. "He called me the other night to send officers to an address in Seattle. His nephew had just phoned to say he'd learned of a covert Soviet plot to overthrow democracy in this country, but the Russian spy needed medical attention badly. Unfortunately, the Russian died. The FBI was there, too. Seems the State Department had them keeping tabs on the nephew, because he'd killed a Russian and some North Koreans when he served in Korea."

"What's wrong with that? It's what we were there for, after all."

"Not after the armistice."

Higgins looked sharply at the admiral. "Special ops?"

"No. Just in the wrong place at the wrong time. Kidnapped. Killed his five captors and somehow got back through thirty miles of mountainous terrain with half the North Korean army after him. Trouble is, State's concerned that two of the people he killed would cause this country considerable embarrassment to have to admit to. Costly repercussions, too."

Higgins rubbed his chin. "And then he uncovered a Russian spy in Seattle? How'd that happen?"

"Casual surveillance requested by the FBI." The admiral looked over the top of his horn-rimmed glasses. "And helping a girl."

"Any more surveillance like that and we should recruit him." Higgins chuckled.

The DCI smiled. "Point well taken." He glanced at his watch. "I want you to follow up on the information he passed on to us about Soviet covert operations. Also I want you to assign someone in Seattle for him to report to periodically to be sure he's alright and not at risk of talking." The admiral stood. "By the way, MacDougall was at the Naval Academy in Annapolis. I've just obtained those records, they arrived ten minutes ago." He left the room as abruptly as he'd arrived.

Higgins opened the MacDougall file and became so absorbed in it the blueprints were forgotten.

* * *

Thursday, March 17. 1960

Higgins sat at his desk opposite Officer Julia Shepherd, who was seated in the early morning sunlight that filtered through the window. She was a student of psychology, fresh out of Camp Peary and specialized profile training—the newest member of the DDO's team. She appeared more curious than concerned. She'd been at the top of her class at Vassar, and at the agency, too, in her training as a profiler. One of his doctorates was in psychology and Higgins had chosen her file carefully.

Julia was in the bloom of life—relaxed, confident, eager. Chiseled features set off by an abundance of auburn hair, groomed in a long, smooth pageboy. An athletic body and the crisp movements of a dedicated runner. Pretty and curvy enough to make any normal young man want to cooperate with her questioning. Determined and smart enough to remain in control of the conversation despite the brilliant take-charge mind evident in MacDougall's files.

"I want you to profile a man in Seattle for me. Jason MacDougall. Talk to him extensively. How reliable is he? He's been through a lot. Evaluate his stability. See if he can be trusted. Get facts so we can fill in between the lines. Report back to me personally."

"What makes him so special?"

"Last week he brutally killed a Russian spy, who he'd just learned was forcing his sixteen-year-old stepdaughter to have sex with him. MacDougall also may have specifics about a Soviet covert operation under way on American soil. But there's more. From his Naval Academy records, he appears to have extrasensory abilities. Just recently twelve sailors in Hawaii drowned in a waterspout due to an officer's bad orders—exactly as MacDougall envisioned several years ago when he was at the Academy. The possibility of paranormal abilities is supported by information in his FBI files. Also, he seems to be a survivor of note." Higgins gazed at the material in front of him as he considered the various ways his agency had explored the paranormal, hiring psychics, testing the validity and usefulness of their abilities.

He closed the folder. "Here's our 'Eyes Only' dossier of everything we have on him, plus your vouchers and plane tickets from National to Seattle. You're scheduled to meet with him all day tomorrow. Your return is open-ended. Don't come back without everything we need to know about MacDougall. I want to know if this man could be some kind of divining rod for covert Russian operatives, who the FBI file says may be led by his Russian twin brother."

Julia Shepherd's head jerked back. That twist was a surprise even in the CIA.

"You have this morning to study the material before you return it to me here, then go pack, and catch your plane. Better get started, Officer Shepherd. Use the office across the hall."

As she started for the door, Higgins said, "Miss Shepherd." She stopped and turned back to him.

"I chose you for this assignment as the best person to get information from someone who may be a very complicated subject, but could prove to have invaluable intelligence for us."

"Sir, I'm a beginner here."

"True. But if your psychic abilities are ever going to help us, I think profiling this man is the way to find out. Either MacDougall's becoming a casualty of war, or he's got the ability to be a key player for us. I believe you're the person best suited to find out which. Pay special attention in the report to the part about Dakota's transformation during their traumatic night together." He placed his hands flat on his desk. "But my decisions are not based on what's in your file—or MacDougall's— it's what's *not* in either of your files."

"Sir?"

"How both of you manage to be exceptional overachievers." With an encouraging flick of his wrist, he gestured for her to leave. "Good luck."

CHAPTER 62
ELECTRIFYING INTERVIEW

Mind racing, Julia Shepherd guided the Hertz rental down Jason MacDougall's driveway. Whatever the man she was about to meet had done for Dakota, Julia wanted to explore for her own sake. She knew she was a special person in the making—and she'd come fully open to whatever transforming experience might be had with this intriguing man.

She parked beside the black Buick at the rear of the bungalow-style lakefront property. She wore spike heels to combine feminine allure with the commanding advantage of appearing taller than her five-foot five height. Now she was glad for the flagstone walkway that led across the grass to the front door at the side of the house. She paused to marvel at the majesty of Mount Rainier towering beyond Lake Washington.

Slightly nervous because she was about to meet a man whose stormy past left more questions than answers, she walked slowly, breathing deeply as she emptied her mind to be at her most receptive. She stopped at the front stoop, smoothed her hair and knocked. Standing erect as a ballerina, she listened within.

She imagined floorboards giving under the weight of silent steps, felt a magnetic presence on the other side of the door and held her breath in expectation.

The door opened wide to reveal a powerful man with electrifying blue eyes that saw everything about her—and were a window allowing her to see into his soul, too.

Taken aback, she stood motionless, holding her CIA identification.

Jason MacDougall reached out and held her hand with the ID. As he studied it, she knew that this man could have no secrets from her—or she from him—and that both realized it.

She'd never experienced this two-way connection before—even with her psychic mother. *Good Lord, we're emotionally naked before each other.* The ramifications were so overwhelming she felt dizzy and clutched the doorjamb to steady herself. She felt a strong arm around her waist guiding her to a chair at an elegantly carved dining room table with a view of the lake and mountain. She placed her leather handbag on the chair beside her.

He cleared his throat. In a hoarse half-whisper he said, "What are you that you can see into my soul?"

She couldn't answer, too shaken by the unique experience—and even more unsettled to realize he knew her shock and fear at finding herself so vulnerable. She watched him pour a mug of black coffee and hand it to her. She let the hot liquid burn its way into her stomach, coughed and relaxed her arms on the massive table, trying to control her thoughts.

"I've never been with another psychic before," he said. "I gather you're here to see what demons have been unleashed in me, to see if my information can be of use to the CIA. Am I right?"

She felt faint, and gulped more coffee. "Are you reading my mind?"

"No. It's just that sometimes I get a feeling or thought about a person."

She sensed no fear or malice in him. "It's that way with me too." She took measured breaths to regain control. "No secrets between us. That's scary territory. How do we proceed?"

It took him a while to answer. "How do we cope with naked truth? Respect and sensitivity works for me."

"Sounds like a winner." She wished she hadn't sounded so relieved.

"I need to make fresh coffee. Would you like more?" he said, walking into the kitchen.

"That would be wonderful right now." She bounced up, removed her stylish overcoat, and joined him at the counter that separated the dining room and kitchen.

Expected in this job to capitalize on her striking feminine figure and muscular legs that tapered to trim ankles, she'd been filled with her usual confidence when she dressed today. She wore a short cream-colored wool skirt and matching cashmere turtleneck that emphasized her wide shoulders, her curvaceous breasts and her small waist. She had arranged her thick hair in a loose French braid to give her the worldly look of a woman commanding respect.

As they waited for the coffee to perk, she avoided his eyes and watched the iridescent green-headed mallards feeding on the lawn by the dock. She was embarrassed that he might become aware of her feelings as she found herself becoming uncharacteristically aroused by him.

She wanted to flee this man who could see into her soul, except she'd rather die than fail on her first major assignment. Instead she stood tall and commented on the view out the picture windows, to conceal her feelings and free him to admire her discretely.

When the coffee was ready, she leaned against the counter and took a sip. "I'm sure you're tired of all the questions about what happened with Leif Olsen last week, but please tell me everything, including your feelings." She moved back to the table, where she could take notes.

Jason started pacing. "My feelings? What feelings? I already knew he probably was duplicitous, or he wouldn't be under surveillance." Jason paused. "Actually, I never thought about my feelings before. He was so charismatic, you had to like him—evil son-of-a ... pardon my French ... evil monster that he was. What upset me was being so naive, plus never picking up signals of his true nature—I think because he really liked me."

When he got to the part about stopping Leif's murderous attack, Jason began acting out every move, as she watched him relive the action, breaking Leif's dagger arm with the tire iron, impulsively castrating him, then swinging the iron to break his adversary's jaw.

Suddenly Jason was looming over her. She cringed with a vision of Jason back in North Korea as the last gladiator standing. Standing on the balls of his feet over her—electrified—lusting for a woman to ravish. *Oh my god, he's out of control! And I'm the available woman!*

She saw his eyes reflect her full comprehension and fright—then her flight phase, as she sought avenues of escape. She slipped her hand into the concealed-carry compartment of the handbag beside her. He stood ready to spring, a desperate need in his eyes. Not to cause pain, she now realized. But to deal with some pain of his own ... ? What pain? Intuition told her to ride this beast and learn the answer. She withdrew her hand, empty, from the leather bag.

His need was so strong she found herself caught up in it. His muscles stood out like spring steel.

Feeling both terrified and driven, she kicked off her shoes, rose from her chair and stood before him.

He placed his hand between her breasts and bent her back against the table, pressing her shoulders onto it. His other hand slid under her skirt.

Maybe she should guide him back to the present. "Jason, this is not North Korea. I'm not the enemy. Do you know we're in Seattle and I'm a CIA officer sent to question you?"

Jason stopped abruptly. He took her hand to help her up.

Standing barefoot, the top of her head barely reached his chin. She stared up into his eyes and sensed his confusion while Jason returned from his other world.

His eyes opened wide. "Oh my god, what've I almost done?"

Watching him carefully, she stood as tall as she could. In this surreal scene, she reached out and gently touched his forearm.

CHAPTER 63
RESOURCEFUL PROFILER

Julia wet her dry mouth and lips. Jason stared at her, looking horrified by what he'd done.

Now that she saw he was in his right mind, she knew what she had to do. "I feel your need, Jason. Do what you need to do. What you were driven to. Let me ease your pain." She reached up on tiptoes and hugged him reassuringly, pressing her body into his in offering.

He ran his fingers up the side of her neck, behind her ear. "You're as crazy as I just was. This has to be taboo for an officer."

"This is about national security." She spoke faster. "I'm afraid we've both been set up by my boss. He must know some things about me I'd hoped he didn't. Obviously, he recognized from your file that you're not going to reveal the sort of information about yourself that a psychologist needs to assess the value of your intel. But put you with a real person who has needs too, and that picture might change."

Jason placed his hands on her shoulders and gently pushed her back. "Let me grab a cond—"

"No need. I'm using the latest in protection. She pulled her sweater over her head and dropped the soft cashmere on the floor. Her skirt followed. "I feel your need, Jason. I want to fulfill that need—whatever it takes. We're kindred spirits who can skip the conventional formalities." She unbuttoned his shirt, unbuckled his belt, then added her underthings to the pile on the floor.

Knowing men's fascination with mobile breasts, she watched his eyes fix on her youthful abundance. She unbraided her hair. It cascaded over her shoulders and he combed it with his fingers.

She unfastened his trousers, pulled them down, and gasped at his arousal. Undaunted, she slipped her hands up his chest and slid his shirt off. She wrapped her arms around his neck and melted into him with an open-mouthed kiss.

She was disconcerted by his insight and couldn't pretend she hadn't brought her own desperate personal needs with her. "It's alright, Jason. I'll tell you all about it later. Promise."

He was trembling. She lowered her heels to the floor and looked up into his eyes. *I've got you.* She took his arousal in her hands.

She was startled by the power of his vice-like grip under the sides of her rib cage as he carried her uncomfortably to the back side of a thick-bodied leather easy chair. He seated her atop the thick back and tipped her upper body over backwards.

With her heels pressing into the back of the chair, she glanced behind her and dropped her hands down on the wide leather armrests to support her horizontal body above the seat cushion. Standing between her thighs, Jason released her waist.

She felt his fingers tracing her collarbones and the tendons standing out on her neck from the weight of her unsupported head. "You make great sculpture," he said, caressing her breasts. "God, you've got it all."

"I want you, need you," she said, separating her legs in offering for the assault she had provoked him to continue. She thrilled to his fingers circling her breasts and felt her nipples swell, her body arch in response. Her nostrils flared, as she breathed heavily, but she didn't utter another word, letting nature take its dynamic course in the man.

He stroked her thighs. "Wider," he said in a deep guttural voice, while he probed for her entrance. She was ready, tensed for the unknown. He plunged in.

"Unh!" What she'd expected to hurt didn't. *Oh, god. Thank you.* She knew she was where she had to be. His warm flesh invading hers felt like the fulfillment of things she didn't know she craved. Sensations she didn't recognize—but was starved for. She relaxed the tension in her groin and wiggled her hips to receive all of him she could manage.

Holding his mouth close to hers, he began thrusting the entire length of her. Again and again, as she felt wonder and bliss.

To her dismay, he said, "Come with me."

"Wait," she pleaded. Why could she never have an orgasm with a man? She thought this time would be different. Jason was different and she felt she was almost there with him. She French kissed him and jerked her pelvis to increase her response.

A muffled thunder rumbled up from his depths. "No condom—too sensitive." He held still and she watched his eyes squeeze shut as he fought his orgasm. When his body-wracking spasms began, he grabbed her hips and drove hard into her.

She let out a sharp cry. "Do it! It's alright. Do it, Jason!"

As gasps were torn out of him, she wrapped her legs around his waist to hold him deep while he exploded inside her.

When it was over, he kissed her eyes, her nose, her lips. She found herself crying silently.

He wiped the tears from her cheeks. "I'm sorry. I hurt you?"

"Yes. But *good* hurt. It's not you. It's me. I've never been able to come with any man. God knows I've tried and tried. At Vassar." She laughed scornfully. "I feel I've been screwed in every model of car Detroit ever built. It became an obsession—as if I had to learn the necessary skills to snag a great husband. Unfortunately, it turns out I'm frigid. From something in your file, I hoped you might—"

His upper body jerked away. "My file? What's in my file?"

"Nothing, actually. Something I deduced from a memo that's not part of the typed records. The director had jotted down a few notes. Your godparents told him you changed a girl's life during a single date where assassins tried to kill you. She said you showed her what she *really* had to offer. Your godparents were very grateful, and mentioned it to show how highly they regarded you."

Without warning, Jason began thrusting into her again.

She squelched an involuntary yelp. "Why aren't you soft, like everyone else after coming?"

He grasped her hips. "What are you trying to do to me? First I get so crazy you reach for your pistol, then you change your mind and make me crazy to have you, and now you suggest everything I do or say can and will be used against me!"

She was leaning back, balanced on her hands and arms. "I'm a stranger to you, Jason Steele MacDougall. But you're no stranger to me. I've read your file. Okay, no psychology mumbo-jumbo between us, we'll just be real people. Admit it, you like this. Well, I need it too." She pressed into his thrusts. *My god, I want some of what he's got for the man I marry.* "This is so good. I wish we could keep doing it all day."

"We can," he said. "You're not frigid. You just don't know the secrets."

"Secrets?" she asked. "What secrets?"

CHAPTER 64
SUKI'S SECRETS

Kirkland, Washington
Friday, March 18, 1960

Jason bent over Officer Shepherd's straining body. "Here's the first secret." He whispered in her ear.

She pulled her head back. "You're kidding!" She looked at him askance. "You're serious. It's okay to do that with you?"

"Or any other lover you're with. It's why you're designed the way you are. Sadly, Puritans considered it shameful, and that became our legacy."

Jason smiled as he felt her hand squeezing between their stomachs. He aroused her nipples to taut peaks while she discovered how never again to be wholly dependent on men for her pleasure. Soon her inside muscles began contracting around him.

"Jason," she squeaked, "can't you feel what's happening? Shouldn't you be hammering the daylights out of me?"

But he just continued his long strokes in and out as she kept up her movements, and tensed in ligament-tearing explosiveness with her as she shrieked and jerked her way through her first-ever orgasm with a man. He silenced her with a prolonged kiss. When her release was complete, he deliberately over-squeezed her perky breasts as he kept thrusting into her.

"Please stop. I can't handle any more right now."

"You'll be okay. Just keep doing your part." He kept going.

"I'm getting really tired on one arm, Jason."

"Of course you are. That's the whole point. To stretch yourself."

"Jesus, Jason. It's happening again!"

Afterwards, he kept going, and she laughed weakly, pleading with him to let her rest. He placed his hands at her back and helped her to a sitting position so she could hold onto him. Still thrusting into her, he said, "Squat on the seatback." She pulled one leg up, then the other. He felt both her hands secure against his back. Soon she was moaning and hammering down over him until they exploded again, masking their shouts with open-mouth kisses. Jason whispered in her ear, "You just had a deeper orgasm. You're anything but frigid."

"I feel so stupid. It's as if I was given a car to go wherever I want, but everyone raised me to believe I wasn't allowed use the accelerator. I let myself be limited to where men chose to drive me. In my own car, no less."

"Good analogy."

"So that's why the Kinsey Report on men was so popular, and the one on women turned people against him." Officer Shepherd pressed her lips together. "The old double standard. Our inhibited culture thought women should be passive and ignorant. What hypocrisy!"

"Do you want to get down now?"

Laughing, she wrapped her legs around him and said in a breathy voice, "I feel giddy and unstoppable. Dance with me, Jason."

And he did, across the living room.

"No, no. Not a waltz. I want to polka."

He looked into her excited eyes. "Are you sure?"

"Yes. Yes. A high-stepping polka. With lots of crazy bouncing. Hammer city, understand?" She gave him a determined look. "Don't worry. I feel indestructible."

So he leapt around the living room while they laughed hysterically, seeming oblivious to discomfort, until she came again—and he with her. Finally, breathing heavily, he flopped them onto the leather sofa, with himself on top, held by her powerful scissor grip.

She looked up at him soberly. "Jason, would you mind screwing me as tenderly as you know how?"

"My god, you're insatiable."

"Think of this as my first honeymoon."

"One honeymoon, coming up." *The Swan,* from Saint Saëns' *Carnival of the Animals* played on the radio in the background. Slowly they climbed heavenward together to the compelling music, being carried forward and upward a delicate step at a time, until they found themselves in the place where heavenly music abounded and eternally beautiful swans mated. When their wing feathers burned in the heat of their passion, and they could handle their bliss no more, they fell, crashing back to earth—where she laughed and laughed and laughed.

When her breathing was normal again, she said, "That was the most romantic experience of my life. Whenever I hear that music I'll think of this moment." As she spoke, she caressed his fingers that were keeping her nipples taut. "Now I know why you sometimes seem heavy-handed with my breasts—it's to keep them at their greatest sensitivity, isn't it?" She hugged him. "I love what you do for me." She stretched luxuriantly under him. "Especially the way when you begin to come, that low thunderous sound begins deep down in you somewhere, and builds to a drawn-out guttural outburst, and finally subsides to a purring jungle rumble." She hugged him tighter, pressing her pelvis into his. "God, even if I still couldn't come, I'd want to screw you just for the groovy sound effects. You are one-of-a-kind."

Jason felt her hand moving between their abdomens. "Do you feel good about contributing to your own satisfaction?"

She smiled. "What I like especially is being encouraged to be responsible for it."

He moved in and out of her. "Delicious" came to mind.

Soon she moaned with pleasure, rising up into each of his thrusts. Her free hand fingered her nipples. When her contractions began she strained her loins up to receive all of him. Her eyes widened. "Oh—oh—oh—my—god ... ."

Her contractions grew stronger. He moved her hand from between them to her free breast and drove into her. He held back with all the discipline he knew, but the power and flexibility of her lithesome loins made him lose control prematurely.

When he came back to earth, she was still hiccupping in orgasm. He felt so rewarded he pressed into her with all his weight while her hard contractions reignited him. Then she was done and he wasn't, so he brought her again, repeatedly, until he came once more among the bursting rockets. Afterwards, she locked her legs around him, holding him within her while she cried gently. Finally, she melted under him, managing a pretty smile through her tears of joy.

"How do you make it all happen?" Her voice was a whisper.

"There's a place inside you that's so sensitive, it can keep you in orbit."

"Where did you learn that?"

"Long ago, from a woman who believes women were given crucibles to be earthly foretastes of heaven. She taught me every woman's crucible is the most beautiful place on earth, that it is housed in the temple of her body, built to entice and fulfill a mate for life. But, she said, 'a woman cannot be lazy, she has to continue developing her mind, her body and her spirit to keep her mate interested'."

Officer Shepherd was silent for a moment. She ran her fingers through his hair, stroked his cheek. "I never realized what could be." She pressed up to receive more of him. "You are a gift."

He felt like a new man. "Would it be appropriate for you to tell me your name now?"

CHAPTER 65
QUID PRO QUO

Kirkland, Washington
Friday, March 18, 1960

Jason watched Officer Shepherd blush.

"Julia. My name is Julia. And I want you to know—the way you first came onto me, there's something terribly wrong with you. It's called war neurosis, and it's a serious mental disorder, probably from your experience in Korea—but I wouldn't fix you right now for anything. Perhaps we could make some arrangement that would give me time to explain what you need to know? Tell me, just how many times can we keep coming together like this?"

War neurosis. The Naval Academy psychiatrist had questioned him about that and Jason had dismissed it. But right now he was enjoying Julia's company and only wanted to answer her questions about sex.

"How many? I think for the man it depends on the woman's needs. Lots more times for you, depending on whether you experience firecracker multiples, or build over and over like me. Then we can rest for an hour or two and begin again."

"Jason. My behavior with you never could have happened without our psychic connection. I knew that despite your temporary craziness I was safe with you." Julia ran her hands over his shoulders. "Now tell me, how many different ways do you know how to make love to a woman?"

"I never really counted—perhaps seventy, counting ways for women to make love to men, my mentor told me." He shrugged. "The chair gig was new, improvised—to challenge you because you came here with the upper hand to cross examine me."

With a burst of energy Julia rolled him onto his back and wound up on top of him. "Like now?" She grinned, stuffing a throw pillow under his head. "I feel like we're experiencing a runner's high, and it's given me an idea for your war neurosis. This is Friday noon. If I stay through the weekend, do you think you could handle me riding your rocket every way you know—while I try to understand what makes you tick? You'll be my coach and I'll try being therapy for your pain-filled battle memories." She ran her palms over his biceps. "Show me whatever you do to keep having orgasms over and over?"

Jason considered her bold request. He respected Julia. And they would be helping each other. "Sounds like fun. But I'd allow five days. You've got that kind of endurance?"

"I run several miles every day. I thrive on the highs that gives me." She grinned.

"Well." He drummed his fingers on the sofa. "It depends."

A worried frown replaced her smile.

"I feel safe with you, too. But I want to be sure you're not going to tell your boss about my little indiscretions with you." He drummed another rhythm on her thigh.

"Only *what* I've learned, certainly no hint of *how* I learned it—if you'll promise to seek help for war neurosis at the veterans' hospital."

"Walter Reed?" That was in Washington, D.C.

"No. Here. In Seattle. Built to care for all veterans with service-connected disabilities."

"You mean like in D.C., for amputees? There are other hospitals for veterans? No one ever told us. Not in the service. Not when we were discharged."

"Well, you've been told now." Securely astride his thighs, Julia stretched her arms toward the ceiling, her body an inviting arc that captured his full focus.

Jason reached for her nipples, using them to pull her mouth to his so she could demonstrate her new-found ardor. When she came up for air, he said, "Conventional sex can get routine, lose its freshness. I'd make you work hard on physical and mental flexibility, I'd keep your interrogation from deteriorating into anything you might expect."

Her eyes sparkled. "Tell me about it. You'll find I'm great at doing several things simultaneously."

"You've learned the first rule of being responsible for your own orgasms," he said. "But what do you think is the body's largest sex organ?"

"Your rocket? My 'crucible'?"

"Your brain. Nothing happens if you can't imagine it."

"You mean if I can imagine it, we can do it."

Jason smiled encouragement. "Picture learning the arts of the quickie and offering yourself in crazy-inventive positions—to be ready any time, any way, at infatuation levels, and never without you having an orgasm."

"Is that what you want in a wife, Jason?"

He looked up, appreciating her loveliness. "I know it's not realistic. A wife who wants to be both my best friend and my mistress, who finds lovemaking several times a day as fulfilling as I do. She'd have to have extraordinary energy to live and work at my side day and night while we take our pleasure in impulsive, imaginative ways. No spontaneity-killing preconditions—like showering, shaving and only in conventional locations. That way, we'll live and work together better."

"Locations?"

"Sometimes doing it where there's risk that makes it exciting."

"Oh, god, I'd love to live like that." Julia shuddered over him in anticipation.

He watched Julia's eyes reading his.

"The CIA recruited me for my profiling skill as a psychic. But I realized I'd never get your trust without perfect candor. Also, something rare for me, and my ultimate downfall, I've been affected by your jungle-like passion—which has kept me hopelessly aroused and self-conscious since entering your house."

"That's a two-way street. Sex is an animal activity where a lot of juices flow."

"Speaking of which, I have to pee."

"Can you hold it? The pressure will make the next orgasm super-sized."

"I thought the last one was pretty spectacular." She raised a brow. "Okay, I'll try to hold on."

He arched up, filling her for liftoff.

She gasped. "Riding you is dangerous! Sometimes it hurts. But I've never felt so alive. I could never tire of it."

"Hope you still feel that way Tuesday night," he said.

"I know I will. At first I was afraid I couldn't stretch enough for your girth. Then I was angry I couldn't come with you. And now I find I can't let you leave me."

"You've kept me captive since we first engaged." He chuckled.

She reached down to practice her new act of freedom. Her other hand caressed his hand on her breast, encouraging his fingers to awaken her nipples. "Tell me, where did you learn to talk so much during sex?"

"Where did you?"

"In cars. Trying to persuade men to wait for me."

"You know, for someone who hasn't had orgasms before now, you're very good at causing them. And you're awfully quick with all the great answers. Is this a special interrogation op the CIA teaches?"

"Maybe for other departments, not for a profiler." She stopped sliding up and down over him. "I'm sure it'll never happen again." She started to pull away.

"Wait." He held Julia's hand. "I'm sorry. I'm not good at the social game. Just blurt out what I think before I ... . Look. I agree to tell you what you need to know. Just keep up that subtle thing you do as you come down each time."

Her sudden anger melted and she resumed her tantalizing stroke.

Jason gave her a reassuring smile. "Every night for almost a year, I fought a ninja warrior for the opportunity to have a young princess teach me three-thousand-year-old secret Oriental sexual arts while I taught her to speak English like a native-born American. It was like living the story of *The Arabian Nights*."

Julia paused in reflection. "Three thousand year-old secrets?" She began working him again, with an air of reverence.

She upped the friction. Jason felt her catch the ride.

CHAPTER 66
GRAND DESIGN

Kirkland, Washington
Tuesday, March 22, 1960

On Tuesday morning Jason awoke to find Julia already out of bed. That was a first. He found her in the kitchen, mixing pancake batter. "It's my turn to ask you your feelings," he said.

Her smile warmed his heart. "I feel free. Happy." She pushed the mixing bowl aside. "Instead of being the inhibited, uninformed girl I was raised to be, I'm free to be a whole person, the woman you and I would have me be."

A flush of energy coursed through his body. "I already feel I've known you for years. And you might as well have known me forever."

"Speaking of which, while you were sleeping I drew a diagram I want to show you."

While he made coffee, Julia added Vermont maple syrup to her mix and poured the batter on the griddle. He watched her roll the thin pancakes individually and sprinkle them with confectioner's sugar. She called them crêpes and set a plate of three on the dining room table. Snatching one for herself, she stood before him mouthing it seductively.

He followed her example, and relished the flavor before devouring the delicacy. "For five days you've practically starved us."

"I want to keep us hungry all the time, so we gorge on each other."

He laughed. "You've succeeded! I've rarely met a woman with your appetite."

"I've had so much to learn and too little time to learn it." She put the remains of her crêpe on the plate and set it on the counter. "And when we discuss my diagram, I want your full focus, so I'm taking care of the distraction first."

He watched fascinated while Julia stood before him and literally willed herself to prepare for him. The energy between them crackled.

She pushed him back against the table so he was half sitting on it. She pulled herself up his body, placed her feet on the table, and settled over him. She was coming as she took him into her. He swirled forward in her passion.

She maneuvered him onto the table, came again, and then rolled him over her, until they took each other through a tsunami. They lay there, sweating profusely, laughing.

"Two athletes with healthy appetites." Julia ran her fingers along his mouth. "Now let's finish the crêpes and we'll be able to think about the diagram."

He admired her understanding of men and of what she'd learned about herself. Now he was ready to see her drawing.

"Come sit beside me on the sofa," she said. "My diagram is a perspective."

Julia patted his knee. "You're a problem solver. When you look ahead, you tend to focus so hard on problems of getting through the day, or the next week, you miss seeing the opportunities and what your life really is about." She placed the drawing on his lap. "Have you ever tried looking *back* to see the broad view of your life, its direction?"

Her leg nestled comfortably against his as he studied her chart of the key people in his life, arranged in a diamond-shaped pattern.

"Early this morning, I drew this, starting with you at the bottom, and your parents side by side the next level of growth up, culminating in your experiences back east and your training at the Naval Academy— which appears to have become the platform from which you've begun focusing in on your objectives to accomplish your purpose in life."

Jason wondered whether this came out of Julia's psychology courses or was an analysis by a psychic. "Looking back makes it easier to see where I'm headed?" He looked up from the chart. "Intriguing."

"*You* are what's intriguing. I'm hopelessly mesmerized by your presence." Julia slid her hand up his arm.

He covered her hand with his. "It's just as well that you're flying back this afternoon. I wouldn't want to become your addiction. I imagine you have suitors in our nation's capital."

"It's very different from my college years." She stared out the window. "There's an officer at work I really ... really like. But I told myself I wouldn't sleep with him until we were officially engaged." Julia looked into Jason's eyes as she kissed two of her fingers and pressed them against his lips. "Because of you, I know what I can give and ask for in my marriage bed."

Jason's gratification was tempered by a wash of loneliness at the thought of her departure. He reached for Julia's diagram, and spotted his name at the bottom.

IVAN

⇅

THE MISSION

↑↑↑↑↑↑↑↑↑↑↑↑

RENAISSANCE MATE

↑↑↑↑↑↑↑↑↑↑↑

?????????????????????????

↑↑↑↑↑↑↑↑↑↑

WAR NEUROSIS & JULIA & FORESTRY

↑↑↑↑↑↑↑↑↑

AGENT FRANK THOMAS & RUSSIAN LEIF OLSEN

↑↑↑↑↑↑↑↑

UNITED STATES NAVAL ACADEMY & SYBIL SIBELIUS
UNCLE DAVID & AUNT SARAH & ANGEL & DAKOTA

↑↑↑↑↑↑

UNCLE EWEN & AUNT RACHAEL & MAGICAL MEGAN

↑↑↑↑↑

IVAN & NATASHA, LEADERS OF SOVIET PLOT

↑↑↑↑

FBI AGENT IN CHARGE FRANK THOMAS

↑↑↑

HYO, SUKI; NATASHA & ANGEL

↑↑

FATHER & MOTHER

↕

JASON

He began reading from the bottom up. "The box in the middle?"

"That represents the culmination of specific growth to prepare you for your destiny."

"And?"

"Now don't overthink this, but tell me what you see when you look back at what your parents gave you."

Jason reflected. "They were both gymnasts. Brains served by healthy bodies. Strength and endurance. Natural athletic abilities with unnaturally fast reflexes. Mother had long blonde hair she could sit on, strong shoulders and arms, a big chest and slender stomach and hips. Mother gave me a passionate love of classical music, art, beauty, nature and animals. She and Dad had extraordinary energy—and from noises and laughter that came from their room at night, lots of testosterone. Dad taught me the physical and mental characteristics of manhood necessary to stand up to any aggressor. Also logging, swimming, boating, shooting, riding, knife throwing, fighting, studying, and above all, being a winner." Jason thought. "The few close friends I've had have been exciting people, like my parents."

Julia jotted key words. "The next level of experience is Hyo, Suki and Natasha and the Angel. Suki came to you because she was desperate for a GI she could trust with her life. Tell me, why isn't she with you?"

"She knew exactly what she wanted, to put roots down in one place where she could be free to build a life. Somehow, she knew my destiny would never allow that."

"Okay. What about your enemy, Natasha? What brought her into your life?"

"She had no choice. It just happens when my twin and I somehow share death defying experiences."

Julia raised an eyebrow. "So if I want to screw your brother all I have to do is be available after you've survived an attack by assassins?"

"Maybe... I don't know. I hope not." In pain, Jason wiped a hand over his eyes.

"And the Angel?"

"I've come to think of the vision as encouragement from a guardian angel. Before I met Natasha in the flesh, I only had a fuzzy image of Natasha's face and even wondered whether she and the Angel were the same. Now I know they're separate entities, Natasha like a physical genie, the other an ethereal messenger. But somehow each empowered me to be here today."

"So how did FBI agent Frank Thomas come to you? What has he meant to you?"

"Orders from Washington, DC. A good guy. I've learned to trust him. Like you. That's special."

"Thank you." Julia smiled. "Now Ivan and Natasha in the flesh."

"Ivan wanted to meet his birth parents. Their death was a fated accident. But because I can identify him and his partner, they consider me a threat to be eliminated. I'm afraid of them. Of what they can do to me. I'm more afraid of what they can do to my country and the future for its children. From my time with Sybil, I've deduced they're working to destroy our republic through our educational institutions, media and legislators, and whatever else serves their goal. I've been told by Uncle Ewen, Aunt Rachael and Grandfather Angus that it's my destiny to oppose Soviet takeover."

"How did the MacDougall Clan become involved in your life?"

"As the head of our clan and my father's older brother, Uncle Ewen flew here to see to Dad's affairs and my welfare. When he discovered I had the family gifts, he took me to Scotland so I could learn about my ancestral heritage. How I admired him and Aunt Rachael. She showed me conservation ethics and qualities of straight talking, natural femininity I want in a woman."

"What about Megan?"

"Megan was a heifer in need of a bull. She transformed me magically into that bull, and taught me the importance of being best friends in any love relationship. Together we learned to make sex an integral part of our everyday life so effectively it became as natural as sipping coffee, with each mug a surprising new flavor. But her life was rooted in the clan she was raised with."

You meant *magic* figuratively, I take it."

"I doubt I'll ever know, just that we were in another time when we were under the auld tree together."

"Alright, what made you go east to live? That became such a turning point in your life."

Jason thought carefully before answering Julia. "My godparents, David and Sarah King, and the Naval Academy, lured me east. Sarah is Mother's youngest sister, and they flew here to help with the funeral and see what might be best for me. They suggested that while I was in Scotland, I prepare for the Naval Academy entrance exams. As a couple they were everything I wanted in life. Sarah seemed like an immortal wife, overflowing with spontaneous laughter that filled any room or house. David was one of our nation's most decorated war heroes from World War II. Together, they made everyone around them feel like they really mattered, which impressed me most of all. I learned to attend church with them. In short, I began learning about service to God and country. And I met Dakota, who showed me that a smoking hot, sexy woman could exist in a bone, sinew and rawhide, formidable warrior like herself. But her life was intended for another warrior. The Naval Academy elicited an extraordinary sense of rapport with our forefathers, who gave their all that we might live in freedom. Unfortunately, it also taught me I was too independent for a military career. Then came Sybil, who taught me I could fight some of my enemies with respect, and even love."

"We're doing great, Jason. Now, Agent Frank Thomas and Leif Olsen. How did Frank come into your life again?"

"Frank persuaded me to keep an eye on Leif by telling me the FBI desperately needed a bona fide college student with my intuition and unusual survival skills, who in no way might seem to be a government agent, and whom they could trust without question."

"And Leif's impact?"

"Terrible. That situation showed me that I was capable of losing control and using unnecessary force to disable a man. That scared the hell out of me because it made me question whether I was any better than that malevolent spy." Jason didn't want to dwell on Leif. "And you, Julia, recognized my war neurosis. The high from our great sex together rebalanced me after I relived the horrors of Leif and North Korea. You showed me what an extraordinary facilitator a woman can be."

"Jason, the grand design for your life couldn't be clearer."

"Clear?"

"Just look at the trail of women behind you. You can call it coincidence if you want, but I see it another way."

He took Julia's hand. "Each of you is a distinct, special person, as if you were from different nations."

"Yet we're incredibly alike. Goal-oriented. Athletic. Smart. Lots of hair. Ample breasts. Small waist and flat stomach. Trim ankles. Seeking someone to give ourselves to for life."

Julia squeezed his hand. "I've been incredibly aroused since stepping into this house with you, even though you had to teach me the secrets that enabled me to experience the joy and fulfillment of sex." She laughed. "Now I'm ready and able in an instant. Mentally prepared in advance." She shifted on the sofa cushion and leaned back to study him. "You love forestry and sailing, I enjoy city life and working with the CIA—and I get miserably seasick. But you have an aura that activates high achievers like me. I got hit with meaningful friendship, erotic chemistry and the hottest infatuation of my life all at once. And I'll bet that goes for each person you've been intimate with." She gave him a knowing nod.

"Each of us is so turned on by you that we drop everything for you—even though eventually we realize we are not the one for you. But each of us has some specific qualities you need in a mate to help you in your mission to stop the Russians. I believe you're being prepared for someone with all of our qualities."

Julia pointed to her diagram. "Look at the pattern that emerged when I wrote out the names for each series of events in your life. The bottom half is shaped like a crucible filled with carefully selected individuals bringing you ever-expanding experience and wisdom to survive in the life that you exist for. The broad base in the middle, at the Naval Academy, is the turning platform where your experiences and war neurosis begin focusing in on your given mission. Ordinarily, real life has no plot, yet yours is the depiction of a carefully crafted life with specific goals and the tools to achieve them. We can't know what lies ahead, but my guess is it's going to lead you to an amazing lionhearted mate who will help you survive and will work with you on your ordained mission to stop Ivan."

"You make everything seem as precise as a math formula."

"But remember, Jason, real life is messy, so don't let that throw you." She glanced at her watch and threw herself back on the sofa, outstretched arms inviting him. "I leave for the airport at 1600. Will you keep me in orbit till then?"

By the time Julia departed for Washington, he felt he'd been through the catharsis of a classical Greek play. This profiler from the CIA was an insightful facilitator who'd proven to be assertive, physical, expressive and loving—a real doer in life and a reminder never to underestimate a woman. Ever.

CHAPTER 67
WHITE HOUSE REPORT

Washington, D.C.
Tuesday, April 5, 1960

Walter Higgins sat at his desk noting the bloom that had not faded from Julia's cheeks since she'd returned from Seattle. Jason's comments about subtle communist subversion of educational institutions had prompted the DDO to pass on the concern to Admiral Zantzinger, to discuss at his weekly meeting with the president and his aids. "The White House has said nothing about your report of the radical teachers' movement. I doubt Eisenhower ever saw it, what with his concerns about Cuba. The FBI needs to investigate this." He rubbed his chin. "Why wouldn't MacDougall tell you how he came by this information?"

"Said he wouldn't reveal his source—and he meant it."

"You couldn't get a glimmer of what was in his mind?" Higgins had serious doubts about paranormal intel, but as long as Julia's information proved reliable, he'd keep using her.

"No way. He used diversionary tactics."

"How?"

She blushed. "Very effectively, sir."

Higgins looked straight at her. "You did a commendable job in Seattle, Miss Shepherd. Keep up the good work."

"Thank you, sir."

"I followed up on your suggestion—your belief—that Jason had an out-of-body, near-death experience when he was sixteen. I had his medical records checked in Seattle. A horse kicked him in the face, smashing his jaw. He was in a coma for four days. The ambulance attendant reported he lost Jason's pulse and the artery stopped spurting, but he pumped Jason's chest and revived him."

"Jason would know that if he told anyone about *his* perspective, they'd write it off as a hallucination."

"In any case, he's a survivor. He managed to carry on with his school work and that spring he won the Harvard Prize—for high scholarship and character."

Higgins wanted Julia to know he valued the practical information she'd obtained. "The name you gave us, Saul Alinsky: he's a Marxist, born of Russian-Jewish immigrants in Chicago. Wrote a book, *Reveille for Radicals*." Higgins held up the book. "Makes interesting reading." He handed it to her. "The FBI has kept an eye on him for years. Apparently Jason knows something more. If Jason's brother is connected with this man, just know your work may have put us onto one of the most important leads of this Cold War."

CHAPTER 68
ONWARD

Fort Lauderdale, Florida
Tuesday, April 5, 1960

Natasha admired the azure Florida sky through the salon windows of their yacht. April was always a beautiful month in Fort Lauderdale—cool, dry weather, wonderfully refreshing before the heat and humidity of the summer rainy season. She and Ivan were so focused on implementing their subversion plan that she rarely thought about Jason MacDougall. When he did come to mind, she felt relief that he seemed to be out of their picture. She hesitated even to mention him, but was curious to know if Ivan still felt some connection to his twin.

"Strange that you should bring him up," said Ivan. "I do think about him occasionally and am relieved that Sybil seems to have been correct, that he wants nothing to do with us, simply wants to pursue his own life." Ivan rose from his desk and began pacing. "I did have a strange feeling a few weeks ago," he mused. "It was just a flash. I sensed MacDougall momentarily faced a deadly threat, but it was over so fast I realized that whatever it was, he got through it unharmed." Ivan crossed the salon and took both her hands in his as a reassuring smile brightened his face. "You and I can focus on our plan for Mother Russia."

Natasha pulled him down beside her on the settee.

Ivan's eyes had a faraway look.

She reflected on their whole covert community. The KGB, the individual Spetsnaz teams, the undercover operatives—all were so concerned about someone being caught and having information to reveal about any of the other operations, that they only shared what was absolutely necessary. Of course, coveting power and being privy to more information than one's comrades was always an underlying motive, despite the egalitarian tenets of communism. And there was constant checking on loyalty and adherence to the party line. Doves within the embassies were just one of their techniques. Natasha figured the paranoia came with the profession. In Ivan's case, the secret about his blood ties to MacDougall was information she and her partner could never disclose. Mother Russia would immediately question the objectivity of Ivan's decisions and his future motivations as mastermind of the Grand Acquisition.

CHAPTER 69
REJECTED BY VAMC

Seattle, Washington
Monday, May 23, 1960

"What do you mean you can't help me?" Jason thundered. He pounded the doctor's desk at the Veterans Administration Medical Center.

Now that semester finals were over, he'd followed through on Julia's request that he check in with the VA. After filling in reams of paperwork and waiting for hours, he was being turned away?

The psychologist cringed, and in seconds two large men in whites stepped through the door. The doctor hung her head and waved the men out. She seemed on the verge of tears.

Jason apologized for his rudeness. "I'm sorry for the outburst. I think it's part of my problem. I'm told the VA is the only place with experience with war neurosis. Apparently I got it in the line of duty while defending my country. So why can't the VA help me?"

She pulled a tissue from the government-issue box on her desk and dabbed at her eyes. "I'm sorry, Mr. MacDougall. Your files from Korea are missing, and without official verification of the incident that gave you war neurosis—"

"I told you, I'm not allowed to tell anyone about the incident. But there's someone who can ... ." Jason stood up, thanked the nice person for her time, and left.

As he walked past a bearded old man in a field jacket seated in the waiting area, the veteran said, "We all heard you." The voice was that of a beaten-sounding youth.

Jason stopped and stood before him.

"Won't do you no good. Congress changed the rules. Won't pay. Makes hospitals assume every vet is lying unless there's witnesses to back the soldier's story. Them who can take care of themselves are too proud to step forward. All you get here is drugs that make you sleep all day and night. Like me. Until I've had enough." The man angled his head to one side, stuck his tongue out and placed a hand around his throat like a noose.

Jason swallowed. "Can you use some money?"

The veteran held out his uncared for hand, while Jason gave him all the cash he had. He looked at the rest of the drugged derelicts in the waiting room. *No way.* He departed the Seattle VA for the first and last time.

* * *

Jason called CIA Headquarters person-to-person for Officer Julia Shepherd, and was informed she'd have to call him back. But no call came.

The phone ringing woke him out of a sound sleep. He turned on the reading light and sat on the edge of the bed. It was 5:15 AM. "Yes?" His voice was always unnaturally deep when he first spoke in the morning.

"It's Julia. I was out on assignment yesterday. Just got your message this morning. Sorry it's so early Pacific Time, but I didn't want to keep you waiting any longer and I have a full schedule the rest of today. Are you okay?"

"I went to the VA yesterday, as I promised you I would, though I've felt great since you were here. They're not going to help me without my files proving what happened in North Korea. And I'm not about to let them drug me like those guys I met in the waiting room."

"My boss told me that might happen, and State won't allow your files to be released under any circumstances."

"What about a letter from you? I don't want to be some kind of time bomb ready to hurt people."

"Turns out my boss's son has the same problem, and it seems Congress won't admit there's a problem and release funds to research war neurosis.

"I'm sorry about his son. I really do feel great, so don't worry about me. I'll be working this summer and starting grad school in the fall."

"Thanks for following up with the VA the way I asked. I think you'll be fine. I imagine you get plenty of exercise working in the forests. Make sure you take time to enjoy a social life, too. It's important to keep a balance."

"I appreciate your call-back."

"And, Jason . . ., thanks for everything you showed me. You've changed *my* life forever."

Too bad she wasn't the woman destined for him. He'd have to keep looking.

CHAPTER 70
REVOLUTIONARY MOVEMENT

Kirkland, Washington
Monday, October 17, 1960

"I have good news, Jason. And some material I'd like to show you."
Jason hung up the phone, cleared his books off the dining room table and put on a fresh pot of coffee in preparation for Frank Thomas's visit.

"The good news?" Jason ushered the FBI agent into the living room.

"We can stop worrying about the Korean general seeking revenge on you. He just stepped on one of his own land mines. A big one, for tanks."

Jason thought a moment. "But I still have to keep quiet so's not to embarrass the State Department, right?"

"Correct. North Korea is still a challenge to democracy, even though it's not in the headlines. And right now, State is focused on Cuba and Fidel Castro."

"Coffee?" Jason looked at the large manila envelope in Frank's left hand and his heart sank. He hoped it wasn't photos for another surveillance job. "You wanted to show me something?"

"Perhaps a little tap water, thank you. Could we sit at the dining room table?"

Seated, the Agent in Charge said, "As you suggested some time ago, I found out what Sybil Sibelius is up to. She's making quite a name for herself." He slid the envelope across the table. "She has a PhD in psychology, you know."

"I only knew she was a psychology student at George Washington University and that she has total recall of information. Oh, yes ... and that someday she wanted to create a sexology institute."

Frank gestured toward the envelope.

Jason emptied the contents to reveal a collection of handbills from campuses all across the nation. A full-body color picture of Sybil dressed tastefully, but in a fabric that clung to her curves. The caption beneath the picture read,

Better Relationships through Better Sex
by sexologist Sybil Sibelius, PhD
Sibelius Institute of Sexology

He flipped through the flyers. Except for the location, dates, and times, they were the same. Mostly colleges in the northeast, some in the mid-west, many in California. Nothing in Oregon or Washington. "Well, that picture and caption says it all. 'She having good turnouts?"

"Sensational. Her reputation precedes her. She's all the rage."

"So I was wrong about her recruiting for radical instructors?"

"Not at all, Jason. As part of her lecture, she offers a sexual aptitude test which in fact is also a test to identify individuals who can be taught *what* to think, instead of *how* to think. After the lecture, her sexy staff sells her self-published book, *Better Relationships Through Better Sex,* while she invites potential radicals to meet her professor friends. A good number of the professors seem to be from the Communist Party USA, who were driven underground in the Joseph McCarthy purges."

"How does she identify the ones to introduce to the professors?"

"The ones with the highest test scores."

"Well, now we know my brother's plan. If they keep at it long enough, they can alter the values of this next generation of leaders in the news media, business, legislature, and State Department. What's the White House going to do to stop them?"

"Nothing, Jason. They're breaking no laws. And there's no hard proof of a grand scheme to take over the country this way—or any other, if I may say it. I used agents all over the country to follow your lead, and all I come up with is a new trend in education."

"Frank, J. Edgar Hoover was on target in that book you gave me. His title says it in a nutshell—masters of deceit: the story of communism in America and how to fight it. Whatever became of Senator Joe McCarthy's lists, the hundreds of communist infiltrators in the State Department and army?"

"As you recall, he was censured by the Senate while you were fighting communist inroads in Korea. Repudiated for his alcoholic, overbearing method of operating, despite the accuracy of his information. It was easy for communists and socialists, who feared the exposure, to brand his efforts a 'witch hunt.' And other, evenhanded people who found McCarthy's approach embarrassing, picked up on the disparaging label." Agent Thomas shook his head and clenched his jaw. "Problem is, when they censured his method, they became distracted from focusing on the need to deal with the problem of communist infiltration."

"What about Saul Alinsky's *Reveille For Radicals*? He claims he doesn't belong to the Communist Party USA, but his focus is on taking over the workers in this country—burrowing into the unions and support institutions. Unfortunately for the poor and the average wage-earners, power-hungry leaders will still dictate their lives, only the new leaders will be Alinsky devotees. Alinsky's followers focus on creating chaos instead of on guiding productive growth with lasting opportunity for all. These guys are clever and pragmatic. They're dedicated. If the rest of us don't continue to demonstrate the superior benefits of the freedom to learn and work according to an individual's capabilities, the freedom to live and raise our families the way we personally think best, and if we don't acknowledge and address the injustices that do exist, these persuasive trouble-makers will infiltrate. I've learned independence and cooperation from living in the forests, observing nature. I would think people who dwell in towns and cities, people who work in factories and sawmills, want to continue living in freedom."

"I agree, Jason. The challenge never abates."

Jason stood and stretched, trying to hide the feeling that if he'd been a cat his tail would be twitching furiously. "You know, Frank, I think it began when a fine haberdasher who became a lawyer, a judge, a senator and then vice-president, ended up in the White House.

Truman was no military expert and was advised, perhaps," Jason shrugged, "by people influenced by some on McCarthy's lists? Truman decided to recall General MacArthur from his U.N. command, to make the general step down from his goal of crushing the North Korean aggressors for good. The White House gave up MacArthur's wins in North Korea and allowed the communist dictatorship to continue as a threat forever."

Frank heaved a deep sigh. "The ways of politicians can be frustrating. They don't live in the same reality as men in the field. They have different perspectives. The same holds true for ivory tower professors."

Jason couldn't hold it in. "What happens when teachers stop teaching that our freedom comes at the price of great sacrifices, that our freedom is based on responsible Judeo-Christian values which produced our Constitution and our Bill of Rights? Our republic encourages individual effort and rewards productivity. The way I see it, families and businesses, churches and synagogues and charities, together, create a constructive society. The communist plan indoctrinates kids to believe government should run everything and government will take care of all their needs. They think massive social entitlements are sustainable, despite all evidence to the contrary. Just look at the people in democratic West Germany and their former countrymen in East Germany now controlled by Soviet communism. If an East German can even afford a car, it takes four years from when it's ordered to when it's delivered—just one difference in the standard of living and productivity under communism."

"It's why Mr. Hoover published his book and why I serve with the FBI."

"You know, Frank, I seem to recall that history teaches us, 'A great nation is not conquered from without until it has destroyed itself from within.'"

PART V

VA HOSPITAL

CHAPTER 71
FLASHBACK

Kirkland, Washington
Wednesday, November 9, 1960

Jason tried to focus on his graduate studies, intent on establishing an environmentally sustainable logging business, no matter what challenges the Russians might pose in his future. But working on a master's degree didn't block out his misgivings about killing Leif Olsen. Sure, the man was a Russian spy and abused his American stepdaughter, yet Jason knew that he'd momentarily lost control, that he'd been possessed by a rage that drove him beyond merely subduing the man who tried to murder him.

Julia had figured he was dealing with war neurosis. He recalled her five days of interrogation with genuine pleasure and now experienced a certain restlessness. But Jason only wanted sex that arose out of a mutual friendship wherein a loving partner wanted this kind of relationship for herself. He felt a deep loyalty to the women he'd known, even though they'd chosen a life different from his and ended up with someone else. Julia was now happily married to the officer she'd told him about. He believed in Suki's and Aunt Rachael's convictions that he would find the woman destined to become his wife. He scanned the campus as he pursued his studies. Was it his own internal struggles that blocked his way to her? During the summer he'd begun having nightmares about killing Leif as well as about the traumatic kidnapping by the North Koreans—Tom O'Reilly's gruesome death, the malevolent woman, the Russian soldier, his surreal escape. The nightmares became so persistent and horrifying that Jason deliberately avoided sleep. Now part way into the fall semester, he went from never having experienced a headache to migraines that lasted three days, to the hour. He struggled to fit a package of meat into his overstuffed refrigerator and suddenly slammed the item in, in a destructive burst of temper that was over before he knew it.

In February, after months of migraines, sleeplessness and occasional explosions out of nowhere, he finally made the decision he had to address his problems while he still could—before he was driven to do something terrible. He made an appointment to see his family's old physician.

"It's been a while, Jason. Good to see you again. What's going on?"

Doctor Packer's hair had turned grey, but he had the same kindly manner Jason remembered from his childhood. He couldn't tell the doctor about the Russian spy or North Korea; that information was classified. However, he could describe the headaches and say that nightmares were wrecking his sleep.

"Jason, your jaw's healed so well where the horse kicked you when you were sixteen, I can hardly see the scars. As I remember, the groom who found you in the paddock lying in a pool of blood thought you were dead and called the morgue. You were in a coma for days. Your grandfather was right to fly in the best specialists from the east coast. Doctor Hand and Doctor Crow performed extraordinary surgeries on your face and jaw."

Jason remembered the valuable horse, Royal Jack. The gelding had returned from surgical confinement in a veterinary hospital and was going stir-crazy in its stall, kicking out the wooden slats. The stable, outside Seattle, was home to several championship horses. Their owner, Clyde Owens, had noticed Jason had a way with animals and was gentle on the bit in the horses' mouths. Mr. Owens asked Jason and his mother, an accomplished horsewoman, to exercise the champions and keep up their training. Jason looked forward to the job every day after school. That particular afternoon, his mother couldn't go to the stable. "Jason," she said over the phone, "we can't put any weight on Royal Jack's back, but he needs to get out. Exercise him on a lunge-line in the lower corral." A passing rattletrap truck backfired and spooked the animal. It bolted, breaking Jason's grip on its halter. Hooves flashed. Jason woke up in the hospital several days later.

He'd never told anyone, except Julia, about his strange experience in the ambulance. In the confined space of the old-fashioned emergency vehicle, he was floating above his legs. Squeezed between the Cadillac roof and his body, he was looking down at the white-coated male nurse frantically trying to find a pulse, clear the breathing passages, administer oxygen and slow the hemorrhaging of the blood spurting from his patient's jaw and soaking his shirt. In contrast to the attendant's anxiety, Jason had felt an indefinable serenity, like basking in the sun with angels of God. The siren wailed as the ambulance sped down the highway, and Jason was asking the angels if he'd lost any teeth, when the desperate attendant began pumping down on his chest and he was unceremoniously whisked back into his comatose body.

While recovering in the hospital he'd wondered if he'd been close to death, but he didn't describe his odd experience. He figured his parents and the doctors would think the blow to his head had made him crazy. After that, he found himself ever more sensitive to his surroundings and receptive to premonitions that others would question.

Doctor Packer ended his examination of Jason's face and sat back. "I might know what your problem is. Recently, I've read about two cases where people with head trauma like yours developed pressures on the brain, years later, that caused symptoms like you're describing. I'm going to prescribe Percodan for the headaches. I also advise you to see a neurologist who has access to the new electro-encephalogram technology. It's so delicate, it can record patterns of neural activity in the brain to reveal symptomatic signs, for medical analysis. Unfortunately, the equipment's so expensive none of our regular hospitals have it, but let me call around to see who does."

Jason left Doctor Packer's office filled with hope. Perhaps his problem wasn't war neurosis, which, as he understood it, was a life sentence. If they could find the pressure on his brain, they could fix it, and he could be himself again.

* * *

The following month, his forestry class made a field trip into the big timber of Pack Forest. Jason was glad to be outdoors, outside the conventional seminar room. Until he reached back to his knife sheath. Empty. What had happened? Where was it—his grandfather Steele's hunting knife? He searched the ground through the lush undergrowth beneath the towering Douglas firs. He swallowed the bile rising in his throat, determined to find the knife his grandfather had passed on to him. It was more than a useful skinning tool. It was a connection with his family. He fought back the panic of yet another loss, tried to swim through the wave of aloneness that washed over him.

He swept aside the ferns as he searched his back trail and peered anxiously at the path in front of his logger's boots. Had someone walking behind him taken it, slipped it out? To make matters worse, he now had a migraine.

Suddenly a classmate stepped out from behind one of the large trees, tucking himself back into his jeans. Both men froze in surprise. The large man exhaled sharply, his breath laden with garlic and in a flash like a time warp, Jason was under attack by a North Korean soldier.

Jason leapt for the startled man's throat to keep him from calling out for help. The man grabbed Jason's wrists and tried to raise a knee into his crotch, but Jason twisted and blocked the blow with his thigh. The soldier's eyes bulged and his mouth worked like a fish out of water as he tried to draw in the air that Jason's crushing hands denied him. He felt the soldier kicking his legs violently and trying to beat his arms away, but Jason continued choking him down onto his knees.

More soldiers appeared. They grabbed Jason's arms and tried to pry him away, but couldn't break his grip on the man's throat. Jason roared in fear, anger and frustration, until something struck him in the back of the head so hard he lost consciousness—

He woke up on his back, looking at the canopy of trees rising a hundred feet over him. He just lay there, his head pounding, in a sweat and still breathing hard, trying to figure out how he'd gotten there. He tried to move, but couldn't. His classmates were on their knees holding him down, two on each arm and leg. Big Fred Mahoney was sitting propped against a tree and trying to drink from a canteen with the help of two other students.

Someone was saying Jason's name. Professor Callahan, their instructor. "Jason, are you alright?"

"How did I get here?" he asked, still groggy. "Why is everyone holding me?" He started to struggle, but was subdued. He made himself relax. "What's going on, Mr. Callahan?"

"Don't you remember attacking Fred and choking him?" Jason heard the concern in the professor's voice, saw the distress in his eyes. Jason's gut knotted.

Slowly, what he'd done came to him.

"Keep that crazy vet away from me!" croaked Mahoney.

"I'm really sorry, Fred."

Jason's classmates loosened their hold on him and he sat up. His head hurt.

Korea. It wasn't at all like World War II, where the soldiers were welcomed home and honored. Americans didn't seem to care about the people who'd fought in Korea. Korean vets weren't made to feel proud by the civilians at home, so they didn't tell their stories, didn't wear their field jackets and keep their uniforms. But now he'd attacked Fred ... thought he was back in Korea ... that his fellow students were the North Korean enemy ... . Jason felt hot, cold, then hot again.

Seeking help for his problem, he phoned Doctor Packer.

"Jason, I've located a facility that has the equipment we need: the veterans' mental hospital at American Lake, just west of Tacoma."

"I've never even heard of the place. The VA in Seattle never mentioned it."

"Jason, before you drive there, you might want to close up your house, in case they keep you for a spell."

"Just what I want. To be diverted at this point in my life." So Jason closed up his house, notified Agent Thomas, and drove to American Lake.

CHAPTER 72
AMERICAN LAKE
VETERANS HOSPITAL

Tacoma, Washington
Monday, March 13, 1961

Jason wasn't sure what to expect, but hoped his stay at this veterans' facility would be brief. The admitting doctor looked across his desk. "We have Dr. Packer's referral and a copy of your records from his office, Mr. MacDougall."

Jason described his headaches, his avoidance of sleep and his attack on Fred. The doctor admitted him right away for observation.

At the hospital, Jason's headaches and nightmares grew worse, but he refused to tell his doctor the subject of the nightmares that kept repeating themselves. He'd given his word to the military, the FBI and the CIA that he'd say nothing to anyone about North Korea or Leif Olsen.

The psychiatrist, Doctor Franke, told him that people often buried memories of horrific experiences and years could go by before some other trauma or recall trigger reactivated the scenario. Jason had hoped his problem was from the accident with the horse and could be fixed. Now he had to accept Julia's concern about war neurosis, too.

The days slipped by while Jason waited for some kind of effective treatment. One of the patients on his ward, a sophisticated, powerful-looking older man, introduced himself as William and befriended the new arrival. William told Jason he enjoyed his intellect and taught him to play bridge. Jason's passion for the game helped him through the interminable days of observation.

One spring afternoon William said, "I'm going down to the softball field for practice. Want to join me, toss around a ball before it starts?"

"I've never played softball, but anything outdoors beats being cooped up in here."

In the days that followed, the team invited Jason to practice with them. He felt so much better that only his relentless nightmares reminded him he was still in trouble.

Two weeks later William clapped a hand on his shoulder. "You're a natural, Jason. And you're the one man I can 'burn leather' with."

"It sure feels good to be out here—the fresh air, playing ball—this is a great sport."

"Ready to learn how to pitch? Hit homers?"

"You ready to coach?"

William had played semi-pro ball before he was hospitalized and now that he was well enough to be discharged, he wanted Jason to take his place on the hospital team. William's belief that Jason was ready to play in the state competition was the best "medical treatment" Jason had experienced at American Lake. Despite the horrible dreams disrupting his sleep and the pounding headaches, he was energized by the prospect of playing in the upcoming ballgames.

CHAPTER 73
MICHAEL

Within the hospital, Jason found the days blending together, one week in the American Lake VA indistinguishable from the next. His medical leave from graduate school had no end in sight. The doctors seemed too overworked to see him more than infrequently. He felt too depressed to write to old friends or relatives on the east coast or Scotland, and he didn't want to burden them with his awkward situation, anyway. He escaped this reality by reading the short stories in every old issue he could find of *The Saturday Evening Post*.

After William's discharge, another patient was moved into the room next to Jason's. During the long, dark hours before dawn, Jason heard the vet crying out with night terrors. One night, avoiding sleep and more nightmares despite their medications, the two men asked the attendant to let them go to the patients' lounge to talk. An unlikely looking pair, Jason mused—the short, emaciated Michael with his haunted eyes and Jason, the strapping softball pitcher. Together they helped each other avoid sleep through the miserable nighttime hours. Neither discussed his nightmares, but the horror they lived with made them brothers who instinctively helped one another.

Michael was undergoing something called electro-shock therapy, and was drugged on Thorazine as well, but he and Jason shared a love of classical music and reading. Jason respected the sensitive, gentle vet and their friendship comforted them both.

One afternoon, Jason had a disturbing premonition of Michael freefalling through space. It became a vision of the young man soaring down a long, long waterfall. The next time Jason met with Doctor Franke, he tried to warn the psychiatrist about Michael. The doctor asked him to describe the vision in detail. As the physician listened impassively, Jason sensed he was being categorized as a hallucinating patient. All he could do was hope that Michael's therapy would alter the course he'd envisioned.

Then Doctor Franke said, "Jason, I believe you could be helped by electro-shock therapy."

Jason saw what heavy doses of Thorazine did to the other patients and didn't want that for himself, so he agreed to the treatment as the least objectionable choice. If he couldn't overcome the North Korea nightmare and depressions, he feared he might end up the way he'd pictured Michael.

During the long daytime hours, Jason began drawing sketches of the angel from his vision in Korea. Finally he felt he had captured not only her look, but her essence. He kept the drawing folded in his shirt pocket and took it out to study often—believing this guardian angel was the reason he had to overcome the suicidal depressions that engulfed him.

CHAPTER 74
SADIE

Natasha and Ivan stood side by side enjoying the view from their corner suite at the Fairmont Olympic Hotel, Seattle's *grande dame* establishment. The picture windows in two walls of the living room looked out on the splendor of the snow-capped Olympic mountain range across Puget Sound to the northwest and Mount Rainier towering in glaciated magnificence to the southeast.

Natasha looked at Ivan. "Does it make you homesick? Being so close to Russia?"

Ivan frowned. "I confess I've grown fond of our tropical lifestyle. The naturalness of it. The feel of the sun and ocean breezes on our skin." He held her close and looked down into her upturned face. "I get such pleasure watching you in the short shorts and halter tops everyone wears on the sultry seacoast. And your bikini," his hand swept across the view, "your curves are more magnificent than these mountains."

She smiled her pleasure. "Really, Ivan. It isn't necessary to flatter me like that. I'm a sure thing, what with our assignments and all. But thank you." She felt his arm tightening around her, ready to put her to the test, when there was a knock at the door.

Ivan released her and stepped back. "Ah, she's here."

"I'll get it." Natasha walked to the door, looked through the peephole, and opened it.

Before her stood a slender woman with the angelic face, waist-long hair and petite figure of a beautiful child. They hugged with enthusiasm, exclaiming their pleasure at seeing one another. "You're unbelievable, Petra—'Sadie.' It's been six years since the rendezvous with Comrade Kanokov in Chicago, over a decade since we trained together in elite forces, and you look as if you haven't aged a day!" She turned to Ivan. "Don't you agree?"

Sadie leapt up to hug Ivan around the neck. Hands around her waist, Ivan held her effortlessly at arm's length and smiled. "I agree." He lowered her feet to the floor.

Smoothing her pinafore, Sadie grinned. "I may not look different, but believe me, I am." She turned to Natasha. "You, on the other hand, have blossomed into one very beautiful woman. I envy you."

Natasha blushed, and poured three shots of vodka. "To the Grand Acquisition!"

"To the Grand Acquisition!" They emptied their glasses and clanked them down on the faux-silver tray on the coffee table. Ivan seated Sadie on the sofa facing the Olympic range, while Natasha increased the volume of the music on the radio and Ivan and she took chairs facing their comrade.

He looked at Sadie. "Obviously, we've checked for bugs." Feel free to talk. What's your problem that requires our help?"

Sadie became all business. "I've finally found out what happened to Leif Olsen and his family. We lost a valuable operative in Leif. I've been pumping a young FBI agent who accidentally let me realize he'd been on the call to Leif's house the night our man disappeared. Said Leif was killed by a student rooming at the boarding house next door. To save Leif's stepdaughter and her baby half-brother from Leif."

Ivan's brow raised in question.

Sadie's voice dripped with contempt. "Seems Leif had her terrified of what he'd do to the baby and forced her to have sex with him, for which the neighbor lost control and killed him with a car jack handle. Apparently the family was in and out of Northwest Hospital in less than a night, then went into a relocation program. My guess is the stepdaughter knew something about Leif's work, but not enough for the FBI to act on. Anyway, the family's lost to us."

Sadie stood and began pacing. "I picked up one of the students residing at the boarding house and eventually learned about everyone who lived there at the time Leif disappeared. One was a forestry student. He moved out at the end of the semester. Normal enough. But when I followed up on him later, I discovered he's a vet going to school on the G.I. Bill *and* he owns a small house and property on Lake Washington in one of the nicer parts of the Seattle area. Nothing about him adds up." Sadie reached into her handbag. "Here's a surveillance photo of him." She handed him the print with an inquiring look.

Ivan took one glance at the picture and caught Natasha's eye, but said nothing. Natasha forced herself to breathe normally as she realized it was MacDougall.

"I suspect he may know about our project," Sadie said.

"The Grand Acquisition?" Natasha asked, alarmed.

Sadie's lips compressed. "Possibly."

Ivan's eyes narrowed. "I'm developing an uncomfortable feeling about this man." Turning to face Sadie, he asked, "How did you learn so much?"

"The young agent answering the call to Leif's house that night was so appreciative of the experiences I lavished on him, he couldn't do enough for me. Whatever I needed to know, he told me—one way or another. Later, he realized what he'd done and reported it to his boss. He told me so. He wants us to run off and live happily ever after." She sighed. "Men are such fools in the hands of a determined amoral woman."

"Are you safe?" Ivan asked.

"Oh, yes. They think I'm a spoiled, rich, thrill-seeker obsessed with seeing how many agents I can score with all across the country. They can't know my questions are from training to exploit men's sexual fantasies and years of psychological training to learn how to ask about one thing in order to learn about another. Of course they suspect me, but my identity is ironclad."

Natasha leaned forward. "How did you manage that?"

CHAPTER 75
CONTAINMENT PLAN

Seattle
Tuesday, September 25, 1961

Natasha wondered how much Sadie would reveal about her cover. The prevailing atmosphere of suspicion in the embassy and the intelligence community kept all of them on guard.

Sadie looked from Natasha to Ivan, apparently deciding how much to tell. "In my specialty—obtaining information from the FBI anywhere I'm needed—my cover has to be unshatterable. I literally traded places with my look-alike college roommate. She was selected earlier when her wealthy parents died in a car crash and our bone and facial structure were found to be almost identical. Our hair too, except I dyed mine black and wore long bangs. Thick glasses and braces, plus me being bookish, completed my image. She sought love from any student who'd have her after her parents died. She desperately needed my friendship, too, and used to explain the ways she had sex with each man we knew. Useful skills for my line of work."

"Is she still alive? Could she talk?" Natasha was almost afraid to ask. Out of habit, she moved to the window and surveyed the area.

"After graduation, we went to Denmark together, where I gave her a choice of trading identities with me or dying very painfully." Sadie cleared her throat. "She became suicidal until I set her up with a Danish count who's a great lover. They married and she started an enviable new life and family with him. She won't talk because it would mean losing everything she now loves. When I returned to the United States, I *was* her—my face, my hair, my handwriting—even had our dental records

switched at her dentist's. Had medical records from one of our European doctor operatives showing I'd been in a terrible auto accident and
had amnesia for a time—to cover for any people or incidents I was at a
loss to remember from my past. I spoke like her. I lived like her. I had an
explanation for any gaps in my memory. Everyone thinks I'm her. So the
FBI's stuck with my cover forever." Sadie gave a wide smile and batted
her eyelashes as she sat on the sofa.

Ivan walked over to the silver tray and poured himself a glass of
water. "You haven't eliminated MacDougall yet?"

Natasha admired Ivan's inscrutable demeanor in light of Jason's
blackmail. That challenge was a secret known only to Ivan and herself,
along with General Kanokov and comrade Sibelius.

"No," said Sadie. "When Leif disappeared, I went to Alaska and
sent the tugboat crew back to Russia. Then I left an agent to hang around
the docks and ascertain that no one's been asking questions about them.
So probably MacDougall didn't know enough to tell anything significant to the agents who came that night. But if he dies unexpectedly, it
could confirm any suspicions the agencies might have."

Natasha hid her relief at the good news of Sadie's strategy.

"Agencies, plural?" Ivan raised a brow.

"The CIA responded to the call to our operative's house, too."

Ivan frowned. "That means they wondered if Leif was doing more
than underwater salvage. They may have suspected he was planting listening devices off the Aleutians to track the American submarine activity there."

Natasha moved from her station by the window. "What's going on
with the submarines?"

"Oil," said Ivan. "It always comes down to oil. Siberia, The Middle
East, the Black Sea, Venezuela, Mexico, the U.S. Gulf States and Gulf
of Mexico, Alaska, the North Pole."

"The North Pole?" Natasha stopped filling her water glass,
puzzled.

Ivan spread his arms. "Vast oil reserves—believed to exist under
the North Pole. Everybody wants to lay claim to the mineral riches
there—most notably our Union of Soviet Socialist Republics, as well as

Canada, Denmark through Greenland, and the United States through Alaska. All want a piece of the action."

"The greed of the rich." Natasha was convinced. "Life will be best when Russia takes control of the world and uses its resources for the betterment of *all* the people, not just the disproportionate wealthy wasteful."

The others nodded in agreement.

"Sadie," Ivan said, "let's get back to our problem. You know he must be incapacitated before he can implicate us. A plausible accident. A permanent debilitating illness. What exactly is it you want our help with?"

Without implicating us, Natasha thought, ever mindful of the blackmail vial of poison and letter.

The elfin blonde drew her legs up sideways on the sofa, but her tone was that of a soldier describing a battle plan. "About four months ago our subject had a combat flashback and attacked a fellow student, almost killing him. He's behind locked doors in the veterans' mental hospital near Tacoma, so he's hard to get to. I have a strategy to neutralize him without drawing attention to ourselves, but I need your help persuading a medical technician who loves his country and family too much to be persuaded by anything I was able to offer with sex or money."

"Tell us your plan." Ivan sat back to listen.

"I've been giving a crash course in fantasy sex to an intern on the psychiatric ward of the VA hospital here near Mercer Island. In return he's given me a crash course about shock treatment, and a hypothetical example of how to give a patient an electro-shock lobotomy. His hospital sends its patients to the Tacoma facility when they need shock treatment." She smiled sweetly.

"MacDougall is receiving a series of electro-shock treatments over the next few days. A technician straps him to a table, puts a roll of leather between his teeth, and at the doctor's command, feeds current to his temples. The amount of current is regulated by a potentiometer on the generator. When the current is turned on, the subject goes into convulsions. If we can arrange for an accident where the potentiometer is turned high enough, his memory will be wiped clean forever, thus eliminating your problem."

Ivan wrapped his hand around his chin. "Very clever. Eliminate MacDougall's memory, not MacDougall. Perfect. Ideally, we'd put your technician on sick leave and I'd slip in there disguised as a relief technician."

Natasha could see Ivan was energized by the challenge.

Sadie shook her head. "This is one place where the security is too good and our time too limited. Even if we fake your identity and get you into the therapy room, afterwards they'd investigate and discover you were a plant." She pursed her lips. "The end of your anonymity and the subtlety of your acquisition plan."

"So," Ivan mused, "the problem is to force the tech to do our bidding and make it look like an accident no one questions."

"Exactly. If anyone can do that, you can."

Ivan stood. "Can you take us to the home of the technician? Right away?"

"Of course."

"Natasha, get our camera bag."

CHAPTER 76
THUGGERY

Tacoma, Washington
Thursday, September 27, 1961

Two days later, Natasha and Ivan lay in wait by the hospital parking lot. Doug Duncan was walking alone to his pickup truck after work. He fit Sadie's description—a big, powerful technician who had little trouble with difficult patients. When he passed a small opening in the hedge that concealed Ivan and Natasha, Ivan sprang out, placed a knife at his throat from behind and commanded, "Stop! Close your eyes!"

Natasha rushed in from behind and tied a blindfold over Duncan's eyes. Sadie drove up in a rental car. Ivan pressed the dull knife hard against his captive's throat and forced him into the back of the car to sit between him and Natasha. Natasha tied his wrists together while Sadie drove them to a remote spot off an old logging road. Sadie turned off the engine and switched off the headlights. Night was approaching, the light fading fast.

Their blindfolded prisoner leaned towards the front seat. "I smell your perfume. This is still about doing you some favor, isn't it? Well, I kept my mouth shut like you said, so you don't have to do this." He straightened his shoulders. "But I ain't gonna hurt nobody for you, if that's what you still want me for."

Natasha noted there seemed to be no fear in the man's voice. Unusual.

After a pause, Sadie replied, "I admire your integrity so highly, I've decided to honor you by asking our most persuasive people to reason with you."

"Do whatever you want to me. I already died in Korea—just been on borrowed time ever since. Now I look after my patients, guys who got wounded worse than me."

Ivan removed the knife from the man's throat and addressed him in a firm, even voice. "Let's see what we know about your life. You and your wife are deeply religious and have home-schooled your teenage daughters. Your eldest is ready for college and wants to be a doctor. Your other will be ready in two years. But the VA isn't allotted enough money by congress to pay its employees adequately, so you live in a rented house and are in debt up to your eyeballs. You can't afford college for your daughters—all because your politicians keep reneging on their promises to care for the veterans it sends to war."

"Mister, I don't do it for the assholes in Washington. I do it for all the people who give their lives so my family and I can live in freedom. I won't do your dirty work just so my kids can go to college. Both my daughters are beautiful and smart and kind. At least they can marry better than my wife did, so their kids can go to college."

Natasha felt a catch in her throat, as Ivan empathized. "What makes you think your wife didn't marry the best of all possible men? It's clear to me she did."

"That kind of talk ain't gonna get you nothin'."

Silence.

Finally Ivan said, "I want you to look at some pictures." Once again he pressed the knife against the man's throat. "If you look at us, you die."

"Mister, that knife's too dull to cut my throat, and you know it. You don't need it. I'll agree to look at the pictures only, not at you guys."

At Ivan's signal, Natasha raised the blindfold and placed two grainy black-and-white photographs in Duncan's hands. She lit the top picture with a flashlight. He stared grimly at the print. It was his wife and youngest, praying alone together at the altar of their church. The backlighting of the sun through a window beyond put them in silhouette and gave them an angelic appearance. Clumsily, he shuffled the bottom picture to the top, and let out a soft cry like a wounded animal.

It was a picture of his eldest daughter standing in the woods kissing her boyfriend. Their clothes lay beside them on the blanket beneath their bare feet. Duncan's tears fell on the photo.

Natasha felt awful as she replaced the blindfold over the man's eyes.

"So my daughter grew up when I wasn't looking. So what?"

"So you have a decision to make." Ivan's matter-of-fact tone might have been asking, "Chocolate or vanilla?" Instead he said, "Either take our money to pay your debts, replace your broken down truck, buy the house you rent and pay for both your daughters' college and then medical school, or I'll give the money to trappers who'd love nothing better than to kidnap your wife and daughters to take them to live in the wilderness and do with them as they please."

Duncan's voice trembled. "Keep your damned money. What do I have to do?"

"You have a small accident that over-volts a patient, erases his memories."

Duncan's back stiffened. "You're not gonna get me to vegetate one of my vets."

"So it's your wife and daughters?" said Ivan.

Duncan was silent for so long, Natasha could hear the slight wheeze of his breathing through damaged lungs. Finally he said, "Who's the patient and what's the problem?"

Sadie answered. "His name's Jason MacDougall."

"MacDougall," Duncan grunted. "Powerful guy. Polite. Thoughtful." He wheezed. "A Korean vet, but no file on him. Was his experience with you traumatic?"

"We think so," said Sadie. "He killed a man and the rest of the man's family disappeared. Eventually he wound up in your hospital because of a murderous flashback incident."

"Might be his experiences with your man set off his problems from Korea. Either way, the shock takes away his memory of traumatic experiences—how long depends on how much current we give him."

Ivan asked, "How could you over-volt him so no one would ever doubt it was a legitimate mistake or accident? Where no one would ever fault you?"

More wheezy breathing. "Not easy. But if I loosen the nut fastening the wrist security strap to the table, back off all but a fraction of the last thread, it will drop off when he convulses, his arm will come free and while I struggle to hold him I could slide my hand over the potentiometer control knob while reaching to switch off the current. That would give him a jolt to make him forget recent trauma real good."

"We require forever."

"We'll leave that up to God." Duncan's voice was firm. "I won't deliberately do forever. It's not necessary. If I over-volt him, his memory will be messed up for life. But he'll still have a shot at a life. That's all I'll do for you. If you don't like it, kill me now—or I'll sure as shit kill you."

Natasha held her breath while Ivan decided if compromise was all he could get.

"I'll trust you. We accept your offer. When will you do it?"

"MacDougall's scheduled for one more treatment tomorrow morning. Have Miss Fantasy meet me at the Esso gas station in Puyallup at quarter of seven after I get off work, and I'll tell her how it went. Then, if any of you ever contact me again, I'll turn you in—or kill you myself."

When Sadie pulled up beside Duncan's old truck at the hospital parking lot, the blindfolded man had parting words.

"Mister, I figure you're a capable soldier of some sort doin' what you gotta do to carry out your mission. But I don't believe you're the kind of low-life who'd go through with what you threatened about my family. Only I can't take the chance I might be wrong. So I'm gonna have to live with the awful thing I'm about to do. And you're gonna have to live with the fact you stole a piece of my self-respect from me. Mister, I think you're a good soldier serving the wrong master. Think about it."

CHAPTER 77
COST OF WINNING

The next morning Natasha awoke to find Ivan already up, withdrawn in thought.

She could read his every nuance from their years of training and working together as élite forces. As his permanent partner, she'd been informed in secret that Ivan's brilliance and extraordinary capability included a borderline manic-depressive personality which she was told she must help him control—no matter what it took.

"You couldn't sleep? Would you like to come to bed and relax with me?"

Self-absorbed, he didn't even look at her. "Not just now. I want to talk. We made a terrible mistake not taking MacDougall out of the picture completely while we had the opportunity."

"Why's that?"

Ivan rolled his thumb, a nervous gesture that meant he was having trouble dealing with whatever was upsetting him. "Because I'm haunted by my conviction that he's not only my birth twin, but my *cosmic* twin, somehow destined to be the key adversary in our project." He turned to her as if preparing for her to challenge him. When she didn't, he said, "He exists to stop us in our mission. I can feel it."

She bounced out of bed. "How can you be sure?" She massaged his shoulders.

"You know perfectly well how. You're the only person who does."

She kneaded his muscular back. "Are you sure you're not just worried about Duncan failing to erase MacDougall's memory, or even that he might turn us in?"

"He's perfectly capable of either. Except he gave his word, which he values too much to break—even to us. No, I'm not worried about him. But it would be unrealistic not to be concerned about successfully altering something as delicate as a human mind, so that's a concern. And I find Duncan's parting statement deeply disturbing."

"You think we're working for the wrong people?" She needed to get him off the cosmic twin tangent.

Ivan ran his fingers through his dark hair. "I think our cause is just. Only right now I'm finding it difficult to deal with the collateral damage sometimes perpetrated on good people in our kind of warfare."

"We agreed to be warriors for Mother Russia, Ivan. We always knew the only rule was to win—whatever it takes." Natasha held his face between her hands. "Let's splurge and have a nice breakfast in the hotel restaurant, surrounded by people not carrying the weight of the world on their shoulders."

After breakfast, Sadie joined them in their suite. They were discussing the day's business when the phone rang. Natasha picked up.

"The desk says there's a long distance call for you, Ivan." She wondered if it was from their boat in Fort Lauderdale.

Ivan rose with a faint smile. "I'll take it in the bedroom so you and Sadie can chat." He closed the door after him.

Natasha listened for Ivan to pick up in the bedroom and heard Sampson on the other end. Hanging up the receiver, she said to Sadie, "Boat problems, as usual. Electrolysis this time. He's going to be on the phone a while."

Sadie squinted at her. "Ivan seems less than his usual upbeat self today."

"He understands the risk of terminating MacDougall outright, but until we know the outcome of Duncan's assignment, our whole mission is at risk. And he's bothered about turning Duncan by threatening his family the way we did."

Sadie gave Natasha a sharp look. "How else was he going to neutralize MacDougall without arousing suspicion? We executed a perfect plan. So instead of letting your partner brood, give him something wonderful to focus on. Surprise him. Be different."

Natasha lowered her eyes.

"Oh, come on, Natasha. He's always cared about you above all others. I know, because after you were raped during training and Ivan destroyed the three Spetsnaz who did it, he never looked at me again—though I certainly tried."

Alarmed, Natasha whispered, "You knew about that?"

"I'm not the best-trained investigator for nothing."

Sadie was a lone investigator and trouble-shooter for the entire country. She lived well and enjoyed her reputation for being the very best in her specialty of intelligence gathering.

Natasha pursed her lips. "Isn't it lonely working by yourself with strangers all the time?"

"Quite the opposite. I meet interesting, capable people. Sometimes in the course of a single day and night I change my clothing and personality to have sex with four or five different men, learning what pleases each and how to extract information from every one. It's fascinating detective work. How could a woman be bored, being so desired all the time? I hate sleeping alone and find something to enjoy about each man. It's like living infatuated all the time. I try to treat every man like I think it's his very first time—to see if I can generate that look of surprise and wonder on his face as he gets caught up in something new and wonderful that makes him cry out like a startled child. You should try it with Ivan. It's exciting. Rewarding."

"But what about you?" Natasha wanted to know. "What do the men do for you?"

Sadie looked puzzled. "That's not what it's about, Natasha. It's about what we can do for men. They're the ones who need physical release. We're just the facilitator."

"Yes, but what do you get in return?" Natasha persisted.

"What do I get in return?" Sadie's eyes widened. "Their desire. Their passion. They give up their careers for us. Die for us. What more could we possibly ask?"

Natasha rarely had the opportunity to talk woman-to-woman and Sadie was someone she could trust and confide in, especially on a topic considered taboo. "Have you ever wondered why women don't feel what men do—that electrifying, tension-building spasm, followed by such grand release?"

Sadie chuckled. "What a silly notion. If we experienced anything like what the men do, we'd be too used up to service them properly."

"When Ivan takes me, I feel like he's Zeus, descending from Mount Olympus, seizing his pleasure from a mortal. If I ever think I've found a man you might respond to like that, I'll send him to you, code-named 'Zeus'."

The bedroom door opened and Ivan rejoined them. Natasha hadn't shared with Sadie what she'd learned from Sybil about the joys of sex. On the other hand, she had to be careful not to betray too much of herself and Ivan and the source of their knowledge.

CHAPTER 78
MISSION ACCOMPLISHED

Seattle
Friday, September 28, 1961

While Sadie was in Puyallup, Natasha felt Ivan's remorse settle again over his normally positive nature.

She tried empathy. "What Duncan said, it bothers me, too. Deeply. But we must carry on."

Ivan shook his head. "It's not that." He stared out the hotel window and drummed his fingers on the marble sill. "MacDougall. I still sense he could remain my nemesis."

She took her partner's hands. "Sometimes your perceptions are simply depression, Ivan. Maybe this is one of those times."

"I wish. But I do believe it, or it wouldn't depress me."

Natasha tried to distract him with a novel technique. But Ivan was in no mood for her. So she teased him relentlessly until he took her with such unstoppable explosion she had no control of how it was done.

Just before eight, there was a loud knock on the door. They opened it together to be greeted by Sadie's dazzling smile. "Mission accomplished."

In the living room, she reported, "Duncan said it went perfectly. He got exactly the voltage and time he calculated. Whatever MacDougall knew, he doesn't anymore.

Natasha gave Ivan a dynamite smile and a pert two-finger salute that said, "See, I told you there was nothing to worry about."

"I even made Duncan feel good about what he'd done," Sadie said. "Told him he'd saved MacDougall's life, that we'd have terminated his vet if it weren't for the 'accident'."

Natasha ordered a celebration supper and champagne brought up to their suite. Ebullient over the success of their Seattle mission and Ivan's return to his normal cheerfulness, she stood before her leader and toasted him. "To victory, and to you, my genius, unbeatable comrade— another success." They clinked crystal and drained the sparkling liquid.

After dinner, they moved to comfortable chairs and the sofa to sip cognac.

Sadie sat with her feet curled under her and looked directly at Ivan. "Would you have used the trappers?"

"Never. It was bad enough just to have Duncan think I might order such evil things. His dignity shamed us."

"Well, here's more," she said. "I gave him a brown bag with a hundred fifty thousand cash. He threw it in my face and drove off. Considering how much that money could have meant to him and his family, the man's integrity is as real as it gets."

Sadie finished her cognac and stood. "Got to go now. It's been wonderful working with you. I've been ordered to leave in the morning for a mission in San Diego. Seems your effort to get smuggling operations flowing over the Mexican border has finally taken off, and my services are required to identify corruptible FBI agents working border security." She hugged herself. "I love my work!"

After Sadie left, Ivan stood before Natasha and raised his glass. "To my extraordinary, indefatigable associate. How could any leader ever ask for more." He downed his cognac, took her empty glass from her, set it on the table with his and drew her to him with another kind of thirst. She was unzipped and unhooked faster than she could inhale.

She laughed, letting her clothing slide to the floor. "I think you want more already. Much more." Exuberant, she pushed away, and danced around him. Suddenly she stopped in front of him.

"What are you thinking about so hard, Ivan?"

"Not much gets past you, does it?" He gave her a wry smile. "I've decided that when we return to Fort Lauderdale, we'll have our lawyers arrange for Duncan's wife to receive an inheritance of a hundred fifty thousand dollars from a distant relative she doesn't know about."

Natasha wanted to shout for joy, but she restrained herself. "I think you're doing the right thing. Don't forget to include enough for inheritance taxes and legal fees, so they get to keep all that they need."

Ivan ran his fingertips over Natasha's perfect skin, heightening her anticipation. But she pretended not to notice his caressing. She reached out and disrobed him as deftly as he had her, and smiled at his readiness. Tonight she would be an experience he'd never forget. She licked her lips. "You're alright now?"

He was fixated on her poised body. He shuddered, oozing lust. "Yes. I made a terrible mistake, not keeping in mind MacDougall is our most important enemy—but we seem to have lucked out anyway."

Forget your cosmic brother, Ivan. She pressed her body against his. "How would you like an unforgettable hero's reward?"

He looked down at her gleefully, clearly reading her signals. "Depends. What's a hero's reward?"

"Brace yourself and I'll show you." Taking a deep breath she wrapped her arms around his neck, leapt up and attacked him with such abandon that both cried out from the fierceness of her offering.

Later, while he slept in her arms, Natasha luxuriated in dreams of conquest and eventual victory over the greedy, spoiled Americans.

CHAPTER 79
SUICIDAL DEPRESSION

Tacoma, Washington
Monday, December 4, 1961

Jason couldn't recall why he was in this place, this veterans' hospital. He just knew that if he didn't get out of here, he was going to go crazy. He tapped his foot impatiently as he sat waiting to see Doctor Franke. While receiving shock treatment he'd felt as if he'd been adrift in a vast ocean, as if he'd been treading water and trying not to drown. Then he'd found himself on the sand beach, just beyond the lapping waves, slowly continuing his relentless breast stroke in the sand, inching forward, climbing back to life among the living ... .

Jason took the drawing out of his shirt pocket where he always carried it, unfolded it and immediately felt at peace looking at the picture. It was a drawing that he found among his things after his electric shock treatment. A beautiful young woman with long hair and splendid features. The woman from his vision. He still remembered the vision, just not when or where he was when it happened. His memory was messed up and that upset him.

The doctor called him into his office and had Jason sit before him. Doctor Franke tapped his fingers on his desk. He seemed to be a nervous person. Jason wondered if that was an occupational hazard.

The doctor interlaced his fingers, turned his palms out and stretched his arms toward Jason, as though trying to decide how much to tell him. "In forestry school you began having migraines, nightmares about something that happened to you in Korea ... and finally a flashback episode that made you seek help here at the VA. We gave you intensive shock treatment to make you forget some of the worst of Korea. As you well know, it has created significant gaps in your memory. But your memories should start returning within a year or so."

Jason turned his palms up. "Why shock treatment?"

"It's one of the therapies for what we call 'war neurosis.' At least, that's the name for it in Korean vets. During the Civil War, it was called 'soldier's heart' or 'exhausted heart.' In World War I it was 'shell shock.' In World War II, 'battle fatigue.' It's an emotional disorder we see in a number of soldiers who experience trauma involving death, serious injury or mass destruction. For some reason we could obtain no records about you, other than your dates of service. You avoided sleep and refused to tell what your nightmares were about. We do know you decided to come here after you almost killed a classmate. Eventually we gave you electroshock therapy to take away the memories that were haunting you."

Jason felt as though he'd been clubbed. "Is my classmate alright?"

"He's fine, Jason, fully recovered. You said you were nauseated by the garlic on his breath. The smell may have triggered your flashback."

"So I'm damaged goods, huh." He tried to sound nonchalant, but fear gripped him. Fear of not being in control. What did all of this mean? He was afraid of the answer, but asked anyway. "What am I dealing with? I mean, what kinds of problems do I have?"

"You already conquered the biggest problem when you drove yourself here in your own car, Jason. Most people won't admit to themselves or doctors that something's wrong. Common problems are depression and suicide. You're going to have to deal with that. The nightmares could return after a while—we call them 'night-terrors.' Anything might trigger you. Certain sights, sounds or smells—like garlic—may be reminders that distress you. Other problems? Exaggerated startle response to loud noises. No sense of future. Overwhelming anger and rage. Hyper-vigilant, survivalist behavior. Paranoia. Each case is different. Time makes the bad memories less sharp; it's the best medicine. We accelerated the time factor with the EST."

"Am I going to do that flashback thing again? Kill innocent people?"

"No one knows. You can be helped with drugs . . ."

Jason envisioned those patients with glazed eyes, subdued, malleable, sometimes drooling and incoherent. He crossed his arms and vehemently shook his head. "No drugs! I've seen what happens to vets on those drugs. If I can't be a contributor in life, I'd rather be dead."

"Could you do that, Jason?"

"Do what?" he asked, buying time to think of an acceptable answer.

"Take your own life?" The doctor leaned back, tapping his fingertips together.

Jason sat up on the edge of his chair. "Absolutely not! I'm too much of a survivor." But was he? The possibility that he might have nothing left to live for chilled him. "Well, lately the idea has held a certain appeal."

"How do you deal with those thoughts?"

He wished he could say that he had them under control, but there was no control, and that scared the hell out of him. He told the doctor only, "I make myself think about something else. Something I want."

"Such as?"

"Like meeting the right woman." Jason stood and looked the doctor straight in the eyes. "Doctor Franke, if I understand you correctly, I'm a time bomb waiting to go off. What can I do to have a productive life that doesn't endanger anyone or involve heavy medication? How can I help myself?"

The doctor smiled. "You've just said the magic words, Jason. 'Help yourself.' Just the way you sought help here before you blew again. But that isn't the way it usually goes, or people wouldn't let things build until they flash back and maybe kill someone."

Jason shuddered at what he'd apparently done to his classmate.

"Here's an example you can relate to," said Doctor Franke. "Who takes Percodan early on while coming down with their first migraine? They probably don't recognize what the headache is, and they haven't yet learned they have to drop the pressing demands of life and prioritize controlling the growing pain. They only learn that priority after they've discovered what can happen to their mind and body if they don't act to maintain control." He folded his hands on his desk. "War neurosis is like that—recognizing the problem and acting early is everything."

The doctor leaned forward, his tone encouraging. "To minimize recurrences, get plenty of sleep and stay out of stressful situations over which you have no control. Exercise a lot. I'll cut back on your meds, and we'll see how you do. Now, before we discuss your future, there're a couple more things you need to know."

The doctor's smile turned to a frown and Jason sensed reluctance in the older man. He sat back again and waited with raised brows while the doctor stood and paced as he searched for the right words. Jason noticed the doctor was developing a paunch, which made his trousers too short. He smiled inwardly when he saw the doctor was wearing one black sock and one brown one, but the smile didn't last long. Something was wrong. What?

Finally Doctor Franke simply blurted out what was troubling him. "Jason, don't try to return to school. I'm afraid you were accidentally over-volted during your shock treatment."

CHAPTER 80
OVER-VOLTED

The walls of the doctor's office seemed to spin around him as Jason tried to process the words: "Accidentally over-volted."

For a nanosecond Jason was looking through the open door of the hospital EST room and saw himself lying on his back in a short gown, strapped to a steel table. There was something between his teeth, and electrodes strapped to his temples. Suddenly his body arched with a huge groan, his muscles bulged, and his neck corded in a tension-filled scene that looked like a horror movie. Unexpectedly, his right arm broke free and the powerful technician-attendant fought it while reaching for a switch on a box with dials. Doctor Franke shouted, "Turn it off, turn it off." Jason had the strangest feeling the white-uniformed tech struggling to hold his arm was counting seconds before he flipped the switch. *Couldn't be.* Duncan was a gentle giant who lived to serve his fellow veteran patients.

Then, as in a dream, Jason was back in Doctor Franke's office, feeling shaken as he heard the doctor say, "While we took away your bad memories, it turned out we also impaired your ability to memorize." Doctor Franke looked intensely uncomfortable, but he went on. "Think of your brain as having channels that carry your memories. The deeper the channels, the better your memory skills. When we over-volted you, we sort of leveled your memory channels. It's like the flow of your memories dissipates into desert sands now. You're only going to be able to remember names, phone numbers, formulas and directions that you use every day, over and over."

Jason felt as though he'd just been punched. As he processed the full implication of Doctor Franke's revelation, something snapped. Furious with the doctor, he leapt up with boxer's fists and thundered, "What gave you the right to do that to me?"

The doctor winced and retreated behind his desk, a hand searching, no doubt for an alarm button concealed there. "I'm sorry. We practice the art of medicine. It's not a foolproof science. And there was a mishap with the potentiometer. But don't misunderstand." He held up his hand defensively and his voice grew louder, penetrating Jason's rage. "Your mind and physical coordination remain as exceptional as ever. We've tested you exhaustively. You can do anything you could do before shock treatment—except for your memorization skills. And those should improve, with time."

Jason forced himself to sit back down to alleviate the man's fears. Pretty stupid to upset the person who held the key to his freedom.

Jason had so many questions. Burning questions that needed answers. "Why is it I remember going to Korea and working there, but not how I got back? Why do I remember a vision I had, but not where I was when I had it? Why do I remember some of the good times with my family and friends, but not the bad? How do you do that?"

"*We* don't do it, Jason. *You* do. More precisely, your subconscious mind does it. When you're ready, the memories will return."

Jason took the sketch out of his pocket and unfolded it. "Who is this woman? Where did the drawing come from?" He handed it to Dr. Franke.

"You drew it before shock treatment. Said it was a woman you didn't know who'd saved your life." The doctor studied the picture. "To me it suggests brains, character and beauty. Humor, too." He handed it back.

Doctor Franke changed the subject. "You've got the money from your father's business. You don't have to work for a while. You can take your time figuring out what you want to do next. I want you to think about leaving forestry, and the Northwest especially."

Jason let that sink in. He felt adrift and disoriented. "Why? Forestry is what I know. What would I do?"

The doctor shook his head, clearly as uncertain as Jason. "I don't know. But I do know Seattle's rainy atmosphere is noted for its high suicide rate. Psychiatrists are just beginning to recognize that certain individuals need a lot of sunlight or they become clinically depressed. You're fighting depression and prefer not to take drugs for it. I'd like to suggest you try a sunny climate for a while. Like Texas, Arizona, New Mexico or Florida. If you choose not to follow this advice, there's a good chance that within a year you, or someone else, will be dead by your hand."

Jason instinctively knew the doctor was correct about needing more sunlight.

Deep furrows lined the doctor's brow. "If you could have anything you wanted, Jason, what would it be?"

Jason thought about it for a moment. What *did* he want? He loved the mountains and forests and wildlife he knew so well. He was fascinated with the sea and loved coastal cruising. And he wanted someone to share his passions. He chose his words carefully. "I'd like to live near the ocean—do a lot of boating." He kept his thoughts about a soul mate to himself.

The doctor nodded agreeably. "I worked on a commercial fishing boat in the North Sea as a teenager. There are many ways to fulfill your love of the sea. There's always a way if you want it badly enough." He paused and steepled his fingers to his lips. "You're at a major crossroad in your life, Jason. The decision you make will either keep you in the Northwest—a dismal life for you no doubt—or send you off in an unknown direction. But you must have sunshine if you're to have hope."

That's not a choice, it's an ultimatum. Jason felt angry and betrayed, but concealed his feelings. He figured he'd be medicated more and kept in the hospital longer if he showed those emotions. "When can I expect to be out of here?"

"We want to monitor your recovery from the ... treatment. And we need time to see how you do without the meds. No promises, but I'll shoot for springtime."

Doctor Franke paused and Jason tensed, waiting for the other shoe to drop.

"Your aunt Sarah was here before your EST. We arranged with your godparents for you to go live with them in Long Beach, California, when you're discharged from this facility. Your uncle David is the new commandant at the cruiser and destroyer flotilla down there. You need a short transition period of living with people who know you well and love you. You'll have time there to try to figure out how to play the hand you've been dealt."

Cards? Was his life just a game? Jason stood up, eager to escape this room, this man, this hospital.

Later, while walking the grounds, he turned to the only source left to him. He prayed for guidance, but his mind was a blank. A blank. Suddenly he felt a welling of emotion.

God, he implored, *if you don't show me the cards, how do I play my hand?*

CHAPTER 81
BRIDAL VEIL FALLS

Bridal Veil Falls, Oregon
Wednesday, April 11, 1962

Michael Higgins checked out of the American Lake VA hospital and drove down the coast, through Portland, to Bridal Veil Falls. He arrived there at five. The falls were as beautiful as he remembered them, especially when a shaft of sunlight made soft rainbow hues in the vaporized water of the fall. Michael treasured the beauty of the moment. *Got to keep moving.* He tossed the Hertz rental car keys into the glove compartment and got out, leaving the doors unlocked.

He hadn't thought about the climb to the top of the falls being so difficult. After a year in the hospital, the climbing exhausted him. The thought that he needed to rest up before the next phase of his journey brought a smile to his lips. The sun was setting, however, and he wanted to see well.

He stepped carefully out onto the rocks beside the head of the falls and looked down over the edge. Magnificent. The volume of water spilling over the lip and falling almost two hundred feet straight down to the rock pool below was the most moving thing he'd ever experienced. Nature at her grandest. He wanted nothing more.

He stepped back where he wouldn't lose his balance and searched his pockets for the note. He unfolded it and read, "Dear Dad, don't be sad for me. I'm in a better place. I'd like to stay here, if I might. I love you, Michael."

He folded the letter, wrapped it carefully in a plastic bag and placed it in one of the lower side pockets of his army field jacket. When he was sure the flap was snapped, he edged back to the brink. He stood there peering down into the shadows as the light faded, loving the sound of the water shooshing over the edge, the quiet thunder of the water hitting the pool below. Home. No more terror. Michael's heart filled with peace.

He raised his arms straight out from his sides. All it took was a simple command to his leg muscles to lean forward on his feet. Then he was airborne, racing the waterfall down the rock face of the cliff. The wind of his passing whistled. He uttered no sound. He breathed in deeply, a smile on his face. The rocks flew up to receive him. Home at last.

CHAPTER 82
HIGGINS' RESOLVE

Bridal Veil Falls, Oregon
Sunday, April 15, 1962

It was three days before Walter Higgins could break away from work. As the Deputy Director of Operations, his was a 'round-the-clock job at the CIA. He now worked from the new headquarters building as it was being constructed at Langley, in McLean, Virginia. What a difference from the original building on E Street in Washington, D.C. In addition to worldwide surveillance, he and the Deputy Director of Science and Technology were plagued with problems installing satellite equipment in the vast and complex operations rooms. The equipment that existed when the facility was designed was already obsolete, and the new gear didn't fit the designed spaces. Higgins recognized that electronics technology changes were becoming exponential, so he'd ordered his operations rooms redesigned. Alternate removable six foot panels along three walls, with eight feet of workspace behind, would permit new control consoles to be installed adjacent to working ones until ready to switch over seamlessly. All this without distracting the operations personnel in the room.

Higgins was a great problem solver. So why the sickening phone call three days ago? Why hadn't he been able to be there for his precious Michael when he was needed? First his beloved wife, to breast cancer. Now their son, who had been a living reminder of her. *Hell!* Some fixer he was.

To keep his sanity, he looked down from the air force helicopter at the vast forests of Douglas fir trees, the principal industry of Oregon and Washington. They flew over the Columbia River where, to the west, he could see the sprawl of Portland in the early morning light, and the river emptying into the Pacific Ocean. Lord, it was an impressive view. Because he wanted to visit the hospital at American Lake, only twenty minutes' drive from McChord Air Force Base, he'd flown to the base and arranged for the helicopter to take him to Oregon.

His thoughts were interrupted by the copter pilot's voice in his headphones. "We're approaching Bridal Veil Falls now, sir. I'll put down in the visitor parking lot. It's already been cleared for us." Through his window Higgins saw two state trooper cars.

The pilot landed and cut the engine. Two officers who always accompanied Higgins opened the chopper door, looking all around in their professional way, and were the first off. As they bent forward to disembark, Higgins noted the array of bulges under their Brooks Brothers jackets. Poor guys were in for a weight-bearing climb today.

The considerate pilot had landed so that Higgins stepped out into full view of the falls. *Oh, Michael, I hope you've found peace here.*

The two state troopers and a state park ranger were momentarily confused that the agents were so much more stylishly dressed than their boss, who was wearing his customary rumpled, brown tweed suit. One of the troopers handed him a cardboard box. Higgins drew in a deep breath and looked at the box as he held it gently, trying to absorb the reality. Then he handed it to one of his men. The officer placed it in a backpack.

"Gentlemen, my men and I would like to make the climb alone, if that's alright with you. Would you please show us to the trail?"

At the top of the falls, Higgins stood for a long time lost in thought as he said goodbye to his son. A wave of loss and guilt overwhelmed him. He slumped and covered his face with his hands. "Are you alright, sir?" one of the men asked, close behind him. Clearly, the man was worried.

Higgins drew himself up. "Yes, Bill, as well as can be expected. Thank you for your concern." *Good men, these.*

He tried again to figure out how it had happened. For security purposes, key personnel in his agency were given psychiatric screening every few months. If they developed a problem, they were taken off the job and given immediate help. Not so with war neurosis. Higgins was convinced there had to be hundreds of thousands of vets out there coping alone because they thought nobody cared. And they were right. Congress wouldn't accept responsibility, and the VA couldn't tackle such a vast problem without the funding. Higgins wondered if it might be costing Congress more to turn its back on the responsibility than to accept it. He thought about the large number of admirals and generals the country was losing to early heart failure—as well as suicide. Filling those shoes cost millions of dollars per individual in training and experience. How badly the VA needed studies dealing with stress, too. So much to understand and so little priority with the people allocating the money.

Nobody wanted to take the time to deal with the problem, least of all the people who had it. Time was always a challenge. My God. His own son. His own son, and he hadn't found ways to make more time for him. Perhaps to have discovered how much pain he was concealing from his dad?

Walter Higgins did something he'd never done before in his professional life—he allowed his emotions to well up to the surface. He felt like a broken old man. He shook his fists in anger and shouted his hurt out over the waterfall. Tears leaked out of his eyes as he let Michael go, releasing his ashes over the waterfall, and watching the breeze scatter them. Then the ethereal flute music of Grieg's *Morning* began playing in his mind. Michael had loved that music and played the record over and over in his room at home. Now Higgins knew why Michael chose Bridal Veil Falls. He stood there a few minutes more, promising Michael he would seek redemption for his failure as a father. Maybe he could help Korean vet Jason MacDougall, who had befriended his son ... . He started back down the trail, determination in his step.

CHAPTER 83
WALTER AND SEBASTIAN

Tacoma, Washington
Sunday afternoon, April 15, 1962

Walter Higgins sat opposite his dead son's psychiatrist at the American Lake Veterans Hospital. Higgins had three doctoral degrees, one of them in psychology. They helped him in his position as Deputy Director of Operations. No more "Doctor Higgins" and "Doctor Franke." These men had a professional collegiality.

"Thanks for coming in on a Sunday. I couldn't leave Langley till last night. Sebastian, how did this happen without either of us having a clue about what Michael was thinking?"

Sebastian Franke looked pensive as he crossed his arms over his chest. "Like most people, Walter, he let us see what we wanted to see. That's a problem with war neurosis. It's easier to ignore than to deal with."

He paused and a silence fell between them. Finally he added, "Are you taking Michael back with you?"

A knot formed in Higgins' throat and he coughed. "I scattered his ashes over the falls in Oregon this morning, as he requested."

"I'm sorry, Walter. I don't know what more we could have done."

An upwelling of anger threatened to suffocate Higgins. *No more we could have done? Like hell.* "Well, I know what more *I* could have done. I could have not been so absorbed in my job day and night that I had no serious time for him." He waved his arms, distraught.

The psychiatrist rose from his desk chair, stepped over to Higgins and placed a hand on his shoulder. "Walter, I don't think it would have made a difference. I don't think anything could have helped Michael live with the horror he experienced. Even shock treatment couldn't. When he was ordered to fire the napalm into the building with the North Korean soldiers, and then all the children ran out with their burning clothes and flesh falling off, he was given a burden no man of his gentle character could live with. If we'd given him more shock treatment, he'd have become a vegetable."

Walter placed a hand over Franke's and looked up in appreciation. Standing abruptly, he paced the room. "Enough talk about what can't be fixed. Let's talk about what can be—Jason MacDougall."

Franke frowned. "MacDougall? What about Jason?"

"I never told you, when I was here a year ago to visit Michael. I have MacDougall's psychiatric profile from the Naval Academy. It mentions that he might have psychic abilities—to sense things others don't usually notice. Premonitions. Even visions. I could use those abilities on an op in Key Largo." Higgins clasped his hands together. "I'm a pragmatist and uneasy with things I can't see, hear, touch or prove scientifically. On the other hand, in my line of work, we're compelled to evaluate the motives of informants ad nauseam. Often our decisions boil down to judgment calls. And on this one, everything in me is saying, 'Don't let MacDougall slip through our fingers'."

"Judgment calls." The psychiatrist took a seat on the corner of his desk. "We have the same problem with the vets. We always have to question everything we hear, unless there are corroborating records. Many come to the VA with stories of what they wished they'd been in war, sometimes for their pride and ego, sometimes just for the disability income and care. Without hard evidence, they get turned away automatically."

Higgins sat down again. "Sebastian, how prevalent is war neurosis?"

"I suspect one in three battle veterans has it in varying degrees."

"My God. How can that be?" He leaned forward.

The doctor shifted on his desk. "How can it not be, Walter? War is insane. Two sides funnel hundreds of thousands of men together to keep killing each other until one side runs out of men or the will to continue the carnage, and ceases—as we did in Korea. The normal response of sane people caught up in the insanity of war is varying degrees of abnormality, or what we call insanity."

Higgins pressed his hands together. "So you're saying, 'If war doesn't make a person crazy, he wasn't sane to begin with?'"

"Precisely, my friend." Sebastian cleared his throat. "Getting back to MacDougall." He folded his arms across his chest. "Jason has a remarkable mind, but he never mentioned anything about extrasensory perception to me other than a vision of some girl—which, frankly, I thought was a product of his imagination. No one here has reported him showing that kind of ability."

Higgins peered at Franke. "It seems the psychiatrist at the Naval Academy decided to give a battery of tests to Jason's nemesis, an upperclassman named Kloski. Jason was certain Kloski would give orders that could get good men killed. Not only did the man test capable of giving such orders, but was actually prone to giving them in emergencies he wasn't trained to handle. Kloski couldn't think on his feet, outside the box." Higgins clasped his hands tight together as he relayed the story of the twelve sailors drowning just as MacDougall foretold. "The lieutenant was eased out of the navy."

Higgins leaned forward in his chair. "Two years ago we were following up on a situation in Seattle. I sent an attractive young woman, one of my brightest profilers, with extrasensory abilities and needs of her own, to debrief Jason and evaluate his reported capabilities. Her report indicates Jason has a good awareness of his weaknesses as well as his strengths." Higgins nodded to himself. "Over several days, he told the officer all about his paranormal capabilities, their limitations, and a story that they were gifts inherited through his Scottish grandfather."

"It's understandable that Jason wouldn't talk about them," said Franke. "He doesn't want to be a misfit. And he knew I thought he was hallucinating," the doctor's voice dropped, "when he told me of a vision he had about Michael." Franke bit his lips together. "I assumed it was the medications talking."

Higgins swallowed his pain and looked into Franke's eyes, determined to find a way to save this valuable life in exchange for the one he didn't save—hadn't taken time to save.

"Sebastian, how reliable is MacDougall now? How bad is his war neurosis? If he has the gifts that have been reported, could he bird dog for me without jeopardizing others working with him?"

CHAPTER 84
STRENGTHS AND RISKS

Tacoma, Washington
Sunday afternoon, April 15, 1962

Walter Higgins waited as Doctor Franke returned to his desk chair, taking time to consider his answer. The psychiatrist chewed his lip before replying carefully.

"Walter, dealing with sick minds all the time, I've required treatment in hospitals a couple of times myself. Does my difficulty maintaining mental balance keep me from being capable? Obviously not. Especially if I use my liability as a tool to help my patients. But each person is different. So I'd be lying if I said I knew the answers to your questions. What I can say is what I believe about Jason at this time."

He leaned forward over his desk and pointed to his fingers. "One. Jason is remarkable, capable of anything, both good and bad—and he knows it. Two. It's very important to him to be in control—of himself, of whatever he does. It's why he won't get drunk or take drugs he can avoid. By the way, he's off meds. I'll even go so far as to say that now he realizes he can have flashbacks, he'll probably recognize what's happening in time to control it. Three. Jason believes he's being prepared to do something special in life. It's how he handles all the tragedy and struggle that's befallen him."

Higgins held up a hand. "You mean like a mission?" Walter hoped for something he could use to his advantage. *I've got your mission, Jason.*

"He doesn't know. He just believes his life has a purpose."

"Okay. What else?"

"Four. Killing the North Korean woman shouldn't bother Jason so much—but it does. Why, I don't know. Until you contacted me, I didn't realize he was under military orders to tell no one about what happened in Korea. Fortunately, you shared critical information with me. For now, the Korea incident is gone from his conscious memory. Five. Jason has a new problem. His short-term memory. We had an accident that caused over-volting during his final shock treatment. There's going to be a lot of frustration and anger over that through the years. Six. Except for his memorization skills, Jason still tests at the highest levels of intelligence we record. I would expect him to out-think, out-perform and out-class anyone else you might select for your special needs." Sebastian sat back, finished.

"Anything else?"

Doctor Franke looked out the window for a moment, as though giving himself time to think before he turned back. "Yes. Jason's deeply depressed, just like Michael. He shouldn't be having nightmares about Korea any more, but he is. The fact he suspects they're true scares him to his core. He's also depressed because he's worried about his ability to function well with his memory impairment. I've told him he can't return to college, advised him to move out of the rainy Northwest, give up his career in forestry, go where he can live in the sun. His anger wells up in him so quickly it's difficult to control. Jason knows he's a time bomb waiting to explode if he can't defuse the triggers. His self-confidence is lower than the ground he stands on. He feels terribly alone and his hope is practically nonexistent. If Jason could find something to give himself to, that could be the best medicine for him. Otherwise, I may have to put him back on anti-depressants."

Despite the doctor's analysis of his patient's liabilities, Higgins experienced a surge of hope. "Sebastian, it just happens that the CIA is losing valuable people to stress and nervous disorders. I've recruited a psychiatrist who was valedictorian at Harvard Medical School and later got extraordinary results with a few vets at the Bethesda Naval Hospital. She's researching non-pharmaceutical ways to deal with the problems because we can't afford to have our operatives lose their edge by being on sedatives." Energized by the possibilities he envisioned with the still unstable but talented vet, Higgins leaned toward the psychiatrist.

"I've got a plan of action for Jason, subject to your approval. Will you continue to hold off on the drugs, to see if Jason can fix himself— so I can try putting him to work?"

"Alright, Walter. But at the first sign, he goes back on Thorazine."

"As soon as Jason is discharged from this hospital and is back on his feet, I want to try using him as a citizen surveillant for my team in Key Largo."

Doctor Franke appeared to be mulling over the ramifications.

"He'd be in the sunny climate he needs." Higgins hoped that would help the psychiatrist with his evaluation of the proposal.

Franke finally spoke. "It's worth a try, my friend. Jason's life could be at risk, but the risk sounds acceptable, considering the good that can come of it. Jason's a fortunate young man to have such a resourceful person as you in his corner."

The risk sounds acceptable. However, that's what they'd said about Michael and look how he ended up. Higgins felt a flush of anxiety. He couldn't let Michael's friend die that way. It just meant he'd have to double his efforts to make sure Jason lived.

CHAPTER 85
VISITING JASON

Tacoma, Washington
Sunday afternoon, April 15, 1962

Higgins hoped for the best and approached Jason in the VA hospital patients' lounge, where he sat reading a short story in *The Saturday Evening Post*. This was a typical government facility. Clean. Well maintained. And furnished with the lowest-bid furniture available. What wasn't typical was the view through the large windows: expansive green lawns and tall fir trees, with the majestic snow-capped Olympic mountain range for a backdrop.

Higgins stopped in front of Jason, who put down the magazine and looked up into his face. Higgins liked the young man's directness.

"Son, my name is Walter Higgins. I'm Michael's father. May I sit and talk with you?"

Jason stood politely. "I take it you already know my name."

Jason looked better than Higgins remembered. The tall young man with the red-blond hair retained his fit body and now his bright blue eyes had a brilliance that was missing when he'd been medicated.

Damn what we do to these boys. "My son was given shock treatment before you. I was visiting him here when I first met you. The doctors told me about your unusual kindnesses to him. Thank you for befriending him and trying to give him hope."

Looking around at the other patients in the lounge, Jason replied, "I'm sorry, sir. I can't remember your son. Which one is Michael?"

Higgins passed a hand over his eyes. Why the fact that Jason couldn't remember his son hurt him so badly, he couldn't say. He just knew he felt like someone had knifed him in the stomach and then twisted the knife. But it wasn't Jason's fault.

"Michael's in a better place now. He ended his tortured memories of Korea. I didn't realize the trouble he was in. I should have been there for him, more than I was." Higgins was ashamed of himself, seeking forgiveness from Michael's friend. For a moment Higgins got caught up in self-pity. First his wife. Now his son to a disorder most people didn't know or care about.

Jason leaned forward and placed his hand on Higgins' forearm. Instead of sympathizing, he said something that snapped Higgins out of his melancholy.

"What a contradiction you are." Squeezing Higgins' forearm, he added, "As hard as nails under the absent-minded professor appearance." Looking Higgins straight in the eyes, Jason asked, "Tell me, Mr. Higgins, what's your real reason for being here?"

Higgins felt as though he'd been slapped. "Am I so transparent?"

"No sir. It's just that sometimes I see what others can't. I still have that gift and sometimes I wish it weren't so. Right now you need to look ahead, not behind you."

Higgins' mind raced. He wanted Michael's friend to make it. And he saw qualities in Jason that he wanted at the agency's disposal. Therein lay the two-edged sword. Emotional involvement with a loose cannon versus unique capabilities perhaps vital to the nation's future. He decided to play this hand straight. He looked at Jason. "You're right. But don't let that discount my gratefulness for the friendship you offered my son."

"So, what's your business, Mr. Higgins?"

CHAPTER 86
RECRUITING JASON

Tacoma, Washington
Sunday afternoon, April 15, 1962

Higgins sat down in one of the vinyl-covered easy chairs in the patients' lounge, leaned back and laced his fingers behind his head. "My business? I'm the Deputy Director of Operations for the CIA. My business is surveillance outside the U.S." Anticipating Jason's next question, he leaned forward and raised his palm like a stop sign. "You've been told the military can't find your records. It's because I have them." He sat there, waiting for Jason's reaction.

Jason raised an eyebrow but said nothing.

"Did you know Doctor Franke is brilliant and one of the foremost authorities on stress disorders, that he works at this VA medical center because this is where the pioneering action is for him?"

"I know he has a fine mind and a wonderful staff helping here."

"My feelings exactly. Which is why I'm talking so openly with you." Higgins leaned closer to Jason. "He believes you won't disappoint me."

Jason's eyes veiled cautiously. "Disappoint you? How?"

"I'm considering asking for your help with something, even though your nervous disorder makes you ineligible for regular employment in the CIA."

"Why would you do that?"

Because every instinct I possess is telling me you have the ability to be a key player for me—that you're worth the risk.

He edged so close that Jason discretely inched back. "Because Doctor Franke and I have discussed you thoroughly and we both agree that you have unique abilities that make you perfect for something I have in mind, Jason."

"You said you have my records. You know what happened in Korea. Why am I here?"

"Only your doctor should ever answer that question, Jason. And he probably never will. He worked very hard to erase it from your memory. I can tell you, you did nothing wrong. You survived something only you could have. Unfortunately, a top-ranking North Korean general was willing to start World War III to get at you. The State Department and FBI provided me with your records, asking me to take care of you."

"Why? To eliminate their embarrassment? Or just my memory?" Jason leapt to his feet, with a clenched jaw, eyes afire.

Higgins threw his hands into the air. "Whoa, son. We don't operate that way in this country." Higgins' officers were moving in. To his relief, Jason sat again, and Higgins nodded his men back.

"The State Department just wanted me to keep an eye on you and make sure you didn't talk. It's when my son spoke about you that I got interested. He knew this idea I had for an experiment to expand our surveillance capability, and Michael thought you were the perfect person for it."

Jason folded his arms across his chest. "Sorry. I'm fresh out of volunteering for experiments." There was finality in the young man's voice.

"I can't say I'm surprised. But let me give you something to think about. Since Doctor Franke believes you need to live and work in bright sunlight . . ."

Jason's face hardened. "Some doctor/patient confidentiality!" he growled angrily.

"Relax, son. One of my degrees is in psychology, which I find useful in my line of work. You wouldn't tell the doctor what happened in Korea. I had to so he could understand the origin of your problem."

Jason sat back, but appeared wary. "Alright. What about bright sunlight?"

"What would you think of becoming an underwater wildlife photographer in the Florida Keys, while keeping an eye on a few things for me?"

"In what capacity?"

"As a patriot, son. As someone who cares about his country. That's important to you, you know."

Jason slammed a fist onto his knee. "Dammit, Mr. Higgins, you didn't get all that from my records."

"Very good, Jason. You're right of course. I got it from your aunt Sarah and uncle David the same time I got to see some of your photographs on their walls. He just made admiral, you know."

"Did he? I'm not surprised. That's wonderful. But stop changing the subject. What do you want me to look for?"

Well, I was warned you like to cut to the chase. "I came here to assess you for recruitment. I think you're a man who could make a difference for us. I want you on my team, son."

Jason sat back and ran his fingers through his thick hair. "Sir, I'm sorry you lost your son. But I'm not him."

Higgins swallowed his hurt and pressed on. "You're right, Jason, because he never could have been you. And you're what I need right now. For surveillance, that is."

"You said your work is outside the U.S." Jason's eyes narrowed with suspicion. "I don't plan on being a government employee or on leaving the country." He sounded like a man who meant what he said.

"You won't have to. The long arms of the enemy have begun reaching into this country in bigger ways. Sometimes it's necessary to backtrack from operations here to discover the sources abroad."

Jason rose, indicating it was time to end this interview. "Mr. Higgins, I don't feel ready to commit to this kind of responsibility. So, if you need an answer today, it's 'no.' But I will think about it if you want."

Higgins decided it was time to back off. "I do want, Jason. I've thought a lot about what you might do with your life once you're out of here." He nodded to one of his men, who handed him a briefcase.

Higgins reached in. "I've brought you this January 1927 issue of the *National Geographic*. It has a wonderful article, *Life on a Coral Reef,* with the world's first underwater color photos made in the Dry Tortugas, near Key West. This year's January '62 issue of the *Geographic* contains articles and pictures, *Key Largo Reef: America's First Undersea Park* and *Florida's Coral City Beneath the Sea,* by a newcomer named Jerry Greenberg. Keep them. They're yours. See if you'd like to join the ranks of pioneers like Jerry Greenberg and Jacques Cousteau—all at government expense, while keeping an eye out for me."

Higgins stood up and began rummaging through the pockets of his tweed suit, until he finally produced a small pad and fountain pen. He wrote a phone number and tore off the sheet. "Here, Jason. If you ever need anything, you call me there. The person who answers this number will have your name and put you through to me, wherever in the world I am."

Looking up into Jason's blue eyes, he took a chance. "Jason, I'm offering you the opportunity that my son couldn't have handled. Use the phone number."

CHAPTER 87
TO DIE OR NOT TO DIE

Tacoma, Washington
Monday, April 23, 1962

Playing the hand he'd been dealt. Jason mulled over Doctor Franke's words and wondered if Higgins might be one of the cards. A week had passed since the man's visit. Jason had studied the *National Geographics*, captivated by the photography and the possibilities. Higgins' offer was tempting.

He stared out the lounge window at the distant mountains, searching for an answer. He didn't feel able to commit to anything while he was still so unsure of himself. He'd been isolated from the outside world for a year—no friendships with men leading normal lives, no female companionship. He was wounded and crippled. Not so anybody could see. But just as damaged as if he were paralyzed. His short-term memory loss proved worse that the doctor had led him to believe—sometimes he couldn't even remember what he'd done the day before. And there were huge gaps in his past, who he'd known and what he'd done with them. He dreaded leaving the hospital and confronting people who knew him well, to find that he had no memory of them.

Anger surged through him and despair numbed him whenever he thought about what the doctors had done to his brain. Until he was sure he could overcome the war neurosis obstacles, he couldn't believe himself worthy of taking on anything more "for God and country," as Higgins had put it. In his worst moments of depression he lost all hope of being able to accomplish anything of significance and was tempted to join Higgins' son. He knew he couldn't hold on much longer. More and more he thought of joining Michael Higgins and the relief it would provide.

Breaking through the fog of his black thoughts, Jason overheard visiting parents talking to another patient about a new movie playing in Tacoma. Apparently the film had been shot in the Florida Keys and there were underwater scenes on the coral reefs. *Coincidence? Destiny?*

It was a beautiful April morning and Jason had day privileges allowing him to come and go from the hospital at will. He drove into town to see the matinee, *Beneath the Twelve-Mile Reef.* In the lobby he spotted a tall woman he'd seen before from a distance. He got a strong feeling he was being followed, but dismissed it when he decided she was too distinctive to go unnoticed. Her full hair framed high cheekbones and a traffic-stopping figure. She seemed comfortable with the fact that all eyes were on her. In her tailored western shirt, Levis and cowboy boots, she got Jason's vote for Miss Cowgirl of the Universe.

Two muscular sailors came up to the woman insisting noisily that she watch the movie with them. "No," she said, her response firm. But one man wrapped his arm around her waist, each one took an elbow and they started drawing her towards the inside doors.

Jason grabbed the Seattle directory from the phone booth beside him and stepped across the lobby to block their path.

"Outta the way, punk," sneered one of the drunken sailors. "Yeah," slurred the other, "this patriotic lady is entertaining two of America's finest."

The lobby fell silent as everyone watched.

Jason inched closer. He spoke in a low, intimidating voice. "Gentlemen, stand down. You're drunk. So I'll let you off, once. But if you don't remove yourselves from this theatre immediately . . ." Jason ripped the two-inch thick phone book in half.

The men looked at each other. "Hell, mister. We didn't know she was yours. C'mon, Jack. Let's go get a drink." They swaggered out the main doors.

The woman stood before Jason and thanked him with a brilliant smile. He stretched up to his full height, but in her boots she remained taller. She grinned and placed a hand on the back of his wrist. "How'd you like company watching the movie?"

They entered the theater and sat together. The film was just beginning and they watched in silence. Partway through the movie Jason realized he was sitting across the aisle from Bonnie, everyone's favorite nurse at the hospital. After a while, he noticed she was sobbing while the rest of the audience was laughing. He excused himself from the woman beside him and went to Bonnie. Without a word, he took her hand, led her outside and wrapped her slender frame in a gentle bear hug while she cried her heart out.

CHAPTER 88
NURSE BONNIE

Tacoma, Washington
Monday, April 23,1962

Jason was quite sure nurses were not permitted to fraternize with patients, but Bonnie desperately needed to talk with someone. "Wait here." He patted her shoulder and went back inside to the cowgirl.

"I know who that woman is," he said in a quiet voice, "and she needs help right now."

"You're very kind." She squeezed his hand. "I'm fine."

What a confident woman, he sensed, as he left the movie house. And unforgettable, even with his memory damage.

He walked Bonnie to his Buick.

She dried her tears. "Just outside town there's an abandoned farm where I like to walk and exercise on my way home from work. We could talk in private out there."

Acres of timber concealed the farm from the two-lane country road. The property entrance was a two-track dirt lane that led them a hundred yards through the dense growth of trees. Cleared farmland appeared on the other side of the woodland. The wheel tracks turned left and followed the back side of the tree line, past burned-out buildings amidst lush grassy open spaces and overgrown fields to the right, an unobstructed view of Mount Olympus in the distance, on the far side of Puget Sound. Beyond what had been a barn, the lane ended at a stream running along the edge of the forest. He parked there and they crossed the stream on stepping stones and entered the woods, which wrapped around to the right and bordered a brook.

He and Bonnie strolled along a path beneath the tall fir trees. They walked and talked and finally sat on a mossy bank under the trees beside the burbling brook, enjoying their view of the mountains.

"Right now, my three children and I are living with my grandparents. I left my husband nine months ago, when his affairs became too much ... ."

Jason had noticed Bonnie at the hospital during the many hours he'd had nothing to do. She was energetic and outgoing, with intelligent wide-spaced hazel eyes and gorgeous chestnut hair. She looked as if she worked out regularly. Any man would be lucky to have someone like her to come home to. *The man must be a fool.*

"Now he's trying to get me back by harassing me with a lawyer and threatening to win custody of our children. I've already lost the man I loved. If I lose my children, I don't know how I'll go on." Once again, she broke down in tears.

Her feelings mirrored his own. How often in the last few weeks had he wondered whether he could go on? Jason felt a surge of anger and intense compassion. He took her hand and gave it a comforting squeeze, hoping she wouldn't think him too forward. She smiled up at him.

"Bonnie, if you could have anything you wanted, what would it be?"

She gazed across the brook. "I already had everything I wanted in life, before my husband started cheating on me. I guess my fantasy is that he could be faithful to me. Us being a happy family again."

Turning toward Jason she put a hand on his arm. "But what about you? What are you looking for?"

What *did* he want? His chest tightened as he tried to put it into words. "A way out of this black hole. The despair just emerges and takes over. I have no defenses against it. It's like a huge snake that wraps itself around me and squeezes the life out of me."

"There are drugs—"

"Look at all the zombies in the hospital," he said, waving his arms vehemently. "They can hardly take care of themselves. Thank you, no. Masking the problem isn't a viable solution for me. I'm looking for something to take it away, kill it, bury it, make it disappear forever."

She looked at him. "Treatment's only temporary."

"Not really. Even when they leave the hospital, patients have to continue on drugs. Nine out of ten return for treatment. They have this fear hanging over everything they do for the rest of their lives."

"You can still have a life."

How to make her understand. He sighed. "Bonnie, I was born to be a player in life, not a spectator. I've read that about five percent of all people are movers and shakers. Fifteen percent of the others are aware of what the movers do, and the rest are the last to know what's going on in the world."

He shifted his gaze to look straight into her eyes. "If I can't function as a mover, I'm worthless. I'd have no reason to go on. After a year of this, I'm flat-out depressed. I wonder if I'm worse than when I came to the hospital."

She shook her head. "You're not. I was on nights when you came. I heard your night-terrors. I watched you suffer with the migraines. Believe me, you're much better, Jason." She stared across the brook. "I've been miserably depressed, but I have the children. My ability to be there for them is a great incentive for fighting depression. And I come here to run until I can't go any further. It gives me a curious kind of energy that keeps me going. She looked at him. "What do you do to fight your melancholy?"

He shrugged. "My family's gone. No one loves me or would miss me, except my godparents and an aunt and uncle in Scotland that Doctor Franke told me about. Not even any cats or dogs. It's as if my depression feeds on itself." He ran his fingers through his hair. "Imagine dying from a hope-eating virus, wearing a leaden cloak of despair so heavy you can't move. This isn't some passing pity-trip. This is real depression, a place where you have to live, even though there's no reason to live. Looking ahead, all you see is loneliness. Loneliness so painful the only way to deal with it is to set yourself far enough apart from the rest of the world that you can't see anything to feel separated from. What they tell me Michael Higgins did."

A furrow between her brows revealed Bonnie's concern. "Could you do that, Jason?"

"Maybe. Probably not. I'm not a quitter. Everybody says they want to go to Heaven, but I notice they do their best to put it off as long as possible." He smiled at the irony.

"When we started our walk and I went back to the car to get the Kleenex from your glove compartment, I found your road map of the west coast folded open. You've penciled in the route between here and Bridal Veil Falls, east of Portland." She cocked her head and raised a brow in question.

He nodded. "On my way to California, I plan to stop and say goodbye to Michael."

"Why didn't you mark the map from Bridal Veil Falls to California, to your destination there?"

He looked into her hazel eyes. "Don't worry, Bonnie. I won't leave while you need me. That's a promise."

She squeezed his hand and smiled. "I really appreciate that, Jason. And I'll hold you to that promise."

CHAPTER 89
HOPE

Tacoma, Washington
Tuesday, April 24, 1962

The following afternoon Jason met with Bonnie again at the abandoned farm. They returned to sit on the inviting carpet of moss beside the brook. He swept his arm out before him. "Look at the grandeur of this earth God has given us. I love it. I don't want to leave it. But now I keep recognizing all the horror that takes place, like a bear chasing down a fawn for food, on the beautiful slopes of Mt. Olympus over there. And at times, man's inhumanity to man. I've learned I can endure anything so long as I have hope to keep me going. At the moment I'm losing hope. That's why I think about following in Michael's footsteps. But I know that's not God's plan for me."

"You can't give up hope." Bonnie's response was passionate. "Find the right woman and you'll always be thankful you kept on trying. Trust me."

The wind blew in a breath of fresh air, fragrant with the scent of evergreens.

"What else do you want out of life, Jason?"

So he told her he loved the ocean.

"I'm sure there's something out there for you if you want it badly enough."

He gave a deep sigh. "Doctor Franke told me the same thing. But if I can't find ways to get rid of the depression and control my anger, it's going to threaten any chances of success. And even if I find the woman, how will I be able to keep her? When I think about the realities, I get depressed as hell."

"Let's keep meeting here when I get off work each afternoon. We'll walk and talk, and run for exercise." Bonnie patted his hand. "Your friendship is special to me." She hesitated. "The nurse-patient protocol—we'll keep our rendezvous clandestine." A long drawing in of her breath. "And platonic. After all, I'm not actually divorced."

Jason tried to sound casual. "And part of you still loves that wayward husband." Nevertheless, he felt a resurgence of hope with this new friendship.

CHAPTER 90

HIGGINS' MOTIVES?

Several weeks later Jason waited at the farm wondering what was making Bonnie so late, hoping she didn't have car problems. When she did arrive, she was grinning. "Boy, have I got a story for you." But she made him wait until they were walking side by side under the tall Douglas firs before she would tell her story. She slipped her hand into his as they strolled along.

"After work I changed clothes and went to my car to come here. Guess who was waiting for me?"

"Your husband? His lawyer?"

"No, silly. I was smiling when I arrived, remember?"

"Then who?"

"Believe it or not, Michael Higgins' father, accompanied by the usual two guys. He had on that same rumpled suit he always wears."

Jason raised a brow. "Don't be fooled. It's all part of his absent-minded professor disguise. He probably has identical suits for every day of the week." They chuckled.

Stopping beneath the trees, enjoying the soft carpet of fragrant needles under their shoes, they looked across the brook and fields at the mountains to the northwest.

"So what did he want?" Jason finally asked, feeling the tension that accompanied thoughts of Higgins and his son.

Taking his arm, she drew close and looked up into his eyes. "He told me how important he believes you are for helping him solve some big problems." Forget Higgins. Jason so wanted to kiss this beautiful face. "He cares about you, Jason. I could tell. He knows about our friendship and wanted to thank me for being here for you when you needed someone. He said no one at the hospital knew about our relationship, but if I did get in trouble over it, I should tell them I was on assignment for the CIA and he'd back me up personally. Come to think of it, how do you suppose he found out about our secret meetings?" She hugged herself and shivered at the thought. Jason had a flash of the tall cowgirl at the theater, and a strange feeling that she knew Higgins.

"What do you think of Higgins?" he asked casually.

Bonnie placed a finger against her chin, then shrugged. "I don't really know the man. Of course, he's in the business of acquiring information and keeping it secret, for the sake of national security. Somehow I trust him and I believe he cares about his people." She smiled quizzically. "What do you think of him?"

"I think he's probably the intellectual equivalent of Shakespeare in the intelligence community ... and the most manipulative person I've ever met. I'm not at all comfortable about being in his sights. I agree that he cares about people, but I'm sure that would never stand in the way of what he thinks is best for his agency."

"Jason ... ." She looked at him sideways. "Are you allowed to tell me why the CIA Deputy Director of Operations is going to this kind of trouble for a patient at American Lake?" Her brows arched.

For a moment he considered not telling her, but decided there was no reason not to. "He knows stuff I've done and survived—things wiped out of my memory by the shock treatment. Says I have unusual premonitions and survival gifts. I do know that I sense what's happening beyond the surface in some situations. I get the feeling he's pragmatic enough to be skeptical about such things, but he hopes my premonitions are real and can help with whatever problem he has. I guess I'm his only available extrasensory prospect at the moment."

"And he won't be disappointed." Her gaze was direct, her smile wry.

Muscles worked his jaw as he thought of the man. "I'm pretty sure Higgins' interest in me has something to do with Michael's suicide. But

that would only be reason to care about me personally, never to be confused with practical decisions about my value to the agency ... Wait, a
minute. Is Higgins still at the hospital?"

She gave a negative little wave. "No, no. He said he was just in
San Diego, 'on company business,' he called it. He decided to fly up to
McChord Air Force Base to see how you were doing before flying back
to D.C. I got the impression he saw Doctor Franke, too. He had all sorts
of questions for me."

They came to the large patch of moss where they loved to sit and
talk. They remained standing, leaning against a tree. "What sort of
questions?"

"The kind your psychiatrist might ask. Astute. Probing. Concerned."

"He's a psychologist, too."

"I know." She flipped her glossy chestnut ponytail. "He seems
to understand how difficult things must be for you right now, and just
wanted to be sure you're okay." Bonnie put her hand on his shoulder.
"Said our friendship was the best possible medicine. I told him it was a
two-way street. He already knew about my separation."

She smiled. Her hand slid down to hold his arm as she stood on
her toes to give his cheek a long, tender kiss.

His urge to kiss her back was tempered by concern that she might
regret her move. He didn't want to overstep the guidelines she'd set.

She settled back down on her heels and squeezed his hand. "It's
late and I need to get home to the kids. See you Monday?"

This he knew for sure, Bonnie's friendship brought warmth and
happiness into his life. Something he sorely needed if he was going to
survive his depression. Monday couldn't come too soon.

CHAPTER 91
BONNIE'S GIFT

Tacoma, Washington
Sunday, June 10, 1962

Jason was about to be discharged from the VA hospital. Finally. His regular rendezvous with Bonnie had anchored his daily life in a sense of normalcy.

The Sunday before his departure, her grandparents babysat for the children. He and Bonnie spent the day on the farm, talking, running, picnicking. Sitting together in their Levis on the moss by the brook, they licked the last of the fried chicken from their fingers and watched a scarlet sunset over the Olympic Mountains. But now he felt melancholy. He was leaving for California and that would be the end of seeing Bonnie. And he hadn't made a decision about Higgins yet. The rosy glow gave way to the cool light of the rising moon.

"I'm still conflicted over Higgins' offer. Tomorrow I leave for Long Beach. How can I commit to something when I'm not sure if I can count on myself? Depression, self-doubt still lurking at the edges." He stared at the dark silhouette of the mountain range. "Staying with my godparents will be fine for a month, but what am I going to do after that? Long term? I have no career, no friends that I can recall, no one to love and to love me."

A moment of silence followed. Then Bonnie said, "I love you, Jason. These days we've spent together have meant more to me than I can ever say. But I can show you. Look at me, Jason." She spoke softly, her eyes illuminated in the bright moonlight. She meant it. Her lips were full and moist and parted expectantly.

Jason sat frozen, not breathing, fearing to break the spell. He wanted her love with his whole heart. Not just her physical passion, but her love. And, miracle of miracles, here it was, spilling out of her— indefensible, undisguised, pure and passionately complicated. He watched in wonder as her expression filled with loving resolve. Jason drew in a long breath, breaking the spell.

There on the bed of moss in the moonlight, Jason's heart pounded in response to Bonnie's outpouring of love. She moved onto her knees, legs straddling his thighs, facing him and placed her mouth close to his.

Nervous, he wet his lips.

Keeping her mouth tantalizingly close, she reached up inside the back of her sweatshirt and unfastened her bra. She pulled his upturned hands inside her shirt and placed her breasts in them. They felt warm and heavy in his palms, comforting and exhilarating. Jason inhaled sharply.

Bonnie moaned. She caressed his lips with hers, teasing him, loving him. Then she kissed his lips lightly. Once. Twice. "I love you, I love you, I love you," she said softly between her next teasing kisses, as she pressed her body down to stroke the enlargement straining against his Levis. She released a pent-up moan that turned into purest content- ment, then purred with anticipation. Her lower body pressed against his fiercely, hurtfully. Then her open mouth crushed his, her tongue promising exciting pleasures to come.

His hands closed around her breasts so passionately she cried out. Pain or pleasure?

She placed her hands over his and pressed reassuringly.

Jason's heart beat wildly. He was a vulnerable child melting in protective arms; a Greek god with his goddess; love joined like two fireflies in the dark.

Beneath the trees, bathed in moonlight, they undressed each other on the mossy bank next to the familiar brook that gurgled over its ancient rocks. The spongy moss felt wonderful under their bare feet. They were far from any other people, free to express themselves however they wanted. He felt confident that he was an experienced lover, even though the women he'd been with had been erased from his memory. He reached for his billfold while she freed her ponytail, shook it out and combed it with her fingers. Her scalloped breasts beckoned him with their prominent nipples. She looked so beautiful in the moonlight Jason wanted to groan with the ache of it. It seemed so natural to lie on the soft moss on their sides facing each other.

She held Jason between gentle hands. Throbbing, he felt heavy with engorgement.

"Are you okay with this, Bonnie? We don't have to do it if we stop now."

She rubbed against him. "I don't want to stop."

They lay on the bed of moss, kissing and exploring each other in blissful anticipation. Then she pressed hard against him. Her voice sounded guttural. "Fill me now, before I die from the need of you."

She rolled onto her back and urgently pulled his anxious-to-please body over hers. She drew up her folded knees and guided him to the slippery source of life between her open, straining thighs. She was so ready he seemed to fall into her.

"Oh ... my ... God," she breathed out.

He groaned with happiness. They embraced tenderly, as he savored the moment, and felt whole. Her eyes, her mouth, her body straining to engulf him spoke the same feeling. This was the difference between love and sex. His love completing another so fully that he could love himself for what he was able to give her.

That was it. For what he could give her. Something out of the past. *In giving is receiving.* That became his focus.

He stared into her loving eyes as they gave their bodies to each other. His muscles felt tight as spring steel as he held himself in check and time slowed, allowing him to appreciate each rewarding movement and sensation.

"Deeper, faster," she cried, meeting him thrust for thrust. She opened cathedral-like doors for him, revealing the magnitude of a woman's capacity for feeling and being and giving. Then it was as if a dam were disintegrating. Unlike him, she seemed to hold nothing back. Nothing.

When her orgasm racked her body, she cried out so loud that he became alarmed and stopped.

"It's beautiful, Jason. Keep going!"

She lowered her feet to the moss, arched her body up off the ground and with thighs of iron began swiveling her hips in surreal seduction. She was underneath, yet making forceful love to him, taking him harder, faster. Her passion and escalating moans grew into cries of ecstasy as she exploded again. Her face in the moonlight shone radiant as her body kept up its plateau of pleasure.

Opening her eyes, her voice husky with promise, she said, "Come with me this time. Come with me now!"

He felt her focus her entire being on giving him pleasure, as she contracted magically around his sensitive hardness, working him, loving him, taking him deeper, harder still … .

Something made him hold back with all his might, until her seductive magic pulled him into the rapids, swirling forward in the river of no return.

Uninhibited, wrenching cries filled the night as they exploded together. His heart felt as though it was bursting out of his chest. Finally he gave a deep sigh and relaxed as they remained together, breathing heavily. Then, unbelievably, muscles inside her began contracting, keeping him hard.

Yes, there's more. He moved an arm under the small of her back to support her. "Don't stop," he said. "I have more for you. Much more."

He resumed his powerful lovemaking and she rejoined him with surprising energy. It was as if he were in another world, a space without time. "More, more!" she insisted, not giving ground as he thrust ever harder into her determined body. His heart thrilled at the memory of rich cello music from Massenet's *Meditation from Thais*. It accompanied Bonnie's passionate cries, transporting him to heavenly places, the crystal-sharp experience so out of body he even imagined he felt the rise and fall of angels' wings.

He embraced the exhilaration, while his body made ready to give his all once again. And they did do it together one more heart-stopping time. They shouted their exuberance, then disintegrated into laughter as they collapsed into the spongy moss. Spent, they separated and lay on their backs beside each other under the stately canopy of fir trees.

He was floating on a cloud of contentment, when he heard her sobbing softly.

"Are you alright, Bonnie?"

"Dammit, Jason. I thought I was okay with being single. Now everything's different."

He wasn't sure how to respond.

"You gave me everything you have to give. Passion. Tenderness. Caring. Holding back. Not holding back ... . I've never felt that from a man before. You've awakened things in me I never knew I could feel. Now my life will never be complete without a good man to share it with."

She lay back beside him and held his hand in silence. They looked up at the heavens.

Finally she spoke again. "My husband and I had it great, until he started fooling around. He really hurt me, wrecked our marriage. But— well, I guess I need to know if we could work things out. For the kids." She coughed. "For me," she added in a small voice. "Can you understand?"

She turned and kissed Jason's cheek.

He could understand. He would have moved heaven and earth if he could have his family back, his old life before he'd been wiped clean of his memories, before he'd been sent off on a military mission that had left him emotionally damaged. But he couldn't. She could. He loved her enough to want that for her. "You deserve that chance."

Sitting up, she sighed. "We have to go."

Both were sweaty and feeling the chill of the night air. They stood and carefully brushed each other off by the light of the moon, then dressed and walked back to the Buick.

Jason started the car as they got in. Sitting on the leather bench seat shivering, Bonnie snuggled against him. He held her close and rubbed her arms and back. She smiled and snuggled closer. When the temperature gauge started to move, he turned on the heater and she sighed, welcoming the rush of warm air. He stroked her hair tenderly, still removing moss.

Through the front windshield Jason could see a moonbeam shimmering in the water of the brook. It was beautiful. He thought back on the past hour.

Despite his knowledge that he was losing Bonnie, miraculously, a great weight had been lifted from him and he felt whole again.

CHAPTER 92
GOLDEN FLEECE

Tacoma, Washington
Sunday, June 10, 1962

Back at the hospital, Jason lay awake, images of Bonnie filling his thoughts. He saw how she'd chosen life for both of them. She'd unveiled the Golden Fleece—the best love was about receiving in proportion to what you were able to give. He knew now that she would forgive her husband and reunite her family. She'd shown Jason what to live for and how to keep going. She'd shown him the extraordinary relationship he must seek to help him through the difficult life ahead. Now if he could just find that for himself.

* * *

The next day, after his discharge from the hospital, Jason waited for Bonnie at the farm. Last night was extraordinary and he yearned for more of that experience. But he knew in his heart that it would not be. Their respect for each other and his hope for the restoration of Bonnie's family would hold them in check.

Bonnie must have sensed that her love was the only thing that would pull him through. She'd given him the hope to pick himself up, to keep going in his quest to find his life's work and the right woman to share it with. Filled with Bonnie's love, he knew he wouldn't join Michael, except to say goodbye.

Finally Bonnie drove down the farm lane to meet with him for the last time. When she arrived, they hugged. He had so much he wanted to talk about. He wanted to tell her she had put him on his feet again. They started walking.

"Thank you for the gift of your love, Bonnie. I'll never forget it."

"Actually, Jason, I'm proud of what I did for my country. Higgins called you an asset that mustn't be lost." Jason was relieved to see she was grinning. She took his arm in both her hands. "You *are* an asset—an important one. I hope you'll always remember that."

He paused. "Will you tell him?" he asked. "About what happened—between you and me?"

"Mmm. Depends." Suddenly she looked up. "What makes you think we'll be talking?"

"Hmmm."

She let it drop. They walked on, holding hands. Jason was the first to break the silence.

He turned to look into her eyes. "So many of my memories are wiped out, but I don't think I ever met a woman who made love quite like you."

"Perhaps you never slept with a married woman. It takes years to learn to make love like that." Her voice reflected the twinkle in her eye.

He shoved his hands into his pockets to keep from touching her. "Is every night like that—in marriage I mean?"

"Is every day Thanksgiving?"

"Well, what *is* marriage like then?"

She placed a hand on each of his arms. "It's whatever you make it, Jason. Nothing just happens. You have to make it happen. Like any garden, you reap what you sow—love for love, grief for grief, disrespect for disrespect, sameness for sameness, extraordinary for extraordinary."

As they walked through the woods, he asked her why she'd suddenly decided to make love to him.

"Because I love you, Jason. I'll always love you. Because I wanted you to believe in that love, to know it's yours forever. Because somehow it became my responsibility to keep you going and show you the kind of love you have to look forward to when you find that special woman.

From the day Higgins met with me, I knew beyond any doubt that you and I had come together for a reason—to give each other new purpose in life." She stopped and turned to put her arms around him. She laid her head on his chest, and remained that way a while.

Then she stepped back and took his hands in hers, gave them a reassuring squeeze. "We're both confident now. Me, about my family and my work. You, in your destiny as a protector of the people and their freedom."

He pressed her right hand to his cheek, then kissed it tenderly.

"Bonnie, Bonnie. How can I tell you what you've done for me?" He paused and stared at the distant mountains. "You've shown me the mistake of carrying baggage from the past that puts limits on what I can do. You've taught me to believe in myself again." Then he looked back into her eyes. "You've kept me alive. You'll be part of me forever."

They hugged and kissed tenderly. It was a sad farewell, but they had given each other the will to embrace the future with hope. Now it was time to get on with their lives. They walked towards their cars.

"What's your plan with your husband?"

She shrugged, but her voice was filled with resolve. "Tough love. I'll take him back, but strictly on my terms. If he violates them, he's out. No third chance. Meanwhile, I'll do my best to love him so fiercely, he'll be spoiled for anyone else. With our work and the kids to care for, I let us get stuck in a rut. I'll never take him for granted again. What do you think?"

He turned toward her with a smile. "Don't see how you can miss." Then he took a deep breath and let it out slowly. "I want you to know, leaving you is very, very hard. If your plan doesn't work out, I'm coming back for you and your children."

She reached for his hand, her expression serious. "Don't promise what you can't deliver, Jason. You'll meet the perfect woman for you, I'm certain."

CHAPTER 93
FOCUS ON THE FUTURE

Tacoma, Washington
Monday, June 11, 1962

Before leaving town, Jason had a mission to perform. This was not just for Bonnie's sake, but to prove something very important to himself as well—that he was ready to be a player again.

At closing time, after dark, he entered the small office in the center of the used car lot. The Clark Gable double was counting cash at his desk. "Sorry, we're closed. Come back after ten tomorrow morning."

Jason shut the door, turned the sign in the window to "Closed," pulled the blinds and locked the door. The owner stared at him, clearly not liking the situation.

"Here," he offered, holding out the tin box. "Take the money."

Jason stepped across the room, ignoring the box. Picking Bonnie's husband up by his lapels, Jason glared at him and stood him against the wall behind the desk.

Weakly, the man slid down the wall to sit on the floor. "Please don't hit me, Mister. I won't fight you. I was wrong. I stopped all that when my wife left me. I'll never touch your wife again. I promise."

"It's not my wife I'm concerned about," Jason rasped. "It's yours! Tell your lawyer never to bother her again. Understand?"

Jason had a flash of Bonnie and the kids playing with this man outside a ranch-style house on the farm she loved. Jason relaxed. But not so her husband would see it.

"Wake up and realize what an amazing woman Bonnie is. She's going to give you another chance. If I hear you hurt her or let her down ever again, I promise you, I'll return and steal her away from you. And depending on what I find, I may not be this gentle with you in the process. Do you understand?"

His eyes opened wide. "She'll take me back?" He beamed. "Damn, that's the best news I've heard in a long time. I'll be good to her—and the kids, too. I swear."

Good. They understood each other.

Jason turned and left, stepping over the dropped cash box and all the money on the floor. He walked to his sleek black Buick a block away and began driving south.

It felt good to be back in the game as his old self.

PART VI

NEW BEGINNINGS

CHAPTER 94
DOUGHERTY ENTERPRISES

Islamorada, Florida
Monday, June 18, 1962

Natasha selected Cheeca Lodge in Islamorada for a secret rendez-vous that Ivan hoped would gain them insider control over their operations in the Florida Keys. Posing as wealthy tourists, they drove a rental Cadillac from Dougherty Enterprises' base of operations in Fort Lauderdale to the exclusive resort on the ocean side of Upper Matecumbe Key.

Natasha used one of their numerous aliases when she made the reservation with Cheeca to conceal their identity for the private meeting—in case it didn't go well. It was crucial that this meeting not be linked to their role as Jeannie and Don Dougherty.

Wearing swimsuits, they sat in the shade of their veranda, contemplating the clear tropical shallows of the Atlantic stretching out to the Gulf Stream five miles offshore, beyond the coral reefs. A weathered old fisherman greeted an apparent stranger, an agile looking man who wore a canvas sun-hat and was walking up the beach. To Natasha's shock, the stranger suddenly sat on the old man at the edge of the foliage and hastily did something to his face, then dragged the man out of sight and calmly resumed walking. He turned towards the cottage. Was he their potential recruit? Natasha handed Ivan his sports shirt and slipped into her short silk kimono.

* * *

An hour later, Natasha stood in the living room of their beach cottage and watched Ivan shake hands solemnly with their middle-aged guest. The clandestine meeting was completed before noon and Natasha peeked out the front door to check that no one was there to see their important visitor depart. A private path cut through the native tropical shrubs and groundcover. There was no one in sight. She signaled their guest to join her on the porch. Just in case anyone was peering through the bushes, she slithered beside the man to make it appear their meeting had been for lust. Pulling his canvas hat brim low, the man departed on a path that would take him unseen to his rental car parked just outside the Cheeca grounds. Once he was out of sight, Natasha went back inside and locked the door. Only then did she allow her face to reflect her excitement as she beamed up at her partner.

"Ivan, that was the most brilliant move I've ever seen you accomplish—winning over the one person with the connections to eliminate the bottleneck. Now we can import all the marijuana and cocaine we need to flood this nation with sufficient illegal drugs to weaken it irreparably."

Ivan grinned at their success. "No question, our sleuthing has found us just the man we've needed. The inability to bring big ships into the shallow waters of the Keys has been a crushing handicap. But this man can assemble a fleet of small local commercial and pleasure boats to ferry payloads from large ships outside the reefs in to the island coasts. Waiting vehicles with concealed compartments will supply enough illegal drugs for the entire East Coast. Within a year we'll increase the flow into America by a thousand percent, at least."

Natasha's body prickled with the rush of victory. "I'm proud of you, Ivan. In one stroke, you've arranged for the old-time population of the Keys—the Conchs—to work for you at what their ancestors did best—remove the cargo from ships offshore and bring in the spoils to be sold throughout the land. Our contact hasn't a clue of what we're doing to his country, and probably wouldn't care if he did."

Natasha shuddered as she remembered sidling up to the departing accomplice.

"What is it, Natasha? You're shaking."

"When I touched that man, I felt unspeakable evil."

Ivan leaned back and looked at her hard. "What do you mean?"

She clenched her teeth and scowled. "I mean that sneaky government employee we've just recruited epitomizes the inherent weakness of capitalism—unmitigated greed with no ideology except self-aggrandizement. We'll turn the United States into a socialist state after speeding the downfall of capitalism. Communism is the greater good for all the people."

She swallowed hard. "Yet I have this peculiar feeling, like I need a shower after that moment with him on the porch. And have you ever thought that, just like him, we're bringing addiction to countless millions of people?"

Ivan stared at her and then shrugged. "The worthwhile people won't become addicts. Our goal for communism justifies this part of our plan."

Natasha thought about their seven years in America implementing Ivan's strategies. Operating from the cover of "Richard Dougherty's" foundation, they'd accomplished many short-term goals and laid the groundwork for the ultimate Russian takeover. Now they needed to return to their ocean yacht at Bahia Mar in Fort Lauderdale. Ivan would write a report about their new success and begin arranging for the necessary ships.

Natasha went into the bathroom to wash her hands. Glancing into the toilet, she saw what looked like a large gob of chewing gum. She looked closer. *Nyet! A tongue ... the tip of a tongue! That poor old fisherman's? Our contact is warning us never to go against him.* A wave of nausea made her vomit.

Embarrassed, she flushed the toilet and hastily washed her face in the sink. As an élite operative she couldn't afford to be repulsed by such vile tactics to silence people. She and Ivan had to be the best. Winners in the Cold War.

CHAPTER 95
PIONEERING

Jason awakened with a kitten snuggling under the bed covers with him, licking his face. He lay there luxuriating in all the love he'd experienced in his godparents' house. He thought about how special their love was—for each other and for their three children. And they had plenty left over for him.

Aunt Sarah took marriage seriously. She tried always to be available in every way for her husband when his workday was done. She organized her days planning for his return so his time at home would be one not of demands, but for resting up to be fresh for the next day's challenges. She set the example of what Jason wanted so desperately for himself. Of course, he was no David King. Yet in many ways he was ... in loyalty, in devotion to cause, in goodness, in natural leadership qualities.

After a while, life had begun to seem possible again. He found he could remember phone numbers and the names of new acquaintances if he used them every day. He spent time at the library developing his love of photography and was encouraged by his uncle David to combine it with his love of the sea. The sea was, in fact, being called the last great frontier. Giant corporations were investing heavily in ocean research. Westinghouse opened a new division for developing deep submersibles.

Jason devoured the information. The sea was already a great producer of food for the planet, a shipping highway between continents and islands, and a repository for mankind's waste, as well as a source of inspiration for poets and storytellers. Now all the talk was about the sea's untapped mineral wealth and potential for medical advances, food farming and underwater habitation for people. Deep sea drilling was bringing up core samples that provided an invaluable source of earth's climatic history. Jason pictured them revealing prehistoric secrets. And who hadn't seen the Academy Award winning feature film *Le Monde du Silence (The Silent World)*, co-directed by Jacques Cousteau and Louis Malle from on board—and below—the retired French minesweeper *Calypso?*

Jason learned scuba diving from Admiral King's best. He found the physics and engineering for self-contained underwater breathing apparatus were common sense to him, so those principles weren't a challenge to remember. And he discovered that hands-on experience with any new equipment stayed with him. Now he felt driven to make a decision about his future. "Go forward; don't go back," his godparents advised.

A pioneer in the sea. With a camera in his hands. Hmm ... . Higgins had suggested that.

CHAPTER 96
HIGGINS' GAMBLE

Langley, Virginia
Thursday, July 19, 1962

In the new CIA building—still under construction—Higgins watched as the CIA Director leaned back in his chair, hands behind his head, looking up at the ceiling, his mustached lips pursed as he considered how much could go wrong. The director appeared to ignore the panoramic view that Higgins found so appealing—looking out over the dense trees sloping down to the Potomac River, the summer foliage now blocking out scenes of the rock-strewn river itself. He could see over the river to downtown Washington eight miles away—workplace of the political leaders to whom his agency was responsible.

Except for a photograph of President Kennedy and a large ship model of a modern navy frigate in a glass-encased stand, the director's brand new wood-paneled office was plain, set up strictly for function.

The Deputy Director of Operations sat slouched in one of the leather easy chairs across from the director's mahogany desk. Now, as he faced Marshall Zantzinger, he tried to relax, but was churning inwardly. He couldn't move further ahead without the director's agreement and it appeared the admiral was not going for his proposal. A Rhodes Scholar at Oxford, the admiral had more faith in the technological intelligence-gathering of NSA than in Higgins' field of human intelligence-gathering.

As the CIA Deputy Director of Operations, Higgins was convinced that with the exploding drug trade and growing threats of international terrorism inside the U.S., the CIA had to find ways for

American civilians to be their eyes and ears. If the agency could pinpoint activities beginning at U.S. borders and track them back to their foreign sources, they could keep most of the fighting off American soil.

Suddenly the admiral leaned forward in his chair and slammed a hand on the thick file on the desk in front of him. "Dammit, Walt! This file reads like a comic book. How the Sam Hill can we justify taking a chance on a nut-case like this?"

Higgins shuddered inwardly but kept a cool façade, a quality that often carried the day for him. "Marshall, we've traditionally relied on scumbags for information. Now Congress is killing that way of operating. Jason MacDougall is a complex individual who's struggled through a whole variety of experiences. Our best agents are the ones who live on the edge and survive. Which MacDougall has repeatedly proven he can do. What could be so bad about investing in a Boy Scout type who's a natural for what we need?"

The director's expression softened slightly. "What if something happens to MacDougall? Shouldn't we train him for the work?"

Higgins smiled inwardly. Maybe the director was coming around. "MacDougall has been training himself all his life. Perhaps better for this work than we ever could. All we have to do is open the right doors for him, and he'll walk through them."

"But to put a man in the field without training . . .?" The director sat back and pressed his fingertips together.

Higgins hiked forward to the edge of the plush leather chair, elbows on knees. "The foreign agents and terrorists are spotting and taking out our best trained undercover officers. Frankly, the enemy has become more effective than the CIA. We need people who are completely outside the mold, who can only be observed doing what they ordinarily do."

On a roll, Higgins became more animated, talking with his hands. "You brought MacDougall to my attention two years ago and we followed up on him, as you requested. Following his amazing escape from North Korea, Jason was sworn to secrecy. Then he uncovered the spy in Seattle and how the Russians are tracking our subs off the Aleutians, also components of their scheme to subvert American democracy from within."

The director tapped a finger on his desk. He shook his head, his former stubbornness returning. "He's a loner, an independent. Unpredictable. He's not a professional. And now he's been in a mental hospital."

Higgins refused to yield. "Yes. But it was *our* VA hospital at American Lake. It's where Michael received treatment for war neurosis. They were there for the same disorder. That's how we got to study MacDougall so thoroughly."

"What about the shock treatment?"

Higgins winced at the mention of shock treatment, thinking of his son, too. "MacDougall started reliving the North Korea incident. He drove himself to the hospital asking for help. But he was under strict orders not to tell anyone what happened in Korea, so he went through hell, yet never broke the order for secrecy. I had to tell his psychiatrist—strictly off the record, of course. It's why he finally got the EST. The treatment means he'll be able to deal with what happened in Korea."

Admiral Zantzinger put on horn-rimmed reading glasses and perused the papers on his desk. His eyes narrowed and he looked at Higgins. "The report says he was over-volted. What the hell does *that* mean?"

"In the final EST session there was an accident." Higgins relayed what Doctor Franke had told him. "It means Jason's memorization skills are impaired. In all else, his mind is as brilliant and creative as ever." He cleared his throat. "Memories of the North Korea episode will likely remain buried so deep he'll never know for sure, if the nightmares recur, that they're based on real events. He can't learn from his Army records. I have them. All but his honorable discharge and dates of service. Just before the shock treatment he was the star pitcher and batter on a team that won the state championship. Now he doesn't even remember playing softball. Most of his childhood has been erased from his conscious memory too."

The director stared at Higgins over his glasses. "What's the downside for us?"

Higgins shrugged. "He's living with it. MacDougall has come through this stronger than any other patient his psychiatrist has treated. The doctor believes that since MacDougall now understands the problems of war neurosis, he'll find ways to deal with them on his own. It's his nature."

The admiral flipped through the pages of the project report as he appeared to think for a moment. "Walt, tell me why you think Mac-Dougall can accomplish, let alone survive, the surveillance work you have in mind."

The admiral wanted the personal details, the kind not necessarily included in a dossier. Higgins responded carefully, weighing his next words.

"Jason MacDougall has a need for acceptance that drives him to exceptional efforts, to take huge risks and do things others wouldn't. Sometimes those efforts surface as poor social graces and apparent lack of empathy—he has an instinct for spotting people pretending to be what they're not. It brings out disrespectful qualities. But of value to us?—he *is* incredibly sensitive and perceptive. Seeing aspects of situations others miss. Knowing things others can't understand. He's got a healthy amount of paranoia, but he's only been delusional the one time that resulted in his hospitalization. In the military and the VA hospital he consistently tests at the highest levels of intelligence we record. He's highly moral and loyal."

The director drummed his fingers on the desk, as though coming to a decision. Determined to press forward, Higgins continued before the admiral could find a reason to dismiss both his DDO and his idea.

"It's as if living between several different worlds has driven him to make efforts to grow in ways comfortable people don't. He's a loner, but a personable loner. He's capable. Creative. Has incredible health, stamina and physical skills. He's strong as a bull—with the constitution of an ox. Speed—his boxing coach at the Naval Academy said he never saw anyone hit so fast and have every blow be precisely placed. He told his coach when things get dicey, everything becomes slow motion except him. A handful of Medal of Honor veterans in life-threatening situations have reported this same phenomenon. When others are in trouble, he steps out of the crowd to do whatever is necessary, while the rest remain onlookers."

He stood up to emphasize his point.

"Go on," Zantzinger encouraged him.

Higgins began pacing the carpeted floor. "He's not content just to read about great people as we are; he actually tries on the role by becoming physically and mentally proficient at whatever those people do. Pioneer, horseman, forester, sailor, career naval officer, photographer. Because of his love of hunting and wilderness living, he taught himself to track and hunt with bow and arrow. And he became an extraordinary snap-shooter with rifles. His accuracy at knife throwing is nothing short of amazing." Higgins decided that revisiting the bayonet incident at the Naval Academy might not help his case, despite MacDougall's exoneration and his uncannily precise prediction about his tormentor.

Zantzinger looked at his watch. "Was there more?"

Higgins sat down again to conclude the practical details of his project. "MacDougall can succeed where others have failed and lost their lives because we'll never ask him to do anything outside the scope of the work he performs normally. I've seen his photographs. He has a discerning eye. With his hunting skills and athletic prowess, he could become a documentary underwater filmmaker. It's a perfect cover. We can send him in any time, anywhere we want, and he'll never be suspected of surveillance work. When he needs support, we'll send in officers to be his film project helpers or dive models."

Higgins suppressed his rising enthusiasm, kept his voice even. "Marshall, this can work. He can get us the information, the results we need. Then we can present our case before Congress and get the funding to motivate Americans to be on the lookout for us, to help put the kibosh on drug and terrorist activities in this country." He reached for the glass of water on the table beside him.

Admiral Zantzinger started to protest, but Higgins stopped him by adding, "You may think I'm doing this because of my son, but I would be doing everything in my power to have MacDougall on my team even without Michael's death. Because I have enough documented facts to suggest this man can succeed where all our best have failed so far."

Zantzinger nodded. He had lost a carrier pilot son in Korea, understood his friend's grief. "Walter, we both know that your personal caring about MacDougall could be a problem. Don't let it cloud your judgment."

"Marshall, you know me better than that. Nothing comes ahead of the agency."

The admiral pinched his chin. "So you propose to conceal your special operative in the high visibility position of filmmaker. And you think drug-runners and terrorists don't have the same aversion to cameras as you and I do to cockroaches? How can a Boy Scout possibly survive the ruthless people we'd pit him against?" It was obvious by the set expression on the director's commanding face that he was buying none of it.

But Higgins was just as determined. The stakes were too high. "Jason MacDougall won't fit any profile they're looking for." He pushed himself forward in the leather chair. "His whole life has been a training ground, a series of tests for what we need now."

The director waved a dismissive hand. "Hell, Walt. You can say that of any gang kid in a ghetto."

"But they work in gangs. MacDougall works alone. And that's what we need. A lone survivor. We're a giant organization that's becoming blind and ineffectual. We need to discover new sources of information we can trust. Marshall, if we don't try to make the most of this young man and others like him, frankly, I think the agency's future is doubtful." He eyed the admiral as he gave him time to process the consequences.

With a lifetime career in intelligence, Higgins was deeply concerned about the agency's weakened information gathering capability. "I want to use him to see if he can learn anything about the new, organized terrorist and drug activities in Key Largo. Already two of my best undercover officers have disappeared. I believe that with MacDougall's brilliant mind and extraordinary survival skills, he would be a natural for passive surveillance. Who would suspect a vet recovering from shock treatment and depression in sunny Key Largo? I rest my case."

The admiral removed his reading glasses and spun them around by the earpiece. "MacDougall has unique gifts, but using someone with his liabilities could be considered a breech of good judgment."

Higgins realized he was losing the admiral. He made a daring career decision. "Marshall, since we and Russia acquired nuclear technology, there can be no open warfare between us without total annihilation."

"Well?"

"Well, what if Jason were a key player for our side in a war for control of America from within?" Higgins stood for emphasis. "Just like Senator McCarthy and J. Edgar Hoover tried to tell us."

Still, the admiral's eyes remained cautious. "Key player, how?"

Higgins decided it was time to reveal his other reason for wanting MacDougall, although he was still worried that the admiral considered psychic connections belonged in the realm of the lunatic fringe. "We know from the FBI report and from Julia Shepherd's investigation that MacDougall seems to have a brother, raised in the Soviet Union." He related the details and moved forward. "MacDougall believes he has some kind of cosmic connection with this Russian, like what's been reported elsewhere between twins. He told Julia he'd experienced it, numerous times. This makes him the perfect bait to draw out the leader of a Soviet strategy inside our borders, a man who's eluded us ever since we learned about him."

"Psychic phenomena?"

Higgins detected a hint of disbelief in his friend's voice, but he stared at the admiral with the confidence of a mathematician who had just outlined an irrefutable math formula. He placed his hands on the desk and waited for the director's verdict.

"So MacDougall is your key to bringing in this Russian." Marshall Zantzinger rose and walked around his desk, straightening his already impeccable tie. He stood squarely in front of Higgins. "You've convinced me of MacDougall's capabilities when the chips are down. Walt, I'm going to trust you on this experiment ... but only if Admiral King agrees, too."

CHAPTER 97
SURPRISE VISITOR

Long Beach, California
Saturday, July 21, 1962

A polite knock on his bedroom door awoke Jason.
"Come in."

The door opened. It was Philippe, one of his uncle's Filipino stewards, with a cup of black coffee. "Good morning, sir."

Holding the kitten in one hand, Jason sat up swinging his legs to the floor. "Top of the morning to you, Philippe."

Philippe placed the coffee on the nightstand beside Jason. "Thank you, sir. The admiral requests your company over coffee. Immediately, sir."

"Tell him I'll be right behind you." Jason gulped down the coffee, dressed and joined his uncle in the dining room.

It was a Saturday morning, and the youthful admiral wore slacks and a Hawaiian print sport shirt. "Morning, Jason. I just received a call from Walter Higgins. He's on his way here from Los Angeles in a helicopter. Wants to meet with you and your aunt and me. Do you know why?"

Jason stared into the scrambled eggs in front of him on the breakfast table, then looked directly at his godfather. "He wants me for some surveillance job in the Florida Keys. I told him no. If he's asked you and Aunt Sarah to attend the meeting, he probably wants to try to maneuver me into saying yes. Don't be deceived by the absent-minded professor look. He's as absent-minded as a shark is toothless."

"You wouldn't expect a man in his position to be otherwise, would you, Jason?" Not expecting an answer, he looked at his watch. "Well, it's only a twenty minute trip for him by helicopter. We'd better shave and get ready."

The helicopter landed with a whirring of rotors, blowing the grass flat on the expansive back lawn bordering the Pacific Ocean. Higgins was accompanied by two men, military types, in civilian dress. He was in his same rumpled suit, face aglow with a broad smile and ruddy cheeks, hand extended. "Admiral King, we meet in person at last. Jason, you're looking well."

Aunt Sarah asked the stewards to move a round table with a big umbrella and four chairs to a spot midway between the house and the rip-rap at the edge of the sea. One of the officers was sweeping the area with a small instrument and tiny earphones.

Higgins was watching Jason. "Just a routine precaution. Nothing to be alarmed about."

They walked over to the garden furniture. "Mrs. King, why don't you sit facing into this marvelous sea breeze so your lovely hair doesn't blow in your face."

Score one for Higgins. What gallantry.

Jason eyed the plate of brioche beside the carafe of coffee on the table. There were four place settings of porcelain butter plates, cups, saucers, and silverware. The stewards disappeared. The officers stood at a distance on either side of the table, looking out over their perimeter. Jason sat opposite Higgins, looking at the DDO under raised eyebrows.

"Admiral King, Mrs. King, my name is Walter. Please call me by my first name."

David King replied, "Sarah. David."

"I trust Jason has already told you I tried to recruit him while he was at the hospital—"

Jason cut in. "I told you then, I'll tell you again, I'm the wrong person to be working for the military or any other government agency."

"Listen to me, Jason. There's absolutely no way you can become a CIA officer. There are strict rules about people with your kind of emotional disorder."

"So why are you here at taxpayer expense, Walter?" All eyes went to Sarah King, exercising her sharp Bryn Mawr mind while looking ever so feminine in her pale yellow chiffon dress. *Three cheers for Aunt Sarah!*

"I don't want Jason as another trained officer. But I do want him as a member of my team. I believe—no, I'm convinced—Jason is what we need in Key Largo right now. I'm not asking him to become our employee; I'm asking him to help his country as a patriot."

Shit, Higgins, you're more devious than I gave you credit for. "Why me, Mr. Higgins?"

"It's your differences I need you for, Jason, not your ability to conform. On your own you've developed skills we can't inculcate into our trainees. What you have we can't buy at any price. What you have, your country badly needs."

"What do I have that you need so badly you'd gamble on my ability to keep my emotional problems in check?" The umbrella flapped in a gust of wind.

"Three things, some gleaned from your records. The ability to survive, no matter what. Instincts such as I've never encountered. And the perfect cover for a new person showing up in the Keys. Those are the things I need in a person in Key Largo right now."

"Why?"

Higgins looked at each person carefully. "From this point on our conversation is Top Secret. Agreed?" Each nodded the affirmative.

Higgins leaned forward over the table. "Something bad is coming our way, and we don't know what it is. I've lost two top officers in Key Largo. Just disappeared without a trace. Probably chained to engine blocks at the bottom of the Gulf Stream. Obviously, we're up against a capable enemy."

Sarah King started to speak, but her husband caught her eye, held up a hand and asked, "Does Admiral Zantzinger know about Jason?"

"Frankly, he was concerned about involving his good friend's nephew. Also Jason's war neurosis. But we're in trouble and need your godson's unique qualifications. The admiral said if you and your wife didn't agree to Jason helping us, he'd honor that."

CHAPTER 98
JASON'S TERMS

Long Beach, California
Saturday, July 21, 1962

Jason decided it was time to speak for himself.

He held up his hands like a double stop sign. "I'll try to make this easy for everyone. My answer is, 'Yes, I'm going to Key Largo. Yes, it's thanks to your suggestion. Yes, I'm going to try a new life and career. But, no, not to become your spy in disguise. I won't work for a government agency in any capacity." He added, "Too many compromises."

"That's three yeses and only one no, son. There'll be no compromises if you work for me. Now what's it going to take to make it four yeses?"

"Sir, I'm damaged goods. You can't be serious about this."

Higgins threw up his hands and looked about him. "Not serious? While you slept, I was flying here in the world's fastest plane." He looked pointedly at the helicopter and officers. "At the conclusion of this meeting, that air taxi will return me to the airport where the brand new CIA Lockheed A-12 OXCART two-seater is waiting to fly me cross-country back to Andrews Air Force Base. I couldn't be more serious about anything."

"How did you know we'd all be free to see you this morning?"

Aunt Sarah blushed. Uncle David took her hand. "We received the call from Langley last night, Jason, after you were asleep."

"Uncle David, you know I love my country. But each time I try to do something for it with the government, I wind up with my neck in a noose. Why would I do that again?"

The admiral looked at Higgins, who scanned the horizon before zeroing in on Jason. "All I want you to do is exactly what you're planning to do anyway. You're a vet recovering in the sun. You have an inheritance that allows you to enjoy diving and photography. Any investigator can easily verify that. Who could possibly suspect you of working for anyone? I want you to keep your ears and eyes open and your instincts sharp. Eventually you'll have information to pass on to me. Just a simple phone call on a secure line. A few rolls of film. Nothing more. Under these circumstances, I don't think this will be more dangerous for you than for any other Keys resident. But I do believe you'll always be glad you said yes."

"Why will I be glad I said yes?"

Higgins smiled. "I've had an officer talk with the owner of the local dive shop opposite the entrance of the new underwater park there. His name is Carl Gage. Reportedly, he's a real character, a chrome dome with a Genghis Khan complex, but very competent. He can be very useful to you. For starters, he says Molasses Reef, right off Key Largo, has the clearest water and prettiest reefs in the U.S. for film work. And he can provide you with the best equipment for your new venture into underwater conservation filmmaking."

Higgins took a swallow of coffee and Jason knew the man was letting the temptation work its effect. "All I'm asking is that you do the patriotic thing and let me recruit you to be an independent operative while you recover in the sunny Keys at government expense."

After another swallow, Higgins placed his cup carefully in its saucer and leaned forward. "Jason, I believe the seeds of enemy infiltration you discovered in Seattle are sprouting in Key Largo. The Florida Keys are a tight-knit, insular community. Residents born there call themselves 'Conchs,' and those families have a history of ignoring federal and state laws that interfere with their enterprises. We haven't been able to penetrate their 'Bubba' system. Something big is going on. Our U-2 reconnaissance planes with infra-red cameras are flying over to Cuba and recording a great deal of well-organized, strictly night-time boating traffic to and from Key Largo."

Jason frowned. "If it's strictly night-time, how can I be your eyes ... unless I'm so obvious that I end up on the bottom of the ocean with your two officers?" He shook his head. "I'm sorry you've come all this way for nothing, but I have to say no."

Higgins looked at Admiral King, who said, "Walter Higgins believes you *can* succeed and I do too. This is a unique opportunity to live out the destiny we all believe is yours." Uncle David looked across the lawn at the comfortable commandant's quarters. "Besides, this cushy pad won't be available to you after September. The Chief of Naval Operations wants me on a project at the Pentagon."

Jason stared out over the Pacific Ocean and his uncle's squadron of cruisers and destroyers anchored there. No one spoke. He looked at the helicopter and the two bodyguards, then back at the ocean. How could he say no to his godfather, the mentor he admired, the hero who had faith in him?

He turned to his aunt and uncle, who looked at each other, nodded, and looked back at him. Despite Higgins' overt manipulation, Jason felt compelled to accept this one assignment.

"Alright, Mr. Higgins. If you'll accept my conditions."

Higgins took an audible breath. "Name them."

"I work only for you, am answerable only to you."

"That was always my intention."

"I work for you as a patriot, not for money."

"We'll cover your costs."

"Your people can reimburse my expenses to live where you want me located and the cost of the equipment I'll need to accomplish what you want. I'll be responsible for my personal expenses. Agreed?"

"Yes."

"I want no papers to sign. No oaths. We simply shake hands on this."

CHAPTER 99
PERSISTENCE PAYS

Long Beach, California
Saturday, July 21, 1962

"Now I want you to answer another question." Jason seized the opportunity to satisfy his curiosity at last. "Truthfully."

"If I can."

"You can. Before I befriended Bonnie, I met a stunning woman in Tacoma through unusual circumstances. She had green eyes and long brown hair and seemed like a rancher's daughter with a brain. And you didn't actually have to see her to know she was there—just notice which way all the men and women in town were looking. Did you go to all that trouble for me?"

Higgins hardly had to answer. His face flushed with embarrassment, and he avoided Sarah King's eyes. Her spontaneous laughter was infectious. Uncle David chortled.

Higgins made the best of it. "You've just proven you're the man for the Key Largo job. You're right about the brain, too. She's a psychiatrist with the agency, who volunteered to be your companion to help you back on your feet. And as a matter of fact, yes, she did grow up on a cattle ranch. With our funding, she's researching the normalizing effect of a behavior therapy on abnormally stressed people. But, as fate would have it, you rescued Bonnie and she rescued you right back. So my psychiatrist got to return to Langley without so much as getting her feet wet."

Slapping his hand on his thigh, Higgins asked, "Jason, how in God's name did you know she was a rancher's daughter, let alone had a brain in her head? Was that extrasensory perception?"

"Sorry. Just experience and common sense. It was the natural way she handled men's interest in her—like someone who's grown up around a lot of breeding and takes it for granted. I got the feeling she didn't just rely on her looks, that she was really intelligent."

Jason sat back and looked intently at the DDO. "Alright, Mr. Higgins, I'll do it—if you'll grant me one last request."

Higgins beamed. "What's that, son?"

"I get the rancher's daughter for a partner."

Flustered, Higgins stammered, "But . . ."

Aunt Sarah burst out laughing and reached a hand along the table to pat Higgins' arm. "Walter, he's pulling your leg."

Higgins' shoulders relaxed as he raised his brow, then stood and reached across the table to shake Jason's hand. "It's going to be interesting." He fished a sealed envelope out of his jacket. "In here is a photograph and instructions for meeting the undercover officer I'm having coordinate with you. She's an amazing young woman and is already in place in Key Largo. She's Cuban and totally dedicated and trustworthy. We need her for her language skills. You'll find her useful for her underwater experience."

Absently tapping the envelope, Higgins said, "Do you remember placing among the best in Advanced Spanish at the Naval Academy?"

Jason shook his head, concealing his frustration and anger at the EST accident.

The DDO handed over the envelope. "Do whatever it takes to memorize what's in here and give it to your uncle to shred—along with the phone number I gave you in the hospital. If your things are ever searched, there must be nothing to tie you to the CIA. Can you remember important phone numbers and code words?"

"If I review them every day." Holding the envelope up for emphasis, Jason said, "It would appear you were confident of the outcome of your cross-country trip."

"Not at all, Jason. I figured you at a fifty-fifty probability at best. But one must be prepared for success as well as failure."

Jason opened the envelope and stared at the picture of the CIA officer who would assist him. Smoldering. He looked up at Higgins, who looked back smugly, apparently pleased with his ace-in-the-hole.

Grudgingly, Jason thought, *Give the man credit. He gets things done.*

PART VII

KEY LARGO

CHAPTER 100
KEY LARGO

The Florida Keys
Sunday, July 29, 1962

What dangers, Jason wondered, could lie hidden beneath this azure sky that arched in an unbroken horizon as far as he could see. This subtropical wilderness seemed the antithesis of the Pacific Northwest. No mountains, no hills, a flat expanse of brackish marsh with an occasional little island of small trees. He cruised along the shoulderless, two-lane ribbon of concrete through the bottom of the Everglades, his photographer's eye registering the incandescent light that shimmered in this environment. The eighteen-mile stretch ended at Jewfish Creek. He crossed the drawbridge, into the Florida Keys at last.

The famous Overseas Highway was built atop Henry Flagler's old railroad bed and separated the Florida Bay side of each Key from the Atlantic Ocean side. This was the final span of U.S. 1, which ran from Maine to the southernmost point in the United States. At mile marker 104 he passed the Caribbean Club, site of the classic movie *Key Largo* with Bogie and Bacall. Only four miles more to the tiny commercial center of Key Largo, where he would meet his partner.

Key West, according to the *Keys Guide*, was a hundred miles farther southwest, over another forty-one bridges and islands. The renowned old city attracted tourists and writers—and Harry Truman, when he was president. It also was home to the navy's southernmost ship and air bases. Ninety nautical miles beyond Key West, across the Gulf Stream, lay Havana.

The sun was slipping low over the bay, so Jason lost no time looking up the undercover officer. Rosa waitressed at the Pilot House, overlooking the commercial fisheries harbor on the Atlantic side of Key Largo. He took a seat at an empty table in the informal restaurant. Higgins' photos made it easy for the two new teammates to spot each other.

The Cuban beauty greeted him with a smile and a lively bounce in her movements as she walked over to serve the "tourist." Jason's first impression was that no photograph could ever do justice to this animated person. Her wholesome Latina body was exquisitely female, crowned by abundant shiny black hair that hung past her petite waist and feminine hips, counterbalanced by soft breasts that flowed and danced easily under her low-cut blouse. More than a beauty, she seemed to embody everything men long for in feminine companionship—energy, cheerfulness, and Bambi eyes that looked at you as if you were the most special person in her world.

Taking his cues from her flirtations for the sake of the locals dining there, they pretended to hit it off in a big way—except Jason didn't have to pretend. When he'd finished his Key Lime pie, she spoke just above a whisper. "You can stay with me tonight, Jason. We'll find you a place tomorrow."

He drank black coffee until her shift was over, then followed her to a tiny wooden house a short distance down the Overseas Highway. Jason parked his out-of-place shiny black Buick with its Washington State tags beside her rusty Keys cruiser. He grabbed his overnight bag and followed her into the single-room dwelling. Absorbing the entire scene in one glance, his attention raced from the double bed, the ceiling fan, and the kitchen appliances, to the wooden table and three chairs, occupied by two hard-case Latinos with pistols in hand and a distinguished looking Cuban *jefe*, the leader.

Rosa blanched.

Jason put out his hands. "Whoa, what's this?"

"Yes, Rosa," the *jefe* said in English, "what *is* this?"

"Nothing, Carlos. This is Jason. A friend asked me to help him get settled in Key Largo. He got into town late and I told him to spend the night here and we'd find him a place to stay tomorrow."

Carlos snarled, "First you save that old man who lost his tongue and bring him to live with you while you sleep on a futon till he's alright, and now you're picking up strangers."

"I told you, he's not a stranger. He's a Korean vet from the hospital who needs time to get well."

Carlos turned on Jason. "If you value your life, go stand with my men." Jason looked at the men gesturing with their pistols and complied, standing warily on the other side of the table between the seated men.

Carlos grabbed Rosa by a wrist and slapped her mouth. She stood up to him with fire in her eyes and spit blood on his embroidered white guayabera shirt as she blurted, "What was that for?"

"Alright, bitch, where is it?"

"Where is what, you insignificant son of a man-hating whore?" She spit out her question with more blood and with obvious hatred for centuries of abuse of women.

"The note on the piece of paper in my billfold."

"Oh, that. It must have fallen out of your wallet when you gave me the extravagant tip for serving your wife and family so well the other evening. I found it under your chair after you left and kept it for you, in case you might want it." She yanked her wrist out of his hand, walked to the cheap dresser, snatched up a scrap of paper and thrust it at Carlos. "Say 'Gracias,' you sad excuse for a man."

He rose from his chair and kicked it out of the way. "You dare insult me in front of my men? I'll show you who's a man!" Holding her wrists between her shoulder blades, he forced Rosa to bend forward over the table and raised her skirt from behind while his men ogled the gaping front of her blouse.

Rosa looked Jason in the eyes. "Don't worry," she said with contempt, "he's too short to reach this way." The *jefe* increased the pressure on her arms and proved he wasn't too short. "Damn you!" She gasped at the pain.

Jason watched the scene morph into slow motion.

With the two pistoleros so distracted, it was easy for him to grab the men by the hair at the back of their heads. He moved too fast for them to resist as he smashed their faces into the table, breaking their noses. Then he yanked them upright and slammed their heads together to knock them out. Carlos never cleared his pistol from the shoulder holster under his jacket before Jason leapt to his right around the table and knocked him out with a roundhouse right to the side of his temple. As Carlos fell, Jason deliberately hit him with his left fist and broke his nose, to shame him in the days to come.

Rosa stood, smoothing her skirt, jaw clenched, chest heaving with uneven breaths. She looked at the devastation, then turned to Jason. "Come outside with me," she hissed.

She closed the front door behind them. "Who do you think you are, coming in and taking control of an op I've been working for months?" She projected a controlled rage. "Waitressing wasn't producing any results to confirm what you learned in Seattle, so when we discovered the *jefe*'s a big recruiter in Key Largo, I decided to become his mistress. I took that note from his billfold two nights ago. It's the location and time of an important meeting, with a list of names." She glared at Jason. "It took you less than a minute to ruin months of trust building with the leader of the Key Largo drug organization. How dare you!" She spluttered to a halt.

Jason squared his shoulders and stared down into her flashing eyes. "What do you think you are, a tiger disguised as a pint-sized woman who obtains information by being raped and beaten?"

Her snarl was so like a big cat's that Jason was taken aback.

"I'm the five-foot-two jungle jaguar you have to survive partnership with, you pompous blowhard!"

"Even so, you're moving in with me, where I can keep you from that sort of abuse. Now go pack your things. That will fit our instructions to appear to become lovers who decide to live together." He frowned, appraising her out of the corner of his eye. "Did Higgins know what you were doing?"

"Of course he did," she snapped. Then she softened. "I told him after the fact."

With Jason's help it only took five minutes for Rosa to remove all her belongings from the simple house.

"I've never seen anyone move as fast as you, taking down the *jefe* and his soldiers." She gave him a quizzical look.

"It's an inherited gift. Everything around me seems to slow down while I move at what feels like normal speed."

"One of your abilities that Higgins would appreciate." She climbed into her rusty sedan. "Okay, Wildcard. Follow me back up the road to the Shoreham. It's on the Old Road, parallel to U.S. 1."

In what passed for a town center, they pulled up beside the motel. Jason rented a room. "I'll take the bed nearest the door," he said.

After showering, Rosa came out of the bathroom wrapped in a towel.

"Why did you call me 'Wildcard'?" Jason asked.

"It's your agency codename." Rosa toweled her luxuriant hair. "Didn't you know?"

"No. I didn't." He scratched his head. "I don't think I like it."

"I can see why. It's a dead giveaway. Don't worry, codenames are never used outside the inner sanctum of Langley."

"What's *your* codename?"

"Aphrodite." She blushed. "I've never known why."

"After seeing you in action with your 'lover' tonight, I wouldn't either." He slammed the bathroom door behind him to take his turn in the shower.

CHAPTER 101
ROSA

Key Largo, Florida
Monday, July 30, 1962

At dawn Jason awoke with a purring sleeping beauty in the other bed.

So, the jungle rumble and resonating purring weren't affectations, but perhaps the product of a seriously deviated septum behind Rosa's perfect-looking nose.

She stirred. "*Hombre. Querido.* I am yours. You will be my conqueror and I will be your sunshine."

Mystified, he said, "Why were you so different last night?"

"Premenstrual bitchiness, I let people think. But the truth is, it's the same post-traumatic stress disorder you have."

"What else did Higgins tell you?"

She stretched, and ignored his question. "We can have breakfast right across U.S. 1 at Hilda's German Restaurant. Ninety-nine cents buys orange juice, coffee, pancakes, eggs, and sausage."

Jason found the food delicious and plentiful, but his focus was on Rosa. He was still trying to figure her out. "Higgins tells me you spent a lifetime underwater?"

"My sister and I grew up free-diving in the ocean. We could hold our breath for five minutes." She flashed a confident smile. "I'll be able to model for you, and show you how to get really close to the fish. Things the other divers don't know. Our cover will be established before you know it."

It sounded too good to be true. "Tomorrow I'll look into cameras and boats."

"Meanwhile, I'll take you to a realtor to look for a place to live. Today's my day off."

They drove to the real estate office, two minutes from Hilda's.

"Hi, Bert. Meet Jason MacDougall. He's a Korean War vet recovering from a long hospital stay. Doctors ordered him to spend a year relaxing in the sun. Needs a place to lease on the water."

Jason nodded his confirmation.

"I thought maybe the lighthouse property, if it's available," she added. "It's furnished isn't it?"

Bert's eyes lit up. "It's just become available." Shaking Jason's hand, he said, "You sure look fit for a guy who's been in the hospital a long time."

Rosa answered. "No broken bones, Bert. Shell shock—a lot of repressed anger. You should have seen him beat up Carlos and two of his armed thugs last night. He's better to have around than a pack of hundred-pound Rottweilers."

"I take it your relationship with Santiago's over then. Good riddance."

"After what he tried to do to me last night," she felt her jaw gingerly, "that's it." She spoke with finality, clasping Jason's arm and looking up into his face with fawning eyes.

What an actress, he thought to himself.

The property sat at the end of Oleander Circle, a developer's alluring name, Jason decided, for a dead-end blacktopped lane. They parked in the yard at the front of the house and stepped out onto the pea gravel. Bert explained that the concrete stilt house was typical for the Keys, with all its living space on the second floor, above potential storm flooding. A canal ran along one side of the property and a wide concrete seawall with wood posts and galvanized cleats seemed to invite a boat to complete the laid-back setting. The vast back yard extended to the ocean. There was even a small lighthouse on the ocean point. Bert said it was privately built and maintained as part of the property. The light guided commercial fishermen to the entrance of the canal, which ended in Lake Largo, the fisheries harbor. *Convenient*, Jason thought. Rosa waitressed at the far end of that long canal, on the other side of the harbor.

The elevated house offered the welcome feature of parking underneath, protected from the blistering sun. Jason eyed the shady spaces on either side of the downstairs enclosure that served as a combination laundry room, workshop and storage area. Next to their parked cars, an outdoor concrete stairway led them up to the front door landing. Catwalks ran around two sides of the upstairs and an L-shaped porch overlooked the canal on the side and the ocean behind.

From the porch, Jason noticed a house mostly hidden by tropical trees and thick shrubbery, on the neighboring oceanside property they'd passed. The other lots nearby and across the canal were mowed weeds, no houses, no trees, giving him a clear view of his surroundings. He'd be able to see approaching water and land traffic from quite a distance. Since Korea, good perimeter visibility was important to him.

"Who lives in the jungle next door, Bert?"

"A recluse bought the place, a writer. His wife's a good-looking American Indian. People never see him. Just her."

Jason studied the site. "The house sure is hidden away among all those coconut palms and hedge-trees. Almost don't know it's there." He turned to Bert. "Any construction planned around here this coming winter?"

"None that I know of. Most of these lots are investments or properties the owners plan to build on when they retire."

Jason and Rosa looked through the upstairs interior. The house was modestly furnished, but there were no bookshelves anywhere. Jason was surprised. "How could they build a house with no bookshelves?"

Bert rubbed the side of his neck, apparently taken aback. "Don't see that in Keys houses. Guess people don't stay indoors reading much." He seemed to think about it. "No wine shops here either. We buy our wine at Lawson's grocery. And forget the fancy stuff, unless you order it special."

Jason took a year's lease and wrote his personal check on the spot, establishing that part of his cover—since Rosa had assured him that any information given to Bert would be the same as telling every member of the community.

CHAPTER 102
LOOKOUT HOUSE

Key Largo
Monday, July 30, 1962

"Ready to unload and move in?" Jason opened Rosa's car door. She reached for a satchel.

He carried two bags of her belongings upstairs and placed them inside the bedroom doorway. "You take this room. I'll use the sofa-bed in the living room."

"You're a chivalrous man, Jason."

"I can put my stuff in this chest of drawers out here."

"Now I can tell you about this lighthouse property," said Rosa. "It was leased by the CIA through a dummy corporation for their support of the *Bahia de los Cochinos*—Bay of Pigs—invasion. The 'corporation' continued its lease until the CIA needed the place for its next operation, which turns out to be you. Bert knows nothing about the undercover arrangement."

"The scope and detail of Higgins' organizing—impressive."

"Speaking of, we have two telephones." Rosa walked over to the counter that separated the kitchen from the living room area of the open floor plan. This is a conventional phone for our personal use. The one in the bedroom is for calls to and from Higgins. Its lines are precisely monitored for any resistance changes produced by wire taps." She gestured toward the identical-looking instrument. "Check it out. Let Higgins know you've arrived and we're settling in."

The phone was answered by a Priscilla. "I'm Dr. Higgins executive secretary."

"Priscilla?" said Jason, as he caught Rosa's eye.

Rosa nodded yes, so he left the message.

"Okay." She picked up her handbag. "Let's get some groceries at Lawson's."

Rosa made Cuban sandwiches for lunch and they washed them down with a couple of cold Buds.

"Can our radio bring in a classical music station down here?" he asked. "I love music. It speaks to me. And those artists soothe my mind, help me stay balanced."

Rosa pushed her chair away from the table. "WTMI. And given the previous tenant, we have the necessary FM antenna to receive it." She turned on the radio and tuned the dial. "Ninety-three point one."

Jason finished his beer. "This is good. The lunch, thank you, *and* the set-up." He picked up his plate and empty bottle. "We can be together every day to exchange information without arousing suspicion."

"An added benefit," she gave a coy smile, "I'll appear unavailable to my lonely male customers."

After Jason cleaned up the kitchen, they relaxed out on the porch in the loveseat swing that hung from the concrete ceiling. He felt at home with the saltwater smells of the tidewater flats and drank in the soul-satisfying view of the canal and the ocean. The raucous call of a great white heron surprised him, so at odds with the elegance of the bird which glided past and perched in a noble pose on a rock by the water's edge.

"The behavior we'll let people witness—they'll know our love is too crazy for us to be government agents," said Rosa. "Everyone loves lovers. I'll keep you aroused in public, as you do me, like now. People must *smell* the sex on us." She sniffed the air noisily. "Cubans are very *machismo.*" She put his arm around her shoulders and inside the front of her blouse. Jason started to pull his hand away, but her grip held him while a fishing boat motored out the canal. She whispered in his ear, "I'm so sorry to have to put you through this."

That elicited a Cheshire cat smile, which he figured was helpful because people would just think he was feeling smug. Which he was. He'd had no idea spy work could be this much fun.

CHAPTER 103
NICE DUTY

Jason turned to face Rosa on the porch swing. "All I can say is, 'nice duty.' I'm going to enjoy being a spirited Latina's crazy, kick-ass lover."

She straightened up and stared at him. "Jason, make no mistake. This is not about free love. It's about saving our republic from communist takeover. We have to succeed. Before I managed to escape from Castro's dictatorship, I experienced communism. Do you have any idea what it's like to live under communist rule?"

"It claims to be a system that takes care of everyone." This was his opportunity to hear from someone who knew firsthand.

Rosa stamped her foot. "Lies to brainwash the naive—*los estupidos*." Her eyes flashed. "My parents were the chauffeur and cook of a wealthy Havana family with a second home in Miami. My parents traveled with them and I was born in Miami. Lived and went to school there during much of my childhood."

No wonder her English was flawless and she sounded completely American.

"We were trapped in Cuba when Fidel Castro took charge in 1959. Under his regime my parents were made responsible for a grocery store in a village outside Havana and I taught English in the local school."

Jason wanted to know how she'd gotten involved with the CIA, how she'd managed to get back to Florida, but Rosa was on a roll.

"Let me tell you what I saw happen in a communist society. Workers' lives are expendable; no one has rights. The local cell of leaders controls everything through fear—neighbor reporting on neighbor, children brainwashed in school to report on their parents. If you speak out, you're thrown into prison. Of course, I know now that Castro's 'new' government is modeled on Soviet communism."

Rosa's shoulders sagged. "I feel sick, talking about it."

This was not the time to ask his questions.

"Russia's leaders claim that communism is superior to western democracies and they're trying to make inroads in every country they can. America doesn't have the economic inequality and rampant political corruption of Batista's Cuba, so there's no basis for a Castro-type revolution here. But most Americans take their freedoms for granted and too few think what I've witnessed can happen to them. Now that I've studied Marxism and the writings of Antonio Gramsci, I recognize the reality of subtle, long-term ideological subversion. If we can't imagine the possibility and be on the alert to prevent it, then someday our government in Washington could be running our personal lives. Like the Soviets and Castro's comrades, the elected leaders will claim to be doing what's best for the citizens, but they'll care primarily about their power and the perks of their positions."

"You don't paint a very bright picture of our future, Rosa." Jason shook his head.

"It's why you and I have to watch and listen, find out exactly what the Russians are up to here in the Keys, help disrupt whatever plan is underway." She stood abruptly, faced him and took his hands in hers. "That's got to take precedence over any personal feelings we may develop while working together."

"Cohabitation is our cover, Rosa, I'm not looking for free love. There's always a price."

"I'll gladly play the part of your girlfriend and be your underwater guide and model. But don't ever make the mistake of taking me for granted. You'll find there's only the jungle with me—that I am an unpredictable, dangerous, demanding jaguar." She narrowed her eyes. "And don't ever mention my PTSD to anyone at the CIA. You're the only one I've told."

Jason was puzzled by Rosa, but giddy at the opportunity to work with such a woman to accomplish their mission for God and country.

CHAPTER 104

KEYS COVER

Key Largo
Tuesday, July 31, 1962

Jason looked into water transportation while Rosa was at work. He decided to call on Carl Gage first and learn from the man's experience operating a dive business.

"Well, Jason, your reputation precedes you. Everyone knows Rosa has moved in with you, which makes you one of the most popular guys in town, as well as a man to envy."

Jason suppressed a grin. The dive shop owner was known for never lacking female company. "Carl, I want to take my experience with photography into the underwater world. What do you suggest for cameras? And where should I look for a reliable used boat?"

"You'll need underwater housings for any cameras you have, and if you plan on movie work, consider a 16mm Bolex. Jordan Klein, in Miami, makes quality housings."

"Can he also house a 35mm Nikon for me?"

Carl was clearly pleased that Jason ordered the housed Bolex, as well as the Nikon housing, through his dive shop. Jason knew he'd won an ally and furthered the authenticity of his cover.

Over the next several days he shopped for a boat and purchased two. The used twenty-six foot inboard would carry him safely offshore for scuba diving. The like-new Zodiac inflatable with a small, quiet Seagull outboard motor should be just right for photographing the birds and reptiles along the mangrove shoreline.

"Rosa, I'm going to start out with the Zodiac to get people used to seeing me everywhere with my cameras. Then on your days off, we'll take the inboard out to the reefs and work underwater together."

"I can hardly wait to go diving again." Her happy anticipation seemed to bubble up from her toes through her smile to the top of her head. "Come sit with me in the porch swing. We need to be seen necking as the boats come into the canal." She grabbed his hand. "Trust me. It's the Latino way of the people we must convince."

Jason played the relationship according to Rosa's terms. She wanted no suspicion about their "affair."

"I'm concerned that some of my customers may be from DGI— *Dirección General de Inteligencia*—the secret intelligence agency of Cuba."

When she worked, Jason often ate lunch or dinner at the Pilot House. Throughout every shift she was bubbly and unflappable. He could see that all her customers loved her, which made it easy for Rosa to listen to the Cubans and Columbians talking at her tables. Later she would be able to compare notes with what Jason heard from the local Keys residents.

On the day his first Kodachromes came back from processing at Eastman Kodak in Rochester, New York, Rosa returned from her dinner shift shortly before midnight. "It's the near-shore stuff, from the Zodiac," he said.

"May I see?" She examined his slides through the hand-held viewer. "Great wildlife pictures. You have an artist's eye." Rosa gave him an admiring smile. "Hmm. You've also recorded boats and people and activities in the area. Some of those could prove useful—maybe strangers or unusual behaviors worth following up on."

"I figure that's what you and Higgins need. As soon as I get the camera housings we'll work out on the reefs."

"In the meantime, while I'm at the restaurant, you should drive down U.S. 1, through Islamorada, at least to the end of Lower Matecumbe Key, and get to know the area. Be seen on land, too, as a wildlife photographer."

Jason followed Rosa's advice. He loved life in the Keys. The sun cheered him immensely. People looked tan and healthy, often barefoot or wearing flip-flops, living in swimsuits and T-shirts. They seemed natural and enjoyed life in or on the water. Like Jason, Keys residents were independent. He relaxed and dressed as casually as the locals. He worked out and ran to achieve the runner's high that reduced the stressor remnants of his war neurosis. His hair turned blond in the sun and salt sea.

Bottlenose dolphins cavorted in an ocean teeming with fish, manatees congregated in the bay that was a paradise of backcountry fishing, great white herons roosted in the mangroves, and white crowned pigeons fed on berries in the tropical hardwoods hammocks. He wasn't even homesick for the forests he'd left behind.

"Today I drove across the bridges from Key Largo to Key West," he said to Rosa. "From the top of the Seven Mile Bridge, the string of low-lying islands looked like a necklace of emeralds in a turquoise sea."

"An artist with words as well as cameras." She untied her apron.

"Everybody's talking about the coming boom. They say that with the water pipe the navy put in from Florida City to Key West, and with plenty of electricity for air conditioning, wealthy people will come to live in 'the Fabulous Florida Keys, sport-fishing capital of the world.' They talk about the destruction from Hurricane Donna two years ago and tell me the islands have already rebuilt."

"Amazing, when you see pictures of the Middle Keys right after Donna slammed ashore," said Rosa. "Bert says eventually the federal government will enact a national flood insurance or natural disasters policy to insure homes against the cost of storm damage. Then the banks can move in to ensure no one has to go without a mortgage. The developers and realtors are ready." She headed towards the shower.

"You mean ready to unleash their greed. Nobody seems to care about the impact of dredge and fill development. This habitat necessary for the abundant wildlife will gradually disappear."

Rosa stopped and peered at him. "You've flipped from cheerful to gloomy."

"I'm remembering I wanted to create a sustainable forestry business, be responsible for the environment, keep it healthy for the future. Now I feel the same responsibility for this part of our country."

"I'm glad we're working together. That kind of thinking makes the dangers worth the risks."

CHAPTER 105

UNDERWATER

Key Largo
Tuesday, August 7, 1962

"I've picked up the underwater camera housings, tomorrow's your day off, the wind is down, we're going diving." Jason could scarcely wait to film the coral reefs.

Up before sunrise to load film in the cameras and stow equipment on the boat, they were anchored seven miles offshore by nine in the morning. Together he and Rosa descended to the sandy bottom, allowing their ears to clear as they breathed their compressed air. Jason checked the anchor, securely dug into the sand, the nylon rode rising clear of the reef so it would neither damage the coral nor be rubbed in two by the craggy outcroppings. He turned in a slow, full circle to admire the living reef. A ridge of corals and seafans rose on either side of the sand, forming a canyon around him. So different from the rocks and kelp and chilly Pacific water off Long Beach.

Careful not to stir up the sand with their fins, he and Rosa swam from one end of the canyon to the other, noting orange and red sponges, purple seafans, yellow-tan elkhorn and brain corals that would become beautiful close-up pictures and desirable backgrounds for his photographs of fish and Rosa.

He had already developed a passion for translating his extraordinary skills as a hunter into wildlife photography and now he could apply those disciplines to the underwater world. He moved within twelve inches of a spiny lobster, without it retreating into its crevice. He enticed a green moray eel to emerge part way out of its hole into the sunlight where he could capture the image he wanted as the eel stared at its reflection in the camera lens.

Rosa's lifetime of free-diving made her a natural in the sea. They waited patiently until the fish grew accustomed to their presence and swam all around the human intruders. Recording the interdependent species in their natural habitat appealed to Jason's conservationist instincts, while his pictures of Rosa swimming gracefully among the yellowtail snappers and grunts created a beautiful new challenge in his wildlife photography.

Time evaporated in this watery world where the dominant sounds were their own breaths in through their scuba regulators and the noise of their bubbles as they exhaled. Jason's tank was getting low on air. He pulled the rod on his J-valve and with five hundred PSI remaining, signaled Rosa that it was time to go. They exhaled the pressurized air from their lungs while they ascended, following their last bubbles to the surface. His head emerged from the liquid blue and Jason knew he'd found a new vocation.

They climbed the swim ladder and removed their scuba gear. "This is fantastic!" he said. "I'll reload my cameras. Are you up for our second dive?"

Rosa's smile matched the sparkle of the water drops glistening on her skin in the tropical sunlight. She moved her regulator to a full scuba tank.

Jason scanned the horizon. The sky remained clear, with a few white cumulus clouds building in the distance. He watched a lobster boat hauling traps a half mile south. Two fishing boats trolled the deeper waters to the east. Carl Gage's "Henrietta" was anchored at French Reef, to the north.

"Not many boats out here. Any you don't recognize?" Drugs and contraband moved easily through these waters and innocent-looking workboats could disguise their real business.

Rosa studied the boats, shook her head, and they prepared for their second dive.

In the weeks that followed, Jason stayed on top of the weather reports. On good dive days, when the sun was bright and the sea calm, Rosa arranged to take off from her lunch shift to help him.

"Let me free-dive while you wait near the bottom in your scuba gear," said Rosa. "We can try for some artistic stills and movie footage and I'll fit in more naturally with the wildlife."

Jason knelt on the ocean floor and looked up at Rosa waiting at the surface, backlit by the sun. He started the film rolling as Rosa broke the surface. Her long hair flowed over her arched back, to her calves. Jason was surprised to see Rosa was nude—and breathtakingly beautiful without the swimsuit breaking up the naturally graceful lines of her body. A school of silversides opened a passageway for her and closed in again behind as she passed through them. Rosa could hold her breath so long that the two-point-six minutes of 16mm film in his hundred-foot load Bolex was used up quickly. He reached for his still camera and signaled for her to pose in a nearby school of yellow-and-black porkfish. The schools of fish provided the perfect degree of modesty for filming *au naturelle.*

Jason spotted a queen angel fish while Rosa was catching her breath on the surface. He tried skip-breathing the way she'd taught him and found that when his regulator was silent, the shy blue fish with its yellow-gold crown stuck around for his photographs. These were the best shots he'd ever gotten.

When the footage came back from processing at Capital Film Lab in Miami, Jason invited Carl over for a screening.

"Jason, you should consider a career as a documentary cinematographer."

Carl's enthusiasm encouraged Jason further. He already felt personal satisfaction in this film work that provided such convincing cover for his surveillance assignment.

After Carl left for the evening, Rosa said "I didn't want to jeopardize our op by telling you more than you need to know, but the sister I mentioned before is my identical twin and she's now living in Miami. We might get some great pictures if I invite Maya to join us for a day of shooting. All I'll tell her is that this is a chance for her to pose with me for some underwater shots."

He envisioned the possibilities. "Outstanding!"

Maya arrived with avant-garde bikinis she'd brought back from Rio.

Jason was not disappointed by the resulting photographs. With such extraordinary models, his pictures were sought after by *Skin Diver* magazine.

He also developed an eye for spotting drug runners. Occasional small boats that didn't quite fit the profile of tourist runabouts. Workboats that rarely fished or pulled traps. He noticed they tended to do their business at night. Sedans and pickups driven by folks whom he didn't recognize as locals and who were too deeply tanned to be vacationers. He greeted them at restaurants and bait shops and marine gas docks. Tourists were generally voluble and full of questions. The more silent guys were the ones to keep an eye on. He was careful never to take photographs where he might arouse suspicion. He reported possible persons-of-interest to Higgins, who had officers from Miami follow up.

The weeks passed quickly. Jason felt more fulfilled than ever by his work for the CIA and his opportunity to help bring the beauty and fragility of the coral reef realm to people's attention. Rosa seemed happy and he treasured her companionship. His outlook thrived in the sunlight. But awareness that the shock-treatment had knocked out parts of his memory and that he couldn't know what was gone worried him. He wondered what clues he was missing because of the memory gaps. He'd picked up no sign that Russians were involved in any Keys enterprise and he and Rosa were still missing concrete evidence of the big, coordinated operation Higgins believed was brewing.

CHAPTER 106
ROSA'S WAR NEUROSIS

Key Largo
Tuesday, September 18, 1962

Jason photographed in daylight and Rosa worked evenings, so they didn't have much time together in their house. Rosa was frustrated that she still had heard nothing about the unidentified *cosa grande*—the big thing—she'd overheard being mentioned by commercial fishermen at a table.

One evening, on her night off, Jason and Rosa prepared supper together. He washed the spinach for the salad, peeled and sliced the plantains for pan-frying, opened the wine to let it breathe and set the table. She had a special recipe for the mutton snapper, served with traditional Cuban yellow rice and black beans. Flan was a favorite desert for both of them. Afterwards, they sat on the sofa-bed in the living room.

She refilled their wine glasses on the coffee table. "Would it be insensitive of me to ask about the nightmares you've been having?"

Reluctantly, Jason shared the dream he had over and over about Korea, and the fact that Higgins practically told him something like that really happened. Jason told her that his doctor said he'd flashed back with a university classmate and almost killed the fellow.

Rosa's eyes were fixed on him. "The Spanish call it *estar roto*. It means literally 'to be broken.' By whatever name, it's all the same. I've told you I have the problem, too."

"Do you want to talk about it?"

She drained her glass of wine. "Alright, I have to tell you some-time. I was married in Cuba, the mother of twin daughters."

Jason looked at her tiny waist with amazement. "I didn't know you had children, Rosa, let alone twins. With a figure like yours that's hard to believe. What happened that makes you live alone performing dangerous work for the CIA?"

She paused as though wondering whether to tell him or not, the sudden tears at the corner of her eyes indicative of the pain. "If I tell you, maybe it can help you understand the importance of the freedoms you enjoy in this country and of the work we do now."

She poured another glass of wine as if steeling herself to speak. "After my parents' wealthy *padrones* fled to Miami, I lived with my parents in a simple country village near Havana, while Fidel's gue-rillas were fighting Batista's corruption. When I was seventeen, I married my high school teacher, a gentle, scholarly man and an accomplished free-diver. As a child, he spent several years in Peru, and for our honeymoon we went to the jungle sanctuary where he'd lived. We had beautiful twin daughters. Lorenzo was so proud, so loving a father.

"After Castro took over Cuba, *el presidente* became a paranoid, power-hungry dictator. Lorenzo and the twins and I had a one-room apartment beside my parents' over the grocery store they ran. When our girls were three, an officer under Fidel desired me. I scorned him. One night he returned drunk with a squad of soldiers who tied my par-ents, my husband, and my precious daughters to trees. He made me and the villagers watch while he accused my husband and parents of spying for the CIA. He had a long, curved sword in his right hand, and a bottle of whiskey in the other."

Jason held his breath, certain that whatever came next wouldn't be good.

Rosa's voice tightened, rose an octave. "The officer began shout-ing, 'Death to spies,' as he cut off my parents' heads. Then, in front of my poor husband, he screamed, 'and their spawn,' and decapitated our precious daughters."

Jason wanted to reach over and hug her, but he knew he had to wait, to let her expel the pain by first releasing the toxin, before covering it with salve.

She took a minute to recover, then went on, anguish distending her neck muscles and tendons and distorting her voice to a squeak. "Then with a shout he cut off my husband's head. When Lorenzo's head stopped rolling on the ground, his eyes were still looking all around until they found me and his mouth was working as if it was trying to say something. That went on for about two minutes. Then his eyes stopped seeing and his mouth remained open."

Rosa's large, sad eyes were dry as she continued her tale in a low, hollow monotone. "The officer threatened to cut off my head, but just held the sword against my neck and said, 'I must interrogate you before I kill you.'

"He dismissed his men, the terrified villagers scattered to safety, and he dragged me upstairs to our room. He stood his bloody sword by the door, took out his sheath knife, cut off my dress, and held the knife to my neck while he forced me to remove his pants and squat over him where he sat on the sofa. His breath was like puke. He kept drinking from the bottle in his left hand, his knife cutting into my throat with his right." Jason studied with new interest—and shock—the barely discernable scars on the left side of her neck, just over the collar bone.

She took several deep breaths and resumed in a desensitized voice. "He made me take his cock. He jabbed the knife harder. I started bleeding on him. All I cared about was living long enough to kill him. Nothing else mattered. Nothing. I needed him to climax so I could catch him with his guard down. But he was too drunk. He jabbed the knife again. I was pounding up and down on him as hard as I could, bouncing him and cursing him and screaming at him to come ... ." Jason sat transfixed in horror, in fury. He saw her eyes brimming. She went on, her monotone giving way to emotion as she gasped for air.

"A terrible thing happened to me. My own body began to respond." Almost unable to talk, her tight voice squeaked. "I couldn't stop it. My family's killer—and I had sex with him like a ... ." Now her tears were flowing out of control, wetting her blouse completely through. She didn't raise a hand to her face, just went on with the story. Her agonized voice tore through Jason's gut like a poison. "When he began to climax, he dropped the bottle on the sofa and dropped the knife to the floor in order to grab my breasts with both hands. I screamed in pain. I grabbed his whiskey bottle and smashed his temple with all my strength. He went limp." Her tearing eyes flashed intently.

"I jumped up. The curved sword that decapitated my family became my weapon of revenge. I seized it with both hands. He was lying on the sofa with his feet on the floor. I kicked one foot up on the sofa so his legs were apart and rammed the blade up between them as hard as I could. It hit something hard and stopped. The three-legged milking stool was against the wall by the end of the sofa. I grabbed it to hammer the sword deep into the bastard. To avenge my parents. Again for my husband. And again for my babies. He came to and started screaming." She grinned crazily. Jason shuddered at the madness he saw in her. As if comfortable in her insanity, her voice normalized.

"I kept beating the sword up into him until he was silent and I was too exhausted to continue." Rosa's tears had slowed to a gentle flow. She began hugging her arms and swaying her upper body with agonizing drawn-out moans, trembling like someone freezing.

When she could speak again, she finished. "One of the soldiers came back and found me sitting at the feet of the body, moaning gibberish. He sneaked me to the Columbian Embassy with my birth certificate and other papers and requested protection for me. The next day I asked them to take me to the American Embassy at the eastern end of Cuba. With the atrocities being committed under Fidel's regime, I felt work with the CIA would be important, if Americans didn't want to be ruled by such monsters, too."

Jason sat beside her and held her, kissing the tears from her eyes and removing the hair plastered against her wet face. He held her tenderly all through the night after she sobbed herself to sleep with her head in his lap.

What a simpatico companion she was for him in this operation. He reflected on the loyalty and devotion that had grown between them because of their shared backgrounds of loss and pain. Could this be the love he'd been looking for? Both had lost all that they loved, and now they were seeking ways to make a difference. They sought redemption together. *Hadn't Higgins said that, too?*

CHAPTER 107
ESTAR ROTO

Key Largo
Friday, September 21, 1962

Jason returned from refilling the air tanks at the dive shop, unloaded them into the downstairs storage room, and took the stairs two at a time, anxious to load film in his topside cameras and go check out the local activity. As he entered the house, he felt a premonition. He stopped, stood motionless, then raced down to the dock and studied his dive boat. Everything looked the same, the lines were still correctly cleated, no discernable footprints in the cockpit. Even so, he sensed something was wrong. He stood well back and rocked the boat with a long pole. Nothing fell. No strange sounds. But he intended to acknowledge his intuition, determined to create a positive outcome.

He stepped aboard very carefully, gingerly opened the cuddy below the steering console ... and held his breath. Four sticks of dynamite were wired to the ignition. Jason spent the rest of the morning removing the explosive device and checking for other booby traps. His instincts told him the sabotage was Santiago's doing, that this was payback and, furthermore, the man was jealous of Jason's relationship with Rosa. He didn't know if the explosion was meant just for him, or for him and Rosa. It could have gone either way.

As he imagined Rosa blown to smithereens, rage boiled inside him. He wanted to go after Santiago and beat him so the man would fear forever trying anything else like this. But that would invite other repercussions and it could expose all their undercover work. He couldn't jeopardize their op.

Instead he telephoned Higgins to report the development. "I'm sure it's personal revenge. The hot-blooded Latino lost face as a leader *and* I've ended up with his beautiful mistress."

"Even so, son, be careful. You know he's a major cog in the local drug ring. Tell no one except Rosa what you found. Act as though nothing has happened." A momentary pause. "And next time call me first, so I can send our unexploded ordinance experts to defuse the device."

Jason tried to quell his imagination and calm his rage. That evening, he showered and went out for supper at the Pilot House. Rosa's happy greeting soothed his nerves. He gave her his order.

Ten minutes later, an inebriated Carlos Santiago came in and sat down at the next table. Jason hadn't been in the same room with the man since the night he arrived in Key Largo and unwittingly ruined Rosa's intelligence-gathering efforts. The *jefe's* nose had healed straight and with his black hair and well-groomed mustache, he remained distinguished looking despite being drunk. Jason's back stiffened, on guard as he watched Santiago's eyes follow Rosa moving from table to table. When Rosa walked over to take Santiago's order, he beckoned her to lean closer and whispered in her ear. Jason saw the color drain from her face. Had Carlos given her bad news? Or threatened her?

Jason's throat tightened. His hands clenched into fists.

Rosa left for the kitchen and returned with Jason's food. As she approached, the macho Latino grabbed her around the waist, making her drop the dinner as he forced her to sit in his lap. He exhaled with a leer and his garlic-laden breath reeked even at this distance.

Jason leapt up, forcibly removed the man's arm from Rosa's waist and started to twist the arm, ready to break it out of its shoulder socket.

"Jason, NO!"

The desperation in Rosa's voice tore through his rage.

He released Santiago, but stood over him with a threatening stare.

Santiago must have seen the wild look in Jason's eyes because he backed down, apologized to Rosa and offered to pay for the lost meal.

Jason returned to his own table, pretending a control he didn't feel.

"You know he's a vet," Rosa reminded Santiago. "*Estar roto*—war neurosis," she explained to the nearby diners, then excused herself from work.

Jason held the restaurant door for her, slid behind the wheel of his Buick and followed her home, checking his rear-view mirror all the way.

"What did Carlos whisper?" he asked in a hollow voice, fearing the answer.

"He threatened that I don't have much longer to live with my Anglo boyfriend. Jason, his machismo ego has to avenge losing face in front of his men."

Jason told her about the dynamite on the boat and his call to Higgins. "It's been a stressful day."

He and Rosa were shaking. She made coffee, but when she carried the mug to him her hands shook so uncontrollably the hot liquid slopped over the top.

"Jason, something big is going down and we can't blow our cover like this. We can't let that happen. I've got to stop shaking with fear and you have to control your temper."

"What can we do?" He was *not* going back to the hospital.

Rosa hesitated, then as though coming to a decision, she nodded. "In order to be with her man, my sister was a guerilla under Castro, while Fidel was still a rebel leader in the Sierra Maestra mountains." Rosa narrowed her eyes and Jason felt as though she was staring straight through him. "Maya told me about *estar roto,* how soldiers dealt with it after combat in terrifying jungle patrols." She paused, as though choosing her words carefully. "They used sex to normalize themselves after high stress patrols and battles. Sometimes with drugs. For hours. Then they would be able to face the enemy again."

Jason felt the heat rise through his body. "You're volunteering?"

Rosa's eyes glinted like black metal as she snapped, "Don't treat me lightly, Jason. This is important. We're on the verge of uncovering something big, so big and so diabolical that I could be with my family soon."

"Please don't talk that way, Rosa." Jason trembled. He wrapped his arms around her and held on tightly. He felt her hands on his face, gently holding him. He read her eyes, they reflected the danger she sensed.

"It's alright, Jason. I'm truly scared, but it's alright. *Via de Christo y todos los santos y los mártires.* I can do it. These men I'm watching are brutal and cunning. They suspect me—the dynamite and Santiago's threat are proof of that. If I'm caught, I know they'll rape me, kill me. But it will only be my body; my spirit will already be with my loved ones. You must remember that and not feel too badly for me, because I'll be in a better place." She gave a deep sigh, then pushed his shoulders away to look at him.

Her mention of the great sacrifice opened his mind to the inevitability of some things. "Oh, Rosa. The only thing we get to take with us when we die is our integrity. It's the belief I live by. Your life is all about integrity, too." He swallowed hard. "But I'm not going to let Santiago get you, I'm not going to let you die. Not in my lifetime." He kissed her forehead.

"You have more integrity than any man I know. And we *must* go forward." She squeezed his shoulders. "I'm trusting you'll discover how important it is that we keep going forward together. We need each other more than ever."

"How do you know so much?"

Rosa gave him a look that chilled him to the bone. "Everything's too quiet, like when the tiger approaches and the jungle becomes still. Higgins senses it too. Some big evil is upon Key Largo. Something so big that Santiago had to behave out of character tonight and back down to you or risk betraying his mission. Jason, we've got to be ready."

CHAPTER 108
CATHARSIS

Key Largo
Friday, September 21, 1962

Jason watched Rosa untie her apron. She slipped out of her clothing, her eyes never leaving his, and stood before him cloaked only in her bountiful midnight hair.

"Rosa, you still love your husband—at least your memory of him. Emotionally, you're still married."

"That's sweet, Jason." She stepped close and caressed his face with a warm hand. "But we're living in the present and the present is full of danger. What if our lack of control tonight is simply an indicator that we're holding too much in and have become pressure cookers with stuck relief valves? You know what happens when pressure relief valves don't function, Jason? There's a big explosion and nobody wins."

She brought her other hand up to his cheek and held his questioning face between her palms. "We're losing control because we're broken and we've got to blow off steam in order to keep from exploding."

She slid her hands down to the top button of his shirt. Jason let out a sigh. He knew she was right. He unbuttoned his shirt and removed it, then his shorts. He couldn't help his male response to Rosa's erotic warmth and beauty.

Rosa's eyes widened, then narrowed with determination as she took his arm and led him to her bed.

He held back. "Wait. I have to get—"

"No problem," she interrupted, "I can no longer have children. And I've seen my doctor since Carlos. No diseases." She pulled him to the bed. "Lie on your back."

Settling over him, she cooed, "It's alright, Jason," and began her determined descent.

The progression of Mussorgsky's *Pictures at an Exhibition* defined his breathless advances into the labyrinth of her welcome. His pent-up turbulence channeled into a consuming focus on Rosa's amorous movements. Once she was stretched to receive all of him, this petite woman became aggressive, rough, hurting them both. Like a cat, Rosa bit hard and dug in her nails, feeding his anger and giving it release. She cried out, her passion escalating along with his.

Jason rolled her over and held himself in check until she peaked, with an awesome strength in her loins—and he brought her to another climax, followed by another that took his all. Her body jerked to the contractions of her ongoing orgasms, her breasts flowed up and down under the skin on her chest. Her eyes glistened and her joyous shouts were joined by his as he exploded within her, thrusting so far she cried out in helpless surrender to the craziness she had deliberately set in motion.

Throughout the night Rosa kept after him, relentless, extracting everything possible from both of their sweaty bodies. She was tender, rough, tireless—presenting herself in amazing ways that kept him wild to have her. The music on WTMI accompanied them. The bass drums and the powerful brasses in Respighi's *Pines of the Apian Way* marched to a crescendo as he and Rosa drove each other's hearts, minds and bodies in blissful frenzy.

By dawn they were too spent to move. "More. More," she murmured weakly. They chuckled as they lay facing each other.

Jason blew out a long breath. "My brain feels like mush."

"Thank you for the compliment." She stroked his forehead. "And I want you to know, you've not only repaired my emotions, you've healed my heart."

"I don't understand."

"When I go to my precious girls and Lorenzo, I won't be carrying the guilt of my night of rape. You've given me beauty to replace horror. You've made me feel clean and alive again. My heart sings once more." She luxuriated on her back, humming through her smile.

Jason leaned over and kissed her eyes. "You said I'd be well today," he whispered. "You're right." He squeezed her hand. "Thank you."

Her finger caressed his lips. "I've never experienced so much. How did you learn such control?"

He looked into her beautiful brown eyes. "You deserve everything good in the world."

"Oh, Jason, now you've done it." Her voice was low and husky. Her eyes brimmed with tears as she reached up and drew his mouth to hers, and they became lost in a long, tender kiss. An eternity kiss.

"Find the woman of your heart," she implored. "Treat her like a goddess. Trust me, she'll keep you well. She's the key to your future."

"Rosa, I'm lying with that woman now."

* * *

Jason was asleep on the sofa bed when Rosa returned from the Pilot House that night. Ever alert to his surroundings, he was awakened by the sound of her car as she approached the far end of Oleander Circle.

"Good tips, but no new clues," she said. "Go back to sleep."

"Sweet dreams."

Rosa closed the bedroom door.

Sometime later, he awakened as she tiptoed across the terrazzo floor of the living room and kissed him on the lips. He cupped her face between his hands and felt the tears on her cheeks.

She covered his hands with hers, then slid her fingers into his palms. "Come to my bed, *querido*."

Their passion escalated and Jason wondered whether the bed-springs would collapse. Rosa gave all her precious love to him in a night that confirmed her readiness to commit to a lifetime relationship.

* * *

Jason faced his days with a new equilibrium. Surveillance and photography by day, a vibrant relationship with Rosa at night—and on her days off when wind or rain interfered with their film work.

"I was determined to stay out of the hospital and to avoid prescription drugs. Our love and intense sex are the best cure there is."

"If not the cure, certainly the best ongoing antidote to control the ghosts from our traumas."

He wrapped his arms around her. "A medicine I look forward to—every day."

"And the patience we need to keep watching and listening until we uncover the Russian-led espionage here."

CHAPTER 109
CUBAN MISSILE CRISIS

Key Largo
Sunday, October 21, 1962

Jason embraced the joy-filled approach he and Rosa shared to manage their war neurosis. No more nightmares. A feeling of well-being. Their intimate relationship was far more fun and creative than traditional calisthenics and distance sprinting to achieve a runner's high. His only frustration was not knowing what memories, what information the over-volting had knocked out of his head.

One Sunday night, Rosa came home from the restaurant and sat down without removing her apron. "I had two customers that I think are DGI. Something's afoot, but I haven't figured it out."

"I don't know what the DGI are up to here," he said, "but I've had a strong feeling over the past few days that something big is going on in your homeland."

"Cuba? I've been focused on action and whispers here in the Keys."

The next evening while Rosa served her customers at the Pilot House and listened to the stories of their day, he sat down to a top round steak at home and turned on the TV news. President Kennedy came on the screen. Jason clutched his fork and caught his breath. The president announced that Soviet missiles were being installed in Cuba. U-2 aerial photographs confirmed the accusation. Jason watched the president of the United States announce a naval "quarantine" on Cuba—a blockade to prevent further shipments of Soviet missiles.

How much had Higgins known, and for how long, Jason wondered. He struggled for patience as he waited for Rosa to return home with the reactions of her customers.

She burst through the front door. "You heard the news?"

"Missiles in Cuba."

"It's all anyone could talk about. That they're ninety miles from Key West. Oh, Jason." She threw her arms around him. "The men I suspect as DGI, they weren't there, so I don't know whether they had any inkling."

He held her close, a momentary cocoon of security. "We need to sit down and plan our strategy."

Jason held Rosa's hands across their little dining table as they sat facing each other. "Higgins will be up to his eyeballs in this crisis. We should wait for him to notify us if he wants anything."

She looked towards the kitchen cupboards. "We already have canned food, water, batteries—all our hurricane emergency supplies."

"Rosa, these are nuclear missiles. If anyone tries to take one out, Key Largo is only a hundred sixty nautical miles downwind. Radioactive fallout. And the navy base in Key West, Homestead Air Force Base— they're targets. We can't escape that reality."

"Maya's just as vulnerable in Miami as we are."

By morning, missiles and nuclear fallout were all any thinking person in the Florida Keys had on his mind. Cars were gassed and bags packed, ready for what could be the most massive exodus attempt in the history of these islands and all of South Florida. Jason and Rosa drove to Lawson's for groceries and watched tourists and Keys residents crowding U.S. 1 on their way north. Convoys of trucks carrying military personnel and towing ordinance were headed the other direction, to Key West. Jason envisioned Hawk anti-aircraft missiles competing with palm trees as the prominent feature of the tropical landscape in the picturesque old city.

Those residents who had nowhere to go in an all-out nuclear confrontation remained glued to their radios and TVs and talked about little else. Jason and Rosa were no exception. Everyone in the country held their breath as the two superpowers hovered on the brink of nuclear war.

Jason wasn't aware of what a mess the government had been making of Latin American relations, but Rosa was and let Jason know about it with vehement passion. What really brought the seriousness of her message home to him was how angry his normally cheerful partner became on the subject of foreign relations and the way Congress had buried its head in the sand by cutting off funds to pay for intelligence from "low-lifes."

After one such outburst, Jason told her, "Change into a bathing suit. We're going for a swim together."

"What if there's news while we're in the ocean?"

"Just do it, Rosa, before we kill ourselves *for* them, from worry about what the Russians might do."

The warm saltwater calmed them and the vigorous exercise restored them. When they returned, Rosa showered, put on a pretty off-the-shoulder blouse together with a flounced cotton skirt and went to sit on the porch swing. Jason showered next and walked out to join her. He was surprised to see tears streaming from her large eyes as she stared out over the ocean—the way home to Cuba.

He sat and held her tenderly. "What is it, Rosa?"

"Oh, Jason, I'm so tired of the stupidity—the blind cruelty. We risk our lives to get information to save our way of life, only to have it ignored by our leaders."

He inhaled a short sharp breath of alarm. "Are you telling me Higgins doesn't report the information we get?"

"No, no. I'm telling you we in the CIA only get the information and report it to the commander-in-chief. What he and his staff decide to do with our hard-earned intelligence sometimes makes so little sense, I just want to give up. It's always the good people who suffer."

Jason caressed her face with his fingers and rubbed her back through her heavy, damp hair. He continued holding her while she cried quietly.

Determined to stay in top physical shape, he and Rosa worked out hard each morning before she went to work. He was amazed by the strength and endurance of this feminine person and enjoyed their shared activity together. He felt blessed to work for a man of Higgins' caliber and with a dedicated officer like Rosa.

What he didn't enjoy was knowing that his government had been blind to Khrushchev and Castro's activity in Cuba. The Cold War adversary had managed to install nuclear missiles just ninety nautical miles from the U.S. shoreline of Key West. Enemy warheads just a hundred and sixty miles from their house. Jason's stomach churned at the thought. Mouth dry all the time from living in apprehension of the worst. Starting at the slightest unexpected sound. *Who needs this!*

* * *

For six tense days Jason tried not to show his worry that potential radioactive fallout could drift from Cuba to Key Largo in as little as half a day. The situation took on a life of its own.

And then it was over. Sunday, October 28th. Khrushchev had capitulated. What wasn't over was Jason's heightened awareness of the importance of keeping all of Central America, all of South America, free from Soviet communist control and free of nuclear weapons.

Rosa hugged him with relief when they learned that the Russian missiles in Cuba would be removed. "But remember, Jason," she warned, "this proves how dangerous Castro is. And the Russians. They're using him, to manipulate the United States."

CHAPTER 110
PICNIC IN PARADISE

Key Largo
Tuesday, October 30, 1962

"What would you like to do on your day off?" Jason asked Rosa. "To unwind after living for a week with our hearts in our throats. Anything at all."

She stretched, palms out, fingers interlocked, elbows taut. "A picnic, in the Zodiac. Explore South Sound Creek, now that they've finished dredging the entrance. Meander among the mangroves before they open it to traffic. Give myself to you as never before, feeling the heat of the sun on our skin, the cooling ocean breeze."

Two hours later, inside the entrance of the wide creek, Jason cut the outboard. The mid-day hush and wilderness privacy was a world apart from the television news of politics and nuclear warheads.

Jason looked at Rosa. Beyond her a great white heron poised on an arched mangrove root, alabaster wings outspread, long beak ready to stab a fish in the shimmering shallows. "Photo op," he whispered, grabbing the Nikon. Audubon's "angel of the swamp" caught its prey and Jason captured the image.

An incoming tide carried the inflatable boat along the winding mangrove waterway. A gentle breeze tempered the tropical heat and kept them comfortable in their swimsuits. After sharing the chicken lunch Rosa had prepared, Jason sat on a stern tube of the eight-foot Zodiac and took pictures. An osprey perched atop a red mangrove. A snowy egret, with its golden slippers, fished from the prop-roots in the shade of the leafy limbs branched out over the water. Rosa relaxed in the bow. Their bronze bodies glistened in the sun. Jason focused his camera on the dark-haired beauty in the boat. Their eyes met through the lens. Jason lowered his Nikon into the camera bag and they peeled out of their bathing suits.

How fortunate he was to be with this awesome woman.

She reached out for his hand. "I cherish your emotional connection when you make love."

"I think the Cuban officer who killed your family and raped you traumatized you so severely you became a bedroom spy with Santiago to punish yourself."

Tears welled up in her eyes.

"You know I pick up on things and say what I think. I'm sorry if that hurt you."

The tears spilled out, glinting in the intense tropical sunlight as they quivered on her chin and fell. "You *are* perceptive and you hit a nerve, but I told you after our first extraordinary night together that you had replaced the horror with beauty. You're a true friend. Since my marriage, you're the only man I've known who *gives* me energy. All the others wanted to control me and rob me of my power. It's another reason I was so bitchy your first night in Key Largo, trying to keep you from taking my energy."

"Your energy?"

"My aura. Yours. Yours is a colorful aura that radiates out to me when we're together, gives me the excess energy I then have for you." Her large brown eyes held him in her spell.

"I saw your aura the moment I spotted you in the restaurant, felt your electricity the instant I approached you." She pulled him closer and reached for his arousal. "Come to me now, Jason, and I will show you how God intended us to see, to feel, to live."

Hypnotized by the magnetism in her eyes, Jason felt himself drawn into another dimension. A radiant rose, she opened to meld with him. As they connected, he was transported to a brilliantly colorful world in a lush jungle. Vivid greens and violets and reds glowed in the golden light. He and Rosa lay on a stone altar in front of an ancient Peruvian temple covered in fragrant flowering vines. Melodic bird songs filled his ears. Iridescent butterflies fluttered about Rosa's head and shoulders and settled on her hair.

Jason became aware of a wonderful warm liquid sensation spreading from her loins to his, sweeping him into a maelstrom through which they entered a garden like Eden. Their pleasure seemed as natural as breathing. Fruit trees and lilies scented the air. Vibrations in the atmosphere, silent to the ear, lifted his soul like ethereal music. Rosa morphed into her magnificent jaguar form as she strode by his side, greeting other supremely happy beings. A mystical world. All seemed perfect. Earthly time did not exist here.

* * *

Slowly, Jason became conscious of the inflatable boat, of lying on his back beneath Rosa. She was caressing his hair and purring like a jungle cat. He tried not to leave the hypnotic dream, but it faded, along with the beautiful colors and mystical feelings. Rosa was keeping him engorged within her. A blissful way to return to reality. He took a deep breath, let it out slowly, and checked his watch. Three twenty-five. God, where had the time gone?

The tree branches were slipping past more quickly. The current had strengthened to its mid-tide peak and they were drifting at close to two knots. Now he thought he heard something. Not birds, or even an outboard, but voices.

CHAPTER 111
OH, SHIT!

Key Largo

Tuesday, October 30, 1962

"Quiet, Rosa," Jason warned in a hushed voice, holding up his hand.

They listened. A man's voice was finishing a story. "And that's how I got to be a hit man!" Raucous laughter. Several men and women. Close by, around the next bend.

Mafia? Jason searched Rosa's eyes. He saw she sensed trouble, too. *Get out. Fast.* He grabbed the starter cord for the outboard. Rosa tapped his knee.

"Too slow. They'll hear us and come after us," she whispered, her shoulders hunched with fear. "We've got to convince them we're lovers enjoying a secluded paradise. Start taking pictures of me."

"Look gorgeous."

In the bow, facing Jason, Rosa sat ramrod straight on the hull tube. She crossed her legs, raised her arms and with her fingers combed her long, luxuriant hair, fanning it out like a peacock tail. He took two pictures. His stomach tightened as they floated around the bend into full view of a seventy-foot Huckins motor yacht at anchor. The bow towered above their little inflatable.

Naked women stood on the foredeck with a man in a robe, one by one noticing that Jason and Rosa were floating their way. Jason shot some pictures of Rosa that included the yacht with the women leaning over the bow rail waving to them.

Through the lens he saw a bearded, muscular man in a swimsuit move in next to the man in the robe. Recognition broke through Jason's electro-shocked memory. His brother! Ivan stared at him with a strange intensity, then said something into the ear of a black-haired, bikini-clad woman who stepped up beside him. Natasha! Jason kept his face blocked by his Nikon and fired off three quick frames.

In that same moment, an open launch appeared around the stern of the yacht and roared towards the Zodiac, making a wake. Jason put the camera down. There were some rough looking characters in that launch.

"Rosa, toss the dinghy anchor to keep us from hitting the yacht's bow."

The anchor grabbed the sandy bottom and swung the Zodiac bow into the current, holding their stern scarcely ten feet ahead of the yacht. Now Jason's back was to the Huckins and Rosa was staring up at its passengers. The launch passed the inflatable and anchored a few feet up-current, boxing them in. *Not good.* Jason saw a moment of terror in Rosa's eyes, which she masked with smiles. *Not good at all.*

Still seated on an aft hull tube, Jason twisted and waved up to the pale, robed man standing on the foredeck with all the playmates. He was a small man, chinless, with dark hair, and he rudely ignored Jason while openly leering down at Rosa. Then he focused on Jason. "What are you doing out here?"

Meyer Lansky, godfather of the American Mafia! What the hell had Higgins gotten him into? The Russians were working with Lansky? Jason felt his face flushing hot and cold. He lowered his eyes so no one would see his fear. Fight and flight were out. He'd have to talk his way out of this one. Something told him, *Be audacious with this man. He's bright. Challenge him.*

"Doing? Isn't it obvious?" Jason looked pointedly at the women hanging over them and taking in the conversation. "I'd say we're doing the same as you, trying to unwind from the gawd-awful tension of the past few days." Then he grinned disarmingly. "Do you know a better way to unwind than to keep doing it till you can't possibly do it one more time?"

The man laughed, looking over his stable. "Obviously not." Then he scowled. "What gives you the right to photograph my boat and the people on it?"

"It's what I do for a living, take pictures of wildlife."

"You mean like birds and alligators and such?"

"Exactly. It's a relatively small niche market. But that wildlife," Jason pointed to the women at the bow rail, "that's the kind of wildlife the whole world wants to admire."

Everyone on the yacht broke into spontaneous laughter.

The man's amusement turned to a glower. "What makes you think I'm going to let you keep that camera?"

Jason opened the back of the Nikon and removed the film without rewinding it, overexposing every frame. He threw the film to Lansky.

Ivan reached out a hand and plucked the film out of the air with extraordinary ease. He never seemed to take his eyes off Jason's face.

"Just who do you think we are?" the robed man snarled.

"I think you're a consigliore," Jason drawled, trying to sound matter-of-fact.

Ominous silence.

Jason fought to keep his voice from going tenor. "The men operating the launch are regular crewmembers of your boat, and the others are soldiers and their girlfriends, who are along for the ride. I expect the incredible redhead on your right is your wife or companion."

The pale man pressed against the varnished rail for a closer look and rasped, "Who are you? *What* are you?"

"Nobody to worry about. Just a war vet trying to recover from some bad time in Korea, while living the good life in paradise with his girlfriend."

"How could you know so much about us, even which woman is my main squeeze, if you aren't the law?"

Jason knew he had to play the consigliore with all the finesse he could conjure up, the mortal danger if his instincts to be bold with this man were wrong. The *padrino* would order their execution and the crew would dump his and Rosa's bullet-ridden bodies and slashed inflatable in deep water, to vanish forever. Higgins would never know what happened to him or Rosa and he'd have to find someone else to monitor the southeast corridor.

Soundlessly Jason cleared his throat. "A no-brainer. The guys at the helm and anchor of the launch are professional crewmen because they have the sort of tan you only get living on the water every day. The rest are soldiers, who are easy to spot from their scars—the knife cuts on their faces and the bullet wound deforming the big guy's forearm because he couldn't go to a doctor with it. God that must have hurt. The redhead has the confidence not to go blonde, wears the earrings, watch and rings befitting an expensive yacht and has the perfect suntan and look of privilege that would be especially exciting to you. The beauty in the bikini obviously belongs with the man in the swimsuit, probably your guests." Jason bowed to the other women. "That's not to slight the rest of you, any one of whom I'd take to live with me on a desert island." The women jumped up and down, cheering, and shouting, "Take me. Take me."

Jason grinned at them, then turned back to the robed man. "You're the brains. You don't have time to soak up the rays and enjoy your toys, so you have to protect yourself from the sun with the silk bathrobe. You make the real money. And frankly, I just love any opportunity to say 'consigliore.' It rolls off the tongue like a thousand-dollar wine. Makes me feel like I've just uttered a secret password to mystical places."

"Hand up the camera bag," said Lansky.

CHAPTER 112
CRUNCH TIME

"Rosa." Jason kept his voice even. "Let out some anchor line so we drift back under the yacht's bow."

He handed the bag up to Lanski.

Lanski rummaged, seeing it was only lenses and film. Then he unzipped the front compartment with the pistol and spare mags. "You think carrying this Walther will save you?"

"Not at all," said Jason. "Frankly, I think we die when fated to, regardless of what we carry or do." He deliberately avoided looking at his brother. Ivan probably had Soviet intelligence reports about the shock treatment, and if Jason seemed not to recognize him, his brother might think that Jason's memory of him had been erased.

"Then why do you carry?"

"Because I never know when I'll encounter an armed robber whose time has come."

"Jesus, you got a mouth." The consigliore turned to Rosa. "He do it as good as he talks?"

Rosa hugged herself and flashed a coy smile.

"Jesus. That good, huh?" He turned back to Jason. "Okay, big guy. You talked your way out of trouble today. We appreciate what veterans go through to keep our country free and prosperous. Now start up your outboard and get out of here." He handed the camera bag with the pistol back to Jason, saying, "You'll understand if I keep the mags."

As soon as Jason steered around the bend, Rosa reached into her beach bag and whispered, "My Smith & Wesson's ready to go." She kept watching the creek behind them and wrung her hands, exclaiming in a hushed voice, "You should have seen the faces of the men in the launch while the women were shouting 'Take me.' Do you know who that man *is*?"

"Sure. I read the Miami Herald. Meyer Lansky. *Un padrino*, a god-father, even if he's not Italian."

"And the redhead?"

He shrugged. "Haven't a clue."

"That's the Miami mayor's wife. Always in the society pages for charities and fund raisers."

Jason rubbed his chin, deeply troubled, shocked by the sudden memory of Ivan and Natasha—flooding into the front of his mind like drowned bodies surfacing from the sea. As though one door opened the next, he recalled the blackmail he'd set up to protect himself from being assassinated by this twin brother. He stared at Rosa. "The gladiator couple next to Lansky, he's my twin brother."

She gasped. "That's Ivan? And his partner, Natasha?"

"Seeing him brought it all back. Or at least this part. After the shock treatment I don't know how much I still can't recall."

"Higgins told me you had a twin, raised in Russia and now working on the Soviet agenda in this country. Higgins said Ivan needed to kill you to keep you from identifying him, but for some reason your brother left you alone after you went to the Naval Academy."

"Right now, our job is to get home safely and report this to Higgins. I'll fill you in on everything I can remember once we're in the security of our house."

They put on their swimsuits for the coastal trip home.

"The mayor's wife," said Rosa. "Guess she gets her thrills slumming with Lansky. Think it's a link between organized crime and city government? Since the underworld gambling operators fled Cuba along with their accommodating host, Batista, they've needed new playing fields."

Jason's thoughts raced on as he surveyed the mangrove creek. "Could be competition for drug activity in the Keys, too. That yacht Lansky has—it's a Fairform Flyer, Huckins' famous hull design for World War II torpedo boats. I read about those yachts just last month."

He steered out the mouth of South Sound Creek as fast as their one-and-a-half horsepower Seagull outboard could propel them, and headed down the coast toward their little lighthouse. Neither one of them spoke. Jason's mind was awhirl. Memories of his brother flooding back; discovering Meyer Lansky with Ivan; the inexplicable mystical trip with Rosa ... .

CHAPTER 113
HEAVEN'S MYSTERIES

Key Largo
Tuesday, October 30, 1962

Jason secured the Zodiac to their dock, and they raced upstairs into the house.

Rosa dashed into the bedroom. "I'll call Higgins."

A moment later she said, "I told Priscilla it's urgent. She'll have him call back as soon as possible." She pulled on a flouncy skirt over her bikini, walked out to the porch swing and patted the seat beside her.

He sat on the cushion and took her hand. "I felt signals from Ivan that tell me we need to be on high alert from now on."

A local fishing boat came in from the ocean and idled up the canal. The fisherman waved at them and continued on to the harbor.

Rosa looked into his face. "What you did today, Jason ... brilliant. Appealing to Lanski's intellect is all that could have saved us. I was so scared of what they'd do to me before sending us to the bottom."

She turned her body toward him, kissed him passionately. "I felt a moment of terror. Now that it's over, I need to make love to you." She tugged his swimsuit.

"Not here, in plain sight of boaters, for Pete's sake."

"Yes! I want people to see how much I love you. It's exciting, and my skirt will conceal the details—if any boats do pass by, they'll not know for certain."

"The kind of spontaneity I love. But now that we've crossed Ivan and Lanski's radar, we can't let our guard down, even for a moment. Sex is the grandest distraction I know. A distraction that also could be deadly. From now on we have to enjoy it behind locked doors." He stood. "Join me inside?"

"Inside." She led the way through the sliding glass door. "Let's start in the shower. It can take us to the rainbowed waterfall in the garden. There's so much more to experience in that mystical world."

"You were really there with me? I wasn't hallucinating in the heat of passion and the noonday sun?"

Rosa ran her fingers through his hair. "We stayed in the Zodiac. But yes, I shared with you the mysticism of the Peruvian jungle where my husband and I lived for a time—to learn to energize each other so we could be on the fringes of heaven, and know our mission on earth."

"My premonitions and visions have taught me there are other dimensions that parallel the earth we live on, that parallel the world we touch, taste, smell, hear, see with our eyes—the one that most sane people call reality." He turned the spigot to draw the hot water up to the shower head. "It's as if a fog lifted for us today, revealing another awesome aspect of life where time is no longer linear—where past, present and future could all happen together."

"Eternity. God's love. As a teenager, Lorenzo was a great spearfisherman. While working in Peru, his open boat was caught in a hurricane and blown ashore, leaving him more dead than alive. He was reluctant to leave the peace and joy he experienced while unconscious. Natives took him to their village where the priestess brought him back to life—and showed him how to experience that beautiful dimension again. It's why he wanted us to begin our life together there. It's what I wanted to share with you. This afternoon we visited only two of the countless areas in those mystical parallels you've discovered." She adjusted the water temperature and stepped in. "Let's travel onward."

He, too, needed release from the tension of today's encounter with Lansky and Ivan. For the first time in his work with Higgins, Jason hoped the DDO was too busy to call back right away.

He embraced Rosa's slippery wet skin and together they slid into nirvana.

CHAPTER 114
ASSIGNMENT

Emotionally and physically wrung out from their roller-coaster day, Jason and Rosa collapsed in her bed, nestled like two spoons.

The jangle of the bedroom phone jolted Jason out of his doze.

"Higgins, returning your call."

Jason held the receiver so Rosa could lean close and hear too.

"Are you and Rosa alright?" Higgins sounded tired.

"We took the Zodiac into some backwater creeks today and came onto Myer Lansky aboard a seventy-foot Fairform Flyer. I thought we were goners." Jason rubbed his fingers through his hair. "Guess who else was on board." He took a deep breath. "My brother, Ivan. And Natasha. They'd been wiped out of my memory until I saw them." Jason jerked upright. "Hey, I'm just remembering they were in Miami years ago." He felt a surge of anger. "Mr. Higgins, did you send me to Florida as tiger bait?"

Silence. Higgins cleared his throat. "We sent you as a keenly tuned-in surveillant, to assist Rosa. And yes, I believed that if Ivan showed up in your area your remarkable antennae would pick up on him. Son, he's eluded us for years and I figure you're the one person who can identify him through all his disguises. Besides, he seems to have stayed out of your life since you left for Annapolis. Do you have any inkling why?" He paused. "I don't know how much you're able to remember."

Jason was sure he'd never told anyone about his blackmail, because the threat of revealing the Soviets' vital deadly businesses and key identities was the only hold he had over the Russians, the only weapon he had to deter them from assassinating him. His enemy knew that so long as he remained alive, the secrets in the blackmail letter would remain sealed. "You know my memory has been messed up. Besides, whatever was true years ago may no longer be the case. Situations change."

Another silence. Rosa looked at Jason and he handed her the phone.

She positioned the earpiece so he could still hear. "Mr. Higgins, back to Lansky. The Miami mayor's wife was with him. Looks like the Mafia and the city government might be in bed together."

"Another layer of connections," said Higgins. "Thanks for that intriguing tidbit. Lansky's original name was Maier Suchowjansky. A Russian Jew born in Grodno in 1902."

Jason jumped into the conversation again. "Should we be watching him for drug activity down here?"

"The FBI and our officers in Miami are keeping track of him and he's not a factor in the Keys. Gambling's his gig. Most likely was on an unwinding excursion after the missile crisis. Perhaps some business on the side with your brother. At least the meeting had nothing to do with you, or you'd both be dead now."

Jason answered with contemptuous irony. "That's encouraging."

Higgins ignored the tone. "But you *can* look for thirty-two-foot cigarette racing boats built in Miami by Don Aronow. These boats do up to eighty knots and are very difficult to detect by radar except on flat calm seas or at close range. They're going to be the boat of choice for many drug runners."

Jason let out a whistle.

"Don't do anything to blow your cover. How's your photography work coming, by the way? Is Rosa helping at all?

"Filmmaking's fine. One way or another, I always work with Rosa on her days off." He grinned at the spirited enchantress beside him. She kissed his nipple and he made an involuntary sound in response.

"What did you say Jason?"

"Just clearing my throat, sir."

Higgins went right on. "We have reliable intelligence confirming that the Cuban missile setup was only one component of the Soviet mega-plan to take over America. We fought that battle in Cuban waters. I'm afraid the next battle will be staged in Florida waters, primarily where you are."

"What battle?"

"Drugs, son. Enough drugs to turn countless people to daily lives of crime to support their habits. A flood of drugs to subvert the moral fiber and character of Americans throughout our country. Massive drug smuggling to dumb Americans down and desensitize them to the degree they ignore what it takes to keep this nation free."

"We've reported the suspect characters and fishing boats we've spotted."

"And we appreciate your good work. We think the Russians are using the drug trade as part of their strategy. It appears Ivan may be involved. I need you to learn what the Russian plan is, if possible."

"Is that all? Because for a while there I thought you were going to ask for something difficult."

CHAPTER 115
ALL BETS OFF

Key Largo
Friday, November 2, 1962

Natasha watched a large semi make a u-turn, completely block-ing the Overseas Highway in Key Largo's little town center. Ivan slowed their blue and silver Rolls Royce Silver Cloud II to a stop. Nata-sha had used a dummy corporation and false ID to lease a vehicle suited to their image in this drug venture. It was only a hundred miles further to Key West, where they were delivering half a million American dol-lars to their contact. Then she was looking forward to a night alone with Ivan at a private resort before returning to their yacht and crew in Fort Lauderdale.

Suddenly she spotted a black Buick Riviera pulling onto the high-way a couple of hundred yards ahead. "Could that be MacDougall's Buick in front of us?" She didn't hide her alarm. "It certainly looks like the picture you showed me."

The sun had just set and the cars had their lights on. Ivan held back to avoid being noticed. When the two-lane road was clear again, he surged the Rolls ahead soundlessly, catching up to the Buick. Sure enough, the car had green tags from Washington State. She could just make out the silhouettes of a small woman kissing the neck and ear of a big man.

"It's MacDougall and the woman from the Zodiac the other day," said Ivan.

"Do you think it's a trap?"

"No. I think the woman's distracting him so much, the radar that ordinarily warns him of my presence isn't working. I've learned that happens to me when we become amorous."

"So you believe this is the second chance encounter in three days?"

"I do. And I believe the time has come to eliminate MacDougall—and his woman, since she's also seen us. Clearly, all bets are off."

Natasha watched Ivan's hands tighten ever so slightly around the steering wheel.

He checked his rearview mirror and both sides of the road. "We'll follow at a distance and see what develops."

She reached for her Florida Keys map and turned on the map light. "What about his blackmail evidence?"

From what Sybil told us, all he can give them is Kanokov's poison and KGB rank, and the embassy's ownership of businesses to eliminate cars and bodies. Those businesses served their purpose and, to cover our tracks, they've now been shut down. Kanokov has diplomatic immunity. At worst, he would have to retire in Russia."

"And Sybil, after all her good work?"

"Nobody's indispensable."

Natasha hugged Ivan's arm. "Not even me?"

He smiled. "You're a different matter."

At mile marker 86, they passed Venetian Shores and crossed the Snake Creek Bridge onto Windley Key. As they rounded the slight curve to the mile-long straight highway ahead, the lights of the Buick had disappeared.

"Where are they?" Natasha checked the map. "The only turn-off shown is for an old stone quarry about a half mile ahead, on the right."

"I'll drive past the quarry road in case MacDougall is checking his tail."

There were no other cars on the highway. "We've been told this is a dead time of year for tourism."

At the next bend in the road, Ivan switched off his headlights and turned around.

CHAPTER 116
TIMELESS LOVE

Windley Key
Friday, November 2, 1962

Jason followed Rosa's directions and at mile marker 85 he turned right onto a lane through the highest hardwood hammock in the Keys. Almost immediately, the woodland lane veered northeast, parallel to U.S. 1. After sixty yards or so, there were no more trees on the left-hand side.

"Okay, turn left here and park," she said in a voice filled with anticipation.

Jason turned the wheel, and the headlights aimed out over the quarry pit to the wall on the far side.

"Leave the lights on so we can see the wall. It's a fossilized cross-section of thousands of years of coral growth."

"Incredible."

"I told you. Let's go see it close-up." She grabbed her ever-present leather handbag and hopped out of the car.

Together they walked across the vast, shallow pit to the neatly cut wall of Keystone, at least ten feet high in places.

"My God, what a sense of history. It's all here—every type of crustacean, algae and coral in centuries of reef-building." Jason held Rosa's hand in appreciation as their fingers traced passages of time in the cross-section revealed by the cutter's saw.

Rosa stepped between Jason and the quarry wall, and he saw the glow of her energy. "This is from the wall, Rosa?"

"All I can tell you is it happens to me here. It's a special place, like the Peruvian jungle." If the car's lights weren't on, we would see the aura of the fossils. I think it must be a place where lovers have come for decades." Rosa placed her purse and sandals on the ground, followed by her skirt and blouse. She stepped onto a coral slab lying on the ground and now stood at Jason's height.

She presented herself so gracefully and naturally, Jason ached to join her. He slipped out of his boat mocs and shorts and dropped his yellow shirt on top. Freed, he stretched to the bursting point. He felt the energy growing between them, charging and recharging each of them until he could see Rosa's aura—especially at her full nipples and between her thighs.

He knew she was ready for adventure as she clasped him with one hand, placed him at her entrance and took him in lustily. "More... more... more.... more... more," she purred. "Yes!"

They were back in the mystical jungle, with all the magical colors and heavenly sensations of love, peaking over and over and over. Wanting ever more of her, Jason stepped back, sliding her feet off the rock. She hooked her heels onto the bulge of his calves and began going up and down the length of him like a jackhammer. Their uninhibited lovemaking sounded like two alley cats. She growled fiercely between orgasms, crying out into the night with him at each climax—until she had his all.

He stood erect while she clung to him with her legs hanging down. Panting, they embraced one another, sweating profusely. When Jason was able, he told her, "You have to be the most amazing creature of God I've ever known. I feel complete with you." Spent with bliss, he felt the softness of her breasts caressing his abdomen as he lowered her till her feet touched the ground. She pressed her lips to his chest.

Jason's muscles tightened like a crossbow. They were not alone.

Ivan's voice spoke out of the dark. "Yes, MacDougall, your partner *is* amazing."

CHAPTER 117
TO THE DEATH

Windley Key
Friday, November 2, 1962

Blackmail or no, Jason berated himself for dropping his guard. "Ivan, I didn't know you could approach without my sensing your presence." Turning to place himself between Rosa and the voice, he saw Ivan stepping towards them, pistol in hand. "Rosa, this is my brother, Ivan. Ivan meet Rosa, the love of my life. Where's Natasha?"

"Behind you," Natasha's throaty voice announced as she stepped out of the dark, pistol at the ready.

Jason politely introduced Rosa.

Ivan said, "When did your memory of us return?"

"When we drifted into Lanski's yacht. The moment I saw you two, it all came back."

"It must have been a traumatic experience. You handled it well."

"I didn't have any choice, did I?" Jason tightened his arm around Rosa's shoulder. "Just like now, right? You've decided, haven't you?"

"Yes, MacDougall. We've decided."

Jason detected a trace of sadness in his brother's voice.

"At least I can give you a fighting chance." Ivan tossed his pistol to Natasha, who plucked it out of the air with practiced precision.

Jason looked at his shorts with his concealed PPK in its wallet holster, but Natasha looked him in the eyes and shook her head slightly.

"He's decided to kill you, is that it, *querido?*" Rosa grabbed a small rock from the quarry floor.

"Have you no fear?" Ivan asked Jason.

"Fear of *how* I die. Of separation from God, of course. Of never remembering who I was before I woke up in the hospital last winter."

"How would you like to help Natasha and me in our mission?"

"What's that?"

"Better use of American resources through better government."

Despite oddly selective memory damage from his EST, Jason was confident in his ability to reason. If Ivan was his Russian brother, the "better" could only be Soviet communism, and he wanted no part of it.

"I'm not the man to help you with that."

"Do you know why?"

"Yes. I do remember it was only a couple of centuries ago that our forefathers risked their lives to be free of tyrannical leadership. And I remember that in Korea the people would give an arm or leg to trade places with the least advantaged American."

Korea. Dr. Franke had said some of Jason's memories would return over time. Jason stared at Ivan. A tugboat pilot house flashed into his mind. "And it's just come back: you killed our parents."

Ivan leapt at Jason, viciously kicking out with his left foot at Jason's head, but Jason perceived it in slow motion.

Jason snapped to the right onto his hands and nailed Ivan's manhood with his left foot, then snap-rolled out from under Natasha's foot, barely saving his head. Still on his hands, he snapped his legs around in a clockwise three-sixty that swept her legs out from under her. As she fell onto him, Rosa's right fist with the rock crashed through Natasha's flailing arms and dazed her with a glancing blow to her jaw. Rosa dropped the rock and snatched the pistols from Natasha's hands.

Rolling over, Jason sprinted toward his brother, who peered at him through an agonized grimace as he struggled to his knees. Jason's left knee caught him under the jaw and snapped him backwards, where his head made a melon-like sound as it smashed onto the rock floor underfoot.

With a ragged breath, Jason stood upright, surveying the damage they'd performed and wondering where he'd learned to fight like that. Natasha looked dazed, but Ivan could have a concussion.

Out of the dark a group of people rushed them and disarmed Rosa before she could regrip the pistols and fire. A giant led the pack.

CHAPTER 118
RESOURCEFUL WOMEN

Windley Key
Friday, November 2, 1962

Jason appraised the group in a flash. A biker gang. Close to twenty of them. Men and women. Looked like they worked out in gyms, ate steroids for breakfast and snorted coke for lunch. *Hells Angels* emblazoned their black leather vests. They sauntered towards him. Several were swinging five-foot chains.

The leader was over six-six, and built like Charles Atlas. Looked like he weighed half-again as much as Jason or Ivan.

The Monster Man knelt by Natasha and pulled her head up onto his knees. He ripped open her polo shirt, revealing her magnificence. He slapped her face into consciousness. When her eyes opened, he gave her a moment to size things up.

"You come in the Rolls?" His voice rumbled from grotesque depths.

She grunted.

"Maggie here will help you."

A young woman with gallon-sized breasts took his place as he stood. He turned to Jason.

"You beat the crap out of 'em. Must 'a been some fuckin' fight. Think you can stand up to me?"

"I think if we don't get my brother to a hospital, he may die."

Monster Man rushed at Jason with outspread arms. Jason snapped into a squat and rolled back on his shoulders, whipping his feet to his opponent's pelvis bones and thrusting up with all his might. The man's legs sailed up over his body in a slow arc. While the man was overhead, upside down in the air, Jason wrapped his arm around the monster's neck and clasped his hands in a chokehold on the man's throat. As the giant landed on his back, Jason throttled him with all his physical strength and willpower. The man kicked his feet and tried to twist out of Jason's hold, but couldn't break free. He tried reaching over his head to beat Jason in the ribs, but he grew weaker and weaker. After what seemed an eternity, he lay still.

Total silence. All at once four pairs of strong hands grabbed Jason's arms, strong fingers digging into the muscle tissue of his forearms and slowly prying his arms straight to break his chokehold—then pulling him to his feet.

The leader's eyes opened hesitantly, confused, as he lay looking up into the darkness of the night sky. He seemed dazed. Suddenly he lurched to his feet and glared at Jason standing between four of his men, two holding each of his arms. Rubbing his throat, the leader turned and stepped over to where two powerful men stood with Natasha, gripping her arms.

The giant reached out and grabbed Natasha's crotch.

"Do that again, and I *will* kill you." The look in her eyes made the giant remove his hand.

Suddenly Natasha threw her weight forward and snapped her head down while she kicked back and up, emasculating both men holding her arms from behind.

The men's faces went ashen as they grabbed their privates and fell groaning to their knees.

Natasha stood before the giant, jabbing with her thumbs into the man's temples, dropping him like a sack of potatoes.

With everyone distracted, Rosa snatched her .38 magnum Smith & Wesson out of her handbag and covered the group. "If anyone moves, I'll gut-shoot them in a nanosecond. Jason, pick up Ivan and Natasha's SIG Sauers and help me disarm every one of these people."

The assortment of chains, blackjacks, brass knuckles, knives and handguns was so great it looked like a flea market for thugs.

Rosa and Jason marched the Hell's angels towards the Buick, two men carrying Ivan carefully, and four men struggling to carry their leader. While Rosa stopped the group in the headlights of the Buick, Jason started the car to charge the battery.

Rosa turned to Natasha. "Are there more weapons in your car?"

"None for this trip."

Jason sensed Natasha was telling the truth. "Drive your car here beside the Buick, and don't try anything if you value your partner's life."

Natasha retrieved the car keys from Ivan's pocket and walked off into the dark, while Jason handed Rosa her clothing. When she was dressed and able to cover the group, Jason took his turn at putting on his clothes.

The Rolls Royce was so quiet it was almost next to them before anyone heard it. Natasha parked and stepped out, her ripped shirt revealing temptation. She walked up to Jason. "I'm asking for a truce in order to save your brother.' Her voice was low and even. "I have a plan."

Jason looked at Rosa. They nodded agreement.

"Alright. Do your best."

Natasha strode over to the gang leader and woke him with smelling salts.

He leapt to his feet—wild-eyed at first—but regaining his wits quickly.

Natasha stood before him, looking up into the giant's eyes. "Before I went for the Rolls, I checked your tags. You're all from Los Angeles. What're you doing so far afield?"

"Just seeing what the rest of the country is like. Kind of one part vacation mixed with two parts opportunism. On our way to groove in Key West. Camped out here for the night. Your ruckus kinda got our attention."

"You've got a brain, yet you're addicted to living on the edge in a physical world of violence. Natural leadership qualities. You're amoral. You kill for business and to protect yourselves—but never unnecessarily."

"Didn't know I was so transparent."

"Tell me, how many are in your California group?"

"It varies. Depending on how many get themselves killed versus how many get to join us. Forty to forty-four's a fair number most times."

Natasha thought a minute, then smiled brightly. "I have a proposition for you."

"Lady, I got one rule in life: Never bargain; just take what's available. And from where I stand, I already see everything I want—your car, your cash, and best of all, you and that beautiful Cuban broad. Why shouldn't I take the bird in hand, instead of some speculative proposition?"

"You forgetting the lady with the revolver?"

"A mere technicality."

"Technically, if you force yourself on the Cuban lady and me, you'd have ten more of the world's best-trained killers just like us, relentlessly hunting down and slowly killing every person who was a member of the Hells Angels in California on this date—starting with you." Natasha said it with chilling matter-of-factness.

Not a soul breathed as the leader hesitated. He grunted. "I take it your proposition would be an acceptable alternative—enough to make me want to change the error of my simple ways?"

Natasha got right to the point. "We're looking for a group like yours to hang out at our six million-dollar estate on the Pacific Ocean near L.A.—to 'protect' our people. I think our leader out there might take a liking to you. She's a tiny little blonde, but likes big challenges—like being completely different personalities while servicing as many as three to five men a day. Think you can handle that kind of energy? Plus, if you do your job well, the money will flow like you've never seen—starting tonight."

"Sounds like a life I could get used to. Tell me more."

"First we let the Cuban and her man go. Then I've got to get my man to a medical facility on the mainland. You escort us where we're going, and I'll give you a hundred thousand dollars cash to get back to L.A. where you can call collect, from 'Zeus,' to a number I'll give you."

"Lady, you got a deal."

The gang let out a sigh of relief.

Jason caught Rosa's eye. "We'll take up the rear."

He and Rosa covered the group with the SIGs and her revolver. Two bikers loaded Ivan into the back of the Rolls. The biker-chicks mounted up behind their guys and the whole gang rolled out onto U.S. 1, awaiting the Rolls driven by Natasha, with Maggie in the front seat beside her.

As soon as they roared up the road towards Miami, Jason said, "We've got to get to the nearest payphone and call Higgins. It'll be too late if we try to get back to the house."

CHAPTER 119
REDEMPTION

The Florida Keys
Friday, November 2, 1962

Jason peered at the small resort motels as he drove past. Harbor Lights. Ocean View. "Of course. Venetian Shores Marina will have a payphone outside the bait shop." He crossed Snake Creek Bridge and pulled off the highway.

Seconds seemed like minutes as he waited for Higgins to answer.

"We've corralled him for you, Mr. Higgins. Ivan. It was a helluva fight and he needs a bit of medical attention. He and Natasha are headed out of the Keys on the Overseas Highway. Probably know of some doctor around Miami. She's driving. A blue and silver Rolls. With a dozen Hells Angels plus their chicks as a motorcycle escort. If you move right now, your people can set up a roadblock on the eighteen-mile stretch, box them in from both ends. Place a back-up in Florida City."

"Jason, you've accomplished your assignment. We'll bring them in."

"We're at the lower end of Plantation Key. They're just ahead of us. We'll be home in twenty-five minutes. We'll call you on the secure line to confirm we got there."

There was only one sheriff's deputy on duty from Ocean Reef to Islamorada at this time of night and Jason ignored the speed limit as he raced up the highway to catch sight of the Rolls and bikers. His phone stop gave the group too much of a lead. Obviously they didn't care about the posted limits either.

Rosa touched his knee. "Jason, I saw you in action with Carlos and his men the night you arrived here, but with Ivan ... I've never seen fighting or speed like that. How do you do it?"

Rosa's awe was palpable. How could he explain his gift to this remarkable partner in mission? He studied the road ahead as he sped on and answered at the same time. "I guess it's like I focus so hard on whatever the action is, my mind dissects it into individual scenes that show me where the action is coming from, where it is, where it's going and what I can do to survive—and maybe even turn an event to my advantage."

"So it's sort of like studying individual frames of movie film?"

"Yes, but only the two or three frames necessary to give me the whole picture in a glance—so there's no conscious thinking involved—just reflexive response that allows me to act in time to initiate forceful counterforce even ahead of whatever attack is coming." That was the gift, but he wondered when his mind might recall where he got the training that his body remembered so well—some of those moves he'd just used on Ivan.

Gravel flew as he turned in to the house. He and Rosa rushed up the stairs and dashed for the bedroom phone. They held their heads together, listening to Higgins.

"Good work, Jason. Our men are in place. I want all the details in the morning."

"Good luck." Jason pictured the roadblock.

"Jason, we can still use you for surveillance down there. You're the kind of patriot this country needs. Good night, son."

Rosa moved her ear away and Jason plopped the receiver into its cradle.

"I've never heard excitement in Higgins voice before." Rosa grabbed Jason's hand. "He really wants you to stay on."

"We've delivered Ivan and Natasha to the CIA. Higgins can learn the entire Soviet plan to take over America. Mission accomplished!" Jason felt a mixture of euphoria and relief. "I couldn't have done my part without you, Rosa."

"I want you to stay on, too, Jason."

"For you." He raised her hand to his lips. "*With* you—the woman I've been looking for as long as I can remember." He chuckled at the irony, but he knew in his heart it was true.

Rosa laughed. "I've been in love with you long before your latest memories came back. We belong together. And we still have all kinds of work to do." Her passionate kiss set him on fire.

She held his face and looked deep into his eyes. "I feel reborn."

"Redemption. For both of us."

He became one with her glow. Morning was a lifetime into the future.

* * * * END * * * *

ACKNOWLEDGEMENTS

Our work never would have seen the light of day without the remarkable patience, coaching and editing skills of Carol Craig, now retired, who taught us the art of crafting our story into novels.

Sol Stein, publishing industry icon, offered invaluable comments. Poet, Leonard Nash, gave guidelines that we hear in our minds every time we write. Novelist, James Hall, encouraged us at the outset. Writer, Elaine Stec, provided a superb analysis of the structure of our novel. Editor, Marlene Adelstein, made important observations. Veterans Administration nurse, Valerie Mazon, supplied corroborating documentation on PTSD and cheered us onward. Professor and author, Rachael Simon, introduced us to the business realities of publishing. We thank each one of you for enabling us to create this book.

The fact and line editing by "Irascible Curmudgeon and Scribe," David Ziegler, has been indispensable. Thank you, David.

We feel blessed to have Betty Kelly Sargent as our current story editor. Book and fiction editor at *Cosmopolitan* magazine for many years, she became executive editor at Harper Collins and is now retired from her position as editor-in-chief at William Morrow. She read our new manuscript and with inimitable skill, expertise and enthusiastic encouragement brought it forward to the book you are reading today.

We're also indebted to the friends who agreed to be beta readers along the way and whose honest opinions helped shape parts of the novel: Vanessa Plascencia, Olivia Hendrickson, Maria Rodriguez, Anabelle Ornelas, Sarah, and several doctors.

To one and all, our sincerest gratitude.

And for our mates, a resounding, "Thank you, God!"

AFTERLIFE

Afterlife is the ultimate gift—eternal life in the light of our Creator. Possibly in the dimension where Adam and Eve began life together—before Eve ate us out of house and home, so to speak.

Where is this timeless place? Everywhere. All around us. Awaiting our spiritual return.

We believe every person has a spirit-breath that enables the telekinetic connection of the living mind-body. The yeast of life is that every birth into this world of linear time commences the eventual death of that earthbound mind-body—whose spirit will then morph into a new beginning in the timeless dimension where we find love abounds, and where we believe God's purpose for each life is completely revealed and perfectly fulfilled.

That is why those who return from near death experiences rarely fear death again. That also explains how it is that *le petit mort* can be the healing gift from heaven as it allows us repeated glimpses of the heavenly life ahead.

How can we be so certain? It goes back to when Jason had his near-death out-of-body experience in the ambulance. The beauty and sense of completeness in those incomparable moments took away his fear of death. He recovered from his injuries knowing the only thing he could take with him when he stood before his Creator would be his integrity—if he had any left. Suddenly his life became simple: he would be known by his choices—sometimes very hard choices—and his actions.

When he came out of the coma in the hospital, he thought he'd come to for a while in the ambulance and then faded back into unconsciousness. It was decades later a doctor told him scientists now know that when his heart and breathing stopped, he'd had no known way of registering the activity around him.

Jason had always wondered how the individual survived after the brain decomposed in death. Now he had the answer. His brain had the equivalent of a back-up hard drive with its own sensors, inputting and preserving his identity forever—even capable of leaving the body and seeing from afar. We're told medical findings have shown that shortly after death, a body loses an infinitesimal amount of weight, and witnesses have told us that as they watch over a loved one, shortly after death a wisp of white mist floats up from the body and disappears through the ceiling. It's called the spirit, or soul. It's that person, for eternity.

Diana MacFarland   The Florida Keys   July 4, 2012

RELEVANT READING AND VIEWING

(Confirming Jason's Exceptional Survival Gifts and the
Soviet Activities to Crush Democracy)
Available through Amazon.com or Libraries

UNDERSTANDING PSYCHIC PHENOMENA:

Entangled Minds: Extrasensory Experiences in a Quantum Reality, Dean I. Radin

Social Intelligence: The New Science of Human Relationships, Daniel Goleman

Blink, Malcolm Gladwell (for a partial understanding of the cutting-edge neuroscience and psychology relevant to Jason's slow-motion survival gift)

PATRIOT HEROES WHO INFLUENCED JASON'S CHARACTER:

Lewis Wetzel: Indian Fighter—the Life and Times of a Frontier Hero, C. B. Allman

America's First Frogman, The Draper Kauffman Story, Elizabeth Kauffman Bush

Cochrane: The Real Master and Commander, David Cordingly

SOVIET ESPIONAGE AND IDEOLOGICAL SUBVERSION IN AMERICA:

Reveille for Radicals, Saul D. Alinsky

Masters of Deceit: The Story of Communism in America and How to Fight It, J. Edgar Hoover

Rules for Radicals: A Pragmatic Primer for Realistic Radicals, Saul D. Alinsky

The Soviet World of American Communism, Harvey Klehr, John Earl Haynes, Kyrill M. Anderson

Venona: Decoding Soviet Espionage in America, John Earl Haynes & Harvey Klehr

Blacklisted by History: The Untold Story of Senator Joe McCarthy and his Fight Against America's Enemies, M. Stanton Evans

One-Party Classroom: How Radical Professors at America's Top Colleges Indoctrinate Students and Undermine Our Democracy, David Horowitz & Jacob Laksin

Deception Was My Job: The Testimony of Yuri Bezmenov, KGB Propagandist, 2007 DVD of 1984 interview with G. Edward Griffin (800-595-6596)

PROBLEMS AND SOLUTIONS FOR DEMOCRACY IN AMERICA TODAY:

Atlas Shrugged, Ayn Rand

Atlas Shrugged: Part One, 2011 Movie/DVD with Taylor Schilling, Grant Bower and Rebecca Wisocky

The New Road To Serfdom, Daniel Hannan

The Miracle of Freedom: 7 Tipping Points That Saved The World, Chris Stewart and Ted Stewart

No Apology: The Case for American Greatness, Mitt Romney

PTSD:

Until Tuesday: A Wounded Warrior and the Golden Retriever Who Saved Him, Former Capt.Luis Carlos Montalván with Bret Witter

Brothers, 2009 movie/DVD with Natalie Portman, Tobey Maguire and Jake Gyllenhaal

The Hurt Locker, 2008 movie/DVD with Jeremy Renner, Anthony Mackie and Evangeline Lilly

The Long Walk Home, Organization to Help Prevent or Diminish Veterans' PTSD www.thelongwalkhome.org

FOR DEALING WITH STRESS AND PTSD IN COMMITTED MARRIAGES:

The Act of Marriage: The Beauty of Sexual Love, Tim and Beverly LaHaye

The Multi-Orgasmic Couple: How Couples Can Share Multiple Orgasms and Dramatically Enhance Their Pleasure, Intimacy and Health, Mantuk Chia & Maneewan Chia, Douglas Abrams & Rachael Carlton Abrams, M.D.

The Orgasm Bible: The Latest Research and Techniques for Reaching More Powerful Climaxes More Often, Susan Crain Bakos

The Cosmo Kama Sutra: 77 Sex Positions, the Editors of *Cosmopolitan*

Position Sex: 50 Positions You Probably Haven't Tried, Lola Rawlins

The Art of the Quickie: Fast Sex, Fast Orgasms, Anytime, Anywhere, Joel D. Block, Ph.D.

AFTERLIFE:

Evidence of the Afterlife: The Science of Near-Death Experiences, Jeffrey Long, M.D.

GLOSSARY

ABBREVIATIONS, DEFINITIONS & TRANSLATIONS

A   AFB = Air Force Base

Aft = at, near or toward the back part of a boat

B   Bow = the front part of a boat

C   CIA = Central Intelligence Agency

Courtesan, Venetian = 16th century high class escorts. They were appealing, talented women capable of fulfilling a man's needs for excitement, intelligent worldly conversation and inspirational, satisfying sex.

CPUSA = Communist Party U.S.A.

D   DCI = Director of Central Intelligence

DDO = Deputy Director of Operations

DGI = *Spanish; Dirección General de Inteligencia;* Cuban equivalent of Russian KGB

DMZ = Demilitarized Zone. The DMZ in Korea is the most heavily militarized border in the world; 155 miles long by approximately 2½ miles wide, it divides the Korean Peninsula in half, across the 38th Parallel.

E   EST = Electro Shock Therapy

Estar Roto = Spanish; "To Be Broken" (War Neurosis, PTSD)

F   FBI = Federal Bureau of Investigation

G   *Govnau* = Russian; "Shit"

Granny Knot = a simple slip-knot, often tied in error in place of a square knot.

Guayabera = Spanish; a lightweight, straight-cut shirt worn outside the trousers.

GRU = Chief Intelligence Directorate of the General Staff at Russian Naval Headquarters

Gulags = as many as 475 government-run penal slave labor camps for all types of criminals and political dissidents in the Soviet Union, some of the main camps comprising hundreds, or even thousands of camp units. Essentially slave labor camps at any given time for an estimated 25-30 million dissenting Soviet citizens.

H   HUAC = House Un-American Activities Committee

I   Intel = Intelligence
         IRA = Irish Republican Army

J   *Jefe* = Spanish; "Chief" or "Leader" or "Boss"

K   KGB = Committee for State Security. The national security agency of the Soviet Union from 1954 until 1991, and the premier internal security, intelligence, and secret police organization during that time.

L   Little girl = polite way society referred to a young woman's virginity

M   *Mach ihm!* = German; "Attack!"
         MI5 = early name of MI6 British Intelligence
         MP = military police

N   *Na zdarov'e!* = Russian; "To your good health!" or "Cheers!"

O   OCS = Officer Candidate School

Op/Ops = Operation(s)

Order of magnitude = tenfold, ten times greater

OSS = Office of Strategic Services—WW II US intelligence agency, forerunner of CIA

P   Pay out the line = aboard a boat, let out the line (rope) a portion at a time

Pazdravlayu! = Russian; "Congratulations!"

PSI = pounds of pressure per square inch

PTSD = post-traumatic stress disorder

   In 1678 the Swiss called it *nostalgia*

   In German it was *heimweh* (home-sickness)

   In French *maladie du pays*

   In Spanish *estar roto* (to be broken)

   In the American Civil War *soldier's heart* or *exhausted heart*

   World War I produced the term *shell shock*

   World War II produced the terms *combat neurosis* and *combat exhaustion*

   In Korea it was called *war neurosis*

   In Vietnam it became *PTSD* (*Post-Traumatic Stress Disorder*), its present name

Polonium Pills = lethal radiation poisoning pills

Q   *Querido* = Spanish; "Dear" or "Beloved" or "Darling"

R

S   *Spetsnaz* = Russian Forces of Special Designation, originally intended to prepare the way for the main Soviet effort during the Cold War. Spetsnaz élite force members were the world's best-trained, most feared operatives of the Cold War, and were often the winners of Olympic events for the USSR

State = the State Department

Stern = the back end of a boat

T

U UN = United Nations
USSR = Union of Soviet Socialist Republics
USUN = United States Mission to the United Nations

V VA = Veterans Administration
VAMC = Veterans Administration Medical Center

W War Neurosis = the original name for PTSD in Korean War vets

X

Y

Z

DIANA MACFARLAND

Diana MacFarland is the pen name for a husband and wife team with a remarkable background. Between them they have paranormal survival skills, top-secret clearance, and access to experts in intelligence and to key government figures.

Educated at Bryn Mawr College, the U.S. Naval Academy and the University of Washington School of Forestry, their exceptional academic and athletic abilities have been put to the test in advanced scuba training by Navy Seals, extraordinary marksmanship, and championship sailing and boat handling.

Together they have performed surveillance work for government agencies and have survived assassination attempts by Soviet Spetsnaz élite operatives as well as the deadly challenges of post-traumatic stress disorder, even as they developed patented breakthrough underwater equipment and created award-winning films.

They live in the Florida Keys with a boatful of furry four-footed friends.

www.DianaMacFarland.com

MAR   2013

Macfarland, Diana
Codename Wildcard : a
thriller

CPSIA information can be obtained at www.ICGtesting.com
Printed in the USA
LVOW131638141012

302783LV00003B/46/P